BERKLEY

DOUBLET

Rob Thurman lives in Indiana, land of rolling hills and cows. Lots and lots of cows. *Nightlife* and *Moonshine*, the previous novels in the Cal Leandros series, are also published by Penguin. Visit Rob at www.robthurman.net.

Doubletake

ROB THURMAN

BERKLEY UK
PENGUIN

BERKLEY UK

Published by the Penguin Group

Penguin Books Ltd, 80 Strand, London WC2R ORL, England

Penguin Group (USA) Inc., 375 Hudson Street, New York, New York 10014, USA

Penguin Group (Canada), 90 Eglinton Avenue East, Suite 700, Toronto, Ontario, Canada M4P 2Y3
(a division of Pearson Penguin Canada Inc.)

Penguin Ireland, 25 St Stephen's Green, Dublin 2, Ireland (a division of Penguin Books Ltd)

Penguin Group (Australia), 250 Camberwell Road,

Camberwell, Victoria 3124, Australia (a division of Pearson Australia Group Pty Ltd)

Penguin Books India Pvt Ltd, 11 Community Centre, Panchsheel Park,

New Delhi – 110 017, India

Penguin Group (NZ), 67 Apollo Drive, Rosedale, North Shore 0632, New Zealand
(a division of Pearson New Zealand Ltd)

Penguin Books (South Africa) (Pty) Ltd, Block D, Rosebank Office Park, 181 Jan Smuts Avenue,
Parktown North, Gauteng 2193, South Africa

Penguin Books Ltd, Registered Offices: 80 Strand, London WC2R ORL, England

www.penguin.com

First published in the USA by Roc, an imprint of New American Library,
a division of Penguin Group (USA) Inc. 2012
First published in Great Britain by Berkley UK 2012

001

Copyright © Robyn Thurman, 2012
All rights reserved

ISBN: 978–0–718–19852–7

www.greenpenguin.co.uk

ALWAYS LEARNING   **PEARSON**

This dedication can go only to all my fans (you are an army), fellow authors, publishing staff, my family, and Web mistress Jayda—all who kept my career intact and alive while I was in the hospital and unable to do it myself. You saved me. Never will I forget it.

ACKNOWLEDGMENTS

To Mike G. and Chuck W., who rescued my computer from being tossed out my car window in frustration; Jeff Thurman, my guy in the FBI for the customary weapons, explosives, and general mass destruction advice; Linda and Richard, whose generosity of spirit knows no bounds; my agent and my editor, Lucienne and Anne, without whom these books wouldn't exist; and, finally, to my personal hero and artist, Chris Mc-Grath. This time you gave me a cover so amazing that it knocked me on my ass at first glance. I had to edit the book ferociously simply because I didn't think it lived up to the cover. . . . An artist that talented is rare. All hail Chris—the one true Art God.

"Are we not like two volumes of one book?"
— Marceline Desbordes-Valmore, *Poésies de Madame Desbordes-Valmore* (1830)

"We cannot destroy kindred. . . ."
—Marquise de Sévigné, *Lettres de Mme de Sévigné: précédées d'une notice sur sa vie et du traité sur le style épistolaire de Madame de Sévigné* (1846)

"Unless we load our guns first."
—Cal Leandros, present day

"What greater thing is there for two . . . joined for life . . . ?"
—George Eliot, *Adam Bede* (1859)

"Exquisite death."
—Grimm, present day

1

Black Sheep

Family . . . it is a fucking bitch.

Just like he was a bitch. I had seen him—wallowing amongst the game, but never tasting of the herd. More perverse, he lived with prey, had been raised by prey, had been taught the ways of the world by prey, when I'd had to teach myself. Clawing myself along, I had chewed my way through knowledge as grimly as I'd once chewed discarded putrid meat and bone. Everything I'd earned, I'd earned with blood, mine or someone else's. I had done what no one else could do.

The castoff failure, but look at me now. Damn right, look at me. Look hard and look good—right before I gut you.

Then there was him, the golden boy, yet look at what he had done.

Naughty and bad, bad and naughty. But much worse: disobedient. Not what they'd expected of their one true success at all.

I laughed at the irony of it.

I laughed, but I hated him, hated him, hated him, hated him, hated him.

Not for what he'd done, but that he'd been the one instead of me to do it.

That was all right, though. That was fine and fucking dandy, as someone I used to know once said. Fine and fucking dandy, because I hated everyone anyway. The only difference was, I was related to this one ... and that made the hate sweeter. Hate was all I'd known. All I had ever been given and all I had ever had. I was created from it, molded by it, lived by it. Hate was like air, necessary to life. I wore my hate as a second skin and let it warm me when nothing else did.

I saw him through binoculars from where I lay atop a roof far enough away that he wouldn't know I was there. It was night, but I saw him clearly. Light was for the fearful herd; the night was for me. Not that it was ever truly dark in this immense mound of misbegotten roadkill waiting to happen.

Yes, I saw him. He had black hair, pale skin, light-colored eyes. Nothing like I was at all. That I didn't hate. That I liked — I was better, purer, closer to the truth.

It was all about the truth.

The new truth.

My truth.

And he was part of that, whether he wanted to be or not.

Family was a hateful bitch; it was. I had the hot poker scars of that burned into my flesh to prove it, but, scars or not, sometimes family was all you had worth playing with. Maybe he would see that. Maybe he would want to play too. I played rough. I played to win.

Did he?

I'd bet he did if given the chance, not that this boring

scuffle I was watching was anything to go by. It wasn't a fraction of the challenge I'd give him.

The Unmaker of the World, they had called him.

Unimpressed, I waggled black-gloved fingers in a mocking wave. We'd see. Sooner or later, we'd see exactly what family and blood meant to him. He might look like one of the cattle, but he would never be one.

Besides, if he could unmake the world, how much more fun would it be for me to remake it instead?

2

Family . . . it is a bitch.

The thought came out of nowhere.

Or maybe not, considering my current situation. There was no denying that it was true. Everyone thought it sooner or later, didn't they? If there's only you, you're good—lonely maybe, but good. You can't fight with yourself. If there're two of you, it can still be good. Your options are limited. You make do and appreciate what you have, unless it's the stereotypical evil-twin scenario. Then you aim for the goatee and blow his ass back to the alternate dimension he popped out of.

A kishi—better known as my paycheck in the form of a supernatural hyena—hit my back with staggering force. I flipped it over my shoulder and put a bullet between its eyes.

Yeah, normally two was a doable number for family. It was when you hit three and higher that things started to go bad. That was when the bitching and moaning started, the pitting of one against another, the slights that no one forgot. No one could tell me that Noah didn't pitch a few of his relatives kicking and screaming off the

Ark long before the floodwaters receded. It was no familial *Love Boat,* and I believed that to my core.

Which brought up the question: Did that wrathful Old Testament God kill the sharks? I don't think he did. You can't drown a shark. I think they were snacking on biblical in-laws right and left. Noah, Noah, Noah . . .

I swung around and kicked the next kishi in the stomach as I slammed another clip home before putting three in its gaping, lethally fanged mouth as it jumped again. It sounded easy, but considering the one I also had attached to my other leg . . . it was a pain in the ass.

Family-wise, I had no pain in the asses. I was lucky. I had one brother and he was a damn good one. Once we were on our own, I'd escaped the curse of screaming Thanksgiving dinners. . . . I had a turkey pizza; Niko had a vegan one. No bitter arguments around a Christmas tree . . . Niko gave me a new gun; I gave him a new sword. Absent was the awkward discovery of first cousins shacking up at the summer vacation get-togethers at the lake. I didn't have to wait for summer. I saw my brother every day when he winged my sopping towel off the bathroom floor at my head or I asked—after the fact—if I could use his priceless seventeenth-century copy of some boring book no one but him and the author had read to prop up a wobbling coffee table.

Summer vacations . . . if you thought about it, what kind of people actually gathered together at a lake with cabins and all that crap anyway? Hadn't they ever watched *Friday the 13th*? Jason? Hockey masks? Machetes? A good time for me, yeah—oh *hell,* yeah—but not as much for the members of your average Prius-driving middle class.

Stupidity is everywhere.

But for me, right now, things were good. My brother

and I kicked supernatural ass for fun and profit. I had a shirt that said that with our phone number. Humans wouldn't take it seriously. Humans didn't know what the world really hosted. But the kind that hired us—nonhuman— they knew a walking billboard when they saw it. Running your own business is a bitch. You have to advertise. Promo. Market. Niko did that. I couldn't be bothered with that crap—unless it resulted in my offensive T-shirt slogan. He and I had been doing this for four years now. Before that we'd done the same, but it had been a hobby, not a career.

Okay, I say hobby, but it was self-defense, pure and simple. When you're half human and half of the worst monster to walk the earth—a creature that ate the supernatural for appetizers without putting hardly any effort into it—you weren't popular with the other monster types. And there were thousands of different kinds. Some immediately attacked me, sensing the half human in me and assuming it would make me weaker—they were wrong. Some ran—they were smart. And some didn't care either way—we hung out and had a beer.

Good family. Interesting and well-paying career. Half monster . . . well, everything couldn't be perfect, but otherwise right now things were good. I was hoping they stayed that way. Except for Niko. I didn't have to hope when it came to family.

The rest of my life might be challenging in some other areas, like at the moment as an adolescent kishi was either trying to eat my leg or hump it to the bare bone, but family? I knew I had that under control. I watched my brother's back; he watched mine. We were a Hallmark card dipped in blood and made of unbreakable steel. I'd never had a doubt about my family and I never would— no matter what the kishi, who had brought the topic to mind to begin with, were doing to annoy me on the general subject.

No, it was all smooth sailing, rather like this current job, until my cell phone rang. "Niko," I said, shooting another adult kishi with jaws stretched wide enough to swallow my entire head. It had leaped downward at me from a fire escape of a condemned tenement apartment building long crumbled in on itself—no demolition crew needed. Gravity worked for free. "Can you get this one off of my leg before I need sexual assault counseling?"

Niko said to not kill the babies, although at one hundred and fifty pounds "baby" was pushing the definition, but I was doing my best, more or less, to be a good boy. Although it would've been much easier to be a bad boy.

So very bad. So very fun.

For my brother, however, I reined in that part of me—that nonhuman half of me, choke-chaining it with a practiced grip. It was the price I paid to keep my brother satisfied. Bearing in mind that if it weren't for him I'd be dead or sanity-challenged ten times over, I owed the man. I was also fond enough of his bossy, anal-retentive ass to die for him.

More important, to kill for him.

And to have chosen the darkest of roads to make that happen.

All that made ignoring a giant baby with an equally giant bite easy enough. As I fished for my cell, Niko was less than awed at my babysitting skills and said so: "If you can't do a minimum of three tasks at once, I have failed you with all my training and instruction. I'd blame myself, but clearly it's entirely your fault, your laziness, your total ineptitude."

Not that we shared the fraternal fondness out loud. How manly would that be?

It wasn't as if I hadn't heard that all before. If adults heard lullabies when they slept, that would be mine. I shook my leg again, shot another kishi bounding down the side of the next building, equally as dilapidated as the first, putting three bullets between its blazing silver eyes. They shone brighter than any streetlights in this part of town . . . until their life seeped away and left only the dull gray of death. I felt bad for them—almost—but they had turned a block that had once hosted scavenging homeless, thriving drug dealers, and sullen hookers into a desolate wasteland. In my opinion, I didn't have a preference for one over the other, kishi or human. The mayor wanted the city cleaned up. The kishi clan was doing the job one block at a time . . . even if it meant eating quite a few people.

Were those people good people? If I knew anything, I knew that these days, starting four months ago, I wasn't in the position to make the call on whether certain people were worth saving or leaving to the predators. That I left up to Nik. I simply stepped over their bodies and went on with the job.

Regardless of whether they were good or evil, those people belonged, whether they knew it or not, to the Kin. The Kin, the werewolf Mafia of NYC, weren't pleased to be sharing their money or their snacks with Johnny-come-lately supernatural hyenas from the depths of . . . um . . . I should've paid attention to where those depths were during the premission rundown—maybe Africa, but Niko knew. That was enough. I didn't think it mattered much. They were encroaching on Kin territory, and the Wolves didn't like that.

Unfortunately for the Kin, the kishi, as a race, howled at a decibel level that would have any Kin Wolf's ears bleeding ten blocks away. Curled up in homicidal furry balls, moaning for their mommies, they hadn't had much success in taking down the kishi. Luckily for Niko, me, and our bank account, human ears couldn't hear notes that high.

And although I wasn't entirely human, my hearing was. That made us the go-to guys for this job. It had seemed easy from the hiring and the half our fee slapped into my palm—if it hadn't been for Niko's research, finding out the kishi were highly intelligent preternatural hyenas, if extremely malevolent. That meant the adults were fair game, but the younger kishi we had to pat on the head and find a goddamn supernatural foster and rescue organization for murderous fur babies to raise them right, socialize their asses, put rhinestone collars on them, and take them off our hands.

How many of those do you think were in the phone book? Nada? Good fucking call.

But the bottom line was, it was all about family, which had to be where that thought had originated. The adult kishi taking down prey for their young, which luckily was only one at this point, feeding him or her, setting up a nest, claiming this place for their own. They were doing what evolution had bred in them to do. Evolution worked the same for nonhumans as for humans. Kishi were predators to their bones. They would slaughter anything they thought they had a chance of bringing down, but to give them credit, they looked after their family.

That's where family became a bitch in yet another way. You eat people for your family, you piss off the Kin for your family, you die for your family.

As a random bully had once said to me when I was a kid in the fourth grade as he demanded my sneakers and backpack, life isn't fair. I agreed with him by punching his annoying teeth down his equally annoying throat. If that's the way the world wanted to be, I'd go along. I didn't make the rules. I only played by them.

Since when?

Since never.

This wasn't a schizophrenic voice; at least, I hoped not. This was just my subconscious, my new subconscious. Since I'd let a small piece of me wither and die months ago to save *my* family, the swamp in my mind that made up the subliminal me was considerably more shadowed. It was more prone to the bad thoughts people think, normal people too, that they shouldn't, don't like to admit to, and don't act on. But as I wasn't normal and wasn't exactly the Webster's dictionary definition of a person, my bad thoughts were much badder than most and I wanted to act on them. Sometimes or often or frequently or very frequently, depending on my mood . . . no judgment needed or wanted. If I thought it, I absolutely wanted to do it.

But I didn't.

The voices/thoughts were almost as much a bitch as family could be, the squabbling, but I'd learned to mostly tune them out. Many psychotherapists would be proud of my progress—the ones who hadn't met me and, if they had any sense, wouldn't care to.

I wasn't good or bad. I was only me, and I was neither.

They'd have to invent a new bizarrely long German psychological description for what I was. How did the German say, "To see him is to piss your pants in fear"? Freud would've known.

I shook my leg futilely one more time and exhaled in irritation at the molten mercury eyes, the dark red coat dappled with silver spots, the milk teeth—as large as a German shepherd's adult teeth—that continued to gnaw at my thigh. "Three seconds and he's a rug under the coffee table. Your move, Cyrano."

Did Niko have a proud, hawklike nose? Yes, he did. Did I give him hell over it? What do you think?

I answered my still-ringing cell phone as I shot the last kishi that leaped through a boarded-up window. Wood split, glass shattered, and bone splintered. The combination made for one dead kishi whose stomach was rounded and full with its last meal, which, I was guessing, had been the last occupant of this street. From the hypodermic the para-hyena coughed up in its dying throes, that meal had most likely been a tweaker.

They say drugs kill, but does anyone ever listen?

"Yeah, Leandros," I said into the phone. "Death and destruction by the dollar. The meter's ticking. Go."

I hadn't had a chance to check the incoming number, not with Kishi Junior both seducing and making a meal of my leg. But it didn't surprise me to hear a familiar voice. Five people total had my personal number. Our business number was an untraceable phone with voice mail lying on the floor of an otherwise empty storage locker. Niko and I'd been sorry before—we went with safe now. "Kid, thank Bacchus." I heard the relieved exhalation. "I need you and Niko at my place now."

The three seconds was up, and I had the muzzle of my Desert Eagle planted between toddler kishi's moon eyes as it gnawed harder at my lower thigh. I had a high pain tolerance—you learned to in this business—but to balance it out, my tolerance for nearly everything else remotely irritable in the universe was low. *Damn* low. Contaminating part of your soul will do that . . . if you believed in souls. I hadn't made up my mind, but either way it was too bad for baby. It was night-night time. I might as well stop the pattern now. The same as its parents, it would grow up to be a killer anyway.

Like you did?

As if I didn't know that.

But I was a done deal; the kishi wasn't, not quite yet. "Goodfellow? You in trouble?" I started to put pressure on the trigger and tried to overlook the shadow of guilt. It *was* a kid. A killer kid, but a kid. Couldn't I relate? On every single level? Then again, did I care if I could relate? Was I Dr. Phil? Hell, no. I was, however, Niko's brother. That had me yanking harder at my internal leash while frowning crossly at Niko as I gave him a few extra seconds to move over and slide his katana blade between my leg and the kishi to pry it off with one efficient move.

"You owe me," I grumbled at him.

While it squealed, barked, yowled, and laughed hyena-crazy through a toothy muzzle, Niko threw the last kishi down and hog-tied its preteen fuzzy ass. My brother—he wasn't a bleeding heart. There were more dead monsters and people in whatever version of hell you wanted to believe in who'd testify to that. He did like to give a break when he thought one was due, though—or when he thought their birthright shouldn't automatically condemn them.

He'd learned that raising me and adjusting to my birthright—a lifetime of habits, right or wrong, was hard to break.

Robin's voice was in my ear, catching my attention again. "Am I in trouble? Ah. Hmmm. It's more like everyone else is in trouble with the exception of myself," he hedged. "I'd rather explain it in person and give you the keys to the bar. Ishiah left them for you."

Ishiah was my boss at my day job/night job/afternoon job, whenever I wasn't out doing what pulled in the real rent money—disposing of monster ass. He owned a non-human bar—not that humans knew the supernatural existed—called the Ninth Circle, was a peri, which was a winged humanish-type creature that had spawned angel legends, and was generally neutral on whether he should kill me or crown me employee of the month for making it a week without icing a customer while serving up their liquor of choice.

Why would he want to kill me? We had a lot of unpaid tabs because I hadn't once made that said employee of the month. But hand held to the empty, godless space that filled the sky, if I killed you, you usually had it coming. Or you just weren't that quick. In my world, the two were practically the same.

"The keys? Why did he ... Ah, hell with it. We'll get the story when we get there." I looked down at Niko crouching on the street, rhythmically rubbing the kishi's stomach. It crooned mournfully, my blood on its teeth, the silver of its eyes surrounded by the white of fear. "Fuck me." I sighed. Before I let Goodfellow off the phone, I added, "By the way, do you know anywhere we could drop off a baby kishi to be raised up all good with God? Religious, righteous, and true? Oh, and non-people-eating?"

"Your imitation of a Southern drawl is pathetic, and yes, drop him off here." He rattled off an address. "They take in strays all the time. But you'd better do it in the next hour or they'll be gone."

"Gone where?" I asked.

"Who knows? It doesn't matter. They'll all be gone. Everyone. Now hurry the hell up. I'm paying your bill this time. I'm a puck, a trickster, and a used-car salesman. Don't think I won't squeeze every penny out of Niko's well-shaped ass if you don't perform this job to perfection." His phone disconnected in my ear.

"Who was that?"

I grinned down at my brother. "Robin is hiring us for a job, and I'm thinking seriously about taking a dive in the fifth, because it's your ass on the line if we screw up."

"Goodfellow will be a good client. He wouldn't cheat us." He'd cheat anyone else—man, woman, or child, but not us. Niko finished the knot on the rope and slitted his eyes at me. "And let us leave my ass out of it. Why I claim you as my blood, I will never know."

It wasn't true. *I* didn't know why he put up with me, but I took it on faith that Niko knew something that made me worth keeping around. Niko inherently knew extraordinary things that most others didn't know and wouldn't ever know. He was like that. Then again, very rarely, Niko screwed the hell up, wasn't the infallible older brother—because no one was infallible. No one. I hadn't kept count before, the times he was wrong, but if I'd known what was headed our way, I might've starting adding them up now.

Number one was a little over sixty minutes away and headed for us like a freight train.

Tick-tock.

Robin Goodfellow, Pan, puck, trickster, car salesman, and more identities than I could memorize in a lifetime, lived off Central Park. That might have had something to do with his being rich and his kind having a history of spending a lot of time in the woods running around nude, which I didn't once picture in my brain—not once, okay? It was a goddamn shame my booty-call werewolf, Delilah, or Puppy Le Screw, as Robin liked to call her, had tried to kill my family and friends, and was considering the same for me if she had the chance, because I really, *really* needed to get laid.

Regardless of my pathetic condition, squatting on the

outskirts of Central Park was Goodfellow's best option in NYC—if he wanted to revert to the old days of forest flashing and if you could call a three-million-plus condo squatting. His condo board hated him . . . something to do with his wanting to install condom machines on every floor, and the thinly veiled orgies. Although in the last year, the orgies were a thing of the past. After nearly a hundred thousand years of debauchery and extreme horniness, he'd embraced monogamy. I suspected it was a puck brain tumor. Or it would pass in another few months. A monogamous Goodfellow was as if aliens came to Earth and didn't want to hunt you, eat you, or screw your women.

Extremely unlikely.

We'd dropped off the kishi kit and now I stood pounding on Goodfellow's door. "Porn and pizza. Asses and anchovies delivered in thirty minutes or it's free." The condo board didn't care for that either, which is why I did it. Unless it was advertising our business, Niko had threatened to kill me in my sleep if I wore any more T-shirts with obscene, violence-encouraging, or just plain fun-with-chainsaw slogans on them. I had to get my entertainment somewhere else now. No big deal. I was versatile.

I'd bandaged my leg, tying a thick gauze strip on the outside of my jeans and popping some Tylenol in the car as we drove the kishi to demonic day care. I'd do a real version when we eventually made it home. If I could help it, I kept my pants up around Goodfellow. A year of monogamy versus a hundred thousand years of frenzied pansexuality kept me cautious. I'd seen him talk a convention of ninety-year-old Catholic priests into a nudie bar. All right, thinking about it, maybe not that difficult to accomplish, but I didn't want to be the next test subject. He did like a challenge.

After dumping the baby, we left Niko's junker on the curb in front of Robin's building. The doormen were used to us by now and drove it to the nearest parking garage for seventy bucks, which was the first charge on Robin's bill. On the way over we'd seen Wolves, vamps, revenants, vodyanoi, and more. They were in cabs heading toward LaGuardia or JFK, in their own cars, slamming their horns headed for the Holland and Lincoln tunnels. Many were so desperate they were going toward the George Washington Bridge. Jersey to escape the city? That told you right there something was going on and it was worse than the ten plagues of Egypt and Chernobyl combined. Some Wolves were just running, no vehicle necessary. People on the sidewalks were glaring around for the dog walker who'd screwed up. Robin hadn't been exaggerating. Everything with claws and paws and fangs was getting the hell out of Dodge.

I banged against the door again. "Pony play and pad thai. Get it while it's hot." I didn't have to see Niko's hand to know it was aiming for the back of my head. I ducked with the instinct of a thousand received swats and stumbled into Robin's condo as he opened the door beneath my pounding fist.

"You," Robin said, catching me by the back of my shirt to keep me upright, "are going to spend months, nay, years of sleepless nights wishing you had never said that, not in this particular situation." I expected him to sound amused, as that was the kind of joke he would make, but he looked nothing but deadly serious.

Once steady on my feet again, I walked in. Same expensive rock-crystal coffee table, same buttery leather wraparound sofa—an identical replacement, rather, as I'd been indirectly responsible for destroying the last one—same enormous flat-screen television set hidden in a recess in the wall behind an original Waterhouse—Nik told me—painting. Same rich and expensive everything, although one addition was fairly new and a gift from me to Goodfellow, or rather from me to Goodfellow's roommate, Salome. She was a Grim Reaper on four paws and I liked to stay on her good side. So a few months ago I brought her a boyfriend.

"Spartacus," I called, "how's it hanging?" Probably not too well. Once you're dead, had your organs removed, and are resurrected as an undead mummified cat, your testicles probably looked like old raisins that had rolled under the couch. Raisins didn't tend to . . . hang. But it was the thought that counted. I caught him as he slithered out from under the couch and leaped through the air, a zombie feline missile. He looped around my neck and purred in my ear. And if his purr sounded like skulls being crushed under an iron boot, again, it was the thought that counted. His bandages were long gone, and I stroked the hairless black-and-white-spotted wrinkly skin. "You're living under the couch? Is Salome giving you a hard time?"

Another purr erupted from atop the massive refrigerator. Salome, unlike Spartacus, was gray with a small hoop earring in one pointed ear. They both had eye sockets that housed flickering lantern lights that reminded me of Halloween. Salome had followed Goodfellow home from the Museum of National History—against his will—and had lived here since, when she wasn't out stalking senile, ancient pet Great Danes in the hallway. Salome had killed man and beast and probably hadn't considered either one taxing. That was why I'd brought Spartacus to keep her company. I did not want to get on her bad side.

A mummy, Wahanket, who'd lived in the sublevels of

the museum, had made Salome and Spartacus. Although a sometime informant, he had tried to kill me twice and he did kill cats. I didn't approve of either hobby. I made sure Wahanket didn't get to play his King Tut games on anyone else, which Spartacus seemed to appreciate. Salome didn't much appreciate anything, from what I'd seen. I gave the cat's bony ass one last pat and plopped him on the floor. "Be a man," I told him. "Show her who's boss." He gave me a dubious glance and disappeared under the couch again. Apparently being a man was overrated.

Niko removed his duster, hot for late summer, but necessary for covering up katanas and various other swords. "You're hiring us for a job, Goodfellow? That seems odd. You assist us so often you know we'd be more than willing to do you a favor for free."

Robin shrugged, his normally cat-that-ate-five-canaries green eyes glum, and waved a hand at the kitchen table on which rested a meatball sub with double cheese and a tea that stung my nose enough for me to know it must cost a hundred bucks a gram at least—the type of tea Niko loved above all others. "There are favors and then there is ripping your own heart out to tape to an extrarealistic Valentine's card. This is the latter."

I moved closer to the table to catch the precise smell of the sub. "Gino's? Gino's extra-sauce, extra-cheese, extra-garlic meatball sub?" Gino's, where the grease was so thick in the air that it contaminated the entire block and Robin refused to even drive down the street. That combined with the stink of a tea that was available only from one ninety-eight-year-old mean-as-a-snake woman in Chinatown. You had to walk across a path of nails to prove you were worthy of this damn tea, and I was not joking. He'd gone to serious trouble to tempt us, and Goodfellow didn't go to serious trouble to do anything. He manipulated, deceived, lied, but not this. Honesty, money, and snacks?

This was bad.

"Shit. I don't even want to know what the job is." But I didn't mean it.

It was Goodfellow. Our first friend when we'd been on the run from the other half of me, a race called the Auphe. The first murderers born of this earth. All the other supernatural feared them, bowed before them, died under their teeth and claws. The Auphe were gone now, as was the handful of half-breeds like me, but I didn't forget that Robin had been the first to help Niko and me.

Even now . . . he was one of very few. The Auphe had been at the head of the supernatural food chain and they had large appetites, torture always being the cherry on top—which explained why I wasn't too popular. Everyone had feared them and no one had missed them when we wiped them out. Although many didn't know that they *had* been destroyed, that I was the last left, not that that would've made me any more popular. Quite a few had taken and still did take that unpopularity and hatred of Auphe up with me. They couldn't kill an Auphe, but I was only half Auphe and half human. And humans were weak, nothing more than sheep. They thought that was worth a shot.

They thought wrong.

Robin, though, had always been loyal, always had our backs. We'd be piss-poor friends if we didn't do the same. I sat at the table and grabbed the sub, taking a large mouthful. "So what's the job?" I asked as I chewed—the Miss Manners of the monster-maimer crew.

Niko agreed with me silently by sitting down and drinking the tea that they probably cleaned gutters with in China. Both of us looked expectantly at Goodfellow.

He exhaled, folded his arms, shifted from one foot to another . . . nervous tics—all the things the ever-smooth, fast-talking puck didn't do. This was looking worse and worse by the second. After several more twitches, he finally managed to get it out.

"It's my family reunion.

"The whole of the puck race here in New York City.

"Tomorrow."

I choked on the bite of meatball, feeling the suck of it into my airway, and halfway hoping it would do the favor of killing me before I could cough it out. Niko gave me an unconcerned smack on the back, which only had the hunk of meat lodging deeper, while murmuring, "We should have asked for more money."

"You haven't asked for any money yet," Goodfellow pointed out.

"It doesn't change the fact that we should have and will ask for more." Niko slapped a hand between my shoulder blades again, saying, "One more cough and if that doesn't do the trick, Robin gives you the Heimlich. The key concept in Heimlich being 'from behind.'"

I promptly expelled the chunk of Gino's finest onto the table and welcomed the darkness that had begun to slice across my vision. If it was dark, I couldn't see. And I didn't want to see . . . pucks, everywhere. All identical, wavy brown hair, sly green eyes, smug smirks, rampaging egos, and an appetite for sex that made Caligula seem like a hundred-year-old virginal nun. One puck had taken a few years to get used to. More than one? Hundreds? Maybe thousands? All exaggerating, lying, stealing, trying to screw anything that couldn't outrun them . . .

The end of the world had come, and not with a bang . . . okay, yeah, with a bang. It could be lots of them—the largest planet-wide orgy to date. If that was true, I was eating my gun right then and there.

"How many of them?" I said hoarsely, taking the tea Niko passed me to soothe my abraded throat. It tasted like donkey piss. The way the night was going I wasn't surprised.

The puck seesawed a hand back and forth. "It's hard to say. That's the point to the reunion. We count how many of our race are left. If the amount is too low, then we have a lottery and the schmucks with the unlucky numbers have to reproduce to make sure we don't go the way so many other of the *paien*—the supernaturals' word for their kind—races have. Extinction. We meet every thousand years. We all hate it, but it's a necessary evil if we want to keep the magnificence that is Puck alive on earth." He took the same hand and opened a drawer to fish out a checkbook. "My best guess: between seventy-five and a hundred will show. See? Not so bad. When you live pretty much forever you don't need that many to keep a race intact. So? Fifteen thousand dollars? Does that sound good?"

"Thirty," Niko corrected. If Robin was offering fifteen it was worth at least two to four times as much. "And you haven't mentioned precisely what you want us to do."

"Babysit mostly." He handed over the check with a sharkish smile that said Niko should've asked for fifty thousand. "All our well-deserved high self-esteems"—unbearable egos from hell—"in one place tends to lead to disagreements . . . some verbal abuse . . . small fights . . . attempted murders . . . large riots. That sort of thing. You'll be like bouncers, keeping everyone in check, the two of you alone. You're the only two in the city who can do this. We'll meet at the Ninth Circle, get it over with in one night, tomorrow night, and then everything can go back to normal."

"What about everyone else in the bar? The Wolves, lamia, Amadan . . . the usual. We saw them running like bats out of hell on the way over here. I guess we don't have to worry about them." I shoved Niko's poisonous tea back at him.

"Indeed. No worries there. No one else will be at the bar, as no one else will be in the city. No one but humans." Robin's smirk had turned into something darker—beyond old, from the impenetrable forests that swallowed travelers whole, and from under a sky where the stars were the blood-tinged eyes of mad gods. "Every living *paien* creature will flee this place. They feel it."

"They *know*."

"The Panic has come."

3

"On the roof two blocks down, did you see it?"

He meant as we'd dumped the car several blocks away in a garage we couldn't afford—there was blackmail involved—and walked the rest of the way home.

I'd seen it, but Niko didn't stop testing me. It was his way of keeping me sharp, focused, and alive.

We'd left Robin's over forty minutes ago and I was more exhausted from listening to him go on and on than from the fight with the kishi. Sitting on the edge of the tub in our bathroom, I continued to swab the puncture wounds on my thigh with peroxide. Then I'd move on to the antibiotic cream plus an antibiotic shot. You didn't know what in the hell was living inside the mouths of half the monsters we came across, and I doubted the CDC did either. I had the immune system of my Auphe half, which was to say the best damn immune system around, but Niko was Niko. Big brothers were big brothers, and I took the same precautions a full human would, necessary or not.

There were a few advantages to not being human. More than I'd used to think, and more than I *should* think. But that's who I was now and I was fine with that. Better than fine.

I answered Niko's question, and it wasn't an unusual one. Anything new in our world was to be immediately suspected and watched carefully. "I saw it. Five blocks back on the roof. You know I saw it or you would've picked me up by the scruff of my neck and shown it to me while swatting my ass with your katana." I applied the cream and accepted the tape from my brother to secure the bandage around my leg. "Something metal. Steel maybe, and black too. It didn't move and I couldn't make out any details, but it wasn't there this morning when we went by."

Niko handed me the syringe and I injected my thigh muscle with the strongest antibiotic you could buy from a guy who had set up a pharmacy in his van. "I am as proud as if you'd actually graduated high school."

He'd homeschooled me, the ass, and his graduation standards had been higher than any public or private school. I'd simply done my best to forget most of it. "Okay, a dark metal thing someone hauled up to the roof. Big deal. We'll keep our eyes open, but I bet it's just someone's hideous idea of art, or a nerd making armor for the next big Ren Faire. I'm more concerned about the Panic." "Concerned" was a good euphemism for metaphorically shitting my pants.

Goodfellow had been at our sides for three or four years now. He was the most loyal son of a bitch around, to us anyway, but every encounter with him put you one step closer to a mental hospital. I'd seen him naked three times, accidentally, and I didn't give a shit which way the guy swung (he swung all ways . . . he swung in directions and dimensions scientists hadn't plotted yet) as long as he didn't hit on me.

And after seeing what he had a license to carry, I was kissing the ground, grateful he hadn't made a move on me. Even if he hadn't been rich, the man would need his own personal tailor to accommodate what he was hauling around. He did chase Niko in the beginning, but as much as I loved my brother, he was on his own there. And good luck. Every story Robin told was about himself, a threesome, a foursome, an orgy, and onward to things that would have jaded porn stars mystified if not terrified. The themes were pretty blatant—ego and sex.

I could take it, though, because he was a friend, a comrade in arms, and all that shit, but one hundred of him? If Niko wouldn't have taken a picture with his phone, I'd have been curled up in the fetal position and sucked my thumb. Worse yet was *how* there were a hundred or so of them. Robin had always been evasive about how pucks procreated and I'd had no inclination whatsoever to push him on it. An all-male race who were completely identical to one another . . . a curious thing, but nowhere near curious enough to ask him or hear the answer. This time we got the answer whether we wanted it or not.

I absolutely did not.

Apparently there was no equivalent in nonsupernatural biology, although Niko tried his best to come up with a close comparison. Apogamy, androgenesis, adventitious embryony . . . all terms I'm sure I knew at one time, when Niko had been shoving biology into my brain with a crowbar seven or eight years ago. But I'd done my best to forget them, and my best was damn good.

"Male apoximes?" had been his last guess.

Robin had scowled. "Yes, Niko. Pucks reproduce exactly like Saharan cypress trees. In fact, we're kissing cousins. Shall I show you my impressively large trunk?"

"Just tell me we don't have to buy you maternity clothes if you lose the lottery," I'd asked at that point during the briefing, pushing the meatball sub far away at the thought of a hormonal puck. "Jesus, I'm going to barf."

"Gods." He stared at me, disbelief dripping from the word. "How do you function when the hamster on the wheel between your ears takes his lunch break? Never mind. Just . . . here. Wrap your tiny brains around zygotes. It's far more complex than that, as we are far more complex than you, but one puck essentially splits in two. The new puck will also have all the memories, personality, and skills of the original, which is another reason we hate one another so much. We yearn to be unique when in essence we all started out the same as someone else. We immediately part ways and the new puck will start developing memories of his own. As he does, his personality changes slowly as well. We all become different sooner or later."

"Except for the ego, sex drive, trickery, lying, stealing, et cetera," I said.

"Well, naturally. Why would we want to change the best of our race's qualities?"

"You actually are family. In fact, you're closer than family," Niko had mused. "You're supernatural clones."

"All born of Hob," the puck said quietly. As the three of us had nearly died at the hands of Hob before delivering him up to a well-deserved death, we skipped over talking more about the first puck to be whelped by the earth.

"How long does it take?" I'd asked, curious despite myself. "Is there a cocoon involved? Is it like *Alien*? Because that would be nasty as hell. Dripping fluids everywhere. Gah. Good luck finding a maid to clean that up."

"Armani does not make a cocoon," Goodfellow had

replied with a sharp frost edging his voice, and fun time was over. He then went on to tell us about the Panic.

Capital *P* . . . for the capital *R* in "Run for your life."

In ye olden times, ancient Greece, ancient Rome, ancient who gave a crap, people had thought that panic was caused by Pan, pucks, whatever, unseen and rotten as hell, rustling and shaking the bushes off the paths to basically scare the living shit out of travelers. Not true. The word was still around today, but that definition wasn't any more true than it had been in the beginning.

What was true about the Panic, Goodfellow had said, was that pucks produced pheromones by the buckets. Normally the chemical led their fellow supernatural creatures, not humans—it didn't affect humans—to trust them. It made it all the easier for the pucks to steal from their fellow supernatural races and for them to believe the pucks when they said they were off for a romantic bottle of wine while in actuality they were shagging their thieving asses to safety, hauling gold, jewels, whatever they could steal. The pheromone also led the preternatural to lust after them—all the easier to get laid and . . . yeah, well, that was more than enough benefit there.

Eventually after a few thousand—or thirty or forty thousand years . . . who was counting—the pucks' supernatural buddies eventually caught on—or at least their genes did—and after generations upon generations of other races being robbed, lied to, and somehow talked into an orgy with five of their best pals, the pheromones couldn't overcome the nature-driven evolution of an innate and rather deserved mistrust.

That was the pheromones of one puck at work.

One.

Enticing in the beginning, suspicious and distrustful in the end . . . but, still, only one puck, Robin had said. But get more than one puck together and things changed. The pheromones mixed into something new, thanks to that evolution of suspicion and wariness—something new and unpleasant. Get five pucks together and everyone supernatural would become extremely nervous. Get ten together and there would be fighting, screaming, and running. Get the entire race in one spot and the chemical overload could conceivably drive lesser species mad or stop their hearts from fear alone. For the hardier predators, it would be as if they were a single small child drifting in the ocean while a hundred giant great white sharks circled them.

That was the Panic.

That was why all supernatural critters were fleeing NYC as fast as if someone had told them the Red Sox were invading. All of that sounded like a good excuse for me to desert Niko to the job. Keep my share of the money. See ya when I see ya. Send up a flare when it's over. But, Robin had admitted sourly, Auphe weren't affected. As with most poisons and venoms, they were immune to the pheromones. The Auphe were never any fun. The Auphe never played fair. The Auphe ate my brothers, sisters, dog, and crapped in the back of my pickup truck. Bitch, bitch, bitch. Here was the one time I thought I could use that in my favor; being half of the genetic monster to first crawl out of the primordial ooze . . . before turning around to murder the second slimy thing to creep out . . . but no.

When did I get my goddamn silver lining?

It obviously wasn't going to be today. I went straight to my bedroom. The fight with the kishi had been light exercise. Goodfellow's briefing had been as brutal as boot camp twenty-four hours a day, seven days a week, five years in a row. I wanted sleep and I wanted it now.

Niko stayed up to read or meditate or trim his bonsai tree while thinking of ten ways to kill a revenant with its tiny gnarled branches and leaves. Those weren't smart-ass guesses; they were what I knew. Niko had many interests, some lethal, some not, but I knew them all. Family. I hesitated in my bedroom doorway. "It's kind of weird," I said.

Niko had been headed for the main area of the apartment after I'd finished the first aid on my leg. He stopped to look back at me as I stood in the doorway of my room. His eyebrows lifted in silent question. "Family," I elaborated. "I was thinking about family when we were fighting the kishi. I thought it was because they were making a home for their own family, but then Robin comes along with every family member on the face of the planet. Maybe I'm psychic; you think?" I didn't want to be psychic. I had enough nonhuman traits to deal with as it was.

He whirled quickly enough that I couldn't avoid the book he threw to nail me in the stomach. I grunted, but managed to catch it before it fell to the floor. Niko's reflexes were the best I'd seen, among man or monster. "Did you see that coming, O psychic one?" He held out a hand and caught the book I tossed back at him.

"No. Ass." But I rubbed my stomach and grinned. He was right. The Auphe hadn't been psychic and our mother only pretended to be. "Let me know in the morning how many ways you come up with to use your puny shrub as a deadly weapon." I changed and hit the bed hard. I slept hard as well. If that didn't prove I didn't have the slightest psychic ability, nothing else would.

But cursed?

That was a different story.

*   *   *

It was eight in the morning when someone banged a fist against our door. Niko was in the shower washing away the sweat of evil exercise. He'd already been out and run his ten miles. As my leg was tenderized and marinated by baby kishi Alpo, he'd given me a onetime break and hadn't forced me to join him. I was still in bed when I heard the knocking, but I staggered up, cursing at the hair hanging down past my eyes and wearing nothing but sweatpants and two pairs of socks. My feet got cold. Hercules probably had acid reflux. We all have our weaknesses.

I passed through the large open space that formed the combination living area, kitchen, and workout gym to the door of our converted garage, and undid the one bolt. Most New Yorkers had several. Unless it was a particularly nasty case we were working, Niko and I didn't have a problem with encouraging break-ins. Spontaneous sparring was like a jolt of extra caffeine in your coffee. Perked you up.

Opening the door, I began to snarl a natural, "What the hell do you want?" It was way too damn early and I embraced NYC manners like a native. What else would I say?

It turned out I didn't end up saying anything at all. I swallowed the words as I saw it . . . him. . . . all in a split second. I saw the dark blond hair and olive skin, the familiar profile, the way he held himself on the balls of his feet, cautious and loose. A fighter. A warrior. I saw it all in an instant and I gave him what he deserved. Not a word, not a demand, not a greeting.

I tackled him in the doorway, slamming him to the floor.

I said I wore just sweatpants and socks to bed. I did. That wasn't a lie. But I always carried something to bed, and out of it, with me. Sometimes it was the Desert Eagle tucked under my pillow. Sometimes it was the black matte Ka-Bar combat knife I kept under my mattress. Sometimes I swapped them. I wouldn't want to get into a habit. Being predictable gets you killed. This morning it was the knife, serrated and ugly. Yet when it saves your life often enough, when it's buried against the flesh of a traitor's neck, it becomes a thing almost beautiful.

"You should be dead," I hissed at him, a wholly inhuman hiss. I had one knee firmly planted in his flat gut, pinning him. He wasn't struggling or fighting me and he could have. I felt the hard play of muscles under my knee. But if he didn't want to defend himself, I didn't care.

I'd thought it when fighting the kishi: I didn't play by the rules. If you played by the rules, you died, and if anyone was going to die in this moment, it wasn't going to be me. "You should be *worse* than dead." This time I cut him, scarcely enough to split the skin ... to let a measly few drops of blood course down to cup in the hollow of his throat.

"You motherfucker. You could've helped him. You could've *saved* him." He could've saved him from our mother.

Saved him from me.

I could live with what I was now. It had taken years and finally an amnesia-induced epiphany, along with an inner sacrifice, but I could cope with the thing I was. That didn't mean that Niko should've had to. He could've had a normal life. Ours was anything but.

Black eyes gazed at me impassively. "Are you going to kill me or not?"

I wanted to. More than anything in the world, at that moment I wanted to. And I didn't see a single reason I shouldn't . . . save one. I growled, my chest vibrating with the sound, and then slammed the blade home . . . millimeters from his head into the cheap pressed-wood flooring and padding we'd put down over the concrete. "It's not my place to, you worthless son of a bitch. It's *his*."

I got to my feet and looked over my shoulder at Niko standing several feet behind. He was dressed in a long-sleeved black shirt and black jeans, wet hair already braided, his gray eyes fixed on me with confidence. Knowing I'd do the right thing, or what he thought was the right thing. But that wasn't it. It was what I'd said. The fate of that piece of shit on the floor was in Niko's hands, not mine.

Gray . . . I was glad his and my eyes came from our mother. It was one thing he didn't share with the man flat on his back. I peeled back my lips and gave a savage grin. "Daddy's home. Want me to make the tea?"

I'd known what my father was since I was five or so. Sophia had told me from the day I was born, I was sure, but to genuinely grasp that Dad is a Creature Feature, you had to have a few years on you. When it came to Niko's father, she'd told us he left before Niko was born, had left a few weeks after Niko was born, had visited once or twice but Niko was too young to remember. Sophia didn't bother to keep her lies straight, because she didn't lie to deceive, not to us. She lied to hurt.

Niko and I hadn't known any truth of his father except he was Rom like Sophia and of the same clan, Vayash. Only Vayash had the occasional blond hair from hundreds of years ago, when they'd stayed in northern Greece for a time. And though it was forbidden to marry or have sex with a *gadje*, an outsider, that northern Greek blond hair and lighter eyes had made their way into the clan regardless.

Horny then was no different from horny now.

But that had been long ago and the Rom were nothing if not practical . . . eventually, which was how Niko could be blond and still be considered full Rom. He had their dark if slightly olive skin, and all Rom knew the quirks of all the clans. My black hair and gray eyes meant nothing when combined with my pale, decidedly non-Rom skin. I'd have been rejected as tainted with outsider blood.

If I weren't already rejected as tainted with much worse.

I bent over and retrieved my knife before going into the kitchen. I wasn't making any damn tea for Niko's sperm donor, but the kitchen was as far as I could get while keeping an eye on him. As for me, normally I would've had waffles with half a bottle of syrup, and coffee. This morning I didn't have an appetite for anything that wasn't red and spilled with a blade. I folded my arms on the breakfast counter, bent at the waist to rest my chin on my forearm, the Ka-Bar remaining in my hand, and watched through the long strands of hair that still fell over my eyes.

A panther watching unblinking through the tall grass.

A last drop of blood ran from the tip of the knife to mar the sand-colored countertop. I lifted my top lip to show teeth at the sight of it and I went back to watching. The man . . . Niko's father . . . didn't miss any of my show.

He stood smoothly, moving the same as Niko moved: effortless and flowing as water. His clothes were similar as well. Dark, not particularly noticeable, would blend into the shadows well. He shifted his dark eyes from me to my brother. "I am Emilian Kalakos. Your mother, Sophia, I didn't know if she told you that—my name." He was confident with the smear of blood remaining on his neck. I almost growled again.

Niko regarded him without emotion before saying,

"No. She didn't. Close the door behind you. Our reputations here do not need any further fuel for the fire."

"I am welcome then?" That was custom among the Rom. They didn't include the *gadje* in it, but Rom wouldn't enter another's home without knowing they were welcome there.

Glancing at me, Niko quirked his lips, a somewhat less homicidal version of my predatory smile. He was letting me know he knew who his family was and it wasn't this older reflection of himself. "No. But if you wait for welcome you will die an old man on the sidewalk. I leave it up to you."

Kalakos apparently knew when to push and when to not look a gift horse in the mouth. He shut the door behind him. "Do you want an excuse or an explanation?" he asked calmly. I hated the sound of his voice. It was wry, amused, self-possessed—it was Niko's voice, and Niko was unique. This shithead shouldn't be moving like him, looking like him, or sounding like him. The fact that he deserted his son meant he shouldn't *be* at all. This time I did growl once more.

"That would be Caliban. Your brother?"

To give him some credit, there wasn't the hesitation I expected before "brother." Nor were there the many other words the Rom had for me, none of which meant "brother" or anything remotely close to it. The Vayash, shamed as they were that a woman of their clan had whored herself out to a thing fouler than the word "monster" could begin to describe, had nonetheless eventually told the other clans of my existence once one hired us for a job. When that had happened, I couldn't be a secret any longer. The others had to be warned.

With Niko at my side during negotiations, willing to dishonor himself by standing with me, the Vayash decided they had no choice. It was their duty to see that the others didn't see me as merely polluted by *gadje* blood, that my pale skin wasn't from a pasty white Midwesterner who lived on diet of deep-fried cheese but from an Auphe. Ninety-nine percent of humans knew nothing of the supernatural world that swirled around them. The Rom knew it all. They knew of the Auphe. They knew what I was.

I'd been spit on enough to prove that on our one visit to our Clan. But I'd been much younger then, half cata-tonic, half homicidal, and a great deal less in control.

Pity I'd had any control at all.

Pity indeed.

This time my conscious and my unnaturally mouthy subconscious agreed.

"His name is Cal. Do not call him the other again." Niko's lips flattened. Sophia had named me Caliban from the Shakespearean play. Caliban the beast-man-monster from *The Tempest*. She made sure I knew what it meant too, and called me by it every opportunity she had. Mommy had been an educated whore.

Niko had never called me anything but Cal. It was naïve for him to think that every one of his Cals could wipe out all the Caliban that came from Sophia's lips.

Yep, naïve . . . but they sometimes did.

Kalakos kept his eyes on me and I knew what he saw. Half-naked, pale eyes gleaming through the curtain of my hair, a bloody knife, and a smile that tasted of years and years of spite—I wasn't surprised he might think So-phia had been closer to the mark.

Good.

"Why are you here?" Niko demanded, his normal . . . his *inherited* calm gone. In its place were emptiness and the chill of the wind across the arctic ice.

Kalakos turned back to him. He looked about forty-five, but not an ounce of fat on him. All lean muscle, like Niko. They were almost exactly the same height. His hair was much shorter than Nik's braid, though. Looking closer I could see one or two silver strands in it. He wore it slicked back tightly in a two-inch-long ponytail. It was good for fighting, not obscuring your vision. It was how I usually managed to keep the mess of my own heavy hair out of my face. Not anymore. Not while he was here.

"The Vayash Clan failed in its watch. We have lost our duty, our burden. They have sent me to bring it back. I know I cannot do it alone." He included us both in his glance this time. "And none of them are fighters, not the kind you two are known to be. No matter what has come before, all Vayash must work to right this. The burden is here in the city. Worse, it knows that you are in the city. If you will not help me willingly, help yourselves. It can sense the Vayash and it will kill all Vayash that it can find."

All clans had a duty and a watch. I thought I'd been the Vayash one. Looked like I was wrong. Or they had a two-for-one burden to carry. Too bad for them.

"All Vayash?" Niko narrowed his eyes. "Then that is not a problem for us. You are the only Vayash in this room and it's been that way for seven years." While we nodded to the clan name when dealing with other Rom, we didn't claim it. It was a truth that became a lie and now was used only for convenience. Rom were honest only with other Rom. But their money spent the same as anyone else's.

"We came to you when Sophia was murdered, burned to death by the Auphe," Niko continued. "When Cal . . ." He didn't finish that sentence. I knew he didn't like saying it aloud; I knew he didn't like remembering it.

I was better off, in a sense. I didn't remember much of that time when we visited the Vayash, and what I did remember was a foggy haze. When I was fourteen, the Auphe had burned our trailer, killing our mother while Niko escaped out a tight back window, and they'd taken me to a place only Auphe can go. Another world or a murderous reflection of this one, I didn't know or remember any of that. I didn't remember escaping and finding my way back home. The fact that only a day and a half had passed at the burned trailer site, yet I'd returned—somehow—sixteen instead of fourteen at best guess, made not remembering that much ... safer. They played with time like they played with lives. The Auphe had had me for two years. Yet all of it I'd recalled, more or less, was the rare sensation of cold or of rough rock against my skin.

Had I actually remembered those years in detail, I imagined the Cal in me would pour down an invisible drain and leave a Caliban-shaped nightmare in its place.

As it was, after I'd returned, it had been a long time before I'd been anything close to functional. I'd rarely spoken. The only human touch I could stand was my brother's hand on my shoulder, and that took a while. I had remembered the Auphe taking me and I vaguely remembered stumbling home naked through a rip in reality, but next to nothing between. But I'd known they'd come for me again. I might not know anything else, but that I knew.

So we had run. We'd crashed in Nik's car or in motels and I'd curled in a fetal position under the beds with my knife and gone days without sleep. Niko ... Niko had rented rooms with a queen-size bed so he could sleep under it with me, to make sure I knew I wasn't alone.

That's why Niko had gone to the Vayash Clan, our clan, for help, but that's not what they'd given us.

I didn't remember much of it. Time had passed since I'd escaped the Auphe, but I hadn't known how long. I couldn't tell an hour from a minute then. Colors were bright enough to make my stomach turn. The light was too bright, sunny days, cloudy days, always too bright. For a while it made me retreat further into myself. When it came to guessing something as changeable as time, a month was probably close, sounded right, and did it matter? Niko had found the Vayash, I didn't know how, and drove us there in the first piece-of-crap car he'd owned. He'd opened the car door for me when we arrived. I did remember that—his face, his mouth moving, although I didn't understand what he said. I didn't always know who I was, where I was, but I knew Niko. He was the only anchor in a world of chaos. He hadn't been as fortunate with me. He hadn't known when I would be less aware, when I would be a whole lot more, and what rabidly unpredictable things I would do if it was the latter.

That day, I thought, had started out a good day. I still ate with my hands—pancakes. Not meat. I refused to eat meat, refused to look at it, and gagged at the sight of pork. Pinkish white like something . . . something I didn't remember. Eventually I'd gotten used to it again. It took almost a year. Pepperoni pizza couldn't be given up forever. But before then Niko had learned not to feed me meat; even the smell of it repulsed me, although I didn't know why.

You knew why.

What do Auphe eat?

Who do Auphe eat?

I had dressed without Niko having to carefully remind me more than twice. English came and went, as it did that day. Sometimes I understood it; sometimes I didn't. While I hadn't said a word that morning, I did dress, although no shoes. The concept of shoes to me seemed idiotic. I couldn't see the reason for them when the random feeling of freezing cold with nothing but jagged rock to walk or flee on was what I expected. Asphalt, carpet, or grass—decadence.

I hadn't needed shoes, but my knife—I hadn't let go of my knife once then. Not to eat, piss, or sleep. My knife I'd kept with me.

Good day . . . it must've been or I wouldn't have gotten out of the car to face a gathering of people with Nik. He hadn't had much choice. Leaving me in a car by myself wasn't the best option. The last time when I'd forgotten how the door handle worked, I had tried to kick my way out through the safety glass with those bare feet and succeeded. This time I had followed just behind him, the front of my shoulder almost touching his shoulder blade. I was oblivious, not really there. Not really anywhere. Good, good day.

Then I smelled meat cooking. Burning. That had seemed wrong to me. Food and fire, they shouldn't mix, should they?

Waste of flavor, waste of blood. I didn't know why I'd thought that. But wasn't it true?

Sheep. It was what sheep did. I pulled my knife from under my jacket. Sheep, yes, but I smelled their rage and fear soaking the air. The rage I'd dismissed.

The fear I embraced.

It had been a good day, but unfortunately for Niko it turned into an *aware* day. I liked aware days.

But no one else did.

Niko had said something to the group slowly surrounding us. All men. I didn't listen to it. "No, Cal." That was said to me. That I did try to listen to. Tried. Tried. Tried. He'd taught me to recognize my name again. "No knife. Our clan." The women and children had fled inside their RVs. I hadn't caught it all, understood it all, or recalled it all. . . . It didn't make a difference. The result was the same. I'd heard him say, "Help." More sounds. "Kidnapped. Killed." And finally, "Family."

For some reason that word I had known clearly. "You are our family. Help us." Knew it because my two years of imprisonment had imprinted on me that those words were only to be laughed at. Weak and worthless. The Auphe had no family, did they? I couldn't remember, but if they had . . . instinct told me that if they did and one of that family pulled up lame, you . . . they . . . would eat that brother or sister. And those sheep gathered around us . . . they were born lame. Lame as a species.

Then Niko had said something that shocked me, even in my condition.

Beg. "I'm begging you."

Fuck the Auphe. I had family. I *had* a brother and these sheep had made him *beg*.

The men had completed their circle and I had turned to rest my back against Niko's. Watchyourbackwatchyourbackwatchyourback. Alwaysalwayswatchyourback. You took down more that way. They moved closer and that had been when Niko had gotten his answer.

"*Armaya khul! Beng!*" He'd been the biggest of the men, their leader. If it had been now, I could tell you if his hair was curly or straight, if he had a mustache or not, but then . . . humans had looked all the same—alien. Wrong. Puny . . .

Prey.

Except for Niko. He was the only one after two years in Tumulus, Auphe-world without the balloons and funnel cakes, who I could actually *see* in detail. He stood out sharp and clear. The rest? The blur of sheep? Who could tell one from another? Who cared if you could?

"*Doshman!*" Another, bigger one had lunged at us

with a blade in his hand, then back again quickly when I shifted my gaze to him and grinned at him gleefully. That . . . oh, yesss, that I recognized. A sheep making threats. It was funny. It was so goddamn hilarious.

"*Johai!*"

The words, they were filthy and full of scorn. They hadn't had to be in English or Auphe for me to know that. They had spit on us as well, forking the evil eye at me; Niko had taken it much more to heart than I did—eighteen years old with a dead mother, a desperately damaged brother, begging for help. Niko who never begged. Niko who had thought all our family couldn't be as bad as Sophia.

Niko, who had been surprised in the very worst way.

"*Marime! Bi-lacho! Za! Za!*" Their leader had thrown out his arm to hold back the rest of the flock and spoken English to Niko. "You are Vayash. Cast off the monstrous *bino*. Or better, kill the mad beast and return to your clan."

I hadn't forgotten or missed a single word of that, I think because I'd seen the look on Niko's face when he'd been given the choice. I was lost in a fog, but that look and the words that had caused it had managed to part it to let me see and hear clearly.

"You are the monsters. We don't need your help. We don't *want* your worthless damned help." Niko's voice had burned with betrayal and hate. Two emotions I knew better than any others. I'd known them when the Auphe had taken me. I knew them a thousand times more intensely when I'd returned.

Niko didn't hate. Niko wasn't like that. He wasn't like Auphe. He wasn't like me. I heard myself snarling. These sheep had made him hate.

I'd made a sound of anticipation and before Niko

could swivel, I met the nearest two who had charged me at the moment of Niko's defiance of the head sheep. I buried one's own blade in his shoulder and mine in the other's thigh. *Don't kill. Don't kill. Don't kill. Niko wouldn't want me to kill.* But it was hard, *hard*. I wanted it. Wanted. Needed.

Niko . . .

I snarled, but honored my brother, not the Auphe. As both men fell, I settled for laughing. I had known then and now that it hadn't sounded anything like a human laugh.

I hadn't cared. They were lucky it had started out as a good day before shifting to an aware one or I would've gone for their throats with my teeth and done more damage than they could have with their pigstickers. Eight years ago I'd barely understood anything around me. I hadn't been right—in my head, in my soul. No, I hadn't been right at all, far from it. The world had been twisted and strange and it was months before I would see it for what it was again.

If I ever truly had.

When Niko had pulled me back into the car ahead of an armed but uneasy mob, I'd said my first and only words of the day.

My voice had been rusty from rare use, but insistent, and the words were my first real step back toward sanity—toward Cal. "Don't hate. Don't beg. Not you."

Because my brother had been better than that. Better than those sheep. Better than me.

He still was.

That encounter with the Vayash had in part made Niko what he was now: honorable if you deserved it, the un-forgiving steel of his sword if you didn't. That would always be a part of him. Thanks, in a large part, to that and this bastard I'd attacked at our door.

The one last thing I did remember . . . Sophia hadn't taught us Rom. Not the language of our clan or the overall language of all clans. While he could guess from the tone what those words had implied, that wasn't enough for Niko. Two days later we had stopped in a library. After an hour on the Internet, he'd taken me back to the car and I thought, in that one moment, that he'd been glad I wasn't coherent enough to ask him what those words had meant. In the years since, he hadn't once told me, and I hadn't asked. He also hadn't learned any more Rom; Niko who ate knowledge and languages like they were Wheaties. He would have nothing to do with it.

It didn't make a difference if Kalakos was his absent father or not. He was Vayash and that damned him as equally in Nik's eyes.

Kalakos nodded once. "I heard what happened, but I was not there. I swear it, Niko. I would not lie to you. Like Sophia, the clan is too small for me. I roam and I rarely see them. If I had been there, I would've spoken for you."

Yeah, right.

"And I never came to you before"—prior to the Auphe's taking me, before Niko's second or third or fourth or seventh birthday—"as I found out about you when you were two years old. I didn't know I had a son until then. But I thought your mother the better choice for you. The life I lead, constantly on the move, the work I do, not so different from yours, it wasn't any life for a child."

That . . . *that* was worth a fucking comment or two. "You thought Niko living with Sophia . . . a bat-shit crazy, abusive bitch of a mother, was a better life for a child? Is that your story?" He was a liar. He'd slept with her, he knew her, he knew what she was—a sociopath. People don't change that much in three years. He'd known and he hadn't wanted the responsibility of a kid, of Niko, any more than Sophia had. He'd just made it out in time before Niko entered the world—or a booze-soaked hell. With Sophia it was the same thing.

Better life?

Shit.

"Guess what, asshole? You were *wrong*." I straightened and threw the Ka-Bar directly at him. I didn't lose control. It was me, all me, and entirely deliberate.

In a move so reminiscent of Niko it was uncanny, he leaned to one side with incredible speed and caught the combat knife by the handle, as it would've passed by his neck or through his neck if he hadn't dodged. The corner of his mouth lifted. I could see the curve of condescension building. For a half Auphe, I wasn't too impressive, not at all—I could see the thought forming behind onyx eyes.

We'd see about that.

Yes, we would.

"Keep it," I said with a mocking grin. "Where you're going, you're going to need it."

The gate I created blossomed into hungry, pulsing dark gray around him and then he and it were gone. All Auphe could build gates to places they'd been to or could see. An endless number of gates. So could I . . . once. Now I was limited, but I had enough ability left in me, and this one had more than been worth it.

"You didn't." Niko frowned, and it wasn't throwing the knife at his deadbeat dad that sparked that statement. "Tell me that you didn't."

I swept my hair back out of my eyes. It was nice to not

be mistaken as the sheepdog entry in the Unshowered Best of Show. But letting it hang, glaring through it, I'd been what Kalakos had expected me to be—wild and tainted. Auphe. That had been worth it—delivering the goods. "Goodfellow said all supers had fled the city last night. Worst that happens is he gets mugged."

"You did. Buddha on high, you gated him to the boggle pit." Niko lowered his head to pound the base of his palm lightly against his forehead. "Cal, there is supernatural and then there is über-natural. The Panic might affect the boggles some, perhaps, but not enough to make them leave. They can burrow under the mud to avoid the pheromones if they have to, but pheromones or not, I have a feeling not even the Panic is enough to drive the boggles elsewhere."

True. Boggles, nine feet of mud-wallowing, alligator-skinned, shark-mouthed humanoids that lived in the least accessible part of Central Park, were the unsocialized pit bulls of the *paien* world—if pit bulls were the size of bears, could talk, and ate muggers and joggers. Very little—actually nothing—scared them.

I groaned at having to admit social responsibility, which was only for Niko's sake or I would've dropped that asshole straight into the pit and had a brewski to celebrate the occasion. "No, I didn't." I opened the refrigerator and grabbed some frozen waffles. "In case the boggles didn't leave"—and I knew as well as my brother what tough mothers they were—"I gated him about one-fourth of a mile away. If he's a fast runner, he'll be back to annoy us—I mean you—soon enough."

He would be too, the way he moved. I saw where Niko had obtained the potential to become the fighter he was. If he hadn't put in the work, studied martial arts, trained in every single method he could get his hands on, the potential might have stayed dormant. But he had put in the work. He had to keep his brother alive from the pursuing monsters until I was old enough to do it myself, and that took effort.

All of his life had been about making sure I kept mine.

Giving Niko a better life, Kalakos had said. . . . That bastard.

I popped two waffles into the toaster. "Is it all right if I hate the son of a bitch for you?" I asked, pretending to search for syrup in the wrong cabinet. "He's a dick and he screwed you bigger than anything, but he's your father. . . . Guess it's polite to ask: Can I hate him?" I already did, but if Niko had a problem with it, I'd pretend otherwise. If Niko wanted to bond with the deserting dick, the absentee asshole, I'd grit my teeth and go along with that as well. I'd despise it, and keep hating underneath, but I'd do it. To say I owed my brother didn't quite cover it.

"Don't worry." Niko handed me the syrup from the pantry, ending my charade of not meeting his eyes. "He didn't come for me and then he didn't come for us both. You aren't his son, but you're my brother and he knew that. Family is family. He is not ours. He deserted not only me, but you as well." His smile wasn't savage as mine had been, but it was far more bitter.

"Trust me, Cal. I hate him enough for us both."

Niko hated.

The younger me, the Cal of eight years ago, felt a pang of regret.

4

Several months ago, I'd killed eight members of my family.

No, that wasn't what I meant, whether it was true or not.

Several months ago there was a somewhat, in some people's eyes, relatively normal Cal—or by and large normal—the best he was able to be as a half Auphe. Occasionally he did lose his shit, attacked and ate deer while on road trips through the woods, created massive holes in between dimensions to shove through malevolently murderous pucks, and once in a while ripped out an Auphe's throat with his teeth. He also opened a gate or two to save his friends, blew up an antihealer from the inside out to save the world, cleaned his guns while watching porn, and generally was a smart-ass to everyone.

Normal.

I opened the front door to the Ninth Circle to start preparation for the Panic. There was nothing normal about *that*.

But I had been normal, considering the world we lived in.

Again, in some people's eyes . . .

Then that Cal was jumped by several Great Dane–size spiders in Central Park and bitten on his way home from this same bar. The venom caused the loss of most of his memories and separated the human part of Cal from the Auphe part for a while. The Auphe genes concentrated solely on fixing the damage located in the section of the mind that stored memory. They ignored the rest of the body and brain unaffected by the venom. And while they were occupied the rest of the suddenly mostly human Cal showed what he could've been—in a fictional world where Auphe hadn't existed, where they hadn't been half of what he was. A dream. A "what if" in a world where "what if" are the cruelest words around. Finally the poison's effects were healed, and not only the amnesia, but something else—a mental split that had existed since birth, a defect, the Auphe would've said—joined back together and there weren't two different Cals anymore: the human one who was snarky and would take you down if you deserved it and then the subconscious Auphe one who wanted out, although it took him nineteen years, wanted free, who thought control was a disease and slaughter the most natural thing there could be.

Those two Cals became one. The venom had activated the Auphe healing to the extent that it had done more than return my memories. It had interwoven what had once been separate. And now there was me. I was improved. I had control, something I believed I'd always lack.

Having control, that was something unbelievable. Incredible. There was no more reverting to the other half of my gene pool and chasing and eating Bambi in the woods, because there was no other half anymore—not mentally. There was something new and now whole formed by a joining of Auphe and human.

Something new, something old, something unlike anything on this earth.

I was in command, darker maybe, but the darkness was worth it.

Darker than dark, blacker than night. Yessss.

Enough, Gollum. Christ. I'd gotten the point already.

But it was worth the trade—I thought. Before, I wouldn't kill you unless I had to ... although I might want to if you pissed me off. Now the whole—the new—Cal wouldn't kill you unless I had to; I'd just *want* to a whole lot more—and you didn't always have to piss me off to have me fondling my guns. The drive was increased, but the decision was the same ... because of the control. I held back, unless you did have it coming to you.

Killer, raper, monster, maimer.

Past Cal would've put you down. I would too, but first you'd have the tour. Down and down, 'round and 'round, through *Caliban's* town. In the past, it would've been quick. Now I took my time. Your pain equaled your victims. Your amount to arrive six feet under, it took longer.

Niko believed in karma in the next life. I believed in karma in this one, and I was a stand-up soldier when it came to delivering it. The decisions I would've made in the past, they hadn't changed. Much. The punishment ... *that* I fulfilled more appropriately according to the crime and the time. I was the right hand of justice and the left hand of the undertaker.

Clever excuses. But why do you think ending the useless needs them?

The spider venom, the biological repair, had stabilized me—Niko, Robin, Promise, and I, we'd all recognized that. I hadn't settled where others in the supernatural community would've liked, but I *was* stabilized. That, for everyone around me, was a relief, because it was one hell of a slippery slope, as they say, when my Auphe genes began to overcome the weaker human genes. Auphe genes always win—that's what a long-gone healer friend of ours had said.

He'd been right—until now. And would be right again . . . maybe . . . sometime in the future.

There were the dreams too. Awash in blood and the hunt. Did I ever have dreams that heart-pounding? That savored?

So wild?

So wanted.

Black thoughts and scarlet dreams, they didn't mean anything in the end—unless they were useful. I was in command of myself now and that was all I needed to know. I would do what had to be done only when it had to be done, and if I enjoyed it a great deal more, then that was a win-win.

I flipped on all the lights in the bar. The last thing I wanted was a dim atmosphere that assisted the pucks in scheming, assaulting, stealing, and a hundred other things.

While at least I was in control of my mind, I knew I was way out of my depth on the approaching situation. The Panic? No fucking way. I tied the black apron around my waist and started lining up glasses on the bar of the Ninth Circle as I used that control to consider something else besides pucks. I thought about consequences—something I rarely did.

Consequences were boring.

Yet sometimes you had to man up and face them.

That wasn't boring. That just sucked. But for my brother, I would do it.

Not that it still didn't suck.

"You think I made a mistake gating that SOB to the boggles before we found out what the Vayash burden is?" I asked my brother, who was working beside me with methodical movements.

The last Rom clan who'd come to hire us to find their lost duty, their burden had been the watchers of an anti-healer known not so euphemistically as the Plague of the World. Suyolak could've destroyed all life on the planet if we hadn't stopped him. The Black Death was just a kiddie party to him, and one he'd started. It made me wonder what the hell the Vayash were supposed to be keeping locked down.

If it was anything remotely close to Suyolak, that was bad fucking news.

Niko showed no signs of being concerned as he shrugged slightly, following my lead with the glasses. "He'll be back, as you said. And whatever the Vayash have lost, we cannot find today. Today is the Panic, and not only are we committed, but I think the Panic may supersede any other threat on the face of the planet."

It should've been a joke, but it didn't sound like a joke, and I was under no illusions that it was.

Goodfellow was the typical trickster with typical trickster ways, but he was sane. Fairly content, even happy now that he was in what used to be the foulest curse word in his vocabulary: a relationship. But he was only one of two pucks I'd met. The other, Hob, had been insane, malignantly narcissistic, and would not only kill you for no reason, but do it more efficiently than anyone alive. When you're the first, born conceivably a million years ago, you learn to fight like there is no fucking tomorrow. My genes were *of* the firstborn, but I was not *a* firstborn. There was a difference—as in unnumbered-amount-of-years-of-carnage-experience difference.

If they hadn't crippled you, it would be different. Much different.

"What do you mean, 'crippled'?" Niko asked, the glass suspended in his hand. His knuckles were white and tense. Shit, I'd actually said that aloud.

The door opening managed to get me out of an immediate explanation. Robin walked in wearing his usual outfit of expensive green shirt, black slacks, and shoes. He sat on a stool and said rapidly, "All right. Extremely important. Before the others get here you are not to mention, hint, or even *think* about how I'm in a monogamous relationship. Are we clear? It would ruin my reputation among the Panic. They'd hang me from the ceiling and beat me like a piñata. So keep your mouths shut. *¿Entienden?*"

"Whatever," I said. "Trust me, I'm traumatized enough. The last thing I want to talk about with a hundred other yous is your sex life."

The green eyes shifted to something less Robin and considerably nastier as he raised his voice. "Come on in, brothers! *Adelfae!* Hear the news." The door swung open again to reveal a streaming horde of pucks. "It's true. Goodfellow is *monogamous*. He's become a freak. A pervert. Depravity on the cloven hoof."

"Or his balls fell off," suggested another puck who came to the bar. "Or his dick. Anyone who would hang about with Bacchus is bound to get a catastrophic genital rotting illness at some point." This one was also identical except his hair was a few inches longer and he had both ears pierced with small gold hoops.

Niko looked at me as the priest must've looked at the guy sitting in the electric chair in the old days right before the switch was flipped: resigned sympathy. "I didn't know he wasn't Goodfellow," I protested, feeling the desperation sharply. Not our Goodfellow at any rate, but his carbon copy. "He looks dead-on Robin. He said he was Robin."

"Implied," Niko corrected, the sympathy turning one hundred and eighty degrees to a mildly sadistic pleasure he didn't make an effort to hide. "He implied it. He didn't say it."

"He's wearing the same kind of clothes Robin would wear"—I kept up the crumbling defense—"and all of them smell the same." I hadn't inherited the Auphe ability to see in the dark, but I had inherited their sharp sense of smell. "Every one of them smells like frigging Irish Spring. All green and minty. It's not my fault."

He put the glass down and patted my back. "It was nice knowing you, little brother. When Goodfellow is through with you and if there's enough left to bury, I'll find you a nice plot." The pucks kept pouring through the door and, immune to pheromones or not, I felt pretty damn panicked as they kept coming and coming. And I wasn't touching that double entendre with a ten-foot pole . . . or *that* one either.

Another puck came pushing through the crowd. As soon as the others spotted him they started singing some ancient seventies song: " 'Do you like piña coladas? And getting caught in the rain . . .' " The tone was pure derisive malice, obviously not a "Hey, great to see ya, brother. Congrats on the boyfriend" song.

A fist banged against the bar, rattling the glasses. "Who told them?" this puck demanded with a poisonous hiss that would've done any rattlesnake proud.

"Goodfellow?" Niko asked dubiously.

"Yes, Goodfellow. Goodfellow who has been outed as a freak monogamist whose shame will follow him to his dying day. Now *who* told?" He didn't wait for an answer. He grabbed a handful of my shirt. "Why do I even ask? We are pucks. Didn't that one brain cell you possess wake up long enough to let you know *we* all lie? *We* all deceive? *We* all hate one another's attention-snatching guts and would do anything to humiliate one another?"

He didn't give me a chance to respond. "Ah, what did I expect? You're a Boy Scout in a con man convention. If con men had the drive and conscience of Jack the Ripper."

Me? A Boy Scout? With the things I'd done? That was a first, but considering this company, he could be right. Releasing my shirt, he dropped his forehead onto the bar and mumbled, "We should've worked out a safe word. Give me three bottles of scotch."

A hand slapped his shoulder and squeezed. "Would you like a mercy killing? I'd hate for a tainted monogamy cell to enter the race should you lose the lottery."

It was the one who'd masqueraded as Robin. I could tell only by what he was wearing. Otherwise he and Goodfellow were beyond identical. It was creepy. The bar was full of about seventy of them, and besides length of hair, clothing, and the occasional scar, they were as Nik had said: clones. Your brain squirmed at the sight of it. It was unnatural—mirrors within mirrors. "No, thank you, Faunus," Goodfellow said smoothly, sitting up. "I'd rather discuss how you haven't had sex *at all* in a year. Did you take vows or is it true that an incubus bit off your penis in disappointment at your pathetic performance?" He grabbed the hand on his shoulder, slammed it on the bar, and pinned it there with a beautiful Spanish poniard gleaming silver and needle sharp. "Let us check and see."

I turned my back just in time to hear the slide of material as pants were yanked down and then a pained groan from the entire bar. Apparently the incubus story edged out the taking-vows one.

"Is this the type of fight you hired us to prevent?"

Niko questioned. I didn't know where his gaze was, on Goodfellow or Faunus, because I remained with my back to the Panic. I might work that way the entire night if it was feasible—serving the customers without facing them.

"Hardly," Goodfellow dismissed. "A fight will be when one of us genuinely tries to kill another. We need alcohol to lubricate that into motion. Give us an hour. And you can look again, Cal—not that there was anything to see." There was a wicked gloat at the monogamy revenge in the words. "His pants are back up. Luckily he does have a belt, as there is nothing else to hold them up."

Warily, I faced the bar again as Faunus disappeared into the jeering and laughing crowd, the bloody blade remaining on the bar. "I think you made an enemy for life."

"We are all enemies, but keeping the race alive is more important than that. And what precisely are you doing?" I ignored his question as I uncapped the black marker I'd fished out from under the bar, leaned across, and wrote "RG" on his forehead.

"Just a precaution." I put the marker back under the bar and handed over his three bottles of damn expensive scotch that he insisted be kept especially for him.

"Actually, that's not a completely idiotic idea . . . unless it's permanent marker." He scowled, but let it go and pointed to several other pucks around him. "This would be Piper, Pan, Shepherd, Paein, Paniskoi, Phobos, Philamnos, Phorbas, Panikon, Puckstein—he converted—Prank, Puca, Puki, Argos . . . and you'll never remember the rest. Simply enjoy the spectacle and if you have to take a break, I'd go together. The buddy system is essential during the Panic."

"Mostly *P*s. Why aren't there any variations on Good-fellow or Robin?" Niko asked.

His face went blank but he smiled ... technically. If someone had taken that poniard from the bar and carved the smile on his face, the effect would've been the same. "That's a good question. I've wondered myself and then I wonder something else. Hob was the first, a million years on this earth. No one dared to take his name. I say I'm a hundred thousand years old, but as I can't remember half of those, what else might I not remember? A million more? Hob went insane because he did remember. All those years and all the things that he had done. In a million years they couldn't all be good things, now, could they? Some might be extremely bad things."

His imitation of a smile became more unnatural as he continued. "Or if you don't care what you do, the absolute number of years of boredom alone would drop you into the deepest pit of insanity. Maybe I'm a little smarter than Hob when I know a perfect memory can be the worst of enemies. Then again, maybes are only maybes. Maybe no one else cares enough for my name to steal it."

The smile disappeared piece by piece, chunks of ice shoved methodically one by one into a freezer. "Do you have any interesting questions to add, Caliban?"

I felt like I'd asked someone what time it was and they beat me to death with Big Ben. Someone was cranky. I juggled more bottles of alcohol, ready to pour. "I was just going to ask why you guys have dicks if you don't use them for the whole baby-making thing, but I think I can live without the info. Go party. Have fun. Stab somebody in the back. We've got it covered."

His eyes didn't become any less opaque, but he did turn and disappear into the crowd. "I think I might've pissed myself a little bit," I said conversationally to Niko. "How 'bout you?"

"A drop. Perhaps two at the most." Niko took the discarded poniard and tucked it away. He did like collecting blades.

"I always wondered why he wasn't afraid of me like everyone else." Or hadn't hated me like everyone else. You hate what you fear. Goodfellow didn't fear me. He never had. "My monster cred just dropped a notch."

Both of us had started pouring drinks when one of the pucks shouted, "Where's the entertainment? The strippers! The whores! I've ten thousand dollars in fives and a crotch on fire! Bring on the orgy!"

"Oh God," I croaked. The glass in my hand fell to shatter on the floor.

And Niko didn't catch it. Niko and his unmatched reflexes didn't catch the glass. For the first time in his adult life, I thought my brother was frozen with fear.

"I thought all other *paien* left when you guys rolled into town," I said. "Goodfellow said so. I remember. Distinctly. Very distinctly." With the possible exception of the boggles, and I didn't see Mama Boggle on a stage wearing pasties over her scaly chest and a G-string made to accommodate her thrashing crocodile tail. Nine feet of croc-a-croc-a burning love. "Oh shit, I think I'm going to pass out." I clenched the edge of the bar.

"Almost all *paien*," one of the pucks corrected. Puckstein—I recognized him by the Star of David around his neck. "Not the lili and lilitu. They can't smell us." He stretched as if he were next up in Olympic men's gymnastics. *Jesus.* "Hope you have a fire hose handy to clean out the place. You're going to need it when this night is over."

Jesus.

I thought about shooting myself in the head. I thought about shooting the puck, but taking out seventy wasn't going to happen. I decided on the simple: running out the emergency exit doors, if Niko didn't beat me to them.

But it was too late. There were three reasons for that. One was the commitment we'd made to Robin—by commitment I meant the money we'd taken and had no intention of giving back. The second was the chains I saw wrapped and locked around the emergency door push bars. Goddamn mind-reading Goodfellow. The third was the worst.

The entertainment had arrived.

Seventy or so lions prowled through the front door. They walked upright, dressed in long raincoats to pass among humans, but they were lions. Until they stripped off the coats as soon as they passed through the door, and then they were lions and eagles. Male and female, they all had masses of hair—no, not hair, but manes, tawny or dark brown or a mixture of both. Sunglasses were dropped as well to reveal cat's eyes in reverse, black with a golden slit of iris. They also had dark brown/black wings springing from their backs. That was comfortingly familiar. It was a peri bar. We were used to feathers here.

But there was something off. I took a harder look. I was used to anything these days when it came to monsters. Yet there was something . . . missing.

Their eyes and full-lipped mouths were so large, you almost didn't notice—that there was only smooth skin between. No noses.

Puckstein was right: Puck pheromones wouldn't bother them at all. Hard to smell when you're lacking noses.

Everywhere else they looked mostly human—human

with the bare minimum of sequined stripper wear to be taken off for money, and lion fur billowing where most women waxed or shaved and some men manscaped. I was half monster, but, yeah, I knew the word "manscape" and if I hadn't, seeing enough fur escape a bulging G-string that it crept down to knee level, I would've *invented* the term.

The music started, the lights lowered and began to pulse in wild colors, and a wall-covering sheet I hadn't given a single thought of going near was ripped down to reveal the entire contents of a porn warehouse. There were sex toys I'd seen, sex toys I hadn't seen but was aware existed, and then there were things I hadn't seen, hadn't heard of, and couldn't begin to guess what in the hell they did.

"I'm surprised Goodfellow didn't go all out and bring in chandeliers from which they could swing," Niko said.

I pointed to a corner where a leather swing was being set up to hang from the ceiling. "Ah." Niko exhaled, to center himself—I'd seen him do it many times before. "You're fascinated with the porn channel. Now you get the three-dimensional version. I'd think you'd be enjoying yourself."

"I like a candy bar once in a while too. This is being stuck in Willy Wonka's Perverted Sex Factory." I started pouring drinks. It was a job. *Muscle through it.*

Niko began pouring as well, as a wall of impatient hands waved frantically in our faces. "The lili, male, and lilitu, female, were born under the sands of Assyria in ancient times. If you're born under the sand, often live in sandstorms, I understand nature deciding you didn't need a nose. They're known to be ravenously sexually predatory, more so than—difficult as it is to imagine—pucks, I've heard."

A naked puck slammed and bent an equally naked male lion over the end of the counter—my end—and I commented in resignation as the bar, glasses, and bottles began to shake furiously, "I think you heard wrong."

I moved around to the other side of Niko, which was tight to be pouring drinks, so I started handing out bottles instead. Whiskey, scotch, tequila . . . whatever I could grab the quickest. Pucks had a tolerance that made a case of forty-ounces seem like a thimbleful to them anyway. I also started drinking myself. Heavily, which I rarely did in a business where you needed to stay alert to stay alive. But if I had to see what I was seeing, I preferred to see it with blurry vision.

The bar was packed, less than inches to spare. Seventy or so pucks, which was equal to about seventy thousand egos, plus seventy horny lions—the Ninth Circle wasn't built for a crowd half this size. But everyone seemed willing to share their personal space in helpful ways such as wrapping their legs around someone else's waist or hips, from the front or the back or upside down. There was also a tangled pile of heaving bodies—I didn't count—in each available corner, skin-to-skin, not a millimeter of space between. Anything to keep the fire marshal away.

Wasn't that obliging?

There were also those who hadn't gotten past the strip shows yet. They were probably the equivalent of pucks with sexual dysfunction. It took them at least two to three minutes to get warmed up for a full-on ménage à whatever the French word for "twenty" was.

The dancers were gyrating on tables, chairs, and an agile two impressively on top of one of the thrusting and groaning mounds of sweating flesh. Female lions'—lilitu's—breasts were bouncing, which I approved of, although the wish on the shaving or waxing issue hadn't changed. The male lions had bouncing going on as well, but it had nothing to do with breasts.

I groaned myself, but there was nothing sexual about it. I looked in another direction quickly, but unfortunately it was where I'd been ready to serve drinks earlier. How'd I forget that? The puck and the male lion hadn't stopped shaking the bar yet. The puck was nuzzling through the lili mane to bite the back of his neck, and the lion was roaring and then purring as his wings flared and he lifted them in the air, the puck's legs clamping around the thickly muscled waist. The lili roared again and there was a sudden rain of russet-colored fluid that smelled of cinnamon and desert sand.

I hadn't seen it, but I'd bet *Brokeback Mountain* wasn't anything like this.

"I am so not cleaning that up," I said, taking another swallow from my bottle of whiskey.

Robin wasn't going to be forgiven for this, not until the day I died and was a year in the ground. Niko was fending off probably the twentieth puck of the night—they definitely liked blondes—with his sword. "Bartenders are off-limits," he was repeating. "Tell your brothers. No means no. It also means I will remove a very different kind of sword from them if they don't respect that."

I looked up to see the air full of sequins that had fallen from tossed-off clothing. They glittered in the flashing lights. Money flew in gusts of wind caused by flapping wings. It was like being inside a giant kinky snow globe. The pucks weren't interested in me, although from their dubious glances they didn't know why, and I drank on. Another puck tackled one of the female dancers off a table and was already inside her by the time they landed on the floor. She laughed as his mouth closed over a dark golden nipple.

Okay, that I missed. "I need to get laid in the worst way," I said mournfully.

"And that would be more than enough alcohol for you." Niko plucked the bottle from my hand.

It passed, the "entertainment" part of the reunion. Rather like the bubonic plague passed: slowly and leaving madness and despair in its path.

Then came the puck version of after-sex. My definition was spooning with whispers in her ear of, "You were fucking hot as hell. You could kill a man with one of your blow jobs," followed by an instant drop into unconsciousness while drooling on her shoulder. With who I screwed, you had to give to not get your throat clawed open in your sleep. I thought I did damn good. I told Niko about it when sparring one day, because two entire sentences before sleep were excessive in my mind. I was *tired*, damn it. I was hoping he could suggest how to pare it down to one sentence . . . maybe four or five words.

Niko, who had a love, not a homicidal friend with benefits, more experience in sex, and a degree in psychology, gave me a lecture on something called postcoital intimacy, affection, and mutual bonding. My way took ten to fifteen seconds; his took thirty minutes minimum. I'd searched our place for whatever romance novels he had stashed away—I was not enabling my brother's pussified ways—but I hadn't found any yet. No way he got it out of a psychology textbook. Men wrote some of those textbooks, and no man would write that. That was insane.

But it turned out that pucks did me one better. They didn't go to sleep. While lili and lilitu curled on the floor in exhausted slumber, drowsy lions on the Serengeti, the pucks bragged and tried to murder one another, and sometimes they did both at once.

"Good Queen Bess, the Virgin Queen, my muscular ass!"

They'd all thrown off their clothes long ago and now were lunging for equally discarded weapons littering the floor between the sleeping lions. That had Niko and me sailing over the bar, as none of the other pucks had an interest in stopping fratricide. Clone-icide. Whatever you wanted to call it.

"She was no virgin, but I pierced that dusty hymen long before you!"

I had a gun in each hand, arms extended to press the muzzles against two puck foreheads. "Drop the swords and go sit the fuck down. This establishment is losing patience with its customers, and when it does, it doesn't refuse them service. It refuses them life. Got it?" They grumbled but gave up the swords and wandered toward the bar in search of more alcohol.

This example cut down on the fighting some, but not the bragging.

"Rasputin? I bought his penis in a jar off eBay. It wasn't nearly as large as I remembered."

"Pity, but absence makes the heart grow fonder."

"Or the penis larger."

"*Thor?* You lie. Thor has never been sober enough to get it up, and he prefers blond women with breasts larger than their heads."

"Hell, yes, I rode with Butch and Sundance, in all the ways there are to ride. It's a forever shame about the Bolivian army. I almost choked up when I escaped out the back with the pesos. Sad times. Good times. This drink is for you, compadres."

"Damn straight, I'm still taking bets on Jimmy Hoffa. For ten thousand you get one guess on where I planted that fat bastard. For fifteen thousand I'll throw in the cannoli he was eating when I popped him one."

"Cleopatra? Definitely a man. Barely looked like a woman even when you were wearing wine goggles. I couldn't believe Caesar never caught on. The kid? That was actually a thirty-year-old toothless dwarf Cleo bought in the market. Caesar thought he had the ugliest baby in Egypt."

"D'Artagnan's best work was always done with his other sword, and size-wise, it was actually equal to the one he used for duels."

Niko circled the next potential mass murder—five pucks squabbling—waiting to see if it got out of hand.

"Did I mention at the last reunion that I screwed Lady Godiva?"

"No, you credit-thieving maggot, I did."

"No, *I* did, and I have a lock of her hair to prove it."

"I didn't care for her. Stuck-up bitch with the worst horsehair wig in the hemisphere. Now let's talk Eve. . . ."

"*Eve?* You *are* an idiot. I was there. That whole show was mine, all mine. It was hilarious. I kept pelting her with apples and shouting, '*Eat it!* Come on, you apple-hating nudist. *Eat it!*' Then I'd hiss a few times from the bushes to throw suspicion elsewhere. I thought I was going to lose my pitching arm before I finally hit her in that incredibly empty head with the tenth one, but she at last took a bite. I know I gave her a fruit phobia for the rest of her life—not to mention death, menses, and painful childbirth, but, more important, that bet was *won*. I had Michael, Gabriel, Azrael, and Lucifer handing over their flaming swords and then their *other* flaming swords, if you get my drift and I know you do. Now, that was a party. I'll bet their daddy paddled their asses good when they dragged themselves home a week later."

And on and on it went. The fighting simmered down, though, until it was only reminiscing.

Niko and I returned to back behind the bar. It felt marginally safer, and why the hell weren't they putting their clothes back on? "Suicide pact?" I said casually, wishing I'd remained half-drunk, but life's not that easy.

"I'm thinking long and hard about it," Niko confirmed. He continued to listen to the pucks, as if anyone had a choice, and looking both fascinated and appalled by turns. History was a sacred subject to him. But when only liars are telling the tales, what did you believe? Not the Garden of Eden guy, that I knew. There were no angels, only peris . . . the seed of the myth.

One of the pucks appeared in front of the bar directly before me as I was handing Niko a leftover hundred-dollar bill that a puck had tried to shove under his apron about an hour ago. As brotherly emotions went, he was less thankful than he could've been. When I was done, I smacked a glass down in front of the looming new puck. "What'll it be?" But there was no drink order. This puck had something entirely different on his mind.

"There is something wrong with you."

It was one of the pucks Robin had introduced . . . Pan. I remembered because of the tattoo on the side of his neck. ∏—the Greek letter for *P*. He was old. I'd never considered Goodfellow old, as I'd never had anyone to measure against him but Hob, and I'd been too busy at the time trying to kill that bastard to make any comparisons. Now, though, with all of them gathered in one place, I could get a sense of the younger versus the older. They might be supernatural clones, but real, earned experience over cloned experience told. Their bragging was much less believable, and I'd have thought it impossible, but they were actually more annoying. Much louder too. Those made Robin seem subtle in comparison.

This one . . . staring at me . . . had hair so short it was nearly buzzed, leather wristbands, a scar that ran from his right eyebrow into his hair by three inches, already had a knuckle-duster knife in his hand, and he was old. He felt like Goodfellow felt—as if he'd known the world a thousand times over and conquered wide regions of it more than once before tossing them aside, bored. Old in the supernatural world didn't mean feeble; it meant powerful and, in this case, aware.

Of me. And wasn't that incredibly bad luck for him?

His eyes didn't blink. "Wrong. Base. Vile." He studied me. "I know you." The green darkened to almost black in surprise and disgust as his pupils dilated. "I *know*." He showed his teeth as he spit, "Impossible wretched *thing*."

It hadn't taken Goodfellow more than fifteen minutes after meeting me to know what I was. This one had taken an hour or three, but it didn't make a difference. He knew and, unlike Robin, he seemed to hold my extinct race's crimes against me. If he did, who was to say how the rest of the Panic would react? This one had completely no reservations about what he would and did attempt to do. He came across the bar at me blade ready with a swiftness that would make the kishi from last night seem as if they were running in mud.

Then again, the kishi had been as challenging as fighting off a pack of Chihuahuas. And this puck was no baby to be socialized and adopted. There was no free ride for him. No shred of conscience to hold me back.

It was the high point of the night for me.

I buried Robin's poniard that Niko had tucked underneath with the glasses into one green eye. I felt the point scraping the back of the inner skull before I flipped him over the counter to land dead and heavy on the floor. Niko tipped over a pile of stacked black aprons and towels on the shelf behind us to cover the body and it was as if it had never happened. In a room full of now-drunk tricksters, it was a magic trick all its own. Pan had been there. Pan was gone. No one noticed where, when, how, or who. Oblivious, they kept drinking and shouting over one another for their bullshit to be heard.

Except for our puck.

Goodfellow, recognized by the *RG* on his forehead and being the only puck wearing clothes, appeared in the precise spot where a second before a wannabe assassin had stood. Not a wannabe in his day or against others, but here and now? He should've paid attention to what he labeled me—because he hadn't been that far off base. "What happened?" he demanded.

"Pan happened," Niko answered flatly. "You didn't say they might know about Cal, or what they would do if they did."

I reached down, jerked the Spanish dagger free from its flesh-and-bone sheath, wiped it on my bar apron, and slid it across the counter to Robin. " 'Wrong. Base. Vile.' " My hair hung forward—still no ponytail for me, thanks to Niko's father—and I grinned blackly. " 'Impossible wretched thing.' Practically compliments. He didn't know me half as well as he thought he did."

He took his poniard and put it away. "Pan is . . . was one of the oldest. If any would recognize your partial heritage, he would be the only one. I should've watched him more closely. I apologize." Swiveling, he took in the crowd and sighed. "Thank Zeus it's nearly over. I've never been at a reunion sober and monogamous. They're somewhat tedious in this state." He sounded relieved when he said, "But they are all finally intoxicated enough to suffer through the lottery. We'll end this now. Again, I am sorry—for what he said and what he tried to do. You know none of it is true, kid." He turned back to give an insistent and reassuring poke of his finger to my chest before he was gone again into the crowd, handing out coins that were each stamped with a number.

None of it? No. I didn't fool myself. Some of it was true—most of it was true, in fact—but we all have our character flaws. You learn to deal with them. I had. I dropped another apron down to cover Pan's head. That was one dealt with right there: covering up the evidence that was the result of an impossible wretched thing. "It was self-defense," Niko said, low—not that any of the pucks could hear anything above themselves. "I know except for the scar, hair, and tattoo, he looked exactly like Robin, but he wasn't. However connected they might be thousands of years ago genetically, he wasn't Goodfellow. He was nothing like him."

He was singing to the choir. I had no qualms about what I'd done. Pan had been an asshole. "No, he wasn't like Robin," I agreed without a shred of guilt. He was more like me, although not enough or he might still be alive, but that wouldn't be something that would ease Niko's mind to hear, so I didn't say it. Instead, I rested my chin in my hand and proceeded to watch the lottery. "Wanna take bets on whether or not Robin gets knocked up?"

He didn't. But from the outraged howls that all but shook the walls, the numbers of about twenty-five pucks came up. Picked out of a large intricate and ancient bronze bowl, Goodfellow held each duplicate coin up to be seen. As the livid shouts continued, I asked, "Does it make your brain hurt? Seeing so many of them so much alike?"

"It does. It's not meant for the human eye to see. Identical twins and triplets are startling, but this? If there were only fifty of them, you could call them pentacontuplets or demihectuplets or, if going by the Latin, quinquagintuplets. But seventy, that curious to search my brain for the term I'm not." For Niko that indicated a weariness usually unseen in him. An unknown father, the Panic, serving drinks while standing on a dead puck — I think we'd both had our fill of this day.

But it was over. The pucks were dressing and leaving, some glum at their reproduction duty, other celebrating at dodging the bullet. The lili and lilitu were doing the same with their raincoats. We'd broken up only ten fights in all throughout the night and killed one puck. Taking into account the situation, I realized it could've gone much worse. I'd told Nik I needed to get laid, but looking back on the entire reunion, I might go the other way and never need to get laid again.

Goodfellow joined us to watch them go. "If they avoid their obligation to reproduce, what punishment do they receive?" Niko asked.

Robin finished off a last glass of scotch. "Oh, we hunt them down and kill them. If they don't do their duty to keep the race alive, they're not much good to us. It's the only puck crime punishable by death. Now that I think about it, it's the only crime we have at all. The first, last, and single law."

"How many times have you lost the lottery and doubled the pleasure, doubled the fun?" I asked with caustic curiosity.

Robin was equally amused and insulted by the question. "Never. There are tricksters and there are tricksters and then there is me. Losing the lottery isn't in my future. Now, thank you for the assistance and, as a token of appreciation, I'll take care of disposing of Pan and calling in three or four cleaning crews for the rest of it—the kind the cops call in to clean up sites of multiple murders, as there aren't enough mops in the building to handle what's on that floor." He set his phone on the bar, ready. "Consider it a tip for Pan. He always was a bastard. Loved watching the lions eating the Christians in the Coliseum. A definite prick, and not the good kind that makes you want to whip out your measuring tape." He waved a hand. "Go, and, Niko, feel free to keep all the dollar bills they stuffed down your apron." There were wads of them. All pucks, not only Goodfellow, had a thing for my brother.

But that was a discussion for, well, not now. I took the opportunity offered and was out the door with Nik on my heels before Goodfellow had a chance to change his mind, which he frequently did when it came to physical labor. "You are splitting those tips with me, though, right?" I asked Niko as the door slammed behind us.

"As frequently as I was groped tonight, all for the greater good and continuance of the puck race ... no. You don't get a dime. I'm donating it to the spay-and-neuter program at the local shelter. It seems appropriate."

We were still on the block where the Ninth Circle was located—a decidedly nonhuman block. It was rare that one wandered down this way. What they didn't know, they sensed: Here there be monsters. And with all the other supernatural creatures gone, it was empty as I'd ever seen it. "You are such a greedy bast ... *shit*."

I'd seen the glitter of metal and the flicker of movement all at once, leaping straight down from the top of the building we were walking past. I threw myself to one side, Nik to the other, and it landed directly between us. The concrete of the street cracked into pieces beneath it.

The force and the weight to cause that . . . I was already unloading my Desert Eagle's normal hollow-points to replace them with explosive rounds especially made for my gun and especially made for this situation. I landed on my hip just as I jammed the new clip home and then was I loaded but locked? Hell, no. I was ready to fire. It had taken barely a second, and I thought that would give me time to get a good aim on what was pissed off that it hadn't been invited to the party.

I was wrong. A second wasn't long enough. It was already lunging through the air and about to drop on top of me. All I still saw was the sheen of metal, but, frankly, I didn't care what it was made of except for what I could best use against it. I rolled flat on my back, aimed the Eagle straight up, and emptied the clip, all eight rounds. I closed my eyes. At that close proximity, I had no desire to be blinded by the small explosions. The only way I knew it had worked was that nothing landed on me to squash me to a thin paste on the concrete.

My face was burned; I could feel the hot, tight pain of it, but that fell into the column of "shit that can wait." I opened my eyes, sat up, and saw it, for the first time, really saw it as it stood. It was shaped like a man, more or less, but it was metal, and not any kind I'd seen. There were scales shaped like the head of a spear but at least two feet long and one foot wide, and they looked to be encrusted with dried blood, and in the thin cracks between the metal plates there was a red-hot substance that I'd swear was lava. There was the faintest smell of sulfur to it, but the smell of old blood was stronger. It stood nine feet tall at least, giving a boggle a run for its money. The majority of it was black metal with a face accented with what looked like dark tarnished iron, but wasn't. That would have been affected by the explosive rounds to some extent, but it hadn't been. Although at least it had been blown backward before it hit me, I didn't see a single dent in its chest or face—only a superficial blackening of the metal. There was a type of metal cowl surrounding its head like a helmet, eyes of the same lava that ran through it, and a snarl of metal lips that showed the tips of pointed black fangs.

Its claws—and that's all it had, claws, no hands—were huge even in comparison to its size, each one at least two feet long, four of them at the end of each wrist.

It looked like your worst nightmare had taken a Terminator, said, "Oh yeah, we can do a hundred times better than that," and combined it with a demon from the deepest pit of hell. But I didn't believe in hell and that made this simply one more monster to put down. One more notch on the bedpost, because I damn sure killed more often than I got laid.

"Nik!" He was on the other side of it. I ejected the empty clip, slammed in a new one, racked the slide, then added one more round. I tossed him the Eagle. "Eight rounds. Seven in the clip, one in the pipe." Niko caught it and was already firing.

He was a master with the sword and I'd rarely seen him need to use a gun, but this was going to be one of those rare occasions. His blades would only shatter against the unknown metal of this thing.

Ignoring the explosions from behind it, the creature swiveled its head completely around, the metal moving as smoothly as flesh, but the sound it made—the motion as scale hit scale—was the sound of human bones being crushed. Two faces. It could watch its front and back all at once. Fan-fucking-tastic. This face wasn't snarling. It was grinning, the metal lips stretched wide and every ebony fang showing. They were as oversized as its claws, and the stench of ancient blood on them was overpowering. I preferred it when it wasn't quite as happy. But my preferences didn't matter right then.

I didn't think the Eagle would do Niko any more good than it had done me; nor would my Glock I already had yanked from my double holster, but I had other weapons. Right now, I had only one I could think of that would work. If we'd had more time to think, maybe we could come up with something else, but we didn't have time.

Or the need.

Our weapons hadn't worked, but I had one that lived in me and it never failed.

I'd gated Niko's father to Central Park. I could gate anyone or anything to anyplace I'd been or could see from where I stood. Twice within a day, at any rate. I could put this thing in the ocean, but I had a feeling that wouldn't stop it. It might give it a long, wet walk to get to land again, but I couldn't know if water would bother it—not when explosive rounds didn't. That left only one place I could send it and be sure it wouldn't come back. Tumulus. The reason I didn't believe in hell, because that was the true hell. The Auphe home away from home—another dimension, another world, a place out of sync with ours—I didn't know or care.

I did know only Auphe—or the half Auphe that was me—could travel there or back. If I stuck this thing in Tumulus, we'd never see its metal ass again. Or I could open a gate *inside* it, but the implosion combined with the explosion—gates were tricky that way—it would send metal shards flying in a shrapnel storm neither Nik or I would survive.

Tumulus it was.

It took less than a fraction of a moment for all that to run through my head, and that fraction proved why I sucked so badly at math. It was on me faster than I'd seen any creature move—and I'd seen the best of the worst. It was too fast to build a gate around it. Too fast for me to build a gate in front of it. Too fast for me to gate myself the hell out of the way.

It crouched on all fours; then it hit me . . . it or a Mack truck, I wasn't sure, but I was positive that I was held down by metal claws that encompassed my chest. They were as long as I'd guessed. I couldn't see them, but I could gauge their length by how far I could feel them penetrate my chest wall, scraping on the outside of my right and left rib cage, pinning me to the street—jammed into the concrete itself. I felt the burn of the metal as it touched my legs. It was as hot as the burner on a stove. The eyes that contained killing magma moved closer until I was certain the molten rock would cascade over me, frying me to an outline of death and charcoal on the street.

Its mouth opened. I could see the red at the back of its throat, but I thought the teeth would get me first. Having your face chewed off or having it melted to slag and ash. Put that down as a choice I was glad I didn't have to make. Neither seemed a time worth having. I lifted my arm and rammed the Glock into its gaping mouth and emptied the clip. Nothing happened except a good gun began to melt in my hand. I threw it to one side before my hand went with it. The last of the Eagle's explosive rounds hit it from behind, but this time it was ready. It didn't move, not an inch. Its mouth, the furnace of heat and metal, moved closer.

Checkout time, and me with no luggage.

I wanted to say something.

I knew this one was it. In our business, it was just a waiting game. When it took me down, my head had slammed against the concrete enough to scramble my brain thoroughly enough that I couldn't gate out. I'd used a gate once today. A second one in one day was doable, usually, but much harder and took a concentration and an effort that a cracked skull wasn't giving me.

Yeah, this one was it.

I heard more explosive rounds being fired and then the sound of running. Nik. Running toward death when anyone else would've run in the other direction. The head facing mine arrowed closer—curious or toying with me, I didn't know. Or care. I was the mouse; it was the cat. Wondering was pointless.

Hadn't I wanted to say something?

Did it matter?

Yeah. It did. Hell, yes. If I was going to die, it mattered. I was going out foulmouthed and spitting blood in the face of my enemy. That's who I was. *What* I was. I'd die, but I wouldn't die screaming. I'd die cursing, and screw life. What had it ever once done for me?

"Swear . . . not . . . Sarah Connor, you piece . . . of shit," I gasped. The weight of the claws was incredible and made breathing almost impossible. "Nothing against Skynet . . . if . . . gets more TV channels . . . all for it, you metal . . . ass . . . hole."

Niko came out of the semidarkness and threw himself on top of the metal mass of claws that held me down. "Gate us out of here," he said fiercely. "Goddamn it, Cal, if there was ever a time to break the rules, it's now. *Gate!*"

But I couldn't.

"Run." I pushed at him with more strength than I should've had, impaled and pinned. "Nik, run. Can't gate." Or I would've gated that windup tin toy from hell far from here. I'd tried. My brain wouldn't cooperate, but it didn't mean I hadn't tried, wasn't still trying. I could feel the blood pouring from my nose, the headache even more crushing than the one I had from hitting the street. The sacrifices of making a second gate so soon from the first were bad, but I'd done it before. Not this time—I pulled all of myself into the effort and nothing happened.

"Nik, *run*," I repeated desperately.

He looked at me with a battlefield, hitching-a-ride-to-Valhalla flash of teeth, unmoving as the head rushed down, jaws gaping, aimed at him. "You're such a fucking idiot, little brother."

It was only Nik who could make me laugh, tasting the salt of blood for the single breath before we died. Nik whose father hadn't saved him and now neither could I.

Fuck, why couldn't I do it? If not for me, then for him. Just one goddamn gate.

Why . . .

And it was gone. Every molecule of metal except the claws still pinning me to the street and an inch or two of metal arm above Niko's back. The gray pulse and black swirl of the gate had appeared, gobbled up the murder machine, and then disappeared before I was sure I'd seen it . . . or done it.

Niko sat up. I could see the smoke wisping up from his back where drops of the lava or whatever the hell it was had dripped onto him and were eating through his shirt and skin next. "Take off . . . shirt." I managed to smack his arm. "You suicidial . . . moron."

He did, but at the same time he used his cell to call Goodfellow for help. "Where'd you send it?" Niko asked. He wasn't talking to Robin any longer. He was talking to me. I blinked at the question and the time lost—a slice of missing reality. He was now off the phone, shirtless, and running a careful hand over my side and down to the street. From his expression, I knew he could feel the claws beneath my skin. Or maybe they weren't beneath my skin. That thing had been big; its claws could be equally big, and I didn't have a lot of spare flesh on me, thanks to Niko's training regimen. That could be why Niko's touch didn't hurt. It wasn't me he was touching, but the claws that had captured me and burst open flesh as they slid along my ribs. I did feel cold, yet I felt a warmth running beneath me.

Blood.

It has a unique, soothing heat that lets you know you might not have bought the farm yet, but the Realtor has the contract in front of you, and the pen is in your hand.

"Cal, where did you send it?"

He didn't look worried, which meant he was. "I don't know," I said, and I didn't. I had no idea where I'd sent it. "I couldn't gate. I hit my head"—more accurately cracked it open like an egg—"... couldn't think straight, couldn't ... pull it together." Not for a gate and not for the faraway Tumulus. "Before, I could ... have." When I could gate with no effort at all, no head wound would've stopped me. No wound would have. "Before it would've ... been easy, but Rafferty *broke* me." I said it resentfully, spitefully. But while the dark part of me meant it, the rest of me didn't, not really. The healer had done what was best at the time, at least what he thought was best, and it had kept me sane long enough for me to find a way to stay that way permanently.

Yet now I was sane but still broken.

"Crippled," Niko murmured. What I'd accidentally said in the bar.

"Didn't mean it," I denied immediately. "That was then. We didn't know." Didn't know there'd be a now when limiting me to two gates with the third one killing me along with the Auphe in me would be more harmful than helpful. At the time gating had brought out the worst in me—the uncontrollable darkness in me. "Rafferty didn't know . . . you didn't know."

I could hear Goodfellow's rapid footsteps coming from the bar. Niko let it go. He didn't have much choice. We could talk and bond and spill our feelings, but as I'd bleed to death in the street at the same time, I thought the girly shit could wait.

A hand rested on my forehead. I opened my eyes. When had they closed? "We have to get this off of you, and with its being embedded into the street, I think you'd rather not be conscious when that happens."

"Just don't mess up the face." I slurred a little. "Only thing left on me worth looking at these days."

He wasn't smiling now. In the face of death, yes. In the face of this, no. But his tone was reassuring. "You'll wake up as good-looking as you ever were, which isn't saying much."

Before I could reply, I saw a skin-colored flash and then I dreamed.

Of smoke and lightning and living metal that would grind you to blood and bone dust.

5

Black Sheep

Interesting.

And fucking annoying.

He was maimed. Spoiled. He hadn't gated away. Couldn't gate away, but why? He was the Unmaker of the World. He had once been able to build a gate to the past . . . to millions of years ago. You can't create a damned and doomed doorway such as that without the innate ability to gate with unmatchable ease.

Nearly unmatchable, that is. There was me, wasn't there? Yes . . . ah, yes . . . there was me.

I took another bite of my dinner and chewed as I put down the binoculars. He had looked dead as the pathetic meat bag of a human and the goat tried to free him from the metal claws of a thing the likes of which I'd never seen. A curious thing too, but I didn't have time for another curiosity. Caliban was my one and only at the moment. I'd gated his attacker to the top of a building far across the city. It seemed to like building tops. Whatever that thing was, it wasn't mine, but it might prove useful to keep around. One never knew when death incarnate would be needed. But in the end my brother was my toy; his miserable life or death belonged to me alone.

I swallowed and took another mouthful. Caliban might have looked dead, but he wasn't. He was family, and our family didn't die easily. No no no no no. I was proof of that. I had lived through twenty years of torture . . . lived and escaped. Twelve more years hadn't made me forget every burn, every sear, every slice of a blade, every week of starvation—none of it, because those memories made me stronger and more determined.

This failure was going to prove to the family that rejected me, the family that was gone but not forgotten, that I was better *than they were . . . so very much better.*

And the success . . . Cal-i-ban, something had happened to him. He had built a gate to the past. I'd "talked" to those who roamed this city: the vampires, the revenants, the Wolves, others. I'd talked to them with my teeth and my man-made claws. I left nothing but shredded flesh, intestines, and death when I was done with them. But isn't that the result of talking? I thought it was, and if I thought it was, no one would tell me anything differently or I'd talk to them as well.

They'd all said the same: He could gate like a motherfucker.

Something had happened. I had only to find out what. Not that in the end it mattered. We healed. Against anything that didn't kill us—we healed. It might take time, but we never failed in that.

We were Auphe.

What didn't kill us only pissed us the fuck off.

I tossed away the leg of the security guard who had tried to stop me from accessing the rooftop of the building at a safe distance from Caliban's party. He wasn't muscu-

lar or flabby, the guard, but in between. Succulent and soft, yet not too soft—the perfect consistency. But I was full. The rest could stay on the roof until someone found the leftovers. I sat up and put my sunglasses back on. Night to everyone else, but the lights . . . it made it day to me. I didn't like the day. I didn't like the tedium of lying on rooftops either. I'd relieve the tedium later by slaughtering one or two people . . . or three or four. With the sudden lack of paien-kind around for the past two days—except for the goats, and even I wouldn't bother with a putrid, diseased goat—humans were all I had, and they were no challenge. It took more to satisfy.

But soon . . . soon I'd find out what had made Caliban less of an opponent, less family, and so much less interesting. I had patience though. Thirty years of it. We would see what we would see. He could again be a worthwhile challenge himself, sooner or later.

I needed a challenge, and so . . .

I would wait.

Awhile.

6

"Nothing for his blood pressure. It's far too high from Rafferty's manipulation, but with the blood loss it should be dropping like a rock. If we give it a chance, the combination should stabilize it in a normal range."

Odd when hearing something like that can be comforting, but it meant one thing: I was home.

It was still dark, but that was fine. I was content to float there awhile. I knew when I opened my eyes that things weren't going to be as pleasant.

Once we had a healer, Rafferty. He could lay his hands on you and knit flesh back together like magic. Except there was no magic, only monsters. He had a genetic gift, one much better than mine. Then Rafferty had left—for good, I thought. He had family of his own to care for.

There'd also been a Japanese healing spirit who had lived in the city, working as a doctor and teaching premed at Columbia. But a time had come when he'd wanted to return home. And me? I couldn't go to a hospital, not like Niko. On the outside I was human; on the inside, I was less so. One blood test, one CT scan, and in would swoop the black helicopters, and the government would take me apart. I doubted very seriously that they'd put me back together when they were done.

That left Niko, who, when he found a problem, found a solution . . . or he took out his sword and beheaded the problem. One of the two. Either way, he got things done.

Which meant that he'd gone to med school—in a way. He had only three months' notice that O-Kuni-Nushi, better known to his oblivious colleagues as Dr. Ken Nushi, was headed home for several hundred years at least, but Niko was smart, the smartest son of a bitch I knew. He spent every spare moment with Nushi for those months, that big brain of his soaking up every piece of knowledge at maximum speed. Nushi had known the only medical training needed for us was trauma, and that had made it easier. And as a practicing doctor, he had access to plenty of medical supplies and drugs to send our way. What he didn't have access to—he worked as a general practitioner, not a surgeon—had to be stolen or bought from highly questionable sources.

Seemed right. I was highly questionable myself.

I slitted my eyes and hissed at the spike of pain caused by the light. Almost immediately the level was lowered. "Damn it to hell. Head?" I mumbled, recognizing the symptoms from too many times before. I then vaguely remembered the bounce of my skull off the street when that thing had slammed into me before trapping me with those massive claws. That would be a big yes on the head injury.

"Head, a few burns to your legs, and sliced open like a side of beef. Oh, and Rafferty's 'gift' that keeps on giving." It was Goodfellow's jovial rundown.

I opened my eyes wider this time. I felt a little loopy, and that wouldn't be from Niko knocking me out. "I feel . . . weird. Kind of . . . happy? Is this happy? I think I like it."

I heard Niko's snort, and his face appeared above me. "Deep sedation, IV. I had to stitch you up, and not just skin, but layers of muscle. When we managed to get that thing off of you I could see your ribs. I could see bone. When I didn't see the blood." His lips tightened before I saw him tuck the image away. "You'll be useless for weeks. Not that you aren't perpetually useless to begin with," he added.

"Love you too, big brother." I grinned and that hurt too. "Ow, Jesus."

"You also have a mild burn to your face from the first explosive round you fired. Fortunately that one knocked the automaton back far enough that the flash from the other rounds didn't reach you. Although if it had happened, I'm certain Goodfellow would be the first in line with the barbecue sauce."

"You engage in one bonding incident of cannibalism to save your life from a pissed-off pack of natives and you never live it down," Robin muttered.

Niko ignored the sulking as he chose a syringe from the metal table beside him, pulled off the plastic cap, and slid the needle into the port to the IV in the back of my hand. "This should help. Not that you need it for your face. It could pass as a sunburn, but your incisions over your ribs and the one on the back of your head are going to wake up and let you know they are there soon enough."

Suddenly I wasn't feeling quite as happy anymore. I looked around, doing my best not to turn my head and irritate the injury there any sooner than I had to. I was in Nik's room. All the more intensive medical care was done there. God knew it was as antiseptic as any operating room. I had bandages that ran the width of my sides, three on the right and one on the left. A blood-pressure cuff around my right arm. There were IVs, one in my right hand and one in the crook of my left arm. Clear fluids on one side and a bag of blood on the other. You couldn't find half-human, half-Auphe blood, but Nushi had assured Niko that the Auphe in my system could tolerate any type of blood: A, B, AB, O. Probably cow blood if it came to it, and that wasn't a joke. Nushi didn't joke about medical matters, Nik had said.

Anesthesia, surgery, blood—it was the first test of Niko's training, not the basic first aid we'd picked up along the way. I didn't think he cared for it too much. I knew the feeling. I'd sat at the side of his hospital bed once, helpless to do anything. Which was worse? Knowing there wasn't a damn thing you could do for your brother or knowing you were the only one who could?

That was an easy question to answer: They both sucked equally.

Niko's scrubs—those we could buy legally, although that wasn't as much fun—were stained liberally with blood. He didn't bother with a surgical cap or mask. With my immune system, a stray hair or flu germ wasn't going to be a blip on the radar. He did use gloves, though, if only to keep the blood off his hands. The gloves had their work cut out for them this time, I saw, as he peeled them off and tossed them in the garbage can that had to be at his feet even if I couldn't lift my head from the pillow to see it. Niko would sooner commit seppuku than toss garbage on the floor.

"Doctor, samurai, weapons expert, teacher, historian, barkeep-slash–puck boy toy, monster killer. You're this generation's Buckaroo Banzai," Robin drawled. He was dressed in bloody scrubs and stripping off gloves as well. A desperately quick surgery required someone to hand over the instruments, hang more fluids, maybe wipe up the floor so you didn't slip in the blood. No one in the room had had much of a good time, except the unconscious guy. But my body would make sure I paid for that later.

I knew Niko didn't care for the doctor part of Robin's list, and that more than anything made me change the subject. "Did you say that thing was an auto-something? Jesus, if it was a Transformer, I wish you would've just let me go. I don't want to live in a world where those actually exist." Things were getting blurry and soft around the edges. The painkillers kicking in. Unfortunately the pain had jumped on the track and was neck and neck with the drugs. I hung in there. I'd hurt worse in my life, more times than I could count. I'd most likely hurt sometime worse in the future. It was the way things were.

"Automaton," Niko corrected as he pulled a heated blanket over me. That was another way to know I was genuinely conscious . . . Niko correcting me. The warmth of the blanket banished an icy chill I hadn't been aware of until then and had me shutting my eyes, interest in my question instantly gone.

But Goodfellow always had a way of getting anyone's attention, anytime, anywhere, any way. I heard his cheerful comment close to my ear: "You know what surgery tends to include?" The next word went from cheerful to wickedly gleeful. "Catheters."

I opened my eyes and glared first at him, then at Niko. "You didn't let him"—I waved a hand at the general area—"play around down there. Tell me you didn't. Niko, I will kick your ass so damn far it'll rotate around the earth like a fucking defense satellite."

He shrugged. "It's a simple procedure, especially for someone like Goodfellow, with so much experience in that area. I could talk him through it while I did my best to keep you from bleeding to death, which you almost did." His impassive gaze took me in. "Do you have anything further to say about the situation?"

No, I didn't. That shut me up as Goodfellow smirked, stripped off his bloody scrub top, and headed for the bedroom door. "I'm going to change while you give him the history lesson, Niko."

"Robin said that from the look of the metal and the description I gave him, the creature was an automaton, specifically a Janus automaton, as it had two faces. It's a metallic, virtually living machine made by the Greek god"—or whatever was pretending to be a god— "Hephaestus. Robin hadn't heard of this particular one, but he said Hephaestus made so many or bought them and passed them off as his own that our mythology doesn't know one-fifth of what he created." The automatic whine of the blood-pressure cuff inflating again had Niko's eyes fixed on the glowing numbers.

I didn't care to look. Either it was so high it killed me, thanks to Rafferty, or it was low enough that I lived. Nothing I could do about it. The warmth and the pain meds finally taking over had me wanting to drift away slowly again, but I resisted it for the moment. "How do we stop it?"

Niko was frowning as he reached for another syringe and injected that into my IV as well. "Apparently we don't. None of our weapons will be effective against it— it's an ancient technology that outreaches ours today. You need to know the correct phrases—a long-dead language, I'm assuming—to turn it off. Goodfellow doesn't know them. He said every automaton has different command codes, I suppose you'd call them in this time. How it was activated is a mystery, the mystery being some Vayash traitor did, at least, know that phrase. That means we avoid it if possible until you're well enough to send it to Tumulus. I am guessing that's where you were attempting to send it."

"No, Nik, to Coney Island for a roller-coaster ride and a giant goddamn pretzel." I tried to snort sarcastically. I wasn't too successful except for the trickle of blood I felt start running from my nose over my lip. Niko took a washcloth and wiped it away.

"Stop thinking, or what passes for your version of thinking, and go to sleep. Second gates aren't supposed to kill you, but you tried too hard and Rafferty's work is too effective. I can't get your blood pressure down yet. So for the love of Buddha, sleep . . . please."

He didn't say "please," my brother, not often. He was polite and honorable — when he wasn't forced to kill you, given — but somehow he avoided the word as if your behavior should be equally polite and therefore no "please"s required.

When he did say it . . . I obeyed. I was about to close my eyes when he whipped his head around and soundlessly put a hand on the unsheathed katana on the low dresser behind him. He was listening. I didn't hear anything except dripping IVs, the low beep of a blood-pressure machine, and a narcotic ringing in my ears, but if Niko heard something, it was there.

I started to sit up, but realized before I did that that was the worst thing I could do. Monster slayer? I couldn't slay a hamster right now. The only thing I would do was get in Niko's way. He stood, not frozen, but waiting. What he waited for stepped into view out of the darkness of the hall. The only light on in the place was in this room, and it was a low light in deference to my concussion at that. It didn't matter. I recognized him all the same.

Kalakos.

He had outrun the boggles. Damn that streak of humanity in me. At the moment I didn't regret anything more than not dropping him directly into their pit. Mama Boggle would've solved this problem for us with one bite of her jaws. Niko's father scanned the bedroom. He didn't seem surprised by what he saw. "You heard me pick the lock," he said to Niko. "I suspected you kept it slightly rusty for a reason. You are like me. No matter what we do, you and I, we will always have our reasons."

I saw Robin in the murk behind him. Kalakos didn't hear him. As long as he had lived or guessed he'd lived, no one would hear Goodfellow if he didn't want to be heard. He had a sword as well, not a katana, more crusader style, but lighter-weight. It was lined up directly at Kalakos's back as the puck took several silent steps closer.

Niko pointed his katana. "Leave," he ordered flatly. "Now." I was vulnerable, embarrassing as that was, and around an unknown variable. He didn't like it.

He didn't like it to the point of being on the verge of burying steel in flesh without a thought.

But that bastard didn't see that as I did. Kalakos's eyes showed no fear, but they did show resignation. "I told you that the burden is one all Vayash are responsible for recovering."

"We have nothing to do with your burden or the Vayash." Kalakos didn't know Nik, had never bothered to know him, but I knew him. I knew that while he rarely lost control, when he did . . . it was one goddamn thing to see. And he was standing on the edge. Teetering.

The black eyes focused on me, on the bandages, the medical equipment, the dried blood that still covered Nik's scrubs.

Just . . . about . . . now.

"I think it seems that you do."

That was that.

"*That* is the burden? That is the duty? It did this to my brother? When you said it could sense Vayash, you meant that literally? Sense us by our *blood*?" Niko's knuckles went white under his olive skin. "And you wanted us to help you fight it. Did you lead it here?"

The point of Goodfellow's sword came to rest against flesh. I could see that in the tightening of the skin around Kalakos's mouth. Sandwiched between two blades, he kept his hands carefully away from his body. It was a smart move.

"I told you that it smells Vayash like a wolf smells a sheep. You chose not to listen. And I did not bring it. It came of its own—"

Niko didn't listen to the rest. His hand wrapped around the grip of the katana slammed into his father's face with brutal force, knocking him down and out. While Kalakos lay unconscious on the floor, Niko spit on him. I didn't think I'd seen Niko do something more unlike himself or had seen him as furious, but then, as Kalakos had said, he and my brother always had their reasons. This was history repeating itself. "This is what the Vayash gave us when we came to you," Niko said coldly. "And this is what you get in return, you bastard. You and your burden."

Kalakos's getting his ass kicked in a truly righteous way for a truly righteous reason made me feel better than all the narcotics in the room. Niko had buried this for his entire life, and it was time that he had a chance to get it out and deal with it. To "emote." It was a fancy word for a beat-down, "emote," but that only made me enjoy it more. I had only one regret.

"Goodfellow, kick him in the ribs for me, would you?" I said. The words were barely understandable. I was going down as fast as Kalakos had, but barely was good enough. As my eyes closed, I heard the meaty thud of Robin's shoe against flesh. It was a good sound to take me into sleep. I probably gave a smile as I went.

One dark and satisfied smile.

"Niko, there is a man in your garbage Dumpster outside. I can see his legs showing from beneath the lid." There was silence, but the scent of heather. I pictured Promise brushing a kiss across my brother's lips. "It is not quite what I would call being inconspicuous."

"In this situation I do not much care about being conspicuous or not." There was the sound of the blood-pressure cuff inflating and the tightened pressure on my arms. After several seconds, Niko exhaled. "Finally. Normal." That was good news. My brain wasn't going to explode. I didn't use it much, but it was nice to know. "As for that worthless garbage masquerading as a human being, if the police show up, I'm quite certain he'll wake up and talk his way out of his mess, because it's not and never will be our mess."

Huh. All that emoting and ass kicking hadn't seemed to bring Nik much closure. I knew about closure, only I tended to laugh a little maniacally when I heard the word. No one knew better than I did that closure was a fairy tale, and expecting Niko to embrace it in a single day wasn't doing him much service.

I opened my eyes to see Promise with her arms wrapped around Niko as he sat in the chair beside the bed. She was resting her pale cheek—like me, vamps weren't much for tans—against his. Her hair was all brown again, the wide blond stripes gone. I coughed and said hoarsely, "No more . . . tiger? I liked the tiger look."

"It was very high-maintenance. Much like you, Cal."

She reached over Niko's shoulder to stroke a gentle hand down my blanket-covered leg. "What have you done to yourself now?" There was nothing but sympathy in her voice, but Niko's face tensed all the same.

"He didn't do anything to himself." He stood up and walked away from the circle of her arms. Standing at the foot of my bed now, he tugged the blanket down a few inches to cover my bare feet. I was a restless sleeper, drugged or not. As for sleep in general, the effects of the lack of it that lined his face were more apparent as he let go of the cloth and folded his arms, brooding. He didn't look at her or me, only inside himself. He'd changed from scrubs into a black shirt and black jeans. "My . . . The man who fathered me is responsible for this. Cal almost . . ." He shut his mouth tightly before relaxing slightly. "Kalakos did this. He is the one in the Dumpster and he is exceedingly lucky that he will eventually wake up. I gave several hours' consideration last night to whether I would allow that to happen or not." Nik must have changed his mind about Kalakos's bringing the Janus automaton here intentionally as opposed to following it or there would've been no consideration and no waking up for his father again.

I cared less about intentions and more about the results, especially when they happened to Niko or me. I would've had no problem killing the worthless bastard if Niko wanted to drag his unconscious body back inside, and I wouldn't need to consider it for hours or even seconds. All I'd need was someone to fetch me one of my guns. But this wasn't about me or the fact that I'd almost been butchered like a pig at the slaughterhouse. Oddly, my human and Auphe sides both agreed on this issue. The first thought was that Niko needed to take care of this himself to come to terms with an abandoned, fatherless life. The second . . .

Unconscious. Human. Worthless. Boring. The dark stretched within me and yawned.

What could I say? They were both right.

But Kalakos would wake up again, and if Niko decided he'd made a bad call, yet hesitated—very doubtful, but if he did—I had a feeling my opinion of what I would do would change, but the agreement within me wouldn't. After all, brothers helped each other out. Besides, worthless and boring or not, it beat TV.

TV . . . Nik should get a TV in his room instead of all those boring books.

TV would be good now.

Where was the remote . . . ?

Niko gripped my leg lightly. I'd almost dozed off again. "We'll have to move you. Soon. Before that thing finds us again."

I yawned. "I know."

"It'll be painful, medicated or not," he warned.

"Your cooking is painful. Moving I'll survive," I assured him.

"Then you can come to my home and I'll have the housekeeper make you a completely nonvegan lunch and dinner." Promise smoothed my blankets again, but her eyes were on Niko. "If your father is genuinely to blame for what happened to Caliban, then I know better than to think you would let him live."

"It's complicated," Nik replied with ten times his usual understatement, "and I am sorry, Promise, but Kalakos is not a subject I wish to discuss, not now."

Then came the knock at the door, and "complicated" was ready to talk to Niko whether he was ready or not. "Maybe the third time's the charm," I said. "Promise, could you get me a gun from under my bed?" I must have been due a dose of pain meds soon, because the pain was growing sharp, but being clearheaded and pissed off pushed it down and made me more than capable of handling a firearm or two. "Or two guns. Yeah, two would be good."

She took a look at me, the guy barely able to move and pissing through a catheter—Jesus, I hoped she didn't know that—and shook her head. "Boys with their toys . . . and their grudges." Niko was already gone, heading toward the door with katana in hand. Promise left as well, but returned with my SIG Sauer and one of my backup Desert Eagles. Chrome instead of the matte black I usually went with, but I'd discovered over the years that color didn't matter. They'd both put a bullet in you with equal effectiveness. I didn't hide them under the covers. I let them rest in sight above the blankets with my fingers curled around the triggers. I wasn't afraid of Kalakos, although he'd damned well better be afraid of me.

I'd have offered one to Promise, but Promise had her own weapons—natural and man-made. She was as lethal as either of my guns. "He knew about Niko before he was born," I said quietly, hardly above a murmur. "He didn't come for him. He didn't take him from Sophia. He didn't save him. The only time Niko has seen him is now . . . when Kalakos *needs* something from him. Remember that."

"I will," Promise, the violet of her eyes swirling with black, said, and I saw delicate fangs lower and lock into place as she did.

"I swear it to you, Niko. I tried to warn you, but leave that behind us. I can help him. It will be back. It is only semiaware; yet that is enough for it to know it hates its captors. The Vayash. Any Vayash, and it will not care if you deny the clan. It will smell the Vayash in your blood."

Kalakos, sounding like Niko, but off just enough for me to make the distinction.

"As if I'd trust him with you. We are moving. It will not find us." That was Niko, but not one I was used to hearing. There was the fury, buried but clawing its way free. Not forgotten, not forgiving.

"When Janus returns from wherever it was sent, it will find you eventually, but will your brother be healed enough to fight? Or still in that bed, able only to die?"

That ass. Granted, Janus had taken me down when the worst I'd had was a baby kishi bite on my leg, but still . . . *That ass.* My fondest hope was that I did have the time to heal to show Kalakos what I could do given free rein. I didn't think Niko would silently hold me back this time.

Unfortunately, Kalakos had offered the only thing that would have Niko letting him in the house, much less not slicing him open for an intestine-fest on the floor. There was a long pause . . . Niko thinking, then: "To you, I am Leandros, not Niko. Better yet, to you, I am nothing—the same as I've always been. To you, I have no name at all. You are too without value to speak them."

He meant it. Niko didn't say anything he didn't mean. That didn't change the fact that seconds later he was in my room with Kalakos because he was that desperate. Grasping at straws. I'd need weeks to heal, if not a month on the ribs. If Janus came back anytime sooner than that, which was a good possibility, as I had no idea where I had sent him except that it hadn't been Tumulus, it would take it less than a second to end me. How many moves, and how often would be enough? How quickly could it find us?

"What do you have that you think can fix this?" Niko demanded, jerking his head in my direction. "Your duty, your burden, it all but ripped Cal apart." And Nik had put me back together, but he couldn't force me to mend any faster than I normally did. "Why do you imagine you can heal him?"

Kalakos looked somewhat the worse for wear since last night. He'd straightened his clothes, his hair remained in a tight ponytail, but his face was covered with dried blood and his nose was obviously broken. Nik's nose. Once proud, now bent to one side. There were also bruises covering one cheek, his right jaw, and half his forehead. One punch had done that. He was lucky. Niko could've killed him with that one punch, easily.

He reached into the depths of a coat similar to many my brother had. The only people who wore coats like that in the summer were people who carried swords or were flashers. With the way things were going, the son of a bitch was a flasher *with* a sword. He retrieved a soft cloth bag and from that he pulled a round iron box about the size of an orange. "This contains something old, very old. An ointment made by the most powerful healer who ever lived." He didn't smile. If he had, with what he said next, I was pretty sure Niko would've taken that second punch to kill him then and there. "The rumors do pass among the clans. I assume you know of Suyolak."

As we were the ones to destroy him, yeah, we knew Suyolak, the Plague of the World, born Rom and died a monster. Knowing him hadn't been the best experience. People had died. We had almost died. The world itself had almost died. Suyolak was the original Grim Reaper ... an antihealer who lived only to slaughter. I didn't see a damn thing that dead bastard could do for me.

"Do you want to die?" Niko demanded, quiet and remote. "If so, return to the main area. There's more room there for me to work."

Kalakos exhaled, eyes shrouded—troubled? Good. He should be. "You are as I was at your age. You fight for your brother while I fought for myself. You fight for better reasons." He lifted the lid from the box, scooped a small dab of dark green salve from within, and rubbed it on his face. In a rewind of time, the bruises faded, the nose straightened, although he winced as it did so, until all that remained was an untouched face and a crust of dried blood that he scrubbed off with one wipe of his hand. "Suyolak was born a healer of the Sarzo Clan. He was a healer for many years before he walked into the shadows. He made this before he turned. As far as I know, it is the last. I think there is enough to heal your brother." He offered the box to Niko. "It is yours. The very least I can do."

Niko accepted the box before searching Kalakos's now-restored face—every inch of it—then passed it to Promise. "I have heard of such things," she said, careful not to touch the contents. "I feel nothing inimical from it. I would touch it but I don't want to waste any. There is little left, and Cal . . ."

Cal was fucked-up five ways to Sunday. If it worked on a half human, half Auphe . . . if it wasn't a trick, I'd need a gallon of it, rather than a small box. But if it did work, Promise was right to be cautious. I'd need every speck of it I could get.

"Cal?"

When Niko said my name, Promise waited until I released the grip on my Eagle; then she handed the box to me. I took a whiff. I remembered too goddamn well how Suyolak had smelled—the one who'd Kalakos had so poetically said "walked in shadows." I'd know a single molecule of his graveyard stench anywhere. There was none of it in what was cradled in the iron box. Iron was what had kept the ointment viscous rather than hundred-year-old dried flakes. Iron blocked the escape of psychic emanations and that's what healing was. Not magic, but a genetic psychic talent.

Our Suyolak wasn't in this. It smelled green, fresh, with a hint of mint and pine. "It's safe," I confirmed. "Our pile of dust had nothing to do with this."

"If this doesn't work, don't bother running. You'll die either way, but it's been some time since I dismembered anyone alive. It takes a while, time I'm willing to spare." Niko had done before what he claimed, but only with monsters and only the extremely horrific ones, but Kalakos didn't know that. "Or I'll let Promise have you. She doesn't drink blood anymore, but has decapitated those who earned it a time or two since I've known her." Now, that was true. I did enjoy watching Promise at work.

Kalakos didn't appear worried. "It will."

Niko moved to the other side of my bed and began to pull down the blanket to reveal my ribs.

"Niko, wait." With Promise watching Kalakos, I felt safe in letting the SIG rest on the covers as well. I tapped my head lightly, and that alone had my vision and the pain doubling. "This is the only weapon we have right now. Wherever I managed to send Terminator deluxe"— and I hadn't remembered yet—"when it gets back, Tumulus and me, it's all we have."

He nodded, then shook his head as he took the box from my other hand. The furrows over my ribs that had torn me open had been ugly, had to have been, and I could've bled out from them. Had almost bled out from them, as I still had a fresh bag of blood hanging from the

IV pole this morning. It was why he hesitated. "If you can't run, if you can barely move and it catches you, you won't have time to build a gate."

"Nik." My lips quirked. "I was as twitchy as Goodfellow in a roomful of polyester suits last night, thanks to the puck grope-a-thon. If there was ever a time I could run like a bat out of hell, it was then. It still caught me."

He frowned. "You know how I feel about your using logic. Turning my own weapon against me. You might as well steal my katana and stab me in the heart." Through the bitching, which was more than likely to distract me from the pain of his tilting my head forward, he took a tiny amount of the balm on a fingertip and applied it to the cut on the back of my head. From the tracing of his finger it was a good four inches long. I felt an instant tingle and warmth and then an annoying pinch. "Hey, ouch."

"Shit." That was Niko cursing yet again. He'd cursed more in the past day and a half than in most of his life. He moved to the supply cabinet against the wall, flung open a drawer, and was back in an instant while stripping open a package. He went to work on the incision with hand flying.

"Niko, what are you doing and—Ow . . . what ·the hell? This isn't the kind of healing Rafferty did." I had my hand on the Eagle, ready to pick it up and nail Kalakos where he stood.

"It's the staples I had to use to close the cut. You're healing around them."

And now he was pulling them out of completely healed flesh, which stung, but that faded too as the ointment finished the job. "Aren't you going to complain that I should've thought of that first?" he asked with the last staple removed, his hand mussing the back of my hair to hide the memory of it.

"I'm not that much of an asshole." Of course I was. "Does it make you feel better that I did at least think it?"

I could see the smile behind his somber mask. "In fact, it does."

Promise and Kalakos waited in the living area while, behind his closed bedroom door, Niko took care of the rest. Luckily the stitches holding my muscles back together were dissolvable, and Suyolak's balm sailed over them. Although the amount in the box had seemed small, a little went a long way and then some. There was enough left for the burns and kishi bite on my leg. After that, I took back the box and scraped a finger inside, gathering just enough left to film the skin. Then I popped the finger in my mouth, the same as a kid with cake batter, and sucked it off.

Niko eyed me warily. "I don't think that's meant for internal ingestion. What are you doing?"

"An experiment. You never know until you try." I sat up, gloriously pain-free, and added, "Now, take out the IVs, tell me how to get this damn catheter out, then give me and Cal Junior some privacy. Knowing Goodfellow, he took a picture with his phone and Junior's an Internet star by now."

Niko coughed once before saying gravely, "Yes, a star. I'm sure." Then he grasped my arm and gripped hard. "I saw you, and I . . ." He didn't have to say it. I knew what he'd thought.

"I'm never dead." I grinned reassuringly. "Heaven doesn't exist, and hell has barricaded the door. I'm stuck here."

"Perhaps, but sometimes you do a convincing imitation." His grip tightened and he left me and Cal Junior with a list of instructions and a syringe—thank God the kind without a needle. I read through the instructions twice and sighed. My damn dick was always getting me into trouble, and never the right kind.

Simple enough that it took only seconds. I then thought about a shower, but I was clean and smelled of soap, and Suyolak's ointment had been absorbed into my body with no lingering trace of touch or scent. The soap meant I'd been given a sponge bath during my narcotic sleep, ridding me of blood and betadine. I'd have been embarrassed, but then Niko would remind me of how he changed my diapers when I was a baby. The last time he said that, I'd considered beating him to death with a box of Pampers.

Best to let it go this time.

I dressed in a pair of Niko's sweats rather than moving naked to my room next door, and thought about how Kalakos seemed to be telling the truth, how he might have saved my life, how, from what he said, he was trying to restore honor to his clan and keep Janus from slaughtering indiscriminately. The only problem I could find with him was that he'd abandoned his son. Could you kill someone for that alone, when compared to all the rest? When all was said and done, the threat defeated, could you? I picked up my Eagle, one in the pipe as always, and opened the door.

I could.

The clang of metal against metal was audible long before I walked down the hall. Niko and I practiced most often with wood. He didn't want to accidentally cut off something essential I might plan on using later. But this wasn't practice; this was something else entirely. I wasn't worried. If Niko needed help against Kalakos, he'd let me know, but as that was unlikely, I decided I was hungry. A good sign. I laid my gun on the countertop, grabbed some cold, petrified pizza out of the fridge, hoisted a hip up on the counter, and watched the show. "What's going on?" I took another bite. "I thought we were leaving. Why doesn't Niko just take his head, shout, 'There can be only one,' and get this over with?"

"They are trying to prove something first. Who is the best? Niko will let him live only because he made you whole again, but your brother requires working out a good deal of frustration regardless." She tapped a light lavender nail to her softly rounded chin. "Hundreds of years and the male psyche still escapes me."

I lifted my head and caught the scent of musk and forest. "Wonderful. Chester the Molester is here," I announced glumly.

The door opened and no one had heard Goodfellow pick the lock. Kalakos didn't know who he was competing with when it came to breaking and entering, and that was a fact. Goodfellow did have a key, but he felt that was boring. Tricksters needed to keep up their skills. He picked pockets too. The used-car-salesman cover was a self-explanatory con of pure evil. "Lazarus has arisen!" he announced at the sight of me. "Not to mention the rest of you appears much improved as well. And I heard your highly inflammatory statement." He put his lock picks away and leaned a wet umbrella against the wall. Had to protect that expensive suit. "You were dying. You're my friend. How can you accuse me of taking advantage?" He sat on the couch beside Promise. "Besides, I can't find a picture of a small enough Santa hat to Photoshop on it for my yearly winter solstice cards. Christmas, to you heathens."

I began to wing what was left of the rock-hard pizza at his head when he folded his arms, leaned back against the armrest, and stretched out, while propping his legs across Promise's lap. "Never mind. I'll torture you later." He glanced at the peek of Promise's fangs over her lower lip. "Greetings, Elvira. Is that an overbite or are you just happy to see me?" He didn't wait for an answer or for her to break his neck, the second being more likely. "Now, this is exceedingly more engaging. Hot, sweaty men in battle. Thank Zeus that Ishiah doesn't mind my looking."

Promise gave his legs the same regard she would have if a giant gelatinous snail had flopped across her lap, but inhaled deeply and turned her attention back to the fight. For once in their lives she and Robin agreed on something. "The only way one such as you could not look is if your eyes were plucked from their sockets." She tapped a painted nail against his chest, but he was beyond threats, his brain completely shut down. I could smell the waves of whatever was the puck equivalent of testosterone rising. He was practically one of those deodorizers they hang around car rearview mirrors.

Scent: horny.

Shape: I wasn't going there.

I went back to watching the fight myself. They were on the workout mats in the gym area. Barefoot, shirtless, and soaked with sweat, both were matched in number of scars, although they were differently shaped and located. Both were also impeccably good with swords—Niko with his katana and Kalakos with what I thought was a Polish saber. The blade was long and curved, more so than a katana, the grip centuries-old wood. A karabela. It meant "dark curse." When I was a kid, Niko hadn't been able to get me to remember the periodic table for love or money, but weapons . . . those I didn't often forget.

It had a few inches reach on the katana, but I had

faith in my heart for my brother. You know what beat faith? A Desert Eagle in the hand that I wasn't using to eat pizza. If Niko stumbled . . . I didn't think he would—not my brother. No. But if he did, we'd have to pay the cleaning lady fifty extra bucks to scrub Kalakos's brain off the wall.

Money well spent.

I finished the pizza as Kalakos spoke, barely breathing hard from the exertion. "I did desert you. I did know Sophia was . . . as she was. But I hunt clan criminals and return them for punishment, or deliver that punishment if the crime is grave enough."

Niko didn't bother to reply. The fight went on. I hadn't seen any human in my life who came close to my brother. Blades, bare-handed, the occasional gun he had little respect for—no one was as good. Neither was Kalakos, but was near enough that I didn't like it. You can be the best in the world, but everyone stumbles; everyone makes that one mistake . . . humans and non. I had, more than once. The fact that Kalakos was good enough to take advantage of that if Niko did . . .

No, I didn't fucking care for it at all.

"You're one of the best I've fought," Niko said. "It's a shame."

He blocked another of Kalakos's blows before the Polish saber whipped under the katana and slammed the Japanese blade upward toward Niko's face; then metal circled metal as the karabela's point plunged toward Nik's neck. That was when Niko kicked his father in the stomach, staggering the older man back a few feet.

He then blocked the hand gripping the saber, slamming fist against fist, started to sweep his leg, then abruptly swept the other, taking Kalakos off guard and throwing him down to the mat. "Elegant move. Rare.

I've seen it used only once before at that short distance."
Yeah, when he practiced it on me. The karabela didn't
bother to come up to block the katana that sliced toward
the man's throat.

Black met stony gray. "Not only did I hunt Rom, but
I hunt the unclean, as you do when they threaten the
clans. A child could not survive that life."

"A child survived worse. A hundred times worse. Your
failure has nothing to do with me." Niko lifted his katana
and walked away. But before he did, he said, "If you had
learned in the beginning to fight for family instead of
money, you would be even a better fighter and less of a
dishonorable bastard than you are now." He was right.
Kalakos wouldn't chase criminals and monsters for free.
We didn't either . . . if the client could afford us. If they
couldn't, Niko may as well have been Sonny and Cher's
lesser-known child, Pro Bono. At least fifty percent of
our work didn't earn us a dime, which was fine. Protecting others was a reward worth more than money. I was
lucky that Niko had taught me that.

Killing is the true payment. Killing is the best part.

I gave an internal shrug. It didn't matter what the
darkest part of me thought. When the goals were the
same, it . . . no, not it . . . *I* could think whatever I wanted.
I was who I was. I didn't need to change that control or
the improved me with the acid erosion of denial.

Know thyself . . . and then know that your brother
knows better than you.

At a stack of neatly folded towels on a shelf near the
paper targets hung on the wall, Nik propped up his katana for cleaning when he was done with himself. Wiping
the sweat from his chest, arms, and back, he added remotely, "You healed Cal. That allows you and only you a
week to recover Janus. Then he becomes someone else's

problem and not ours. The Vayash will have to send others to do what you could not."

He stood, no better off than Niko, but not much worse either. He might have sweated a little more, breathed a little harder, but the difference was small. I liked that less and less. Niko was younger and more motivated, but Kalakos would have picked up tricks along the longer years to stay alive doing what he did. The dirtiest of tricks. *My* kind of tricks, but I wouldn't turn them against my brother. Would he?

Kalakos started toward Niko, refusing to give up. It was a good thing for him that he left his saber behind. "There is no one else who can—"

I gave a low whisper of a hiss before slicing a hand across my throat, and he stopped talking immediately. That smell, the trace of rotten eggs . . . sulfur. I looked up at the metal ceiling far above. "*Shit*. Niko, now!" He didn't question. He propelled himself across the room, lunged, and landed on top of Robin and Promise, which was a Goodfellow wet dream come true, and then I threw myself off the counter onto Nik. As I landed on his back, there was the tearing of metal and the shattering of our floor as Janus came to visit.

Suyolak's medicine had healed me, but Rafferty's rewiring was still in place. That meant I couldn't make a gate as fast as my first one yesterday—it took me three days to recover fully—but it was faster than it normally would've been. Too bad it wasn't fast enough.

Janus's two-faced head was swiveling, its one claw missing. It was checking the soon-to-be battlefield, slower and more cautious this time. It then moved, deciding it had all enemies in sight, and was almost on us when Kalakos threw himself in front of it. He slid a sword into one of the glowing red seams in its chest. It wasn't the saber. This was a Greek sword, true as any ancient warrior charging Troy had held—a xiphos made of the same dark metal of the automaton. Kalakos slammed his feet against Janus's abdomen and pushed hard, ending up half on the couch. Janus jerked and staggered back a single step, the floor cracking beneath his feet again. It was for only a second or two, but that was all I needed.

In those seconds we were as much history as Janus himself.

7

Black Sheep

I liked games. It was true few others liked the games I played, but I didn't care what they liked. It was a waste of their breath. I had discarded my sunglasses as the rain continued to fall and the lightning flashed. It was good weather. The air sizzled and danced and it was dark enough for certain curiosities to travel roofs and not be seen by the mass of ignorant humans that clogged the sidewalks of this place, insects overrunning their anthill. I tossed down the binoculars and laughed. That thing, that metal thing, had come back and dropped through the roof where Caliban lived.

Little pig, little pig, let me come in. *The first book I'd learned to read in my days of freedom. My teacher had been proud. I was a literate predator and that made me more dangerous than the first Auphe had been. When the prey was so many, you had to know them, truly know everything about them. My teacher said a mind was a terrible thing to waste. She was right, and when she taught me all she could, I ate hers. I thought it a compliment to her teachings. She thought differently.*

That meant I taught her a lesson as well: You shouldn't say things you don't mean.

Ah, but back to the good part, the now part. That wasn't the best part, that metal thing, metal toy, showing up. It remained as interesting as I'd thought last night, but it wasn't on my agenda now.

I was Auphe—the New Coming.

Toys could wait.

But Caliban . . . I couldn't see him. The windows were too high, the angle wrong, but it didn't matter. Blocks and blocks away, I had smelled the blood last night . . . Auphe blood—much more pungent and real than human blood. It would've been too far to smell him, whole, but the blood . . . its scent traveled . . . and traveled yet more. But then it had faded, disappeared this morning. Somehow he had put himself back together, all those pieces, and I wanted to know how. I would know how. He'd be happy . . . very happy to tell me. Or I'd be happy to force him to tell me. At times I mixed up the two—a mistake easy to make when you didn't care one way or the other. I clicked the man-made metal claws that encased my one gloved hand against the dirt. It was an apartment building, and I hid in the greenery they had forced to grow there in pots against its will, choking on the fumes of this place. Such a minor evil that I felt disgust and rage. Humans—their wickedness was so dismal and feeble that I wanted to rip out the trees and bushes and throw them over the side of the roof.

What had I been thinking again?

What had I . . .

Yes, games. I'd watched Caliban for three months now in this place. I'd had twelve years of freedom, but I'd returned for three years to piss around the home of my former prison—Nevah's Landing—because I knew Caliban would as well. Sidle told us so. Sidle, our warden . . . our torturer . . . Caliban's victim without a single look . . . the bullet through his brain.

Not one glance as he pulled the trigger.

It was beautiful.

Games. Whether he'd admit it or not, I knew he liked games too. I'd followed him from Nevah's Landing, a place he'd sooner not remember, living with cattle, picking up boring cattle emotion. He'd wiped out eight of our kind, useless kind, barely worth the carnage. But I might be wrong. Maybe he didn't mind remembering what he had done—I wouldn't. Maybe he had enjoyed it. Killing his brothers and sisters. I didn't blame him. I'd have killed them too. They were weak. They couldn't gate. Worthless maggots.

A fun game I'd wanted to play in the three years I'd been back, but I couldn't. I'd especially wanted to play with Sidle. I would've dragged it out for weeks and weeks until his vocal cords ruptured from the screams. But no, no, no. I left them for Caliban.

The trap. The bait.

I'd watched him from the swamp, too far for him to sense me, and I'd learned about the last of our kind, or so he thought. I'd followed him back to this disgusting stench of a city and I'd learned more. He couldn't gate. At first I assumed I just didn't happen to be watching him at the right time. I had needs. I couldn't watch him always. But then last night, he gave me nothing . . . which made him useless and not the Caliban I'd expected, the one whose name was snarled by all the nonhumans. Not the Caliban who the Auphe had tried to use to travel back and wipe out the humans before they infested the world like billions of locusts.

Caliban, but not the one they spoke of with fear and hatred. Not the one worth my time. I was on the verge of impossible-to-bear boredom, ready to kill him as he'd killed the others, if he didn't die during the night. But not for revenge—he wasn't worth revenge, but because he was the same as the ones he'd killed in my onetime prison:

Useless.

But now he wasn't. He had gated.

I had felt it. Auphe could feel one another, sense the presence of the superior, from a certain distance, which had kept me farther than I wanted from my target. But a gate was different. One could feel a gate much farther. Sidle had told us so. He enjoyed telling us the murderous tales and lethal abilities of the true Auphe, and of the shameful shadows we were of the true Auphe race.

But there is true and then there is better.

I was better.

I would prove it to Caliban now that he was worth my time.

I would prove it to the memory of the first Auphe. The first race had gone and the second had come.

Evolution, bitches.

8

The couch ended up at a sharp angle, one end propped up on the sofa in Goodfellow's condo and the other on the floor. The expensive leather of Robin's furniture ripped and tore. It was the second time I'd destroyed the puck's wraparound couch. I only hoped the other end hadn't landed on Salome or Spartacus. Spartacus didn't deserve that, and Salome would gnaw off my leg and balls and be the first to bring the game of pool to the mummified cat community. It gave whole new meaning to "rack the balls." I shoved Kalakos off of me. If we'd hit Salome, let her take her wrath out on him.

"You brought him too? Your generous nature surprises me," Robin drawled; his end of the couch was the higher one. He looked comfortable. Good for him. He used to puke when I had to gate us away. Eventually he'd gotten used to it, as had Niko. Kalakos was all but doubled over, doing all he could to keep from vomiting. Humans didn't like gates and gates didn't like humans. "And you will pay for my sofa, I promise you."

"I had to," I snapped, wiping the slow ooze of blood from my nostrils. I was healed, but normally even in the best of conditions, the nosebleed would gush like a river. The headache would be the same as being hit in the head with a baseball bat, but now it was only a lower-level migraine. Not that I'd ever had a migraine, but I thought it was a good guess. "I didn't have a choice. Any hands, legs, any piece of any one of us at all that was outside the gate would've been left behind in our apartment. Fingers on the floor draw rats. And I like our couch. My ass imprint is the perfect depth. I wasn't leaving it behind."

"Yet my furniture means nothing to you." Goodfellow stayed in place, hands behind his head, as the rest of us slid off and onto the floor. "The two of you are quite the experts with swords." He addressed Niko and Kalakos, who was recovering. He was less green. He'd head back into the nausea range, because Goodfellow was talking and didn't appear to be stopping anytime soon.

Janus—no big deal. A sweaty version of *American Gladiators* right in front of him, that was worth discussing. "It is almost as if Niko inherited some talent from you, although he is superior. He fights with his skill and his heart. You fight with your skill alone. Too bad. A strong heart usually wins. We pucks hate that, as it makes trickery more difficult. Unfortunately it is true."

Kalakos still held the xiphos in his hand, the one that had actually seemed to make a mild impression on Janus. "Niko is impressive. I will not deny. All the male line of my family is the same and has been since . . . I cannot remember. Blond hair, fighters. There is a story that a man impregnated a girl from our clan back in Greece hundreds of years ago. Northern Greek and blond, he was supposedly descended from the Trojan war hero Achilles." He shifted his shoulders. "Foolishness. Mythology, the historical rumors that never die."

Robin crossed his ankles and raised his eyebrows.

"Mythology. When will you humans ever learn what is true and what is not? Achilles existed. There is no myth there. He was human, however. No goddess dipping him in a river by his heel. He was a human soldier and a superb warrior." He moved a hand to pat his stomach. Salome appeared, jumped, and curled up, dead and purring. Her feline grin was the same as always—the Cheshire cat crossed with Hannibal Lecter. "It does explain a good deal. The inherent genetic talent of hundreds of years of warriors since Achilles, hundreds of more warrior ancestors before him. The general appearance: the blond hair and epic nose. You could be his brothers, both of you."

Niko, ever prepared, had held on to his towel and finished cleaning up. "Or his cousin, Patroclus?"

"No, contrary to useless historical myth, they didn't look much alike. Patroclus had dark hair. He also had a tendency toward a foul mouth and insubordination. When they were younger, years before Troy, he was whipped on one occasion, his back turned to rags of flesh ... or at least he was until Achilles returned to camp and broke the neck of the *antisyntag* ... the lieutenant colonel who was doing the 'punishing.' The man wasn't fond of mercenaries to begin with. We had a time covering that one up. But as all the men hated him anyway, a few barrels of wine and it was forgive and forget."

"They existed? You *knew* them?" Kalakos asked with a healthy dose of disbelief. "Achilles and Patroclus?"

Robin looked down his nose. "Were they worth knowing? Yes. Ergo, did I know them? Yes." He stroked Salome's wrinkly bare skin. "When Patroclus died, Achilles cut off his own hair to mourn him." He stared into the light of Salome's eyes as he said that, as if he could see it all over again in the dusty glow. "I handed him the dagger."

"That tradition extended that far back?" The Rom had picked that up when passing through Greece. "To cut your hair?" Niko wondered, a shadowed memory passing over his face. Why wouldn't he be curious? He'd once done it himself.

Robin didn't answer the question, instead saying, "Niko, you can borrow the shower and some of my clothes if you wish. There is also soy milk in the refrigerator. Wine for Promise. Nothing for Cal, as he keeps destroying my condo. And when we are settled, I'd like to hear about the xiphos Kalakos has that didn't kill Janus, but made the automaton at least hesitate for a second or two. Who knows how long we have? This is perfect weather for a war machine like Janus to move about unseen among the local populace."

"We could've been hearing about the swords sooner if you weren't telling us goddamn bedtime stories," I growled. "And it's a war machine? We have an actual war machine on our asses?"

The puck gently rang the gold loop in the tip of Salome's ear. "I like stories. And obviously it's a war machine. Do you think it was built to pick olives?"

What the hell did you say to that?

Niko showered, as did Kalakos, although he hadn't been offered an invitation. The condo had three bathrooms. He took advantage. He wasn't lacking in intelligence enough to take any of Robin's or Ish's clothes without the offer. He did ask politely for shoes, which Robin grumbled about before giving in. "But no shirt. If I have to give you shoes, I get a nice view in return. And if you could throw in a boom-chika-bow-wow once in a while, I might even give you shoes that fit."

Kalakos slapped the xiphos lightly against his leg. "I've not killed a puck before."

"And you never will. Achilles-lite. Vaguely similar taste with half the lethality. Now go take your shower or your generous host, me, will let you walk around New York shoeless, shirtless, and perhaps without your balls."

Salome knew that word. Her hairless muzzle turned toward Kalakos and she showed him her bored let's-play smile. I couldn't figure out how she fit the dentures of a T. Rex in her cat-size mouth, and Kalakos didn't waste time pondering the issue either. He was already moving for the hall and the bathrooms. When he returned he was re-dressed in his black pants and put on his long coat I hadn't noticed him seizing before I'd gated. It must have been where the xiphos had been concealed. He also had the shoes Robin had promised him. He didn't mention anything about the very visible fang marks in them.

When all was done but not said, fifteen minutes later we gathered around the dining room table and I said, "Spit it out, Kalakos." He was at the opposite end of the table from me, not that that would do him any good. I had kept my Desert Eagle with me when I'd gated and it shone bright and deadly on the table in front of me.

"Niko will cut you some slack for your Suyolak-jacked-up Neosporin, but he's my brother. He cares if I live or die. I have different priorities. 'No life for a child.'" I was no Salome but I stretched my mouth into a grin that outdid your average crocodile. "I lived that life with him. And if it comes to me living or me dying and taking you with me because you discarded him like *trash* to live that life, I don't have to flip a fucking quarter to know which choice I'd prefer." I picked up the Eagle and aimed it at where his heart would've been if the son of a bitch had had one. "Tell us the story. Goodfellow told us one. Now it's your turn.

"And, Kalakos," I added, casual on the outside, but on the inside was the blackest of rage, "you know what I am. The entire Vayash clan knew from the day I was born. They kept an eye on Sophia, making sure the wild, crazy, sociopathic bitch didn't get them in trouble. She laughed at that. And they knew the Auphe. All the Rom know the Auphe. The clan knew from the beginning and so did you. The Auphe don't play games like me without a reason. When they *make* things like me, even they don't know for certain how I'll turn out." I turned the Eagle on one side. "More human?" Then to the other side. "Less human?" Then I aimed it back at him.

"But you left Niko there anyway. You know what?" My finger tightened on the trigger. I wanted to pull it. God, I wanted it badly enough that I felt my finger cramp from the pressure of holding back. "That's the bigger crime than leaving him with Sophia. I could've been born a monster. You could've left him with a monster."

Kalakos tensed, fingers curling around the grip of the xiphos. "You *are* a monster."

"*Now* you get it." I felt Niko's presence behind me, but my trigger finger didn't relax. Neither did my predatory grin. "Now you know why Niko is willing to give you a week, but if I think you're lying, I won't give you a second. I'll kill you, and the best thing you can hope for is that I use a gun to do it." I finally let the tension drain away and leaned back in my chair, Eagle still aimed at him, but my grin gone. Niko moved up to my side, although if it had come down to it, I didn't think he knew himself if he would've tried to stop me from pulling the trigger. He sat around the corner of the table from me. "So tell your goddamn story."

All Rom clans have a burden and a duty. That's where the story began. I didn't know why they all did. I didn't think they remembered when or why it had begun either, but this I did know: I didn't give a shit. Janus was the Vayash burden. Created by Hephaestus, who claimed to be a Greek god ... again, didn't care ... he gave the automaton to the Vayash those hundreds of years ago they'd squatted there. It was inactive, a dead machine, if machines could die. Only certain spells could bring it back to life, control it, or disable it again. No one knew the words, the incantations to do any of that. Hephaestus had not trusted them with that. Fake god or not, he was no fool.

"Incantations. *Spells*." Robin clunked his forehead lightly against the table. "Isn't the absolute magnitude of the supernatural enough for you? Must you humans continually offend us with your fairy dust and your talking, colored, egg-crapping rabbits? There is no magic. None. There is a technology that came far before that of humans and built by races long extinct, but there is no magic. Hephaestus without a doubt bought the thing, already an antique in his day, and passed it off as his own work. He wasn't capable of anything like that. Could barely build a mousetrap, the lying bastard." He tunneled fingers through his brown hair, squinted against what was a clearly massive headache. "But, to be perfectly clear one more time, there is *no* magic."

"No Santa, huh?" I snorted.

"No, there was a Santa Claus, but a seven-year-old werewolf ate him," he answered, distracted before turning his ire back on Kalakos. "And who knows this better than anyone? That magic is a trick and the cheapest one there is? An embarrassment to all?" He rearranged himself in the chair to lean closer to Kalakos. "You do. The best of the human tricksters, the Rom, yet you fake it nonetheless, giving us all a bad name."

Closer still as he emphasized. "Do not *think* to play trickster games with a trueborn *paien* trickster or I'll take Cal's gun and put it where he wouldn't think to before I fire it."

Kalakos took that as a strong hint to continue the account with less of that magical bullshit, the only thing that offended Robin: trying to fool a puck. "Although it was assumed no one knew the codes, especially after so long, someone had. The Vayash had found Janus's metal casket empty and the body of two Rom by it. One had had his throat slit neatly.... Blood must have been been part of the activation, combined with the correct command, or that's what the Rom had guessed. It wasn't as if we had a guard on a creature that did nothing but sleep. No, this was very deliberate and ritualistic. The scarlet was smeared liberally on and in the casket. The other Rom had been torn apart. Arms, legs, head, they were all scattered. The traitor. He had been the one to bring Janus to life, but the words used to control it beyond that were obviously not correct. Janus was gone. The clan was parked in Pennsylvania at an RV park and fortunate to be in the closest small town running a rickety fair, earning the day's pay."

If they'd been there when it had happened, Janus would've killed them all, Kalakos said. Hephaestus had warned that should Janus escape it would have enough low-level awareness to hate its captors and destroy them. Beyond that . . .

It would go home. Whether it was a beacon or some bizarre programming from the Greek geeks beyond time, it would return to the place of its creation. Greece before it was Greece. That was why it had headed to NYC. In a straight line from Pennsylvania, it was the closest to the ocean, and the ocean had to be crossed to reach home . . . but that was before it became distracted by the presence of three Vayash in the city. Kalakos didn't know how it sensed us. Did it smell Vayash blood? He had no idea. But find us it could and would until we destroyed it or put it back to sleep, and as none of us knew the *incantation*—Robin glared when I emphasized the word evilly—that wasn't going to happen.

Kalakos had placed his xiphos back onto the table. Facing a monster like me versus that threat of a colonoscopy given to him by a puck with a borrowed Desert Eagle—cooperating was in his best interest. From inside his coat he produced another xiphos. As I'd noticed before, they were the same dark metal that formed Janus. "We were given these with our burden and we were told they wouldn't kill it or even harm it, but that they would cause it pain, give you the moments you needed to hopefully escape. I have only two." He regarded Niko. "As you and I are the swordsmen here, I believe one should go to you and one to me. We will make the best use of them."

"Logical. Reasonable." Niko took the xiphos handed to him and passed it to me. The xiphos left on the table before Kalakos he took for himself without compunction. Niko was about logic and reason, but most of all practicality—the kind that suited him. He didn't bother to look at Kalakos when he ordered, "If you have something to say, do not bother."

"I have something to say. I'm a better swordsman than all of you put together," Robin groused. "Why don't I get a chance at one?"

"You don't have Vayash blood," Niko reminded him, running a hand over the dark metal. "Janus has nothing against you, although it will still eviscerate you if you get in its way. Do remember that. But this mess is not of your making. Stay back and stay safe. You as well, Promise. We have three more days before Cal's gating ability will have recovered to solve all of this for us." That gate I'd built to escape Janus today had set the clock back. Between the first and second gate I had no limit, although I had pain. Between the second gate and the third, which would kill me . . . it took three days to reset me back to gate one.

"Kicking metal butt and sending it to another dimension. That's me." Three days was a long time when Janus could find us as if we had a GPS stapled to our asses, and we all knew it.

I examined my own xiphos, for the first time putting down the gleaming Eagle. Goodfellow was on the money. He was a better swordsman than all of us, but hundreds of thousands of years—or longer . . . as he'd said in the bar, long enough to be forever—after that kind of time spent with a sword in his hand, he couldn't be beaten by anyone human. Perhaps not even by anyone less or more than human. It made me think of what Robin had said in the bar. How old was he—genuinely? Why had no other puck poached on his name? What did they all know? Consciously or subconsciously?

The Auphe weren't the only firsts. The first in time, but not the only first of a race or the only ones who had lived millions of years—a number that went hand in hand with insanity, unreasoning hatred of everyone and everything, and pitch-black malevolence. Hob, the first puck, had been that way, and although he was now dead . . .

He screamed. Didn't he scream like a baby? First born—last torn.

It was a warm thought. He had tried to kill Niko and Georgina, a girl I'd loved. He had deserved to scream. There was no denying that, and most would scream their

lungs inside out when ripped apart by the mass of unbe-
lievably pissed-off Auphe I'd tossed him to. I had no re-
grets.

It didn't change my original thought, though.

Hobgoblin—Hob to all others, as shorter names made
it quicker in getting to the running part—was the first
trickster and had been as much a murder-loving bastard
as the Auphe. A combination like that we could use until
the days passed and I could gate Janus onto the bones of
those now-dead Auphe and the bones of the first puck as
well in Tumulus. Good company for an ancient war machine. "Goodfellow." I ran a careful thumb along the
blade. "If he had to face Janus, what do you think Hob
would do—to at least slow it down?"

Robin's lips flattened. "I do not know."

"You knew him better than most. You've said so. He
was the first trickster. He would have a chance to put this
bastard off for three days at least. What would he do?"
Robin was one of the best tricksters out there, but he
wasn't what Hob had been—a blood-spilling psychopath
created out of insanity and violence. He *was* violence, or
had been, walking and talking, but so sly and slippery
you didn't see him coming until you wondered why your
guts were on the outside instead of the inside. It would've
been a challenge for him, but I'd seen into that bastard's
eyes. Pure poison was all that lurked in their depths. His
tricks, they always ended in death. He would've known
how, if not to take out the automaton, then how to delay
it. I knew from personal experience that sometimes it
took a monster to outthink a monster.

"I *don't* know." It was more that he didn't want to
know, didn't want to go down that path. I didn't blame
him. I had my own path. I knew what it was like. Moving

along the path slowly, controlling each step, but I was walking it all the same.

Halfway there now . . .

"Okay," I said. I wouldn't push him on it yet. I'd give him a chance to think about it before I brought it up again. "No big deal. We'll just—"

That was when I felt it. Behind me. A gate. Jesus Christ, a fucking *gate*.

Once I would've thought, No. Not again. Not anymore. I was the last. I'd made sure of that. There were no more. *No*. No more kidnappings. No more threatening to kill my brother, my friends. No more red eyes, white skin, metal teeth. No more Auphe hell.

God, no more.

Of course, I was somewhat of a chickenshit then, not that everyone—or anyone—agreed with that. But I had been more human.

Not that I hadn't had my moments back then, but they were Auphe moments, lost in a blind genetic rage. I wasn't blind any longer. With help, I'd killed every last one of these bastards on the planet, culminating with eight half-breeds like me in Nevah's Landing.

What were my thoughts now?

Shit, not again. And the emotion that went with it wasn't fear. I was mad as hell. I'd destroyed our race. Our entire goddamn race. What the fuck did this out-of-thin-air, leftover asshole think he could do to me?

Arms wrapped around me from behind, steel bands. Stronger than me, stronger than Niko, who was hurtling toward us, but it was too late. The coldness of the gate swallowed us and the condo was gone. But I heard the words that floated behind.

An unfamiliar voice but with an all-too-familiar sarcasm, the same as mine—at someone else's expense—said, "You could cover your windows, goat. I go where I see, and I saw far too many perversions through yours."

It was bad when an Auphe thought your sex life—your monogamous sex life—was a perversion. Or it could be it wasn't the sex but the emotion that went with it. Yeah, Auphe were creatures of few emotions and they were all malignant as biohazard waste filling their skulls. Hate, disgust, slaughter-glee, arrogance, ravenous hunger. No affection, though—that didn't exist to them.

And we were gone, bodies and voice.

The gate dumped us in a dark basement with a concrete floor with one flickering bulb overhead and the rot of dead bodies—gone, but the decomposition lingered in the cold air, as did the taint of Auphe. I was used to my scent. I'd had it all my life, after all, but the smell of another Auphe was somehow different and repulsive. It . . . he released me and I whipped around, the xiphos between us. I missed my Desert Eagle as much as I'd miss my hand. "It was the feathers, wasn't it?" I grinned, showing all my teeth, top and bottom. The predator's grin—the better to eat you with.

If there was one thing I could say about an Auphe, it was that I didn't have to conceal what I was in front of him.

Guard up, using every ounce of swordsmanship Niko had taught me, I drawled, "Spying, were you? I think that makes you the perv. Did you see the feathers flying around the bedroom as the peri"—he didn't need to know Ishiah's name—"spunked goose juice everywhere? Did he look like a pigeon that swallowed a grenade and exploded? That's my mental nightmare."

The Auphe. No, the half-Auphe, like me—I'd seen

that at the same time as I'd smelled it—grinned back. He was even dressed all in black, as I was, although he had a leather jacket, T-shirt, jeans, and combat boots, whereas I was stuck with sweats and damned socks.

Ever had to face death while wearing a pair of socks? It's somewhat humiliating.

He had human teeth, straight and white, until a second row of hundreds of hypodermic needles snapped down over the top of them. That made him more Auphe than me, as did the red irises he revealed when he took off and dropped dark sunglasses to the floor. His hair was white, the Auphe winter tint with the glitter of ice, but the same length and don't-give-a-shit style as mine. It was on purpose, to mock me. I knew it. His skin wasn't pale as mine was, though. His was a healthy human tint. Light tan. He was me, but the opposite of me.

"Peri and puck. I had to eat a pit bull to rinse the taste from my mouth after that show." His voice was deeper than mine, with the faint grind of broken glass to each word. Semi-Auphe vocal cords. He shook his hand, the one that I had already seen gripping a black matte Desert Eagle, to show off the spiked dog collar wrapped three times around his wrist.

"What's life without souvenirs?" I said. The gun he held was well-known, a black matte Desert Eagle with a scratch on the grip. Mine.

He saw my eyes flicker toward it. "Yes, Caliban, it's yours. I picked it up off the street where that cattle you live with dropped it as he tried to save your life. I like it. It's a good gun. I do like a good gun. In death I like all things. Guns, knives, swords." His other hand clenched, then flared with fingers spread, silver bright. He wore black gloves over his hands, but over his empty one was a metal set of claws that encased his fingers and hand, a modern imitation of an extinct Auphe taloned one. When he made a fist, four to five inches of metal would extend past his knuckles to carve you apart. "But I like the old ways too. And if you're not born with them, you make them. Or have someone or something make them for you."

"You know my name? Caliban?" I asked without emotion, sword between us but closer to him now. No feelings—none human, at any rate. Others, though ... they were there. But if I did let those come, it would get down and dirty before I was ready for it.

"All in the Nevah's Landing prison knew of Caliban. The golden boy who would return the world to what it should have been. But you didn't, did you? You destroyed the Auphe instead. Then you shot the failures and burned down the house until the bones were fiery dust. I didn't see the others, years after I left, with the windows boarded, but I saw what you did to our keeper, our torturer—Sidle."

Proud, irritated, satisfied. Those emotions all showed on his face ... because he let them. Why would he bother to hide his feelings? Auphe didn't hide from anyone or anything. "Ah, that was the best. The way you scattered his brain and bone and blood without looking. You pulled the trigger and kept walking. I threw down the binoculars and laughed, laughed down the night sky, or at least I tried."

Binoculars. That's why I hadn't felt him. He'd been far away ... watching.

"I was jealous you were the one to do it. You always had all the good times, didn't you, while I spent eighteen years in a cage, chained, tortured, and fed like a tame *dog*. That, Caliban, was not a good time, but the past doesn't matter anymore. Because that was the moment I knew I wasn't alone. You killed Sidle without a second or first thought. You killed him because he was weak. I knew then I had a worthy competitor." Then he said worse. "A brother."

Irritated and satisfied I couldn't care less about, but I didn't want this thing proud of me, and the very last thing I wanted him thinking was that I was his brother.

I'd killed Sidle, part Auphe himself, because he'd kept seven half-breeds—now I knew it had been eight—like me in cages all their lives, manacled, splashed with acid, tortured with a cattle prod, and who knew what else. I killed his prisoners because they *were* Auphe: insane and ready to butcher any living creature they came across if their cage doors were opened. I gave them the only escape available to them in this world.

I killed Sidle because he deserved it.

I hadn't lost a moment of sleep over it, hadn't spared a thought on the piece of shit since.

"That one empty cage in the house," I said, taking another step forward with hand tight on the grip of the sword. "Sidle said that half-Auphe had died. He lied, didn't he? He didn't want to get in trouble with the masters. He was too stupid to know that they would've been doing a homicidal dance of joy at the first half-breed to gate. The first success, long before me. You said years of captivity . . ."

"Twelve of freedom. Born six years before you and caged eighteen of them. Too bad I didn't learn to gate sooner." The metal teeth gleamed. "But once I did . . . I killed and killed and killed, but finally I learned. You cannot take down an enemy that would drown you and the world in a mass of their flesh without lifting a finger. Not if you don't know them. I had to learn, and now I know. Reading, writing, history." He said it singsong, as a kid would—if that kid was possessed. "I know the cattle better now than they know themselves. I know how they think. I know how they smothered the Auphe, breeding like rabbits, and I know how to do the same to them."

The first Auphe who knew that to learn about your enemy made killing easier, planning more efficient, wholesale massacres closer to reality. This son of a bitch . . . *Jesus*. "You went to *school*?" I lunged at him with the Greek sword, but he was equally quick. Hell, this wasn't a situation to be lying to myself. He was quicker. He swatted the blade aside with what I knew were the metal claws he wore. I had to depend on knowing, as I didn't see anything but the afterimage of a silver flash.

"I have a GED." This time he swung at me, and as fast as I moved I didn't escape the shallow slices across my chest. My adrenaline levels had tripled, and that did let me see the claws this time, if not avoid them. "I'm an educated monster. The top of my class. I had many teachers, all very proud . . . until I ate them. No spirit of celebration in them at all. Humans are incredibly dull. Barely worth the slaying." The talons clacked against one another, ringing out his disappointment at the lack of challenge. "They would be enough for the half-breeds you killed in the Landing, but I am not the same as them. I'm like you, Caliban. I'm an improved version of you, you who are not quite that *special* and *unique* after all."

It was true. He wasn't like the ones in the Landing, all of them mentally and psychotically dysfunctional. They also had bodies twisted and mutated beyond the hope of passing for human. Not like I could. Not like he could. Worse, he wasn't the same as them on the inside either. He was clever. He infiltrated the enemy; he was more than functional. He excelled.

He wanted something or we would be fighting to the

death now instead of him holding back with baby slaps of his claws. I wasn't one of the humans who bored him. It would take effort to kill me and he would crave that trial of himself, the escape from tedious prey to face an equal. He said he was my brother. He wasn't. Sophia wasn't his mother, and I knew there had to be plenty of Auphe sires at the time he or I was made. We were not brothers, no matter what he thought. He and I were the last of a half-breed race; that was all. In his eyes, however, I knew that was enough. It was the week for family reunions, unwanted and bloody. Niko and Kalakos. The Panic. And now me and mine.

Better to deny yourself than offend a brother, after all.

Oh, shut the hell up. I mentally slammed a hard foot down on my lurking internal smart-ass and, worse, the tingle of interest.

The last two of a race that shouldn't have existed to begin with if there'd been a God or if nature had had any judgment. This was a reunion, but it had nothing to do with family. It had to do with an opportunity to put nature's screwup right.

"Who the fuck are you, anyway?" I growled, slashing at his claws with the sword before reversing to knock my Eagle from his hand. He didn't appear upset. His glittering teeth flashed, satisfied, as if I were a dog who'd done a particularly difficult trick.

"My name was the same as all the others were given. Failure. But once free I named myself. Now I am Grimm . . . for aren't we the grimmest of brothers?"

"You're not my brother." Auphe were bad enough. Add the original Grimm Brothers fairy tales, with zombie horses and wolf-eaten grandmothers who stayed dead and half-digested, and "disgust" was a word that didn't begin to cover the combination of the two.

"When we are the last of one race and the beginning of another, we are brothers." The claws slashed again and this time I managed to just dodge them. "I've made you my sole interest." The smile became sly and secretive. "A large interest. Blood and killing, like the sun rising—together they always come first to our kind, but that's not to say you can't serve as both."

"That sounds pretty fucking convenient." I stabbed at him with the xiphos.

"For me? It is. It very much fucking is." He was gone in a darkling flare of gray light. I twisted to see him behind me. "Fine and fucking dandy, as Sidle used to tell us through the bars of our cages. Fine and fucking dandy."

"Kill me already then," I snarled, "or we can kill each other. That's the best end to the fairy tales you named yourself after."

"Kill you?" He laughed. A milder echo of the pure Auphe's breaking-glass sound. "Why would I have gated that metal monstrosity off of you and your cattle if I wanted to kill you?"

"Janus? You were the one who stole it from the Rom? I hope you had a good time screwing around with it and me outside the bar." He needed to believe I knew I hadn't gated it. I'd thought I had, with my last effort, though I'd had no idea of how or where. Grimm couldn't know I was weak and gateless for days.

But I wasn't, was I?

"Baby games." He smiled, teeth sliding back up, and he looked more human. I preferred him Auphe. I preferred knowing in every part of me what he was. "Not that I won't kill you now that you've proved worthy, but I have things for you to do for me first. The blood I want from you is not to spill; it is to spread. When that is done, then finally we'll have our real games, and don't tell me you don't want them as much as I do. That you don't want to play . . . at the end. Prove who is the best."

Cal wants to plaaaaay.

Maybe I did, but that didn't mean I would.

Spread my blood. That gave me a strong sense of déjà vu. I hated déjà vu.

But the hell with all that. If I hadn't gated Janus that meant I had a third gate waiting in the wings. The final gate. I could try it on Grimm. I'd happily die to take this bastard with me. One gate opened inside of him and he'd be decorating all four basement walls. I had barely a chance to think of triggering it when the pain searing through my head gave me double vision. Opening a gate and taking Grimm with me was worth it. Opening the third gate and dying while Grimm looked at my twitching body with disappointed puzzlement—no more play—wasn't.

The pain faded as I let the thought of the gate go. I could kill the bastard with my hands and my sword in the place of a gate and walk away from his cooling corpse. That was a better option. Better because I'd live, but better also because I'd be the reason he didn't.

"I have questions too." He gated again, gone from the room. I rushed the door, but before I could reach for the knob, he was back—directly in front of it—directly in front of me. Bare inches away. "You could have gated a hundred Auphe to a million years ago, if you weren't the insolent badass you were and had refused. When I heard of that, I was . . . What do you call it? What's that word? Happy? Happy as hell," he said, pleased. He hadn't wanted the Auphe to succeed any more than I had. He did hate them as much as I had—or hated them more—and seeing the prison, the cells, knowing what had been done to him, I didn't blame him. He deserved that hate to banish those memories. In his place . . .

In his place, I would *be* him.

His expression changed to confusion. "After that you could gate as you pleased to the goat's abode, but dying on a street last night, you couldn't gate at all. That makes me curious. It also makes me annoyed. Annoyed enough that I was going to kill you and the cattle that wrung their hands to keep you alive—until things changed."

"Cattle?" I noticed for the first time that he was the only supernatural creature that didn't use the more typical word for humans. "Not sheep?"

He pressed the metal claws against my face. "Nooo, Caliban. Never sheep. I am the sheep. The black sheep of the Auphe. Blackest of the black. That is my title. They thought you a bad boy. I wish at least one remained to see what I am and what I will be. Bad enough that they would've bowed before me."

The claws clutched my face lightly, but not so lightly that I didn't know he could have removed my face if he'd wanted. I could see through the space between the talons as I felt their chill. "You gate, you can't gate, and then today you gate again. And you heal from something when it should've taken you weeks to recover. I want to know what you have become. I'm intrigued. Life was so boring before you, Caliban. *Borrrrrrring*. You cannot know."

"What things do you want me to do for you first?" I asked abruptly. "What do you mean by 'spread my blood'?"

His red eyes flared brighter in anticipation or something close to it . . . GED, short attention span. He was more like me than I cared to admit. "Humans, they breed and breed. You know. This is why we were made. To go back and warn the first Auphe. Destroy the humans before they gobble up the world, gobble it all up when it belongs to us. It's too late for that now, but it wouldn't matter if it weren't." The talons loosened some, not for my comfort, but as he was caught up in what he had to say, his . . . hell . . . vision. "We are better than them. The Auphe are gone, but you and I remain. We are the Second Coming, the new wave that exceeds the first. We are meant to take their place and do what they could not. But as the Auphe in us breed slow, as we live so long—"

Keep dreaming on that one, asshole. I'll outlive you; I promise you that, even if it's by seconds, I thought, my grip tightening on the hilt of the xiphos.

"—I needed to find what else we could breed with besides humans. Something that matured faster, fast enough to equal the humans in a few centuries, at least." He tilted his head until his forehead rested on the metal claws that pressed against my skin, his eyes bloody mirrors of mine, so close the gray of my own reflected in his. The same as the red of his must have reflected in mine. Not brothers, but something as binding, that called to every Auphe cell in me.

An obligation. The last. We were the last . . . until he proved we don't have to be.

I pushed the thought away. *Yes, we did have to be. The last.* That's what the remains of my conscience said, and it was right.

"And I did find what would breed the fastest." His eyes remained fixed on mine. "Succubae. They lay eggs, but not with us. With Auphe they have litters, and those litters mature in a year. Three hundred and sixty-five days and you have a full-grown member of the Second Coming."

Spread the blood. That's where the déjà vu came from. I'd had this "invitation" before by the real deal. Pure Auphe, not the watered-down versions we were. I'd jumped off a building to turn that particular one down. I wasn't any more enthusiastic about this one, no matter what other thoughts might slink about in the lowest levels.

"Succubae? They hate us, especially the taste of us." I knew that from personal experience. Succabae lived on sexual energy, any sexual energy from any being, except one. Auphe energy revolted them. I'd had one nearly upchuck in my lap after tasting me. "They wouldn't breed with an Auphe," I said with all the ego-bruised confidence in the world. "For any reason."

The jagged voice was mildly curious. "Who said I asked their permission?"

This was what I'd traded part of my humanity for . . . control and something else. Control for situations such as this. The something else was Niko's life. Those months ago, while facing the Egyptian life-sucker whose pets had made me forget my life—all of it—things had taken a turn. I'd finally been on the verge of regaining my memories, and not only my memories but the biogenetic skills that resided there.

I couldn't function properly, the useful part of me— the *bad* part of me—unless all was whole, memories that resided in brain cells and Auphe abilities that resided in both. I'd been close, minutes away, but they were minutes I didn't have. Half a minute and my brother would've been dead. What I'd needed I'd needed right then, not in minutes.

You have to give to get.

The better Cal had pushed a part of his human self down and let the Auphe flow over it. Devour it. A small bite only, but large enough that I was myself again—less/more than myself again, the true Cal with an added cloud of a dead race. Thirty seconds then was more time than I needed to tear out the heart of that Egyptian snake goddess and watch it melt at my feet.

I'd saved my brother and gained control of my former attacks of dangerously *unaware* violence. The Auphe had been many things, but not unaware in their violence. They were very aware. With more Auphe in me as the human portion was swallowed up, I gained awareness.

Control: The Auphe in me spoke of obligations to what was left of our race—the Auphe in me that was yet only half, shit, maybe three-fourths as both time and genes multiplied, as I sacrificed, but whatever it was, it wasn't enough for Grimm's plan. That was my newfound awareness.

As for permission . . .

He did say he hadn't asked the succabae's permission.

Control could also mean violently *aware* attacks. It wasn't as limiting as one might think.

I didn't ask for permission either when I sheathed the xiphos in Grimm's stomach.

Grimm was more Auphe than I was, with their speed, but he also had another quality of theirs . . . enormous arrogance. That worked to my advantage. It made him assume things he shouldn't.

Things such as: You're my brother, because why wouldn't you want to be?

I already have a brother, better than you.

You know you want to prove ourselves deadlier than the first Auphe.

Been there, done that. The T-shirt shop was closed.

You have to want to reclaim the world. You want to rule it and everything on it.

Rule the world? Too much damn work.

You want to kill whoever or whatever you want, whenever you want.

I already can.

You want to kill.

I do.

You need to kill.

In his conceit, he was right on that one.

At this precise moment, I did need to kill.

So thanks for the opportunity.

"What?" I twisted the blade and felt his blood pour over my hand. "Should I have asked your *permission* first? Like you asked the succubae?"

The talons tightened on my face. He said he liked guns, but I knew all Auphe save me liked claws and teeth the best. I didn't want my face ripped off like a Halloween mask, yet it felt good to get down to the basics of flesh and blood, the cutting of one . . . the spilling of the other. As long as he died with me, it would be worth it. Here was the plate and here was me stepping up to swing the bat. I could save the world from him. Was that the martyr in me? It would sound better to say yes, but it would be a lie. It was about the world, but with the smell of blood, the warmth of it covering my sword hand, an enemy pinned by my metal and his arrogance, it was more about something else. It was about the *game*.

I could kill another Auphe, defeat him. He wanted to play? Let's see who won.

But was it that easy? No. When is it ever that easy? From behind I felt five gates open. "Father?" The hiss was pure succubae/incubi, the smell mostly Auphe. Some visitors for Daddy. There went my opportunity to finish the game with Grimm.

Which pissed me off to no fucking end. Not good news for those available for me to take it out on.

I pulled the xiphos free. I was going to need it. Grimm smiled, that perfect human smile, before dropping his claws from my face. He didn't appear upset about the black-red blood leaking from his abdomen. It was already clotting. With us human-Auphe half-breeds you couldn't begin to know where the vital organs were. We were all different — although maybe not as different as I wished we were. "No, Caliban, we're not ready for that game yet. We have things to do," he said, before pointing a gleaming talon past me. "Turn and greet your new brothers and sisters."

I did. It was the past returned to life, or very nearly. They looked as ghastly as the Auphe, but unlike the half-Auphe in Nevah's Landing, these all appeared the same. Identical — same father, perhaps same mother. They were Auphe pale, nude, with the slippery long white hair, the whiteless red eyes, the small pointed ears, but there were no hundreds of metal needles in each narrow jaw. They had succubae/incubi fangs. Metal, but snake fangs all the same, each five inches long and curved, their black tongues forked. Here and there on their skin was the glint of a pearlescent snake scale. You couldn't tell if a pure Auphe was male or female except by smell; the females had no breasts and the males' reproductive organ was withdrawn until needed. It was the same with the new ones.

I usually didn't bother to tell the difference. It was easier to think of them all as its.

It killed, *it* mutilated, *it* needed to die.

Grimm had done what he'd claimed. They appeared as deadly as the real Auphe had, but I felt a contemptuous disdain coiling in my gut. They were one-fourth Auphe, half of what I was. I felt about them as the original Auphe had felt about me and the others. They were lesser.

Pathetic corruptions.

Great. I was a monster, I had a nightmare family that

would not die no matter how many times I killed them, and now the Auphe in me was not slaughter-prone alone; it was also a bigot. Whatever. It wasn't as if I'd intended on welcoming them with a slap on the back and a six-pack anyway. And if they were sending off any cuddly-puppy vibes, I was missing them totally.

They crouched by the back basement wall, the five of them, fully grown, as Grimm had said they would be. Fangs bared; black natural talons that their father would envy were poised in the air. They continued to hiss. Despite my inner scorn, I'd try to be careful and do my best to believe that they were at least half as dangerous as the Auphe and Grimm. Arrogance had been his downfall. I wouldn't let it be mine. There was one way to know—the tried-and-true way. The oldest way. Every Auphe proves himself an Auphe. Survival of the fittest. Time to prove myself part of a family I didn't claim and hopefully prove it more lethally than they could, ending all of this at the same time.

I pointed the xiphos at the nearest one. "Call me Uncle Cal. It'll make me feel all warm and fuzzy when I chop off your head." Grimm was older than I was, but I was by far older than these new Auphe. They matured in a year?

I'd introduce them to twenty-four years of being the real bogeyman in the closet of every other weak excuse for a monster.

So much for careful.

Useless shadows. Garter-snake doppelgängers. Show them what a real Auphe is.

A real Auphe—a real predator—didn't wait for its enemy to call it out or for its daddy to tell it what to do. It didn't wait at all.

And I didn't.

9

That Kalakos was the one who took the last of the five Auphe-bae hit team out of this life was a surprise. To me some. To him most of all.

But that came a few minutes later. Right now the first four I had to take care of myself.

The Second Coming slashed at me with claws and jerked their heads forward in reptilian fashion to try to bury their fangs in my flesh. Succabae and incubi weren't poisonous. They didn't have to be. With the size of the fangs, these kiddies could cut through you ten times more efficiently than any butcher knife. The hissing ... it didn't stop. It was almost worse than the fractured-glass sound of an Auphe voice piercing your eardrum. That had been once in a while—not big talkers, the Auphe. This was constant. Trying to tune it out while listening for the movement of Grimm's grown children was almost impossible. Add that to their gating when they pleased—and they pleased a damn good deal—and I was fighting what disappeared before me and what I couldn't hear coming up behind me.

I loved every damn minute of it.

The adrenaline rush. The feeling of righteousness. Sometimes I thought the only time that I felt truly salvageable was when I fought something truly evil. Grimm's doing—they were evil. They weren't meant to dwell on the skin of this world. I didn't get that feeling when I took out a supernatural hyena. They belonged. Yes, they ate people, but so did lions, given an opportunity. They weren't evil as the very definition of the word, but what I faced was, in every sense and bitter syllable of the word.

I whirled as out of the corner of my eye I saw one reappear to my right. I sliced it from neck to pelvis with the xiphos. It didn't matter where its vital internal organs were with that kind of wound, as basically every organ it had cascaded out onto the filthy concrete floor we fought on. Another one vanished from in front of me to appear behind me—directly behind, as I felt its weight on my back. Claws sank into my arms and I knew fangs were angling to tear my throat out. I didn't waste any time. I saw another Auphe-bae gating out and I swung around to put the majority of the one leeched onto my back into the gate as it closed. That meant it took whatever part of the Auphe-bae that had been inside the gate with it. As pieces of him fell around me, I guessed it had been about three-fourths. There was half of a head left, the red eyes dulling but the jaws snapping slowly as black brain matter pooled outward. There were arms and legs, but a good deal of his torso, including his spinal cord, was gone.

They didn't have the proper respect for a gate that they should. And not one had thought to open a gate in me, as I'd tried with Grimm. Grimm had said they matured physically in one year—mentally as well, from the cursing they sprinkled in with their hissing. Yeah, they were all grown-up and cussing with the big boys. It was efficient for breeding to retake the world, if you were only going by numbers, but one year of fighting experience didn't make the grade.

I grinned at the three left, the one now having gated back. I had the blood of their siblings dripping off the blade of the xiphos. I liked the sound it made when it hit the floor. The pitter-patter of a slow and soft rain. "Daddy didn't tell you what else was out in the big, bad world, did he? What else could put a boot up your pasty snake asses without half trying? Kids, you don't know what a *bona fide*," I drawled, "Auphe is, and now you never will."

I could understand Niko's appreciation of swords now. You felt the thud of the metal entering the flesh. You knew, by the vibration that traveled up your arm alone, whether you'd ended a life or only damaged it. Niko would value it for different reasons: giving your enemy more of a chance, having more time to decide if they deserved that death you were handing out as freely as Halloween candy, challenging yourself to be a superior fighter.

His reasons were principled; mine were not, but we ended up at the same place. I didn't know if the difference mattered, and right then I didn't care.

I dived to the floor as two gated out and one sprang toward me. I rolled onto my back, the one thing you didn't want facing an enemy. This one was the biggest by a few inches, broader in the shoulders, heavier. If there was a runt in the litter, this one would've eaten it.

It almost vaulted over me as I'd planned, but was able to stop itself, if only barely, to land on top of me. "I have killed men and women. Children and babies." Its breath was not Auphe hot on my face, but Auphe-bae cool, cold-blooded as its succubus-snake mother. The tang of truth was in what it said—that tang being rot and decomposition. "Vampires, Wolves, hordes of revenants, and you think me not Auphe?" The hissing soared, filling the small room with its rattrap, claustrophobically low ceiling. "You think me not worthy of the name?"

No, senseless little snake. No. No. No.

"In fifty years or so, you might be worthy." I'd knocked my Desert Eagle from Grimm's hand to land on the floor earlier. Grimm had forgotten it or wanted to see if this batch of Auphe-bae noticed, testing his progeny. They failed. They didn't look at anything in the room but me. That wasn't smart. I could've smashed the overhead lightbulb and jabbed the delicate sliver of glass into the eye of one of them until it pierced the brain. Anything can be a weapon.

"Maybe a hundred years," I amended. "Give me a call then." I reached behind me, hand scrambling against the concrete, seized the grip, then inserted the muzzle of the Eagle into one pointed ear and gifted him with five rounds.

"Thanks for reloading it," I said to Grimm. I had time to see the quickest flash of him; his back hadn't moved from the door. He was making sure this game played out to the end, whatever end that might be.

He had too—reloaded the Eagle. Niko had used all the explosive rounds in it. These were nice, normal hollow-points. I had to worry about wearing my victim's blood and brain matter, but not roasting off my own face in the bargain.

"I went to school. So should they. Survival of the fittest is the best school," I heard him say, nothing in his words but careless amusement. I killed his children and it didn't trouble him. Why should it? He could make more.

A hundred years, you told the Bae. Together in a hun-

dred years Grimm and I could make a hundred thou-sand. . . .

"Can't afford the child support," I muttered to myself as I pushed the body of the one I'd shot off of me and impaled the one that gated out of the air above me be-fore I could sit up. It kicked, flailed, and screamed with rage as its chest rested against my hand that gripped the xiphos while I finished it off with the Eagle, this time three rounds in a scarlet eye. That blew the dead body back, and I gave a jerk to the xiphos to let the child of the Second Coming go flying across the room.

Two more to go, and I had no expectations, belly wound or not, that Grimm would be anything like the Bae, who were so easy to dispose of that they no longer deserved the name Auphe. He was older than I was, had been free long enough to be more experienced in deal-ing death, could gate, was closer to true Auphe. If Grimm wanted to kill me, there was a chance that the best I could hope for was a suicidal tie.

It was time to find out.

His last pick of the litter had vanished in a vortex of silver, gray, and black before reappearing as I stood. It also had come out in midair, but not over my head. It ap-peared next to the ceiling, getting as much height as it could, and to the side, giving it an angled downward speed. As it did, I heard the force pounding against the basement door. I threw myself backward and sideways to let the Bae tumble and charge past me. Janus could fol-low the Vayash as if a GPS were stapled to my ass—funny, huh? But it wasn't a serious consideration I'd had earlier about the war machine. It was a serious one, how-ever, when it came to other matters.

When I'd been attacked by a mass of giant spiders and disappeared by gating out onto a beach at high tide in a childhood sanctuary in South Carolina, the only reason Niko had found me wrapped in a cocoon of amnesia was because of the GPS in my cell phone. It had washed down the beach by miles as it gave its last location before the ocean shorted it out. As the tidal drift had added days to his finding me, he decided that a brother who could gate hundreds or thousands of miles deserved something with added efficiency over a cell phone.

They made identification chips for pets small enough to be implanted under the skin and not seen, but not locator chips. They did make locators, but they were large enough to have to be fastened to a collar or an ankle band, as they did for sexual predators. Some could track one mile; some could link up to a satellite and cover at least half the country. The trouble with those is they were noticeable right off the bat, either by an amnesiac loony who'd yank it off his ankle, by someone who lost the control he was so certain of and did the same, or, in this case, by a kidnapper.

That meant that under the flesh it had to go. It was the size of a pacemaker and fit under a fist-shaped scar I already had on my chest. It filled the shallow crater some, and although the shape was squarish, it didn't make it look much worse. It was experimental, and the FDA would keel over at the thought of it implanted in a human or semihuman being, but when Niko had asked me point-blank one day out of the blue, my answer had been as matter-of-fact as the question. And the fact that he had to cut me open to put it in and then again once a year to change the batteries, that made me *know* it was necessary. For his peace of mind if nothing else.

Who knew that it would come in handy so soon?

"My family," I affirmed to Grimm. "And that, asshole, will never be you."

He moved away from the door as his last child I'd dodged passed him. "We are something new."

"We are something old," I said automatically, the words beyond my power to swallow.

"We are something unlike anything on earth," he finished.

I'd echoed those words, the same that a healer had once said about me, as I'd burned that South Carolina house of horrors to the ground. And Grimm, despite being far enough away that I couldn't sense him, had heard me.

"That makes us one. One, Caliban, and that is more than brothers, more than family. Plus it's poetic. My teacher would've liked the symmetry. That is, before I ate her." Did my grin, sarcastic and sinister in its eager violence, look like his? No wonder no one tipped me at the bar.

He finished, back on topic, "One." As the Bae hit the door and turned to charge back, a gate began to outline Grimm. "Until I kill you. Games are games and we'll play—back and forth, give and take, but death is the ultimate move. And once you've given in, given up, given your all to the Second Coming by siring a tidal wave of our spawn, then you'll die in the game." He glowed. The gray-and-silver light. The metal claws waving a dark good-bye. The grin brilliant white then luminous mercury. He moved as if my sword hadn't touched him, much less been buried in his stomach. "And this world will be mine to do with as I please."

I didn't grin this time. I smiled, and it was a cold and hard slice of hell, as that part of me I normally kept silent decided to get mouthy. "Who says I'll lose the game?

Who says I'll share?" And I said it in Auphe. My human vocal cords couldn't duplicate the sound of the seven years' bad luck of a mirror being smashed inside your ear, cutting your eardrum to ribbons before the shards burrowed into your brain, but the words I knew.

From the flicker of anger that crossed his face, Grimm didn't. He couldn't speak Auphe at all. He hadn't lived among them for two years as I had—even if the language was all I remembered—and none had wasted time teaching the caged failures the motherfucking tongue.

"You'll die and that won't change. The game is mine to win. You, Caliban"—the glow brightened—"you might have been the Auphe's fondest ambition, but you, bastard brother, are not *me*."

The door shattered to three large pieces and several smaller ones. The Bae staggered back as one stake-shaped piece slid perfectly into its chest as if it were the unlucky extra in a vampire movie. Niko passed it, dismissing it as the lesser threat. He swung a katana I didn't recognize. That would mean it was one of Goodfellow's many swords. It had greater reach than a xiphos. It should've cut Grimm in half, but he was gone. The closing of the gate did take half the katana's blade with it. If I were an optimist, I'd hope it had done some damage before the half-Auphe disappeared.

But if I were an optimist, this wouldn't be my life we were talking about, would it?

The Bae gripped the wood to pull it from its chest, then swiveled its head to hiss and lunge at the next person hesitating in the doorway. Kalakos cursed in Rom and took its head off at the shoulders with his saber. The move had been instinctual. That could be seen in his brown skin that now almost matched the color of the Bae as it fell in two pieces. Paler than pale. He hadn't seen what was attacking him. It had been too quick, in the middle of a rescue, the moment too muddied. Kalakos had seen a threat. That was all. It wasn't until it was down and dead that he saw, for the first time, an Auphe. Or the closest thing next to me to qualify as an Auphe.

I watched it twitch and changed my mind, my former scorn sulking. I'd more or less told it that give it fifty years' experience and it would be the next thing closest to me. Now I thought that in fifty years I'd be the closest thing to it instead. It had the equipment, the ability, and Grimm would make certain the Bae would learn to use them. Grimm knew education was an advantage above all others.

"Makes me look pretty good, doesn't it, Kalakos?" I said. "Given half a century or so of murder and mayhem and it would've become the *shadow* of an Auphe." A thousand years and it would leave the Auphe in its dust. "Tell that to your clan, the cowardly sons of bitches. Afraid of a sixteen-year-old mentally damaged kid like I'd been. I doubt they'd have done much spitting if that had come calling in my place."

He took a step away from the Bae, regained the equilibrium a warrior needed to survive, and looked at me for the first time. Or rather saw me for the first time. All my ... heh ... quirky imperfections aside, I wasn't the Bae. There was some human in it, but there was humanity in me. I wasn't overflowing with it, but it was there.

"I apologize," he offered in that familiar if older echo of Niko's voice, "for myself and my clan. This ... this is a monster, not you. We misjudged our own blood and we are shamed for it."

That was unexpected, kind of decent, and the right thing to do. If it had come eight and a half, nine years earlier, it might have made a difference. It hadn't, though, and my grudge was about what he, decent but not decent enough to be a father, and the Rom had done to Nik. I didn't give a shit what they thought about me.

Niko paused for the briefest of moments at the apology before overlooking it to grip one of my shoulders hard enough to get my instant—*ow*—attention. "Who was that? *What* was that?" He wasn't talking about the dead Bae on the floor or the others. He was referring to the one clever enough to take me from the condo alive, fast enough to escape my real brother and survive—all while making an edgier game of it than I'd thought. I'd been down here less than fifteen minutes, listening to Grimm, attacking him, fighting the Bae. He hadn't bothered to go any farther than what I had to think was two or three buildings down from Goodfellow's. Niko didn't have his tracker with him. That had been left back home when we'd fled Janus. Goodfellow had one, though, as did Promise and Ishiah in a locked safe at the bar.

"He's one I missed in South Carolina." I wiped some of the Bae blood from the xiphos carelessly onto my pants. "By twelve years. He was the Auphe's first success, not me, and they never knew it. He's also head of the Auphe Second Coming. Big, bad Auphe messiah." I ran a hand slowly through the space where his gate had been. I could feel the pain and the wound of reality knitting itself back together still. Every gate had a price. Mine too, as much as I tried to forget it.

Kalakos had thought I was a monster and then he saw the Bae.

I'd thought I was a monster when I'd been old enough to realize what a monster was.

I'd eventually reached a point where I didn't care anymore if I was one. I'd admitted it without shame. Sad to say I occasionally enjoyed it on the sly lately, but now I knew.

Accepting that you were a monster wasn't the same as being the real thing, full-time, every single second of every single day.

Grimm had shown me that.

He'd also shown me that he was right. He was superior to them. He was as ruthless as the Auphe, but smarter. More adaptable. Thrived on change. Nature had taken her fuckup and created a rung higher on the ladder, and Grimm was standing on it.

"Nik," I said, calm, not that that was what I felt. I didn't know what I was feeling other than it was a seething mass of confliction. "You need to know. He's better than me ... even on my very best day." Best day. Worst day. My Auphe days, the ones that were now gone or at the very least viciously choke-chained and powerless.

And why wouldn't they die? Auphe. Half-Auphe. I killed them over and over, three times now.

Why wouldn't they fucking *die*?

Yet ...

Welcome back, brothers and sisters. I missed you.

I missed the game.

10

My brother was surprised I was smart, smarter than him.
That I'd gone to school and Death had a degree. I sat in
the New Mexico desert, back against a rock, eyes closed,
and slowly healed. It was cloudy even here today, but
warm, and it felt good as the stab wound in my stomach
bitched. It wasn't a critical wound—that was the best part
of being half-and-half. You never knew where our bodies
kept the important parts. All of us had been different, but
I'd lucked out and Caliban hadn't. He'd skewered me all
the way through, but hadn't hit a single worthwhile organ
when he did.

Of course, it hurt like a motherfucker, which was good.
I'd learned to like pain. Sidle had taught his prisoners
that. He, my very first teacher, had taught us to love it.
Hate and pain—they were the only things we could love.

So, so good.

Caliban had given me a present. I'd give him one too.
Whether he'd learned to like pain the way I had, I didn't
know. He hadn't had a Sidle.

Time enough to find out.

Sidle with his lessons had been my first teacher, but not

my only one. There were no degrees in pain among the cattle.

I'd had several teachers as I traveled looking for Caliban before I caught up with him in Nevah's Landing. For some reason the fight made me think of a teacher I couldn't remember. A woman. Red hair? I didn't recall. But the wound in my gut made me think of something I couldn't think of. Something I'd done to her. Senseless, that. It was a lost memory and I didn't lose memories. What Caliban had done to me was the same as birthdays and balloons. What I'd done to her was a hole in the ground with maggots your only party favors.

But who was she?

When had I sliced her open?

Maybe it was but a dream. A good dream, but a dream.

I traced a gloved finger over the clotted blood covering the slash in my stomach, then tore it away to let it bleed again, up the pain again. Ah, good, good. Pleasure and pain, pain and pleasure. I watched the blood course out.

The dream, which was all it could've been, made me think of martyrs. After hearing my long-gone warden read the Bible over and over, for the good parts—smiting, killing firstborns on either side, selling your daughter, sacrificing your firstborn son because God told you to before saying Psych! *Destroying cities—I knew what to do with a martyr: Stone him or cut off his head. Stoning would take far too fucking long.*

I could be logical and martyr a teacher too in a dream. What could be better?

The memory of the dream grew sharper.

Shit, what a giving, kind, love-everyone-in-the-whole-wide-blessed-be-world cow she'd been. It was unbearable.

I couldn't remember her name. Georgia? No, not it—as if it mattered.

She'd been a freshman in college, worked as a waitress to pay her tuition, worked the soup kitchen on alternate weekends—I like soup, or how it seasoned the homeless man who I'd eaten in the alley, and she'd volunteered her time to teach classes for GED candidates. She'd grown up in New York City, and shook her finger at us to not make fun of her accent. One day someone had asked her why she left and ended up in Columbus, Ohio—for college, and she thought she needed a change, she'd said. She'd been tired of the city. Tired of its not being what she wanted it to be and of knowing it never would. The world wouldn't change. The world was the world and it had rules, and because it wouldn't change, neither could she. The best you could do was change where you were in it, and she had.

Fuck, she's one of those, *had been my disgusted thought.*

There'd been no waiting then. I couldn't sit there every day with that in the room.

"Patience is a virtue," *I'd read, curling my lips and nodding at the saying she'd written on the blackboard.*

She'd laughed, red hair springing around her shoulders. "I know. I'm such a hypocrite, aren't I? Patience for everyone else is a virtue, but I lost patience for patience or for virtue. But that's who I am now. We are who we are and sometimes there's a cost. And that is how it will always be unless you decide you don't want to pay it anymore. Now, this isn't philosophy. Turn to the chapter on Charlemagne."

The rest of the students were puzzled and generally not that bright when it came to things they couldn't see or touch. They had been sitting with their history books open, thumbing through to find what she was talking about. Idiots. Never did they want to think for themselves; they wanted knowledge handed to them like a blood-

coated can. Drink it down. Ten seconds later they were goddamn geniuses. They didn't know. Our teacher was human, but not all humans were golems of mud slouching from here to there, thick tongues with nothing interesting to say, no interesting ways to die.

But I would've given anything to make a buffet of them all, scratching, and chewing gum, and poking me in the back to ask for a pen. That student hadn't come back to class; they did tend to drop out once in a while, but this one did get his pen—jammed in his eye before I'd dumped him in the Ohio River.

The teacher had begun class and I'd paid close attention. Cattle had things to teach me if I bothered to listen. They taught me how to imitate them, think like them, and end them. It was work, but after eighteen years in a cage, vengeance isn't work. It's a gift.

After the class was over the teacher let the others go but had called me over to her. She'd sat on the edge of her desk, her gold-and-brown long skirt drawn primly around her legs. Her eyes had been brown, I'd thought, but, no, that was wrong. A gold light had glowed behind the brown. She'd known things. Some humans did. The ones who loved money told you what they saw in the dark of their minds. The ones who thought they knew their place in the world and the universe, they said what would be would be, and the knowledge they saw would only hurt you. You simply had to accept that there was a greater purpose. And what you did ask them they wouldn't breathe a word of an answer to you. Greater purpose. Pat on the hand. They were as bad as the first. They thought they knew, but they didn't. No one knew.

The universe was a coin spinning on its edge. When I gated, I could see it. Violently unpredictable. You didn't know which way it would fall. It was chaos and nothing more. But the peace-loving Gandhi wannabes thought differently, because they could see, but they couldn't see what one like me could see. She was right. She was a hypocrite, but she didn't know why. None of the good ones did. None of the good ones knew they lied to everyone and they lied to themselves. They told all that nothing big could be changed and you were stuck with what life gave you.

But I had proved them wrong. It took a while, but I wasn't stuck now.

Not once did they stop to think that they took hope instead of giving it. Not that I needed hope or a denial of my fate. I made my fate.

What will be will be.

Suck that shit up.

It was too bad. She'd been an adequate teacher, one of the best I'd had. But sometimes you had to move on.

Because "what will be will fucking be." As much as I despised her fucking kind, I couldn't let her be anymore.

As I'd stood by her desk, she'd taken my hand, the dark gold of hers a contrast of the light tan of mine. She met my eyes through the sunglasses I refused to take off in class. "I knew someone like you when I was a year or two younger." *Younger . . . when she'd lived in NYC. Someone like me. There was only one like me, except . . . I felt the grin start, but held it back.*

Cal-i-ban.

"I loved him." *She'd squeezed my hand, but her eyes held only calm, no sadness. No fear. If she'd known me, she should've feared.* "And he loved me. Too much, I think. He said I was born of peace and he was born of blood and death. He told me it wasn't a guess, but that he knew I wouldn't survive in his world. And he was a killer, but he wouldn't be responsible for killing me just by being with me. I was willing to trust fate. He wasn't."

Then there had been sadness. It had made me smile. "He was right, but he gave me a chance," *she'd said.* "He'd let me look at our path and where it led. I told him no. Little things can change. The whole of your life or death cannot. I refused to look and he refused to risk me without a guarantee I would be safe. That I would survive. I've thought since I came here of my sin and my lie. I loved him so much that I broke my only rule. I did look. And then I left. He was right and neither of us should have to see it happen." *Her voice was soft and would have been boring had it not been for the information on Caliban.*

She'd put her other hand against my face. I'd felt the warmth of it through the hair that fell across my cheek. "I know you won't believe me, as he didn't believe me, but the first day you sat in my class I knew you. I broke my rule again and looked into your future too. I won't run and I won't blame you. You were born to be who you are, Grimm. We are all born to a purpose." *I hadn't told her my real name in class, yet she knew.*

I really hated those damn seers.

"Balance in this world is far more important than those who live in it." *She'd leaned forward and kissed my cheek.* "But, Grimm, you will not tell him what you think to do here."

Not tell Caliban I sliced up one of his old girlfriends? Yeah, that was a promise. Stupid bitch.

Her hand on my face had burned, and the brown—no, what color?—of her eyes had turned to pure glowing golden amber, and I thought felt something leave ... no, something stolen from my mind. It was there. It was about Caliban, who was in NYC, but what ...? I wasn't supposed to tell ... tell him about my teacher? Why would I?

I'd forgotten her name and face the second I used a

switchblade to slice open her stomach. It wasn't like she was important. Finding Caliban, after all these years, that was the only thing.

I'd retracted the blade to put back in my pocket, shook my head, and removed my sunglasses to rub at my eyes, my headache fierce. The teacher, Georgina . . . George . . . G.

Eh, it was gone. Why would I waste a brain cell on her name or her face anyway?

I'd left her sprawled across her desk. Blood pooled around her. I couldn't really tell what color her hair was— brown? Black? Red as her own blood? I did see the palm of her hand—it was the same silver-white as my hair. Freaking bizarre.

But she was gone and so was I. And the world was better off with one less psychic. I'd planned on killing her when the GED class graduated anyway—martyrs and psychics. Hell with them. And I knew where Caliban was, NYC—I didn't know how I knew, but suddenly I did know—and teachers were a dime a dozen. I was on the move. Blood dripped to the floor. I vaguely remembered gutting her, but not with the intensity I normally did. I loved a good gutting. I liked to lie in the grass or abandoned buildings or even a bed and relive them from time to time. I shrugged. She must not have been that interesting.

Now the blood began to splatter the floor.

But that's what happened when you broke your own rules. My kind had no rules. We lived—or had lived—in the same place, but dwelled in different worlds.

I was sure she thought she'd gone to a better one. They always did. There were other worlds, I knew. Whether she went to a good or bad one wasn't up to her, whatever she thought. It was up to that ever-spinning and capricious universe. And if it had made me, it couldn't be very good and generous, could it?

She had been a good teacher, though.

I took the apple out of my jacket pocket, polished it on my sleeve, and left it in her limp hand before I left. I'd brought it to be ironic. An apple a day will never keep an Auphe away.

I walked out into the hall and closed the door behind me. I thought I heard the sound of something being tossed into a metal trash can, the kind by the teacher's desk. With my Auphe hearing, if I heard something, there was something. I glanced back through the frosted glass and saw a misty outline of a crying woman, face in her hands, red hair. . . . I rubbed my eyes again and it was gone.

Just a dead human on the altar of a teacher's desk, martyred as she'd meant to be. A human without a face or color or a name.

"I'll find a way to change it. I will. I don't care if it's never been done. The world can't stop me. No one can stop me."

It was a woman's voice choked with tears and determination. Familiar. I turned to look again, but then I'd found myself on the first floor with no memory of coming down the stairs. Too much excitement, too much glee at the games to come. My brother. Fighting, blood, family joined again and maybe a few hundred deaths or so.

Because he was in . . . She'd said he lived in . . . Fuck.

I'd known.

I'd just this second known and it was gone too, like the other things . . . like . . . what other things?

Absently I put my sunglasses back on, left the building, and stepped down to the sidewalk. Why was I standing here doing nothing? I could be in the library searching the Internet for Caliban. Or I could be off showing one of

*those gangs downtown that when they said they were go-
ing to take your money and shove your head up your ass,
it was harder than it sounded. You had to break a lot of
vertebrae to do that, have some real upper-body strength,
and a machete to make that back door a few sizes bigger.
I had the ability and the motivation. Tonight, I'd thought,
I'd be the teacher.*

*Out of the corner of my eye, I'd seen a face in the win-
dow . . . colors of brown, red, and amber. I'd smelled the
pumping heart and the circulating blood of healthy life.*

I'd heard one word.

Forget.

*The desert heat made me sleepy as I tasted my own
blood from the tip of my leather-covered finger. It had
made me dream. An enjoyable dream.*

Forget.

*I could see the blood, brighter than any other blood I
could think of. It was all I could see. It was a curtain
pulled over everything else. But I didn't mind. I liked
blood, and I liked red. As I began to tumble into a healing
semicoma, I had an image of me handing Caliban an
apple and laughing. Laughing. Laughing. Laughing.*

Forget.

I could hear a woman crying. "I'll find a way to change
it. I will."

Forget.

*Had I dreamed? It didn't matter. If I had, I would sleep
again and dream of better things, things that I could remember. Such as Cal's sword in my stomach. The Second
Coming.*

Family.

The end of the world.

The beginning of mine.

11

I told Niko, Robin, and Promise about Grimm, the Auphe-
bae, every detail I could remember, except for the specific
ones of what I'd done in South Carolina to the other im-
prisoned failures. That I glossed over. Niko already knew
them. I'd told him the day I'd returned home. I told Niko
almost everything, and not only because he was my brother.
He was all that stood between me and the world. I wasn't
worried about myself. Of the two, the earth and Cal off his
leash, I wasn't the one that needed protecting. I was sane
currently, and I did go back and forth on whether that was
a good thing or not, but who knew if that would last?

Not if. How long . . .

I didn't tell the puck and Promise the particulars of
what I'd done in Nevah's Landing at the beginning of the
year, that I'd shot seven half-Auphe manacled in cages
like fish in a barrel, because it was my only option. I
didn't want to and I didn't have to. They knew what had
happened, as it was the only thing that could've happened. They didn't need me painting them a mental picture. It hadn't bothered me when I'd done it, and it didn't
bother me now. There was nothing else to do.

But I didn't want to see them look at me with that mental image in a continuous loop behind their eyes. On the other hand, Sidle, the warden and torturer ... When it came to killing him, my only regret was that I couldn't do it again ... and again. He merely wasn't worth mentioning to the others, as he had been a useless *thing*. He'd been proof that you didn't have to gate or look like an Auphe to be a monster. You could be a weak one with an advantage that he hadn't deserved. The half-Auphe had been in cages while he roamed free to find instruments of pain to make them behave.

It was in that one instance that Grimm had been right. I should've made that bastard suffer instead of putting him down instantly and painlessly like a rabid dog.

"I've killed, Caliban," Promise said, curled on Robin's couch after we'd pushed ours off of it. She'd said the male psyche was a mystery to her, but that wasn't true. Not with five deceased elderly husbands. As far as I'd seen, Promise knew any thought that might run through a man's head. And she saw mine.

"In the old days before we had ways other than blood, I killed to live. You shouldn't feel that you are worse than I was—or Goodfellow, for that matter." She slanted a knowing glimpse of violet and velvet his way. "I have heard tales of his escapades, and pretending to be a god wasn't the worst of them."

As far as Robin was concerned, the vampire wasn't there and the subject she'd brought up didn't exist. He didn't want to talk about it, apparently. And that was more bizarre—alien-pod-person bizarre. Goodfellow was incapable of "not wanting to talk." From the first time he'd opened his mouth to introduce himself and try to sell us a car, he hadn't shut up once, and that had been close to five years ago. He'd been kind of ... off during the Panic. I'd thought he'd gone back to his old self after it was over, but now I wasn't as sure. I watched as he continued to pretend Promise wasn't on his couch—or on the planet, for that matter. The dismissal of her was that complete.

He was rearranging notification cards on the table. When we'd returned to the condo, I'd read them upside down as I'd looped around the coffee table to grab my spot on the couch. They said that he was not monogamous, and should he find the originator of the rumor he would drench his dick in Tabasco sauce, piss in his treacherous mouth, as that was all it was good for, and then draw and quarter him before letting a horny mule hump his remains.

Sounded like a great start for a new line of greeting cards to me. They were clearly meant as damage control for the attending members of the Panic. Next to them was a stack of smaller personal cards spelling out *Robin Goodfellow—monogamous since 2011,* with the suicide hotline at the bottom for those who couldn't face the fact. Side by side sat the contradiction. It didn't make any difference to the puck. What was one lie to a trickster? Especially when it was to other tricksters?

A lie would be the first words out of a trickster's, especially Robin's, mouth the moment he woke up in the morning.

Of course you're not average size. You're enormous, he'd say. Unbelievable. I was stunned, momentarily blinded by the vastness of it. Now . . . is it a penis or a clitoris again? Sorry. I drank entirely too much last night.

Or he might tell the truth if it was worse than a lie. A puck knew how to do the most damage, and the best weapon to wield.

It's not me; it's you. It's really, really you. It could not be more you. You should carry a bucket for your sex partner to hurl into when they wake up and see you in the daylight.

But that was before monogamy with Ishiah. I didn't want to know what he told him first thing in the morning, but it crept into my mind all the same. *Having sex with a walking, talking feather duster doesn't make me sneeze at all.*

I sneezed through my entire shift every shift at the bar. I knew that would be a whopper of a lie. As a matter of fact, I sneezed as I finished telling my grimmer-than-Grimm fairy tale and scattered Goodfellow's cards across the coffee table. It was psychosomatic, since I hadn't seen Ish anywhere since the Panic had come and gone. I didn't know if he'd returned or not. I thought he and Robin still kept separate apartments, but I didn't ask, as I had no desire to know. I liked the boss/employee relationship the way it was ... with me not knowing shit about what he did after hours. Now, though, with the mess we were in, it seemed odd he wasn't around. "Where's Ish?"

Niko went to the door to let Kalakos inside. The Vayash wasn't privy to Auphe, half-Auphe, one-fourth-Auphe secrets. As far as he knew, the pure Auphe race existed yet. He didn't know they were extinct. Very few did know that, rumormongering tricksters included, difficult as that was to believe. Mainly, Niko had put forth, because no one wanted to talk about the Auphe. They were the original "see no evil, speak no evil, hear no evil"—with an emphasis on "speak no evil." If no one talked about them, then no one could know they were gone.

Kalakos didn't need to know anything about our lives, and as Niko wouldn't have trusted him with our plastic tableware, he'd been left in the hall while we'd talked.

Although I had to give it to him: He had charged into that basement behind Niko and ended up decapitating the last Bae. He'd watched Niko's back—far too late by twenty-seven years, but it meant something all the same. Maybe.

I'd think about it.

But regardless of what Kalakos had done, it wasn't my call to make. I elbowed Robin, who was gathering the cards into neat piles again with impatient, quick movements that made a professional cardsharp appear to be moving in slow motion. "Ishiah?" I prompted.

"He's in Vegas. Lucky bastard," he grumbled. "The peri have something rather like . . ." He rearranged the cards again. If it had been anyone else, I'd have said he was buying time. But this was Robin, trickster extraordinaire. He didn't need to make up a lie. He already knew every one there ever had been or would be. "They have something like the National Guard. Ishiah is retired, but he's been reactivated for one mission. It shouldn't take more than a few days. A week at the most."

Why peri would need a National Guard was my next question, but the puck cut that off promptly with a suggestion. "I've been thinking. Cal, note that—you can think *all the time*. It's true, but I digress. My first thought is this: Janus will be showing up soon, as it's still storming and he can move about unseen. Which means we should move before he tracks the Vayash among us here. As if it would hurt any of you to use an effective war machine–deflecting deodorant?" he complained. "My second thought is that perhaps Hephaestus could assist us with the situation."

As Kalakos came through the door, Niko closed it and asked verbally what I longed to ask physically, with my hands wrapped tightly around Goodfellow's neck.

"He's alive? He traded whatever currency of the time for that monstrosity before years later passing it on to the Rom to guard, and you only thought now to bring up the fact that he's still *alive*?"

Robin snorted. "If it were that easy, don't you think I would have? No, he's not alive. He's dead. Deadish. Yes, deadish would be more accurate, and he's wildly insane, quite naturally. All Greek legends end up insane sooner or later. It must be something in the water." He shrugged, as I put a water purifier for him on my mental Christmas list. "But he was insane long before he became biofunctionally challenged, which makes it that much more difficult."

"Is he in Greece?" I asked. "Because that's a long trip. But if we go with you, Janus will probably jump the plane and ride it all the way there."

"Greece? No. Very few of us are there now. When the people stopped believing in us, we left. Too many painful memories of better days." He checked his watch. "Conveniently enough, Hephaestus is in Connecticut. With traffic we could be there in two and a half hours."

"He's in Connecticut. Dead and in Connecticut? Less than two to three hours away?" Niko said dubiously. "I find that difficult to believe. Greece, very well. But if he's dead, why isn't he in Hades or the Elysian fields?"

My brother the Buddhist believed in life after death—of all different sorts. An afterlife for every belief that has been and will come. I didn't give him grief over it. After what he'd lived through in this life, he was entitled to believe whatever he wanted. But I knew after death there was nothing but emptiness and nonexistence. I had no problem with that. It was heaven in my book.

Goodfellow answered Niko's question by holding up

two fingers. "Two words: industrial revolution." He added, "And guns. He loved weapons, anything that could inflict death and despair. We all have our hobbies. He was late by a hundred years or so. As I said, wildly insane, easily distracted, and behind on the news, but by the time he caught up, weapons were that much more advanced. I'm sure he was quite the happy camper when he discovered the concept. They don't have guns in Hades or the fields, so he went where the guns did."

"I repeat, you didn't bring this up sooner?" Niko's voice lowered to the same threatening rumble of the thunder outside.

"Niko, he's madder than a syphilitic-ridden Al Capone, not deader than dead, but deader than he should be, and he hates me. Ares's steroid-induced rages, does he hate me. You don't need to know why. If I thought he had an iota of sanity or cooperation in him, I'd have mentioned it, I don't know, perhaps while Cal was dying, while you were beating your father like a Turkish rug, when we were again attacked by Janus, while Cal had been kidnapped and we were frantically searching for him as if he were a microchipped prizewinning Westminster Labradoodle. So many wasted opportunities when we were lying about while lacking in any pertinent activity, I realize, but it's a chance in a thousand anyway. He despises me more than any creature I know, and that, considering my extraordinary reputation, is saying much." He gave up on the cards and pushed them off the table.

"Was I put in my place?" Niko asked me ruefully, not entirely used to the feeling.

I was, however, and didn't mind seeing someone else suffer. "You were puck-slapped but good. Okay, we're taking two cars and I'm not wearing a sweater."

Goodfellow was shocked and appalled. Everyone wore sweaters in Connecticut. He was ninety-nine percent positive that you couldn't cross the state line without one.

"Two cars. No sweaters," I stressed.

Then I leaned closer to Robin and did something I shouldn't have, that made me feel like crap, but could be necessary. I murmured, "Hephaestus hates you, but what does he think of Hob?"

He feared him. He had to. Alive, dead, or halfway between, all feared Hob.

And no one except Niko, Robin, Promise, Georgina, and me knew Hob was dead. And not deadish, as Hephaestus was, but as dead as they came. Gone from this world for good. It was something to think about.

Until Goodfellow gave a low hiss back, inaudible to everyone but me. "What would he think of an Auphe? What would he think of you if you threw away your sanity, your ability to tell right from wrong, and lived only for every life you could extinguish, to ask him a question? All while knowing if you did, you couldn't come back. No second chances like you've had before, not this time. You would never be Cal again. Never sane again. Never *right* again." In that moment he wasn't Robin. "The next time you speak of Hob is the last time we speak," he added without emotion, but cold, hard promise.

I knew I shouldn't have brought up the subject again. Unfortunately I knew too late.

The sly, snarky, patronizingly sarcastic, fast talking, horny, name-dropping Goodfellow was gone; this Robin I didn't know. He wasn't my friend, and as I had only the one besides my brother, I wasn't going to risk losing him. I leaned back before the others noticed the exchange and gave the best and most honest apology I could. It was one my friend would recognize for what it was and hopefully come back.

"Okay. Shit." I grimaced. "I'll wear a goddamn sweater."

It was ninety degrees in Bridgeport, Connecticut, unusually hot, the radio said—before I kicked it. It wasn't the kind of weather you layered for, and I was wearing a bright green cashmere Lacoste cardigan over a pink polo shirt, pleated khaki pants, white socks, and loafers. I'd also been offered a holster for my Eagle and something called a Members Only jacket to cover that. I knew the names because Goodfellow had labeled each plastic bag in which they were immaculately folded, along with a catalogue page of some blond, blue-eyed, tanned, blindingly white-toothed man wearing the same outfit while standing by a boat. With a blond woman. A blond kid. A blond damn dog . . . wearing a matching damn sweater.

Douche bag.

It covered the catalogue dick and Robin both.

"What did you do to piss off Goodfellow this badly?" Niko asked, edging away from me as if I were color-contagious. He was dressed in the black-and-gray clothes the puck had smugly given him. Normal clothes. The kind that didn't make you look like someone pulled the head off a Golfing Ken doll and stuck a catastrophically pissed-off serial killer's head in its place, which was a look I was pulling off in spades. I let my black hair hang where it wanted. Still no ponytail for me, until Kalakos was gone despite what I'd talked to Niko about in the car.

"You don't want to know," I said glumly.

We stood by the rusted chain-link fence at the abandoned Remington Arms factory. Despite its being early afternoon, it wasn't a safe place to be for most. It was the typical bad part of town, but it would be more peculiar if I were in a good part of town. An industrial area near the water, no shadows, no alleys, nothing green—not a blade of grass pushing up through the sidewalk. Or what was left of the sidewalk.

Nothing but our rusty fence the armory stretched far behind, a wide street with dilapidated houses on the other side. Nik and I were waiting for the others to get out of their car, parked by ours at an empty house across the road with a battered For Sale sign. Promise climbed out of the car, her gloved hands keeping her face well shadowed by the hood of her cloak. She wanted to see this through as much as we did, if only for Niko's sake.

Following her out of the car was Kalakos, who, as Goodfellow had said, was like a terminal case of gonorrhea with a side order of herpes. You couldn't get rid of him no matter how hard you tried.

As the three of them were crossing the street, I looked back down at the clothes that were my punishment for pissing off Robin. "Nik, if Hephaestus kills me, strip me, would you? I don't want my corpse seen like this." None of the clothes had been worn before. Robin had been waiting with this vengeance bomb for a while, and I'd been the one to set it off. He wouldn't be caught dead in any of it himself. He dressed expensive and sharp always, but he leaned more toward James Bond than whatever this crime against humanity was. I scratched my stomach, then an arm. "I think it's burning my skin. Like holy water. I thought that was only in the movies." I scratched again. "I'm sweating like a pig. Jesus."

"Stupid assholes. Shitheads. Give me your money or

I will fuck you up so bad your mama won't know you on the slab."

Finally. I didn't think he was ever going to make it down our way with that slow shamble.

He was a mugger, gangbanger, junkie, homicidal shit with a knife, probably all four. I'd seen him stumbling down the cracked and crumbling sidewalk as soon as we'd parked the car and hit pavement. He hadn't been an issue then. If he'd had half a brain to look past me to Niko or to look at my face instead of the opposite of camouflage I was wearing, he wouldn't be an issue now. But I'd been hoping, and when you wish on that kick-him-in-the-balls star twinkling high above at night, sometimes you get your wish.

Another douche bag, and I couldn't *wait*.

"I'm not going to bother to ask. You need him more than I do," Niko said. "Try not to kill him. We're not one hundred percent certain he deserves it."

I was already stripping off that stupid jacket. It was lightweight, though, and that could be useful at times. "Today my percentage on the curve has dropped from one hundred to twenty-five. Maybe fifteen."

I couldn't tell if he was white, biracial, Hispanic, young, or middle-aged, as he was so covered in filth, hair matted for years, teeth all but gone from meth, clothes layered rags, but what did it matter? I did know he was a son of a bitch with no bark *or* bite and he'd crossed me on the wrong day.

Any day would've been a wrong day, but with his knife—a kitchen butcher knife, pitiful—I would've given him the less humiliating "go away." I would've used a round to his leg from one of my guns or put my own knife, the kind you don't steal from your grandmother, through his hand to make sure I cut enough tendons that he'd not carry a weapon again. But today . . . today wasn't any day.

I strangled him unconscious with the Members Only jacket.

It rolled up nice and tight. It wasn't a wire garrote, but it did get the job done.

Better yet, he had a friend, a buddy, a compadre, otherwise known as the dumb ass who came over the fence to help cut us up. This one was wired on meth or crack. That meant he was snake-mean, gave him the sad illusion that he was immortal, and made him a cheetah in speed compared to his friend, who'd done a believable imitation of the living dead from an old zombie movie. My opinion about those movies had been formed from minute one: If you could trot or even speed-walk, there was no excuse for your not surviving that apocalypse.

"Give! Give it! Fuckers! Give it over before I cut your goddamn head off!" This one had a switchblade he stabbed in my direction with frenzied, wild motions. I shrugged off my holster and tossed it over my shoulder, knowing Niko would catch it. Then off came the sweater, which surprised me by rolling up as nicely as the jacket. Cashmere, huh? Shelling out the dough on expensive fancy douche-bag clothes was worth it. Who would've believed it?

I dodged the stab of the switchblade. Yeah, he was a cheetah next to the other guy, all right, but Niko had taught me to be the actual article, with lessons starting when I was about eight. I snared the guy's arm with my new weapon, broke his wrist in a particularly nasty way that would never heal right, and then strangled him with the sweater until he was down and out to match his partner. That improved my mood enough that I kept going, kicking off a loafer and beating Mr. Switchblade in the head with it. It wasn't as effective as the other pieces of clothing, but it was still entertaining.

Imitating my shoe-beating squat, Niko crouched across from me, gazed down at the drooling mugger and then at me. "You didn't kill them. That's something," he said with a noticeable lack of conviction. "Should I be concerned or is this a new type of crime-fighting superpower hitherto undiscovered in those comic books you read as a kid?"

"I still read 'em." I gave a wicked grin, able to forget about Janus and Grimm—*better than me on my best day*—long enough that I could enjoy myself for a minute. "Find me five more. I still have a shirt, pants, two socks, and one shoe left."

There was a flash out of the corner of my eye. I looked up to see Robin considering the picture on his phone. "I have the shot of the infamous Leandros penis—infamous like the Loch Ness monster: Most thought it a rumor. I have a preppy demon spawn armed by Nordstrom assaulting criminals. It's a start to a porn site. I just need a theme."

Kalakos spit on the sidewalk; the Vayash clan did love their saliva and sharing it. We didn't know how Janus tracked us. Kalakos and Niko both thought it was likely the genetic signature of Vayash blood. I had a different theory: the unique chemical makeup of Vayash spittle. It had been exercised fiercely enough over the generations that it was better, stronger, faster. Steve Austin couldn't hope to deliver the loogie that a Vayash could.

"We are wasting time," Kalakos said with frustration boiling over the stoicism he'd worn, head to toe, since he'd arrived. "The burden needs to be returned to sleep or destroyed, and you are playing games like . . ." There he was stuck. Like a child? Hardly. Like a monster? Not if he wanted that apology from the basement to stick.

Goodfellow didn't wait for him to sort it out. "The wannabe Achilles is right." He put the phone away and tossed me the black combat boots he held in his other hand. "Time to go. You're without a shred of doubt going to have to run for your life in there. You can't do that in loafers."

I caught the boots and snarled at the smirk that had been thrown with them. It was a halfhearted snarl, though. Robin was back and that made all this worth it. Almost.

"In there" was the thirteenth building of the Remington Arms factory. All thirteen were identical and connected by a massive bridge that matched the brick outside of the buildings. It loomed, the entire structure. It was only four stories high, but somehow it loomed. That this was a place that had made weapons didn't surprise me. They sure as hell hadn't been turning out toys. It had been built in the early nineteen hundreds to make guns, all kinds, from handguns to machine guns. Equal-opportunity methods of death and destruction.

The thirteenth building was hugely cavernous inside. Some of it was divided into four floors, but in some areas—the metalworking ones, from the equipment left behind—you could see straight up from the ground floor to the underside of the roof. In those large spaces light trickled from the small windows from what would've been one wall of the fourth floor. It was a dim light spilled from a thickly overcast sky, but Promise was cautious, pulling the hood of her silk cloak farther forward to shade her face. A stray hit of daylight wouldn't cause her to combust, although it would go a long way toward explaining the urban legend of spontaneous "human" combustion. What it would give her was the vamp equivalent of a third-degree burn. While vamps were quick to heal from any other wound, those took months to heal, and aloe didn't do a thing for that level of crispy.

Robin stopped to take the room in, eyes closed in concentration. "No, not here. Ah, I feel him now." He indicated a hallway that ran the length of the building. "Not far, and asleep, I think, or we wouldn't have made it this far without some difficulties." I didn't wonder how the dead or deadish slept. When I'd discovered there were undead mummified cats that followed pucks home and made themselves queen of the condo, I stopped questioning dead right then and there as too complicated for me.

He took out his sword from beneath a coat, the same long duster style as the one Nik always wore and was wearing now, thanks to Robin's owning several. He didn't carry a sword every day as my brother did, but enough that he needed the spares. Kalakos had his own. They were all virtually identical. Give them sunglasses and they'd be supernatural Men in Black.

Niko was carrying his xiphos and he handed me the second from inside his coat. Hephaestus hadn't built Janus. Someone from a race older and more skilled had. If the Janus metal that formed the xiphos made the automaton stop and think, it might do worse to Hephaestus if he went off the deep end. Turn him from deadish to deader than dead. I had my holster back on and already had the Eagle out. I switched it to my left hand and carried the xiphos with my right. "Let's go find out how to take out the batteries on that thing."

"Yes, yes. Running toward imminent death rather than away like a sane person would. Your hobby, I know. Wait a moment." He looked past me to Promise. "You can't come, not yet."

"Why not?" she demanded coolly. "I know you don't doubt my abilities in a fight." She didn't have a collection of revenant heads she'd removed in the past, but she could have . . . if she was into that sort of thing. I know I didn't doubt her or her abilities; after seeing her in action I knew for a fact that a revenant made the worst kind of Pez dispenser.

"Doubt? Hardly. And if I were ignorant enough to question the matter, I wouldn't say so," Robin said dryly. "I like my dick attached to my body. No, it's Hephaestus. The sight of a woman, any woman at all, ups his insanity level considerably. But we will need you to come in as a distraction if we're on the verge of a hideously painful death, which I strongly anticipate. I need you to stay here until you hear the screaming and the dripping of blood start. When you come in, say something idiotically syrupy, such as, 'I am here, cherished of my heart, the sweet spring air that gives me breath. It is your beloved Aphrodite.' Yes, that's perfect. Her to the letter, not that she could read. A more vacant-brained person I've yet to meet."

"Aphrodite?" Promise said with a suspicion I could hear if not read under her shadowed hood. "Wasn't that his wife? Wasn't her cheating on him with the god of war why he went insane?"

"Do we need to go into this or can we draw the usual conclusions?" Robin responded irritably. "And anyone can wear gold armor and pass himself off as a god of war, especially when the real one is *off at war,* as anyone with a brain cell would know. It's not as if she asked to see any ID. Besides, I told all of you that he hated me beyond all things, yet here I am." He started toward the dark hall. "Risking my life, as always. Brave and self-sacrificing. Noble and . . ."

I stopped listening, as Robin wouldn't stop talking until Hephaestus was choking the air and life out of him. "Where do you think he keeps his little black book?" I murmured to Niko.

"In chapters, and they require approximately a thousand semis to haul from place to place." He jerked his head, indicating to Kalakos that he should move ahead of us. Just in case. If he had to be at someone's back, we wanted someone watching him, despite my elevated status in his eyes from monster to "not that bad." That was practically a gold medal from the Vayash, the status of "eh, he could be worse."

"Your exercise outside has improved your mood," Nik went on to note.

He wanted to talk about Grimm. I'd given over everything I knew . . . when it came to facts. My emotions I'd kept to myself, locked down tight, and not from everyone else, but from Nik too. He knew it and he didn't like it. I shook my head. "Later."

His eyebrows lowered. He wasn't happy. No matter how old you are, big brothers, at least the good ones, never stop thinking it's their job to look out for you and to watch your back. I knew if I lived to be eighty and Nik eighty-two, sharing a room at the nursing home, he'd be asking why I sent back my tapioca pudding and beating the nurse's aide with his walker for losing my dentures. And I would be damn lucky.

I didn't have to try to find the words he wanted. They were already there, ugly and useless. "Grimm is me, Nik. He *is* me." My palms sweated against the grip of my weapons, and not because of what we were about to face. "Only without whatever conscience you managed to shove down my throat." And that I managed to hang on to—an extra-small portion for the healthy monster on the go. "If things had been different and the Auphe found out about him first and locked me away in that cage, I would be him. I would think the same thoughts. I would be doing the same things."

Although Grimm had six years on me, which meant I might not be doing them as efficiently. "Shit, our sense of humor is even the same." Bloody and sarcastic to the bone.

I lifted my hand holding the xiphos and had a vision of Grimm's black glove hosting curved metal claws. I'd liked them. Me, the gun guy, was wondering where I could get a set made. *Jesus.* "I can't tell you how I feel because I don't know. I do want him dead. That isn't going to change. I gutted the son of a bitch the first chance I had. It didn't faze him much, but I did it and I enjoyed it. Don't worry. I know how I feel about him." I wanted him six feet under or in pieces.

"What I don't know," I concluded, "is how I feel about me. As soon as I've decided if I'm scared as shit or pissed as hell or both, I'll tell you."

I could've been Grimm and I could still be—someday. The first I accepted. The second . . . it was harder to deal with when it was in my face and not the occasional nasty thought whispering in my ear. The mental prodding was a potential. Seeing myself in Grimm was the reality, and I wasn't ready for it.

Liar.

Niko started to open his mouth. He was going to tell me it wasn't true. That the other half Auphe and I were nothing alike. If worse had come to worst in the past, caged or not, I wouldn't have grown to be him. The things brothers are supposed to say. I shook my head again. "Later," I repeated, "okay?" The "okay" was my version of "please." Nik would recognize it, but no one else would. Goodfellow already had a picture of me beating a man with a frigging loafer. He didn't need soppy dialogue to put on his planned Web site to go with it.

"All right," he agreed, bumping my shoulder with his. "But the clock is ticking." That small push meant that he needed to know what Grimm was going to do to my head as much as I did. Because he was my brother, but also because he needed to know how I'd handle the next battle with Grimm. It didn't matter how ready your body was for the fight. It was a given: If your head was up your ass and your brain didn't know up from down or what that smell was, you were dead.

We came to the end of the hall; the weak light from the room beyond was all that had helped us pick our way through jagged pieces of metal and garbage littering the floor. Stepping out into it, I saw it wasn't a room; it was almost the twin of the echoing space we'd left behind. Open all the way up to the roof, it contained rusted beams and a floor where every step would have to be cautious or you'd step on a shard of metal, flip it up, and slice your leg open or off completely.

Robin's list of his heroic traits finally came to a pause; there was never an end. "We're here. The foundry," he said quietly. "I told you Hephaestus was a fraud and could hardly build anything when you compare his work to Janus. Tinkertoys would practically puzzle him."

"There's a 'but' coming, isn't there?" I asked. "I hear a 'but.' Why is there always a 'but'?"

"I hear a 'yet' or a 'however,'" Niko corrected, "but I'm more gifted in the vocabulary skills than you. Good-fellow?"

"That doesn't mean he couldn't make something that could kill you," the puck answered grimly. "A sword is simple compared to the inner workings of a gun, but it can be equally as deadly. Don't underestimate whatever he might throw at us. As they say, it's not what's on the outside that counts; it's how many arms and legs something's inside tells its outside to remove from our bodies."

"I don't remember the saying going like that and I think I would've remembered that version. Nik?" I said.

"It might not be accurate, but I'd argue it has merit." He took several impossibly silent steps to the side. There wasn't a single sliver of metal that rang out. Kalakos, as impossibly silent, followed his lead but in the opposite direction.

Goodfellow had one more piece of advice for us. "Besides toys he might have an employee or several hanging about. I'd tell you that the eye is the best place to hit them, but if that's not self-explanatory on sight then you need to go back to preschool."

Then he raised his voice in a shout that rang all of the metal in the room. It was like standing in a Buddhist temple while every monk gathered around to smack you in the head with four-foot-long wind chimes. Despite that I heard Robin's voice plain as day over it all. "Hephaestus! You humpbacked bastard! Wake up! You have a visitor—it's Goodfellow and I've come to apologize!"

When he quit shouting, the metal slowly fell into silence and I heard him mutter quietly, "Although I shouldn't have to. It was the best thing to happen to him. The woman was so empty-headed that if your ear was close enough to hers, she would literally suck thoughts out of your head to fill hers. Where most have minds, she had a miniature black hole inside her skull. What she could do with her tongue, which *was* absolutely unbelievable, wasn't worth having to listen to her go on and on about butterflies and flowers and how she wanted to spend a month doing nothing but smelling the milk breath of puppies. . . ."

Hephaestus woke up.

I was thankful. I'd already pissed off Robin once today. I didn't want to do it again by pistol-whipping him into blissfully silent unconsciousness. Hephaestus made that unnecessary by shoving himself to the front of the line.

"*Puck.*"

Hey, he'd picked up English from the long-dead workers that had toiled over and around him nearly a hundred years before the factory was abandoned. That was convenient. I wouldn't have to listen to Goodfellow and him insult each other in the seven-thousand-plus past and present languages Robin claimed to know. I had picked up some good Greek curse words from him, though, for the times I was craving a gyro from the short-changing jackass street vendor who set his food truck up on the sidewalk ten blocks down from our place.

"That's me," Robin said with a manic and reckless cheer that didn't bode of good things to come. "I've come to apologize for soiling your wife. I was in the wrong. I'm deeply sorry. I now can admit to my illness and am seeking help through Sex Addicts Anonymous. I am here to make amends, offer you a stale doughnut from one of the meetings if you'd like, and, oh, coincidentally"—as if it were the most casual of thoughts to pop up—"I have a question for you about Janus. You must remember Janus. I'll bet you sold it for more gold than you could carry. An incredible piece of work. Staggering in its brilliance. Unparalleled in its mixture of art and efficiency." Giving credit and flattery where it wasn't due—it was a trickster's best weapon, according to Robin. "Now, how do we turn it off?"

"*Puck . . .*"

The rumble faded into nothing. He wasn't a morning

person, was slow to wake. I related. And he was dead, deadish, whatever. The combination could make no time a good time to wake up. I was thinking we should've brought several gallons of caffeine when he spoke again. This time he almost brought a few of the beams far above us down. I dodged a rain of smaller pieces of falling metal while avoiding impaling a foot on those already on the floor around me.

"*Aphrodite. Where is Aphrodite? Virgin to my bed, petals of the rose, she who owns my loins and heart. Come home. Come home. Come home.* You . . . *Puck* . . . *Goodfellow, good—fellow. Good . . . But where is the good? Where? Nowherenowherenowhere. Wife stealer. Life stealer. Liar. Wretched thief in the night, tainter of all that is pure, death awaiting its day. This day. This day. This day.* My *day. Puckpuckpuckpuckpuck.*"

I didn't think Aphrodite, named as the goddess of love and sexuality, had been any kind of virgin on her honeymoon. But I did think Robin had been right: Hephaestus was bat-shit crazy, and getting anything out of him on Janus wasn't looking promising. His voice shook the entire building. It was the sound of an earthquake that brought down cities, islands, nations. The grate and thunder of the earth losing its patience and shifting to throw anything living off its skin or bury it deep beneath itself.

I shouted at Goodfellow, "Where is he?" From the ear-bleeding echo, he could be anywhere in here, but the puck didn't hesitate. He headed straight for what squatted in the center. It was a vat about twelve feet tall and wide enough around to mimic a giant swimming pool. Robin said some *paien* knew other *paien* sometimes, some knew most of the time, and some always knew. Goodfellow always knew.

Following him, I saw him start up the ladder mounted

to the side. I circled to the other side in hopes of finding another one and bingo, there one was. I holstered my gun, but held on to the xiphos as I climbed. The rungs were filthy under my hand and carried the strong smell of stone. It was the same smell as the rock in a deep cave. Rock under the sun and sky didn't smell that way. They had the scent of life to them, although they weren't alive. A cave had the same scent/taint of an underground tomb of someone buried alive and chained to a forge: despair, exile, and death.

At the top I hooked my arm around one curved hand-hold on the ladder and leaned over the edge to see. I didn't have to lean far. What had once been eight feet high and who knew how many gallons of molten metal almost a century ago was now a cold, frozen pool of steel. Robin pointed at the mass with his sword.

The guy was right. If Hephaestus was embedded in that somewhere, drowned in metal, melted fragments at one with his executioner, he'd have to be deadish at the very least.

I leaned further and tapped the metal with my sword. "Goodfellow's a bastard and a son of a bitch. Everybody knows it. And his 'sorry's aren't worth a fart in the wind." In the past I'd found out the easiest way to reach some-one as crazy as a shithouse rat and prone to removing visitors' arms and legs frequently enough to warrant only a casual verbal warning label.

And that method was to agree with them totally.

"Tell us about Janus, and what the hell, we'll kill the puck for you," I promised.

Opposite me, Robin grimaced and lowered his face into the palm of his hand. He hadn't said anything, but he hadn't needed to. Before it was covered, his face had said it all: We are beyond fucked now.

That was my reward for thinking like the human I wasn't. Would I, Caliban—not Cal—want someone to kill my worst enemy for me, or would I want to do that wet work myself?

Stupid question. Stupid attempt. Stupid me.

"*No! Mine! Mine. Mine. Mine. Mine. Mine.*"

That's when everyone else woke up.

It was also when I wished for one of the few times in my life that I'd kept my mouth shut. But those that came from beneath, they were willing to shut it for me. Or remove it altogether.

So many pieces of flesh to be devoured.

And all the time in the world.

12

From below the floor they were reborn.

The floor was concrete, but they broke through it with as little effort as if it had been a bar napkin, the cheap kind that disintegrates if one drop of liquid is spilled on it. They swarmed loose of earth and man-made rock and opened mouths filled with large, square, thick teeth, each one a different size, each mouth a child's drawing. Crooked and slanting inward, outward, large and some larger—made for chewing stone to mine the metal needed for Hephaestus's forge. The teeth reminded us we weren't as solid as stone, and the mouths stretched wide to roar at us.

But didn't.

There was no roaring. There was worse. It was the sound of thousands of years of crackling, white-hot flame and the hiss of steam hot enough to boil your flesh from your bones. They were crouched until they were almost doubled over, backs curved into sharp, unnatural peaks. That didn't keep them from moving fast, scuttling side-ways like crabs. Their hands matched—a thumb and a thick extension of flesh, four fingers fused into one. Each, thumb and the rest, had a single talon each. Longer than the hand itself and of a gleaming metal that would score rock as easily as the bulldozer teeth.

The single eye was fire. Red, orange, yellow, white, it burned. Every single eye burned and the pale flesh around it was scorched and blackened. But fire could see, or Hephaestus could see through the fire. I wondered if the fire burned in their brains too. Were the roars not roars but screams of long years of agony? Was the sound of flames and corrosive steam their way of screaming?

Burn.

I burn.

We burn.

I didn't know and I didn't have the luxury of caring. They were here to butcher us, and whether putting them down was self-defense or a mercy killing, the end was the same. "Cyclops," I heard Kalakos say, incredulous. He said he hunted the unclean, but he hadn't hunted anything close to this. With the Auphe-bae, these, and Janus all in two days, he might hang up his sword.

"Welcome to the big time." I slid down the ladder to stop at the last rung and step carefully into the minefield of metal and broken concrete. At this level I could see that the hunched backs of the Cyclops stood about five feet tall. If they could've stood upright, they would've been tall. NBA recruitment material, but not literal giants, as Niko had taught in mythology when I was a kid. I told Goodfellow so.

"Work twenty-four/seven in a small cave and smaller tunnels mining ore and it will take barely a hundred years to take you from giant to this." Robin had gone down his ladder simultaneous with me, but I heard him from the other side of the vat over the Cyclops venting Hephaestus's rage. "But they're no less dangerous for it.

They are wholly pissed and they do not care who they take it out on."

The one closest to me moved sideways a step, head rocking back and forth, soot stains coloring its mis-shapen chin, but with the eye always on me. It had moved less than a foot, but that was enough for me to see in the cloudy, weak light that it had silver painted in swirls all over its sunless body. I thought it was a tattoo. I was wrong. It wasn't a tattoo and it wasn't silver; it was more like mercury. It flowed. And it wasn't on its body; it was in it—channels eaten into its moon-slug flesh. But where mercury was poisonous, it didn't burn. These coiled chan-nels were lined on each side with thin ribbons of black. I could smell the flesh burning. I could see the wisps of smoke rising. If there was pain, that I didn't see.

I did see the scuttle and lunge through the air, the madly grinding teeth aimed at my heart, the mechani-cally thrashing hands and claws aimed at my gut. Not good. I put two rounds directly in the furnace of an eye.

I hadn't been solely tattoo watching after I reached the bottom of the ladder. I'd switched the xiphos to my other hand and drawn my Glock. As Goodfellow had said, if you're going after a Cyclops, guessing where to start isn't a problem. If they couldn't play "I spy with my one Cyclopian eye" because I sent a bullet through it, that put them at a disadvantage. If it passed through to their brain and killed them as well as blinded them, that was a bonus.

If bullets worked on an eye made of fire. If their brain was high-functioning enough to be bothered by losing half out of the hole blown in the back of their skulls.

This one did have a problem with it. He threw back his head and the hiss and crackle became a real scream, deep and hoarse and full of fury. The eye flickered but didn't go out, not until he staggered backward, with each step impaling or slicing his legs with metal, and finally fell. His crushing hands grasping nothing but air, he screamed one last time. No fear, no despair, only unfulfilled rage.

Then he was still, his eye a dead black socket and the quicksilver running out of the curving, carved canals that covered him to disappear into the concrete and metal beneath the body. I studied my gun, the body again, and shrugged.

Okay. Cyclops. Not that big a deal.

I kept thinking that as I saw Nik with his back to the wall strike, his sword in the eye of another Cyclops. I thought it right up until I was gauging who was the nearest and next in line. I was looking in the wrong direction. Out of the corner of my eye I saw Nik disappear, the ground opening up beneath him. He was swallowed, the teeth of broken concrete and discarded metal chewing at him as he went. I knew it because I smelled it: the too familiar tang of his blood, bright and healthy as it came—when it was inside his body instead of out.

I ran. I wasn't as agile as Nik at dodging the minefield of a floor, but I didn't care and I could move close to as fast as a purebred and faster than any half-breed except Grimm. Who didn't matter now. As the pain didn't matter. There was no pain. There was the empty space where my brother had stood. That was all.

I reached it a second behind Kalakos. He'd been closer to Niko, close enough that he reached down and yanked him up and out, hands to wrists, before the Cyclops below Nik had a chance to turn him into the flesh-and-blood version of ore, a crushed pulp of bleeding tissue and shattered bone. I came to a stop between the hole in the floor and Nik and Kalakos. Seeing the eye, a miniature sun, below in the dark, I fired. The scream, maddened, was the same—as was the eye extinguished to the darkness of death.

Feeling my first Vayash impulse—to spit on the body packed tightly in the earth below—I instead growled and turned to look Nik up and down. He was bloody from being pulled through the floor, an inanimate monster all its own, but aside from scrapes, cuts, and abrasions, he'd live. He'd be sore for a while, but he wasn't going to bleed out.

Kalakos had come to the same conclusion and had his sword back up for the next charge. "You don't have to thank me," he said, "either of you."

"You think I would?" I snapped, and fired at another Cyclops across the foundry.

"No, because I know now it's something a father must do instead of supposed to do and should've been doing since the day his son was born. I see now." The rushing Cyclops came low, his eye down. Kalakos half removed his head from the thick neck, slammed it backward with the flat of his sword to bring the target in view, and quenched the flame. "Gratitude for that would be no different from gratitude for breathing. The Vayash have a duty. I've learned I have more than one."

He moved away then. He didn't wait for a comment. The fight was only warming up. There was blood to be spilled, lives—our own—to be saved, answers to be wrenched from an insane god.

"I hate him more now than I did before," I muttered. "Sanctimonious ass." Whether he meant it or not, it was too late.

"Perhaps he meant it and we should take it at face value, but that window of opportunity has unfortunately long closed." He added, "And he managed to get the last word." His clothes were saturated with blood. I could feel the warmth of it against my back as I did my best to press him hard enough against the wall to pin him, leaving no room for him to be sucked down again. That meant there was no avoiding feeling his blood, all but seeing the cloud of bright copper in the air floating around us.

"Unfortunately," he'd said, which meant regret, and my brother deserved much more than regret, thanks to that Vayash son of a bitch.

"Last word. That's the worst." No—regret was. "*Bastard,*" I said, wishing for the first time that Kalakos hadn't been one as I watched for the next Cyclops. "You okay? I can smell the blood. Not enough to take you out of the fun, but could be enough to slow you down."

"Other than your crushing me into what I'm beginning to think is a piggyback position, I'm all right. Fully functional, certainly not slow, and definitely not your papoose." I felt his hand urge me away; he was ready to rejoin the battle. I thought about stalling, but this was Niko and he was right. He'd have to lose half the blood in his body to slow down.

As I began to move, I heard a groan from above. The beams that had shaken earlier at Hephaestus's voice were moving again . . . and Hephaestus wasn't talking. They were wrenching free of their mounting and joining together over our heads, booming as they struck. The movement . . . it wasn't falling. Not falling down, but moving fast and inevitably, as if they were falling sideways. Tinkertoys would puzzle him, Robin had said. I didn't think so. I was looking at the most badass set of Tinkertoys on the planet, and Hephaestus wasn't stopping there. Metal hit metal and was held in place with the sudden intense red, then white glow of a forge I didn't see.

"Hephaestus is also the god of volcanoes. Fire and metal." Niko's hand had altered from pushing to fisting my shirt—Jesus, I was going to die in this pink shirt—and yanking me to stand still. "What is he making?"

A brilliant mind asking a question with the most obvious of answers. Or let's be honest. Just a damn *stupid* question.

"Something to kill us, Dr. Oblivious," I hissed, hoping whatever it was didn't have great hearing, or any at all. The beams were joining faster, other metal flying up to it to enhance its status as the bestselling murder machine for kids four years and up. It was the size of Janus, no bigger, but a framework with no head. It had arms, though, four of them, with grasping metal claws. I could hear the creak of the ratchets as the hands opened and closed. And it had two legs. Thirteen feet tall in length, it hung above like a waiting spider. Would it climb down or leap inst— *Motherfucker*.

It was on *fire*.

All of it.

Like the Cyclops's eyes but thirteen feet of it. A metal skeleton became an inferno. Metal shouldn't burn like that, unless Hephaestus wanted it to—as if it were an endless fuel. There was a darting of flaring coat, brown hair, and sword. Robin was getting out before he turned to charcoal. I thought that was a damn good idea. Fighting monsters was one thing. Fighting a god and the industrial age combined, we weren't properly armed—like with a fire truck and several bulldozers and earthmovers from the nearest construction site.

Shit, it fell. Just . . . fell. Didn't climb. Didn't jump. The building shook under the earthquake of it.

No sense of survival, no pain, no mind to manipulate, on fire, and could play with our charcoaled remains until

Christmas if Hephaestus wanted. "Robin was right. This was a bad idea." Niko's hand still wrapped in my shirt, I began to weave my way toward the door, then flat-out run as it rose to stand upright. Sliced feet I'd worry about later, if there was a later.

I saw Promise at the entrance to the hall. An earthquake was a good cue that we needed help, but unless she had a couple of tanks with her I'd stick with the running. "Hephaestus, it is I. Aphrodite ... O sweet Virgin Mary in heaven." Under the hood of her cloak her eyes widened and stared upward.

There was the sound of a footstep behind us. Metal against metal, it was the peal of the largest of bells—the one tolling for our asses. The heat had been intense when it had hit the floor. It was getting hotter now.

Idiot Puck. Dying for the answer to the simplest of questions.

Then Hephaestus laughed and the hundreds of shards of metal rang again, this time church bells for a funeral ... ours.

Robin ran past Promise, hooking his arm in hers and dragging her after him down the hallway. He wasn't deserting us. If he had made it out, we could too. And if we couldn't, other than adding himself as another piece of coal to the furnace in a heroically martyred brothers-in-arms gesture, there was nothing he could do. And if it doesn't save anyone and you're still dead, it's hard to appreciate all the perks of martyrdom. Like having his dick preserved as a sacred relic.

I didn't look for Kalakos. He had saved Nik, said it was his duty, but it was my duty too and had been long before he came into the picture. Of course, Niko felt the same, and no one outdid him at the job. He was behind me, beside me, and then in front of me, decapitating a

Cyclops. Flames were a fountain out of its neck before it collapsed and we ran over the top of its body.

Another step from behind, another earthquake, another rising of the heat until I thought the earth was crashing into the sun. I started to look over my shoulder before deciding I had no desire to see the world of shit about to drop onto us.

"The Cyclops," Niko snapped.

The last of them were clawing free of the earth—in front of us, on each side—and I snatched a glance behind me ... yeah, there too, right in front of something that made me rethink that whole atheist, nonhell philosophy of mine. A gigantic scarecrow of pure hellfire, made special for us on some black altar. No, the devil wasn't close to this. When it came to taking names and incinerating asses, Greek gods had it all over him.

Step.

I felt my skin began to tighten against the heat.

The Cyclops surrounded us in a closing circle. It wasn't too many, but it was too little time. We were out of it. Out of goddamn time. Not martyrs, but dead just the same. Didn't that suck? Didn't it just ...

No.

Hell, no.

Fuck that.

"Niko, down!" I yelled as I raised the Glock. He hit the floor instantly and I started shooting.

Ten Cyclops, I'd counted. You carry guns, you count your ammunition, and you count the enemy. I spun, firing as I went. Every eye a target, every target my whole world. One ... four ... seven ... ten. Ten and the end. Ten shots in a fraction over a second—check the speed-shooting records—and each Cyclops a dead, eyeless heap on the floor. *This* was why I carried guns. This was why I loved them. Some felt the need for speed and some were about the result: Kill 'em all and let God sort them out. I was a fan of both. I came to a stop where I'd started, the first and last Cyclops to die lying side by side. "I think I'm ready to shoot in the Olympics now."

"You were ready for the Olympics seven years ago. Stop stroking your ego and your penis extension and *move*." Niko was up and running flat-out for the entrance. I was on his heels. Goodfellow was waiting for us there. He had come back, knowing he could do nothing but die with us. What a friend—and an idiot, as a god had told him seconds ago.

I told him so as Niko and I slammed into him, carrying him along in the rush before he had a chance to turn around. The fiery proxy hand of an infuriated dead god, like a plummeting comet, crushed the hall three feet behind us. We erred on the side of caution and kept running. Promise waited for us in the next room and she joined our escape. When we made it out of the building, we all stopped and turned to see if this was far enough. If New Jersey would be far enough.

It was. Hephaestus wouldn't reveal himself or his machines to the outside world. I guess he'd gotten comfortable in his coffin of solid metal, mouth filled with it, eyes blinded by it. Or he was crazy enough that "out of sight, out of mind" was a literal term. I didn't know. I didn't care. I sat on the ground and then lay back, eyes on the sky. My legs and feet were hamburger; those godawful khaki pants Goodfellow had forced on me were more red than tan now. If Niko hadn't been wearing black, I'd have seen the same on him, except from the neck down. We both had cuts on our faces. Robin was also in dark colors and I did smell blood on him, puck blood—green and earthy as a forest—but not as much. Goodfellow could move when he wanted to. A hundred thousand lifetimes and more of outrunning jealous husbands or wives—he should be.

We were alive, though, and "surprised about it" didn't begin to sum that up. I waved a hand to get Promise's attention. "Sweet Virgin Mary? Yeah? I didn't know you were Catholic. Didn't know vampires were anything."

"My housekeeper is Catholic," she said, still staring at building thirteen of the factory. "I must have picked it up subconsciously from her. It did seem oddly appropriate. In all my days . . . Gods." She pulled at her hood, her hands gloved in silk against the sun as well. "I never wanted to meet one, and I don't plan on repeating the experience."

"I warned you he has a bad temper," Goodfellow said. "And the insanity issue. I said this probably wouldn't work. But did you listen?"

I lifted a weary arm and aimed the Glock at his knee. "I have one round left. It's all I need."

Kalakos came around from the side of the building, where he must have escaped out the back. The cherry on top of the fucking sundae.

"Never mind." I let my hand flop back. "I think I'll save it for myself."

13

Black Sheep

Home is where the heart is or where you bury the ones you want to eat later.

The cattle with their idiotic sayings, mooed by lungs not fit to breathe the same air as mine. The new world would have sayings that fit the mouth of the predator, not the bleating prey. But the new world took time, and I had too much work to do to bother inventing new ones until the Second Coming ruled—hundreds of years yet. It wasn't so long for those with Auphe blood. A pureblood Auphe had lived thousands, hundreds of thousands of years. I did the math. I didn't like it. I'd used a calculator for it and to keep track of my growing horde of children, but I'd done it. I would survive a few thousand years easily. Hundreds were nothing.

A drop in the bucket.

Humans. I dragged my claws through the dirt and wished it were flesh. Boring in what they did, boring in what they said, boring to hunt. Criminally boring.

Bored, bored, bored with them and bored, bored,

bored here. But I did have to check on the family. Didn't want naughty thoughts developing in tiny meandering minds or escapes being planned by the incubators. I had picked them out a nice place, more room than the cage that had been my home. Prison. Homes were prisons; prisons were homes. Were homes, were homes . . . No.

I snarled, then pulled my talons out of the dirt they'd ended up buried knuckle-deep into. It was a good place. Good enough. A cavern in the New Mexico desert, unknown by man or forgotten, it was a small opening three feet across that led straight down. It opened up into four large caverns. I kept the succubae in one guarded by their own children, the Second Coming in another, the dead bodies or the live waiting their turn in the third. The fourth was left for the children to spread as I made more. Room for the family to grow, little bundles of death and teddy bears everywhere.

Cute. Sweet. Look at Junior and Junior and Junior and Junior.

I'd need a new cavern soon.

Worst part was keeping the fifty succubae fed. It was human after human. Fifty every month to be drained of their sexual energy, all energy, unto death. It became tedious when I was the single one intelligent enough to steal them away without alarming the herd and bring them back from all the cities I'd ever traveled to be dropped down the cavern. Some children were grown, but not experienced. Stupid, in fact. Goddamn stupid. They weren't ready for hunting trips, and nobody delivered this far from a city, no matter the tip.

Life was hard.

It was strange about the sex. Humans were supposed to enjoy it, and it was everywhere you looked where the cattle massed together as their herding instinct told them to.

On every building, every wall, every TV or movie screen. It was . . . pervasive. Ah, that was the kind of word an educated monster like me would know. It was pervasive, and yet despite that none of the human husks were smiling when I sent in the children to clean out the succubae's lair. Not a one. Screaming was a better name for the open rictus of frozen jaw. All of them the same, and I'd seen many. Too many to count, not interesting enough to bother with a calculator. Many said it well enough. Succubae liked to eat as much as I did.

I didn't respect them. They weren't as weak as humans, but only several slithers above them. I did respect the she-snakes' philosophy, even if it was another human one made their own. They turned it into "if you can't fuck it then eat it" and did both at the same time. It was efficient, economical, and twice the fun.

The earth began to tremble. Finally. This was what I'd been waiting for while chasing nonsense thoughts around, seconds away from teaching a few of the children about inexperience and stupidity as Caliban had taught the others in that basement. My brother had had my gift of them. Toys. He had many toys, the golden child. Here came one now.

I'd gated to just outside Caliban's own cave after I felt him gate out as the machine plunged through the roof. I'd shot the lock out of the door, no windows to see through—inhospitable. I walked in and saw what I needed, the inside of the room and what it held. You can't go where you have never seen and you can't take anything from there either. This was about taking. I took Janus and gated it far down another cavern that was more of a well tunneling through rock several stories down. Then I had gated sand and dirt on top to complete its desert burial plot for safekeeping.

The tremble of the earth changed to a shaking, with plumes of sand erupting several feet high. It was impressive. Strong, quick, and useful for testing Caliban. How he reacted and fought it told me things, things I needed to measure his worth in the Second Coming. Unfortunately the things I learned were contradictory. No gate, then gate. On the verge of death, then whole again. Intriguing and annoying.

Janus was simpler. Intriguing and a tool, that was all. I planned on sending him back to New York and Caliban again soon enough. So much to learn . . . and while it wasn't the ultimate game of Auphe against Auphe, it was a good game. I hadn't been bored once it finally began.

Sand stopped flying up and now sank down under the earth, into a new pit as a hand, darkly gleaming in the hot sun, broke its way into the air and freedom.

On the downside: "You are a pain the ass. I've had body parts in a cooler without ice that kept longer than you." I was also a truthful monster. When you had no one to fear, you had no reason to lie. "There was a teacher once. She had a saying she wrote every day on the blackboard. 'Patience is a virtue.' It made its mark on me, those words of the cattle. From weakness came truth. Those words have let me come as far as I have. From blood and filth and bars and cages, no way out. No way, no way, no way . . ." My thoughts circled viciously, 'round and 'round, then slowed. I pushed my sunglasses closer to my eyes, which I kept aimed on the sand. I didn't look at the sun. It burned. It didn't like me and I didn't like it. But I would take the burn over the cage. Always. "Until one day I found a way out. I took it, and I plan to take everything else. All there is— because of patience. But while patience is a virtue, pissing me off is not." I gated it down again and refilled the grave. I'd be back to check on its blind progress.

When I wasn't watching . . . judging Caliban. Fitting those conflicting pieces of him together—if I had to tear bits of them off to do it. Finding out how he worked—if I had to open him up and see the wheels go 'round and 'round in his guts and his brain.

Patience is a virtue. . . .

But only sometimes.

14

It was heading toward evening and as I'd gated us and Kalakos yesterday, all of us from home to Goodfellow's penthouse to escape Janus this morning, that still left me with three days before I could build a new gate to take that thing out of this world. Janus's waiting those days didn't seem likely; neither did Niko's letting me attempt the third death gate in the hopes it would move the titan. But no guarantee.

That meant we moved to the last idea Robin had: the black market. As it involved sewers and underground tunnels, Promise decided that in addition to demented gods and a leviathan of fire and metal that had almost destroyed us while nearly converting her to Catholicism, she had had enough for the day. She wished Niko thought the same, given the much more passionate kiss she shared with him by the cars. Both of them were usually more private in their affections.

We decided to clean up on the way. We couldn't go back to Niko's and my place, thanks to Janus, or Promise's, thanks to the time limit. Same went for Goodfellow's, thanks to Grimm.

Grimm, whose own timing was suspiciously coincidental when it came to Janus.

In the car, I made Robin sit in the back with Kalakos and hoped for one day that he could at least pretend to let the monogamy slide. Man hath no fear like a closed-minded Rom chased by a puck ready to tap that, knock some boots, bang some balls, whatever those puck kids were calling it these days. If I had cut Kalakos's throat when he first showed up, as I'd been tempted to, it wouldn't approach the punishment of a horny puck thinking you reminded him of Achilles.

We all threw down Tylenol as I drove back to the city. "I was thinking," I said, fiddling with the radio, putting it off, as I didn't want to say it at all, "Janus and Grimm showing up at the same time. Maybe it wasn't a Rom family in the clan that passed down the frigging secret password to get Janus's juice flowing. Grimm has been around thirty years, free twelve of them. The son of a bitch went to adult-education classes to get his GED. He knows how to research and problem-solve, not just slaughter. Probably reads Sun Tzu and Machiavelli, like Nik." I added, "I hope he doesn't sleep with them like Nik does. That's not Auphe; that's just sick."

Niko snorted as he was cleaning the blood where he could, pulling up his pants legs and taking off his shirt. He was using surgical sterile scrubs from the first-aid kit he'd brought with us. We didn't go much of anywhere without one. "I sleep with someone much warmer. Can you say the same?"

Not since I'd booted my ex, Delilah, out of my life and was waiting to put her down like a rabid dog. In a way she was. She was a Wolf, taking over the werewolf Mafia—the Kin—and had tried to kill me, Niko, and two other long-gone friends. The other Wolves, Alphas or not, feared her. She had no limits, no conscience—only ruthlessness and the certainty that no one counted in this world but her. Rabid in the mind and soul.

But in better days, she *had* been warm in bed.

Robin accepted the kit handed back to him. "You think Grimm is capable of that? Finding out how to wake up Janus and stealing him? Being what he is?"

I flipped down the visor and wished for sunglasses. The clouds were thinning, and the sun, lower in the sky or not, was directly in my eyes. The radio did say the rain had stopped in the city. That should keep Janus out of sight until nightfall.

"Grimm is me on crack with eighteen years of torture, locked naked in a cage, fed nothing but raw meat, and then escaping to twelve years of freedom. He hates the Auphe more than I did, and who the hell thought that was possible? Think what I would've been like if I'd lived his life. If I were more driven, smarter, so sociopathic that they need a new name for it, and *not* crazy."

If he'd had the Auphe kind of crazy along with their skills and predation, that could've actually helped us. Arrogance and insanity—they had been their only weaknesses.

"You like him?" Robin decided he didn't want to think about it and brushed it off with, "I wouldn't have tried to sell you that first car. I promise you that." He had taken off his coat and then his pants entirely, not bothering to roll them up like Nik, to scrub down the slashes and cuts on his legs. I could see in the rearview mirror that there was enough red splattered for an entire finger-painting class gone wild. My legs felt as his appeared as I drove, but since Niko had been pulled beneath the earth, scraping metal as he went, and Robin was about as bad off as I was, I'd rather have him tormenting Kalakos while I claimed the driver's seat.

"You would be more driven, in a positive way, if you were less lazy," Niko pointed out doggedly. "And you are intelligent. You lack some on occasion in the knowledge base of what we hunt, but again . . ."

"Lazy," I grumped. "Well, you can take it to the bank Grimm is not. He's motivated, obsessed, and since the Auphe aren't here for vengeance, he's decided the world will do instead."

"Who is Grimm? Another Auphe?" asked Kalakos, who hadn't been allowed in on the debriefing of my kidnapping, "and why isn't this *ţap* wearing any underwear, his *koro kani* waving free in the breeze?"

"My dick is not blind nor a scrawny chicken, and if I was going to die fighting Hephaestus, I wanted its glory witnessed one last time," Robin replied, offense lurking nastily behind the trickster facade. "And if I weren't monogamous, *arthida*, you'd find that a Rom can't run far or fast enough to escape what I'm carrying. But no worries, I do not sexually assault, in the traditional fashion. I'd strangle you instead with my nonblind, nonchicken dick. I have the reach to circle your neck and some to spare."

From Kalakos's saber suddenly lying across his lap, he believed him. I laughed, didn't try not to. He had healed me and saved Niko, but trust is earned, and not in two actions or two days. "Your arm's bleeding a good deal," Niko commented, while still cleaning blood from his skin. He unbuttoned the sleeve at my wrist as I noticed the entire material starting six inches below my shoulder had gone from pink to solid red. It was worth it. I'd take red over pink and anything over those damn buttons, no matter how I had to get it. Goddamn Goodfellow.

He rolled up the sleeve until he revealed the cut. I took a quick look, then eyes back on the road. It was a keeper. Monsters . . . *paien* . . . whatever Robin wanted to call them, they respected scars. In our life we'd eventually come around to that way of thinking as well. Not as badges of honor, or attractive to the opposite sex, but signs you'd fought something big and bad and lived to show the proof. We didn't care about the first two, or Niko didn't; I kept the second one on call if needed, but the third . . . it was a warning that something nasty had fucked with me and not walked away. You'd best make certain you were bigger and badder and nastier than hell if you didn't want to make their same mistake.

Bleeding in the gush of a slow waterfall, the wound was long and ugly, starting in the front of my biceps, curving to the back of my arm, and was about half an inch wide. A Cyclops's talon isn't as sharp or precise as a scalpel. One thing did relieve me. It was two inches below my tattoo. Messing that up would've pissed me off.

Kalakos, once Robin's pants were back on, leaned up to see. "'*Fratres* . . .' Part of your tattoo says 'brothers' in Latin. What does the rest say?"

"It says, 'If you're close enough to read this, I'm going to pluck out your eyes and use them as Ping-Pong balls.' Mind your own damned business." I ducked instinctively as the first-aid kit came flying back over. Niko caught it. "You want your stitches while you're driving or in a fast-food parking lot?"

I *was* hungry. That tipped the scales. While we were at McDonald's, I ate a Big Mac with my other hand while Niko stitched my arm. Goodfellow refused the food, saying he'd seen pigs at troughs who dined better. Kalakos had brought back the Big Mac, fries, and chocolate shake for me, a salad for Niko, and two plain hamburgers for himself.

"You are stoic. Admirable." Kalakos watched Niko's precise work. "I've sewn myself up often enough and cursed most of the time. On the first and last occasion that I killed a werewolf, I may have screamed in finishing the stitching of the last of the seven claw marks."

"I'm not stoic." I reached for the shake wedged between my legs. "I'm used to it. Big difference. If I screamed or yelled every time I was cut up and Nik had to turn me into a craft project, I'd lose my voice."

"We face Wolves every day. They don't attack us often anymore, but for years it was almost a daily event. You, Emilian Kalakos"—it was the first time I'd heard Niko say his entire name—"are out of your league here. When Janus is dealt with, you should leave. The creatures that live in the city make Wolves seem as puppies." Niko finished washing off the stitches with another surgical scrub.

"And I'm not wanted."

"You may have saved Cal. You did save me. It's appreciated, but it doesn't wipe out the past. Your opportunity to make amends has long come and gone." He slipped his shirt back on and put the first-aid kit back together and handed it to Kalakos in case he needed it. He didn't want him around, didn't want him at all, but Nik, contrary to what he was saying and unlike his father, did do what was right from the very beginning. Not a lifetime later.

Kalakos proved to be as stubborn as Niko. Genes do sometimes tell. "You have a tattoo as well. Same black and red, but a different language. I do not recognize it." *What does it say?* went unspoken, as Niko wouldn't threaten to make Ping-Pong balls of his eyes; he'd do it first, warn after the fact.

But Niko did answer. " 'Brothers Before Souls.' Cal's gift, albeit drunken, to me."

When I had a choice at one point to revert to human, at least temporarily, or stay as I was born and far more able of keeping my brother alive, I'd made my decision and it needed no thought. I would do anything for Nik, whether it be light, gray, or the dark at the end of the road. Before the father of my half brother, before my friends, before my life, before the world itself, and, yeah, before my soul. It was my promise to Niko, and he might not have wanted it, but it was his and he knew what the tattoo meant.

Exactly what it said.

"Can you match that?" Niko asked.

"No." Kalakos settled back as I checked the mirror again. He turned to face out the window. "No, I can't."

At least the bastard wasn't making excuses anymore.

"There's a tunnel under Atlantic Avenue?" I asked skeptically standing in the parking lot of a funeral home in Brooklyn. I felt out of place not wearing a heavy gold chain with a thick patch of chest hair showing. I knew I didn't belong behind a funeral home. I was alive, and if I weren't alive, my body would be scraps in some beast's stomach, not laid out like a plastic doll in a coffin.

"More than a tunnel," Robin answered with exasperation. "Niko, I know he can read. I've seen him do it. Can't you deprive him of food or bathroom privileges until he learns one new thing a month?"

Niko was stiff and limping, but we all were. "I could, but then bathroom privileges would become the kitchen sink or the corner of the Dumpster outside. He's an adult. I don't like it, but that means he's entitled to embrace his ignorance. Cal, beneath Atlantic Avenue . . ."

"Is a tunnel built in ye olden days. It was big enough for two locomotives to pass each other side by side. They closed it down before the nineteen hundreds. Now it's a tourist attraction. You can go down a manhole back at the Court Street intersection on some guided tour." I'd reloaded my Glock and tucked it in the back of my pants and pulled out my shirt, the blood on it now reddish brown, to cover it up. The xiphos I gave to Niko to tuck away in his coat. "So bite me. Who's the genius now?"

Robin slapped his forehead. "I forgot. Ishiah has those crass 'unknown facts of NYC' bar napkins that were delivered by mistake. I saw them at the Panic."

With an internal shudder, I wished that had been all I'd seen at the Panic.

"Yep, a mistake," I said, pushing the Panic far from my thoughts, "but that doesn't change the fact that I read them, because I'm not dense." In reality I would've, as Niko said, embraced that lack of knowledge thoroughly, but bartending had its slow moments; a Wolf had thrown another Wolf through the TV and the wall behind it, and porn was not allowed in the Ninth Circle. Your boss and your best friend doing it was no problem, but no porn in the bar. I didn't get it either. Ishiah had some weird rules.

Until the new TV arrived, I read napkins.

"Regardless of your newfound brilliant knack for trivia, not all of the tunnel is a tourist trap. At least half of it was walled off and that is where the market is." Goodfellow walked us to the back of the funeral home and knocked.

A few moments later it was opened by a man in his fifties with a long, narrow face, eyes moist with unshed sympathetic tears, a charcoal suit, a deep, somber voice, and a box of Kleenex in one hand. "You've come to the wrong door, but how can I direct you in your time of sorrow?"

"Relax, Jackie boy. We just want to go downstairs," Robin said.

The eyes overflowed with tears and Jackie snatched a Kleenex, which I'd thought was for distraught clients, to blow his nose. "Sorry, Rob. I'm trying out some contacts and they're eating my goddamn eyes alive. I can barely see ya. Sure, get your asses in here before Pinky brings the police running with all that blood."

Me being Pinky. Goodfellow and that damn shirt he'd forced on me would make sure that nickname stuck around for a year or so.

"How's the wife? She up front?" We followed Goodfellow up the stairs and inside while he talked up Jack the Snot Machine.

"Yeah, snooty bitch." He frowned. "She wants me to go by Jacques instead of Jackie while we're working, so's we seem fancier. Then we ran out of embalming fluid a week ago—a shortage on fricking embalming fluid, you ever heard of shit like that? And that's when the bus wreck happened. Family reunion. Been coming to our funeral home to be stuffed in overpriced boxes since great-great-great-whoever. So's I'm out raiding every grocery store in Brooklyn for that runny maple syrup. Almost like water, cheap-ass shit. But it runs through the embalming machine like a dream. And I'm thinking, Praise Jesus and halle-fucking-lujah, 'cause twenty of those suckers are stacking up in the morgue and starting to go off in a bad way." He opened a door off the hall marked, JANITOR ONLY. DANGEROUS CLEANING SUPPLIES. FLAMMABLE. "But that ain't the end of it. The next morning Grandma Nosy wants to know before the service why her father smells like a pancake breakfast." He stepped back out as we stepped in. "Eh, what can you do? It's always something."

"That, Jackie, is truer than you know. Good luck with the wife and the waffles." Robin gave him the Brooklyn aim of the finger and firing of the thumb before closing the door behind us.

"He's human," I said.

"That he is." Robin unlocked another door on the other side of the room. It was double bolted and had a security pad for a password.

"He doesn't know about Monster Mart?" I persisted.

"No. That would only mess with his tiny mind, and Jackie has far too little to endanger. Besides, a zombie or vampire running a funeral home? What a cliché," he noted with disdain.

The door opened. "He thinks I'm a drug dealer or a gun runner or run a white slave ring. As long as I pay him something every month, he minds his own business." There were more stairs and no light as the door shut behind us. Robin clapped his hands and half domes of plastic sprang to a soft white light. They sat on the stairs and up against the wall. "Pick up the pace. We have a few blocks to walk, and every once in a while I get blood leeches nesting down here. Fourteen feet long. Not something you want to get tangled up in because you're too slow."

All of us limped faster while Robin explained the marketplace was in the part of the tunnel walled off from tourists, civilians, and the homeless. Also all the monsters had their own ways in. Some species shared: the Wolves, the revenants, the vampires. Others, like Goodfellow, preferred their entrance private.

About two blocks later we walked through a massive brick arch that had to be as thick as a man was tall. The ceiling was brick too and about ten feet high. And beyond the arch were booths, tents, tables . . . anything you could imagine from an ancient bazaar to a white-trash yard sale was here.

"You . . . stained with blood. I see your past, right before me. I'll tell it to you for a sip of fresh blood." To my right, a creature crouched on the wet brick floor. He . . . I thought . . . he was stirring a spidery seven-jointed finger around a cracked plate of intestines. I didn't have to think twice on that. I'd spilled enough that I knew what they looked like. Eyes of dark gold streaked with fungus green studied me, the slippery mass before him, and then me again. It could've been a salamander from its moist skin—if its mother mated with about twenty South American face-eating spiders at once and a snake to top it off for the mottled green-and-gray forked tongue.

"No, thanks, froggy. I've lived it once. I can do without the rerun." I kept moving until the hand wrapped around my forearm twice over.

"For two sips I'll tell your present and future. I see those as well," came a needy, sibilant hiss. "Everyone wants to know what lies beyond and what lies within."

He stood four feet tall and I could've bent down to his level, but I didn't. I grabbed his neck and jerked him off the ground up to mine. I stared into his eyes—close enough that I could see a perfect reflection of myself in the black pupils. "You have no idea what lies within me," I said, soft, smooth, and *hungry*. Not for food, but for fear. "Go back to your bowl of Campbell's Cup o' Guts before I let you see if you can read your own intestines with more fucking accuracy."

To give me credit . . . it had been a long day.

I dropped him then with the unpleasant sound of a snail squashed under your shoe. "If that's the best this place has, Goodfellow, we are wasting our time and I'm spending more of *mine* in a pink shirt."

"Lighten up, Pinky." Robin grinned. "All fairs, carnivals, markets, bazaars have their fakes. Be grateful he isn't a real expert in extispicy and doesn't have the true sight or he'd be screaming the ceiling down. We'd die in an avalanche of brick."

"I focused on the one word that interested me. Extra spicy?" I stepped over the tentacle of the Bride of Cthulhu who was browsing a jewelry stand.

"No, Taco Bell. Back to the bar napkins for you. Extispicy . . . the ability to read omens and predict the future by reading entrails."

"Cal calls that lunch and hasn't delivered a prediction yet," Niko said dryly. Kalakos stayed behind us, but not too far. He thought he'd seen and hunted the unclean. He was a babe in the woods. *I* didn't recognize one-fourth of what was roaming around down here and I hoped I didn't run into them upstairs.

Sometimes things are so nasty that you don't want to get close enough to do your job. Carrying a gun in one hand and a barf bag in the other because their ugliness was beyond extreme wasn't worth the money. But then I saw something else. There was a shimmer to one side. Not the love-at-first-sight idiocy shimmer, but a true shimmer of what I thought was a silver-blue light. But when I glanced over, there was no light. There was a woman.

As I stopped to get a closer look, she was already facing me. She, like Cthulhu's main squeeze, was at a jewelry stall. A choker of polished black tears and garnets or rubies cut into star shapes hung from her hand. "It's beautiful and it's sad, isn't it, sugar? But family is that way. I had it special-made to remind me. Life is shorter than we know and we'd best get our asses out there and kick up our heels."

The choker looked nice on her when she held it to her throat. Her accent reminded me of my trip down to

South Carolina, Southern, although not quite the same Southern, but neither of those things were what caught my attention most of all. Not close to it.

She looked like me.

Her skin was as pale as mine, and that was hard to find. Her eyes were the same exact gray, her hair the same black only with a slight wave to it. If we were together—not that we were, and where had that thought come out of in the middle of this mess? I felt a twitch below. Oh yeah. That's where. If we were together, we'd look like one of those bizarre brother/sister-looking couples you see. Walking mirror images—she was close to my height too; not quite an Amazon, but definitely not fragile. Her smile, it was all me too. Wicked and wild, but without the shadows. "What's the matter, sugar? You look like you've seen a ghost."

I started to get a scent off of her. She wasn't human, not down here. So what was she? Goodfellow put an end to that quickly. "Ah, *gamiseme tora*. No, no, no. I can't. . . . Trixa would kick my . . . No, no. I apologize, Ms. . . . ?" He knew her, but he didn't know her name? Or from the shifting from foot to foot was he waiting for the name she was using?

"Charla Tae-Lynn." Despite the name, she was no countrified Alice down the rabbit hole, this chick. No way. "But this one"—her hand straightened the collar of my bloody, torn shirt—"he can call me Tae. Three names can be a mouthful and then some. And if I want a mouthful, there are lots more pleasurable mouthfuls to be had, ain't there, sugar?" My brain fried at the double entendre. She winked, slapped my ass—which enjoyed it thoroughly—and disappeared into the milling crowd.

"Who . . . ?"

"No." Goodfellow shoved me along in the opposite direction.

"But . . ."

"*No*." He kept shoving. "You think Delilah is hot shit? That one would eat Delilah alive and have room for the whole Lupa pack for dessert."

"What is she?" Niko asked. "She has a . . . presence."

"Presence? Presence? You've no idea. And we have enough trouble. Given another day, Cal won't have a dick to insert anywhere anyway. He'll be Janus mush or locked in with a pit of succubae that he wants nothing to do with and they want even less to do with him. Either way, his sex life is on hold. How about we get to work and try to do something about that . . . and save our lives, if that's not too much to ask for?"

We ended up at the last stall next to the bricked-up wall. This place was unbelievable. It reminded me of the trade shows where, hand to God, the guns were all within the law, Officers, until five minutes later when the cops were gone and you were being shown the latest in the highly illegal, mean-as-rattlesnake-poison, newest design of machine gun to come out of Israel. So new you could feel the packing grease on the stock.

"This is, as I said, my last guess. We hit the black market to see if anyone had been asking about a nine-foot artifact of assassination, and there's no one better to ask than my old friend the Artful Dodger." He was trying to summon up the old Goodfellow energy, but the shape we were all in, none of us felt like being upright, much less bargaining with a thief. And if he went by the Artful Dodger, he was a thief. But so was Robin and he had no equal.

Dodger grunted, unimpressed with Goodfellow's praise.

"Although it's probably pointless, as Janus's type are gone for all time or not for sale. But if someone needed Janus, whether he already possessed him or stole him, a Rom perhaps or someone more Grimmly inclined, that doesn't mean we make the assumption he had the words to activate him. If they didn't, and as Hephaestus isn't talking—sanely—this would the only place to find them. Words sell for more than gold or anything else often enough."

Dodger grunted in agreement on that one.

"And if a Rom did buy them, it would be here, as I doubt more and more that Hephaestus entrusted them to some of the Vayash; it would be like giving your car keys to a two-year-old and telling him to take a drive around the block. Disaster." Robin leaned against the booth, yawning, exhausted as we all were. "If it were Grimm, on the other hand, he'd drive Janus like Andretti with a Viper."

The Dodger grunted at him again—a "get off, you lazy bastard" one. I had to admire him. He could grunt with the best of them.

Hoping the stall was sturdy, I watched Robin lean harder, as equally unimpressed with Dodger as Dodger was with him. He yawned again before returning to his train of thought. "If those words were found here, then we might find the second set. The ones that put the Statue of Liberty's boyfriend back to sleep. Dodger, can you point us in the right direction? I know you're more about the glitter and shine than that boring reading and writing."

"Money, lives, and blood no object?" The grunt became a question. "And I learnt me some lettering. If it makes money, I learn."

"Good for you, and price no object? Who do you

think you're talking to? Who got you the Trojan horse *while* Troy fell? And it was on fire at the time. If my business wasn't serious, I'd take it to Walmart." He lifted a shoe off the damp black-green fungus creeping across the floor and the rivulets of sewer water that seeped into anything belowground in the city. "At least they mop at Walmart. I've heard people say so."

"Lemme look, guvnor." That he mixed with a grunt and grumble to keep his vocal cords in the game. He swept jewelry, silver and gold teeth, metallic nuggets— all that was shiny and covered the threadbare black velvet into a large Tupperware bin. Robin didn't go to Walmart, but this guy did. Putting them away, he then pulled out and slammed down a book as thick as a NYC phone book but wider, bigger, and the cover was definitely made of tanned, dark brown human skin. It was the frigging Necronomicon, and if it wasn't, it should've been. "I've expanded me business." Dodger chortled slyly. "On my way to being a right proper gentleman now, I am. I am. Rich I'll be, sitting up in some fancy roost like you."

Goodfellow groaned. "Don't start that again. Not that accent. If you can't do it correctly, don't do it at all. I cut your tongue out once. Don't make me do it again."

Cut it out, huh? It'd grown back nice, though, hadn't it? Which meant . . .

The guy was short, had to be six inches under five feet, and he looked odd, as if the face of a ten- or twelve-year-old boy had aged while the rest of him, including his child-size hands, didn't grow. He had a face that would substitute for a prune, mud brown hair cut in a bowl cut, and eyes that matched the mud of his hair. He looked human, but I'd bet Kalakos's left nut, right one too, that he wasn't. Down here Niko and the gypsy were the only humans walking around. As for me, there was no dual citizenship in monster–human land.

I leaned a few inches closer for a whiff to get a trace of what he really was. I narrowed my eyes. All I was getting was human, every last cell. I tried elsewhere, the last refuge of a human on the outside but a *paien* on the inside, their minds—that was always the difference. It took but one cell to get you in the club, and where better to hide it? And from the faintest trace I detected, it *was* one cell. One damn cell to have him crossing the line. That was a trick.

And developed into a bigger one than I thought, as Dodger was giving me the same once-over.

"Monster."

This time I wasn't the one saying it. Dodger was. He said it to me as he grew two feet taller, his arms became wings, his head narrowed, his mouth became a beak, and black feathers covered him. The irises of his now round eyes were a white full-moon shine. They made his feathers appear blacker. The night and the moon, as one.

"Monster," he croaked. "*Auphe!*"

No one else had heard the "Auphe" over the loud bickering of the customers as Niko wrapped his hand around the beak, shutting it tightly. The wings flapped desperately as Robin did his best to calm him down. As he did, Niko said, "The Artful Dodger from Dickens. His real name in the book was Jack Dawkins. Jackdaw. A jackdaw is one of the known tricksters. Very clever. I wonder who fooled who? Did Dickens fool his readers or did Jackdaw fool Dickens?"

"He's very . . . free . . . with his knowledge," Kalakos said, eyes fixed on Jackdaw, but the comment was meant for Niko.

"And you just noticed?" I asked wryly.

Goodfellow wasn't having any luck with the convincing or restraining until he snapped, "He is what he is. Do you want to annoy him enough that he tells us to let you go for him to handle your squawking death wish?"

I pulled out the Glock and slapped it down on the book. "I've never seen a trickster turn into a bird before, but Thanksgiving is only a few months away. I'll bet you wouldn't taste that different from turkey." Then I picked up the gun and aimed it at one MoonPie eye, the muzzle a half an inch or less away. "So shut the fuck up, as plucking feathers all day from your dead ass isn't my idea of a good time."

Jackdaw stayed a bird, one that bowed his head to hide his eyes and the tears dripping from them. I didn't know birds could cry. "This is what I am," I said flatly to Kalakos. "Whether I try to back down from the *paien*'s insults and attacks or I am *this*, I am always treated the same once they know. Terror or attempted slaughter. I learned that a long time ago."

Kalakos watched as Dodger rapidly turned the pages of the book. "How long since you were able to try to back down?"

"Sixteen. The day I escaped the Auphe." The two years of captivity I didn't know. I didn't remember if I'd backed down or fought. I did know one thing: I might have backed down in the beginning, but I must have learned to fight. Or I wouldn't have made it back with teeth coated in black Auphe blood.

The pages of Dodger's book were flying faster and faster. It was a good indication that this wasn't a conversation he wanted to be a part of and as soon as he was rid of us the happier he'd be. "Humans only notice once in a while that I'm not ... right. But I don't live in a human world anymore. It wouldn't be safe for them. Eventually . . ." I shrugged.

"Everything is not eventual," Niko refuted sharply.

"But eventually everything is," Kalakos said. It wasn't a counter to Niko. It was as if he were saying it to himself.

"There is nothing. There is no Janus." The crappy cockney accent had disappeared and the voice was that of a bird, a harsh caw, but an improvement. "I am sorry. I am sorry. Please. *Please.*" The tears had slowed but not stopped. He'd been about to scream my identity to every monster in the place, and I recognized crocodile tears whether they came out of the eyes of a bird or not.

Sometimes I took off my mask and showed who I was, could be, would be.

There were times it was necessary . . . like with a giant screeching tattletale of a blackbird.

There were times it was purely instinctual.

And there were times I enjoyed it.

"Dodger." I leaned closer and picked up a fallen black feather, ran my finger along it. "I've been looking into goose-down mattresses. Good for insomnia. But expensive as hell." I considered him before smiling—a sociopathic shopper finding a bargain. "But you . . . you'd be free. And better than cable when I have you pluck your own feathers out one by one"—I let the one I was holding drift away—". . . by one."

Dodger dived his beak back into the book, turned a few more pages, and then: "Here. It says here. There are commands or spells or phrases, but none specific in a way they can be written down for the sake of history. They are . . ." He peered at the word, puzzled, as a last fake tear fell from the end of his beak. "Mutable? Indefinable? Erratic?" He hunched. "I am sorry, Lord Auphe. That is the best I can decipher."

Lord Auphe. Now I did feel like shit, crocodile tears or not. He was afraid; I knew it was true. The tears were an act; the fear wasn't. Almost everyone who knew the truth was afraid. I grabbed Robin's wrist and took off his five-trillion-dollar watch, shiny and gleaming as they came, and tossed it on the book. "Sell it. Buy Mrs. Jackdaw something nice. And keep your mouth shut until we're gone or a jackdaw mattress won't have a chance to hock anything."

As I was turning to leave, with Goodfellow bitching and snarling about his watch before demanding the location of other book stalls with more helpful information, I saw it, a black blot overhead. Bad things come from beneath, beside, and overhead. I didn't skip a location and hadn't since I was fourteen.

It hadn't been there before. It had been brick shadowed in the gloom of torches and lanterns, but now it was pure black with the sheen of dirty oil. "Goodfellow, stop your bitching. What's that?" I pointed up.

"Zeus's pubic lice. We took up a collection. They were supposed to be exterminated three weeks ago or I never would've brought us here." He already had his sword drawn. "The blood. The blood our clothes are soaked in. It woke them. They sleep in the side tunnels. It's the manananggals." It was the sound a cat would make coughing up a hairball or Salome would make coughing up a Great Dane, but apparently it was serious. Goodfellow was already moving back toward the entrance. "I'm going to eviscerate every last one of those lazy exterminators. Run. *Run!*"

Strange, twisted heads lifted from their bargaining to watch with suspicion and nervousness as we tore through the market, trusting that if Goodfellow thought it was bad after facing Hephaestus and his crew, it was plenty goddamn bad.

"Manananggals," Niko said as we ran, his own sword out, "are descended from the ancestors of bats. An off-shoot. They're similar to vampires, although vampires are descended from Homo sapiens, humans. They suck blood through a hardened, long, tube-shaped tongue, sometimes even taking the blood directly from the heart if they strike deeply enough. They form in colonies as real bats do, but are much larger. They—"

A dark olive-skinned hand came up to smack the back of Niko's head like the countless times my brother had smacked mine. Kalakos growled, "We are about to die. Could we do it without the enlightening voice-over? *Khul!*"

"I still hate you, Kalakos," I said, "but that is a memory I'll keep to my dying day." Which might be this day.

I looked up to see the stream of silent wings in rippling motion, a river of night streaming over our heads. Niko's general pissiness at having his lecture interrupted was apparent. "Fine. One last fact. They don't attack one at a time or even two or three. The entire colony will swarm down on us the same as a school of piranha. They will blanket us. There's no way from beneath that. They'll suck us dry in seconds."

Jesus. Could this day get any worse? And dying in a pink shirt was still in my future. *Goddamn it.*

We were halfway to the arch when I raised my eyes again. One of them hit the wall, tumbled, and, before it straightened, its flight let me see more than I wanted. What fresh hell was this? They were cut in half at the waist. No legs. Only a waist and a heavy sac of intestines that should be cascading out . . . but weren't.

"Holy shit, why are they sliced in half? What keeps their guts from falling out? That is disgusting. Niko . . ."

"If we live, you can Google it when we get home. I don't want to weigh you down with so much information that it slows your running." If we lived . . . I was currently on Niko's shit list, which made one not that invested in living.

"*I* was listening. I didn't do anything. It was Kalakos. I marvel at every fact that falls from your lips, I swear."

"You'd best hope and pray we do die." One drop of vengeance in an ocean of head slaps I'd received over the years and Niko was holding a grudge. After the past two days, the calming effects of his meditation were taking a beating.

It didn't matter. It looked as if my suggested hopes and prayers were coming true. Now I heard them, the rustle of their wings. They were coming down, the shroud to cover the dead—and we were the dead. The size of a medium beagle, they had pinpoint eyes of milky white, ears huge and pointed, snub muzzles pouring gray mucus, clawed hands at the juncture of the wings, and a curved dagger of a tongue plenty long enough to reach my heart. I lifted the Glock, but it was hopeless. I could take out ten Cyclops, but these were in the hundreds. Three swords and a fast reload and we were screwed all the same.

Until it came through the arch we'd been running for: a flying serpent with intensely blue scales, black wings, four taloned feet and legs curled under its belly, a sleek head with a sunburst of black spines, and eyes that rivaled the sun at noon.

It also breathed fire. We'd had some serious run-ins with fire today. We dived to the slime-covered floor as the flames of an entire forest fire turned the colony of bloodsuckers above into ash. It continued with its flight and smashed through the far wall, and here was hoping this was not the day for a scheduled tour or that ticket was going to be really worth the price.

"That was a dragon," I told the puck accusingly. The blackened ash continued to fall.

"I'm aware."

"You said there were no such things as dragons."

"There aren't." He tried to wipe the ash from his face and hair, making it worse. "And don't ask. Just embrace a little mystery in your life and that you have that life left to embrace anything at all."

That wasn't going to happen. I wasn't done. . . . I mean, shit, a dragon. Who as a kid doesn't want to believe in dragons? But I didn't get a chance to push it. Dodger, puppy-dog tears and a watch he could trade for a condo, started squawking loudly enough that the whole market heard this time. "Auphe!" A wing pointed. "Auphe! With the black hair! Auphe!"

I'd said there were creatures down here I hadn't seen before topside. There were creatures I couldn't have dreamed up or have made out of a squid, a vampire, a revenant, an entire pack of Wolves, a shark, a Sasquatch, a pig, a chain saw, and a hot-glue gun. "I think I want the bats back. At least that would've been quicker," I muttered, holding out my left hand to have the xiphos slapped into it.

It would've been.

I'd told Kalakos at Dodger's booth. This was my life. Massive unpopularity and/or fear. Anything between was as atypical as it came.

Vendors and customers both attacked. It wasn't all of them. Some were too small and harmless for the weapons we were carrying. Some were too huge and gelatinous to move more than an inch every fifteen minutes.

Some, led by Jackdaw, were watching from the side and taking bets. A trickster, a lying, betraying, crocodile tear–spurting trickster, could figure the odds with no problem.

"When have any of your informants ever once not ended up not trying to kill us?" I gritted.

The puck lifted his shoulders without a trace of guilt. "I warn you each time. I can give you the information, but I can't make your brain absorb it or your ego swallow it." He swung his sword and sliced a clump of those fourteen long blood leeches he'd talked about earlier on our way through the tunnel. They had reared up over his head, their tails knotted for a base of balance—a base that also tangled and wouldn't let them separate to flee when Robin's sword cut through rubbery flesh. Sucker mouths lined with a circle of teeth all made the sound of a fox-caught rabbit.

Ever heard a rabbit scream? It's the sound of a burning house full of trapped children. I haven't heard anything worse for fear and pain, and I hoped I didn't.

I avoided the flopping of their death throes. I hoped it was their death throes and they weren't like worms: Chop one in half and you suddenly have two. Niko took off two heads of a three-headed humanoid lizard with one stroke of his sword. A creature that was either a Turkish Karankoncolos or a down-home Sasquatch—I couldn't keep them straight—was leaping toward Goodfellow and me as if it were a spring-loaded grizzly bear. I shot it in the chest three times, which knocked it sideways into Niko.

"*Shit!*"

I tossed aside monsters and planted the Glock in the bear-thing's humanlike ear and put two more rounds in at the same time a silver blade came through its throat and out one slitted purple-black eye. You could say that took care of it. I pushed and helped roll its three hundred pounds off Nik, who staggered to his feet.

"'Kay?" I asked.

He nodded, somewhat out of breath with katana and xiphos in hand. He pointed to the arch, which was a good substitute for "run" when you didn't have the air to say it. He went with me on his heels until another freak I'd yet to see rushed me. It was shaped like a woman, a wild tangle of black, brown, and gray hair. Her nails were corkscrews of years of growth. She was nude, not that that went into the positive column. Her teeth were perfect pointed triangles in her gaping mouth—all of her teeth and all of her mouths. She had one mouth on her chest, her stomach, each arm, each leg, and they all made the same *mmmmm* sound I made when I was extra hungry and smelled a chili cheese dog.

Today I was the chili cheese dog. I shot her in the one place, oddly enough, she didn't have a mouth: her face. She tumbled backward into something that might have been . . . Hell, I didn't have a clue. It was tentacles, a seven-foot-tall writhing mass of transparent tentacles, each tipped with a black seven-inch-long thorn and equipped with crimson suckers. It should've been a claw or a talon, but it was a thorn, and I could see the tears of dark red poison welling from the tips. Worse, I could see the poison pumping its way down the tentacle through the translucent flesh. It was like a thick vein, and beside it was a much larger tube of the same color that nothing was coursing through. It led to the suckers, and I imagined the flow of that vessel worked in the opposite direction—to suck up flesh from a paralyzed or dead victim. The poison might not be a poison; it could liquefy instead for easier consumption.

It could be both.

Rob Thurman

After this party, H. P. Lovecraft could suck my dick. This was one of his worst nightmares or wettest dreams. What had been *wrong* with that ass?

With no face. No mouth. No orifices at all that I could fall back on to aim a bullet up in a desperate time of need. I shot it in what was roughly its middle while chopping off the tentacles that flashed toward me with the xiphos. The bullets were swallowed into its mass with no effect. The sheared pieces of tentacles fell and didn't move again. Relief, yeah, but when the thing had a hundred of them, tipped with poison, I couldn't put a sword into a major organ, if I could find one, without getting close enough to get wrapped up like a mummy, all while being stabbed by toxic barbs.

I was part Auphe and resistant to many venoms, but this thing had gallons. If it worked fast and Sushi-zilla ate even faster, I could be sucked up like a milk shake in seconds, nothing left but bones and bad clothes. But not today. I'd had enough today. I'd had Janus nearly land on us, a tribe of Cyclops, bat-shit crazy gods, a monster of metal and fire too unreal to be believed. I was done for the day. *Finito*.

I holstered the Glock to fish in the pocket of those stupid pants Goodfellow had forced on me and closed my fingers around one of my favorite toys. "Nik, Robin, Kalakos! Go! The whole place is going to be covered in seafood stew in six seconds!"

We'd been close to the arch and I could see the three of them battling like hell. Heads were flying, limbs; monsters were taking them down right and left, but they didn't fail to get back up again and again. I waited until they made it to the arch itself. And they weren't doing it for themselves alone; they were clearing me a path, because I was going to have to run like a son of a bitch.

I chopped several more lashing tentacles with the xiphos while lifting the grenade. I hadn't used it at the armory when the Cyclops and the fire giant had attacked. Throwing a grenade into a room filled with thousands of pieces, shards, and splinters of metal? The shrapnel from that would've killed us before Hephaestus's creations had a chance.

I removed the safety clip and pulled the pin with my teeth. It looks great in movies. In real life it hurts like a mother and can screw the hell out of your teeth, which was why this was the first time I'd done it. With one hand swinging a sword, I didn't have much choice. "I'll think of you next time I'm drinking sake," I said, then turned and ran. My path was paved with bodies of prejudiced *paien,* but that didn't slow me down. Once I released the spoon on the grenade, I had about six seconds. I had enough left in me to be standing up on the street hailing a cab in six seconds.

Or that's what I thought, until I checked behind me and saw how fast that thing was coming up behind me. Too fast and too close. In six seconds I'd be dinner and half-digested. I let go of the grenade's spoon, counted to three, whirled, and threw a homer.

It hesitated at the blow of what had hit it and flew through several layers of tentacles to embed itself there. That's what I hoped, that curiosity would kill the Kraken. I didn't stop to check. But while three seconds was enough to stop the thing before it reached me—fingers crossed—it wasn't long enough for me to reach the arch to hide behind its six-foot-thick walls. Niko was starting back, to throw his martyred self on top of me or to kick my ass for not exercising more, running more, running twice the hours every day to be faster. Robin grabbed him around the chest, yelled my name, and pointed to the side.

I blinked and thought, *What the hell?* If it didn't work, it was that much more convenient.

One second later, the grenade blew. I tumbled over and over until I lost count. If I was in a wreck and the car rolled, it would feel like this, but without a seat belt. I had my hands over my ears, but I thought I heard the splat of exploding Jell-O. It was my imagination, more likely, as I heard nothing but ringing when I lifted my hands away.

Dizzy, I was trying to get enough equilibrium back to tell up from down when Niko threw open the lid of the coffin. He said something. I didn't know what. I couldn't hear a thing, but it would be along the lines of, "Are you all right?" "That was the bravest thing I've seen." "You were Indiana Jones, Han Solo, and Batman combined." "I'll do the laundry for the next year."

The ringing began to clear as he helped me out of the black steel coffin with its plush red-cushioned interior, and repeated what he'd said. It wasn't what I'd thought. "You *idiot*. A three-legged turtle dying of leprosy could run faster than that." He gripped a handful of my hair and gave my head the lightest possible of shakes. I had a headache already and he'd know that. "I'm going to run your lazy ass every day until I think there's a remote hope you could make a preschool track team."

"Jesus. Fine. I didn't get eaten. Doesn't that count?" I didn't wait for him to give the inevitable no. "I thought vamps weren't into the coffins these days?" I asked Goodfellow.

"The majority of them aren't, but there's the old-school. Too old and set in their ways to give them up. And the younger ones who are growing up now. They're about fifty, the equivalent of a human fifteen-year-old. Some of them are into Voth—vampire Goth. Idiotic, isn't it?" Goodfellow wasn't waiting on us. He was leaving through the arch. Many bodies were still twitching and alive. It was a good decision. "Goths derive from death and vampires and now vampires have developed Voth from the human teenagers."

"If they're vampires wouldn't they already be that way?" I knew I was talking too loudly, but my hearing wasn't completely back. "Well, not now, but wouldn't it be more retro than made-up?"

"Hades, no. Vampires never dressed like that. Capes and black makeup, huge fangs more likely to bite off your own tongue than anyone's neck, long black nails. That's no way to blend in with your prey. And if you don't blend in with your prey, you don't eat." We were up the stairs now, Niko smashing the head of one last blood leech under his boot.

"Which reminds me," the puck said, "I'm starving. Who's up for Chinese?"

15

Goodfellow had been serious about the Chinese. We had a cab drop us off at Canal Street, right in the middle of Chinatown. It left us standing in front of a small green-grocer with a red-and-green awning as the sky darkened to night. Fruits and vegetables were piled in bins for people on the sidewalk to pick up and examine. An orange and white cat stared at us from inside through the window of the store itself. It knew what cats dragged in and that it would look much better than we did.

"I don't cook. Unless they sell corn dogs in there, there's no food here," I grumbled.

A fiftyish small man with slicked-back black hair and a wide grin of white teeth except for one silver one that flashed cheerfully greeted us. "*Luō bīn xiānshēng, wǒ hěn gāoxìng zàicì jiàn dào nǐ. Nín zuò wǒmen de róngxìng yǔ nín de guānglín. Nǐ shēntǐ hǎo ma?*"

The smile disappeared and the brown eyes drooped as he took in our scratches and cuts, and my shirt covered in dried blood. "*A, wǒ kàn yěxǔ bùshì.*"

"He is asking about my well-being. Something that would've been nice to hear from the two of you after I faced a god that hates my guts." Goodfellow answered the man in Chinese. "*Zhè shì yīgè fēicháng jiānnán de yītiān, Liú xiānshēng. Wǒ shì lái yòng le yīduàn shíjiān wǒ de fángjiān, rúguǒ zhè shì nǐ méiyǒu bùbiàn.*"

The owner responded in English for politeness' sake. "Of course, your room is prepared as always, Mr. Fellows. Come inside. Welcome, welcome." He led us to the door, through the tiny store and the door at the back. We went down the stairs, passed through a room where knockoff designer bags were being produced among giggling and impossibly fast chatter, to another door, more stairs, and finally a subbasement. He took us to the largest room, which still qualified as small, but with expensive, comfortable furniture, a computer, and a TV squeezed into it. "I will have my great-grandmother bring you food, medicine, hot tea."

Robin collapsed on the overstuffed couch. "And, Mr. Chen, alcohol, please. A great deal of Baijiu. You know what I like."

The man bobbed his head. "Of course. Only the best for our friend and benefactor."

"You're genuinely going to send your great-grandmother down those stairs? You still don't trust me with your daughters?" Goodfellow drawled.

"I will help her, and no, Mr. Fellows, I do not trust you with my daughters." The sad eyes brightened again, the skin wrinkling around them in a laugh. "I also do not trust you with my wife, my grandmother, or my lucky cat that sits in the window to watch for the police."

The great-grandmother must've mainlined ginseng, because she and the owner were back by the time we had all picked out a place to collapse. She looked a hundred and fifty years old, but her feet moved at the speed of light as she balanced a tray on either hand. "I will ring the buzzer if the police come," Mr. Chen said. "Haters of capitalism that they swear by, *tsk*, but I fear there is no way out down here."

"You can say that again." The puck sighed, referring to our situation rather than a lack of a basement door. "Thank you. You are a true friend."

Mr. Chen had carried a large box loaded with clothes, bandages, and ointments, as well as a more modern first-aid kit, and balanced on top of all that was a tray with six small ceramic bottles and smaller cups that reminded me of the kind you served sake in, but shaped differently. Goodfellow lifted the tray out and placed it on a low, black lacquered table and started pouring. "That's a lot of alcohol?" I snorted. "If we had a teddy bear we could have a tea party."

"They'll bring more when we finish," Robin promised. "Here. Try it. It's honey fragrance. It will help with the pain until more Tylenol takes effect. Oh, and it's not like sake. You shoot it. No sipping. Treat it as a shot. It enhances the flavor."

I should've known by his offering me the first one. But I was tired, hurting, and if this took the edge off, I'd take that. I tossed it back and promptly choked, positive that kindly Mr. Chen had put diesel fuel in that innocent bottle. My throat was liquid lava and for a moment I thought I saw a tunnel and a bright light. "Honey fragrance?" I coughed several times before gasping. "Then their bees must be flying around sipping paint thinner instead of nectar."

"But it's such a small amount." Robin grinned, pouring one of his own and throwing it down as if it were mother's milk. "I'll be sure to tell Chen how disappointed you were. He's a good host. He'll hurry with more and stand there until you drink it to make sure all is satisfactory." He gave up taunting me long enough to point to a small dark alcove in the back of the room. "There's a shower. It's not much, but finding underground facilities bearable to use as an emergency bolt-hole isn't easy. However, I learned a long time ago that it pays to keep them. I'm hoping that in whatever manner Janus senses Vayash, buildings on top of buildings on top of the ground and us beneath it might slow him down."

"It's almost night, when he can travel unseen. We will find out then." Kalakos rummaged for clothing and claimed the shower first.

I didn't mind. I was more hungry than worried about the blood and dirt. I left the alcohol alone and moved to the trays of food. There was rice, several bowls of different soups, dumplings, a dish of poached vegetables I passed to Nik, a hot pot of steaming beef, and on and on. It was less a dinner for four than a buffet for ten. I grabbed a fork and started loading up a plate. As long as it didn't look like fried chicken feet, I scooped it up.

"Had your time to think about Grimm?"

"You couldn't eat your grass clippings and let it go, could you?" I kept eating but with less appetite.

"I can listen and graze both," Nik said, dry as dust, but serious too. I'd had my time to think and come to terms. And the thinking had been done. The terms, they were harder to swallow than Mr. Chen's alcohol.

The room was too small for Robin to give us any privacy, making the assumption that he cared about anyone's privacy. He didn't. But this time he turned on the TV and kept drinking to give us the illusion of it. That was a first, but we were all having a bitch of a time with relatives these past two days, including one he didn't want to talk about either. This once he understood and gave us a break.

I took another bite of something spicy and loaded with chicken. After swallowing, I used the fork to push the next bite around the small pot. "Grimm has a damn good shot of taking me out anytime he wants—he could gate circles around me and cut me to pieces, but he needs me to build the new race. The Bae."

The puck immediately gave up pretending he wasn't listening. "No. The Bae."

I frowned. "'Succubae' or 'succubi' is plural for 'succubus.'" And they sounded the same whether spelled different or not.

"Yes, that was true until copyright law came into effect and I copyrighted the word and/or syllable 'bi' used in any remotely sexual way, which includes a succubus. You may call them 'Bae.'" Pronounced 'bay.'"

"You really are a freak, aren't you?" I considered stabbing him with my fork. It wouldn't be the first time . . . or the second. "But whatever, okay. Anything if you'll go back to watching TV." I addressed Niko again. "He needs me to build the *Bae*. And he needs me cooperative."

Which the Auphe, when they had tried this same plan over a year ago, hadn't required. They'd had access to Tumulus, a place that would drive me insane in minutes. Frothing at the mouth or catatonic, I didn't know, but insane enough that they could've either used my crazed rage or a catatonic body, posable and reactive as any other male body—but without anyone home in there.

Grimm, an assumed failure, hadn't been taken to Tumulus. He didn't know the way. He couldn't get there. And if he could, he wouldn't have known its effect on me. He probably didn't know I'd spent two years there at the mercy of the Auphe while being trained for the big day—gating them back far enough in time to wipe out the human race.

So that was out.

No insanity equals no involuntary cooperation.

"And since the succu*bae* aren't willing and I'm not willing—it ain't happening. I don't think he'll try to hurt you or Promise, Robin, or Ishiah. He's been watching me since I put down the other half-breeds in Nevah's Landing. He knows there's no way in hell he'd get me on his side if he did anything to you. I don't know how many succubae he has or how many Bae offspring, but replacing the Auphe as top ruling race on the planet is going to take a long time. He can't hold you all hostage while I help him knock up"—I let go of the fork and said it for what it really was—"while I rape succubae for a few hundred years or so." Assuming I inherited the Auphe longevity. "Robin, Ish, and Promise would still be around, but you'd be . . . gone. It's not smart or efficient and Grimm is both."

"You think he is that much more of a threat than the Auphe? They deserved their place at the top of the evolutionary ladder when it came to predators. We were lucky, very lucky to beat them. That and you were incredibly stubborn, as usual." Niko tapped my plate and bowl with his fork. I might not feel like eating but I couldn't fight if I didn't fuel the machine.

"The Auphe were cunning. Grimm is smart. He has a goddamn degree. What kind of Auphe gets a goddamn degree?" I ate some more. "The Auphe had no problem dying for their cause, bringing the good old days of murder and mayhem back. Grimm will *live* for his cause. If he thinks you or I are about to take off his head, he'll gate and come back to play the game later."

"That is troublesome." Now Niko stopped eating, but he'd nearly finished his meal, depriving me of fork vengeance. "What do you mean by 'game'?"

"Trying to kill each other," I said uncomfortably. This was something new: to Nik and me. It was something I'd not felt with the pure Auphe and probably wouldn't feel with Grimm if I hadn't given up part of my humanity months ago to get back all of my memories and to save Nik's life.

"I thought you said he needed you alive and cooperative, and trying to kill each other is a game?" he demanded.

"Yeah." I speared a piece of chicken and looked at it instead of my brother. He had never looked at me with disappointment, but I didn't want to see the first time if it came. "It's the only game Auphe play with one another. I didn't know before the Nevah's Landing amnesia-fest." I heard the rasp of Niko's hand touching cloth and knew he was touching the tattoo through his shirt. I didn't regret it, becoming less human and more Auphe. It'd been for Nik. Even without a single Auphe gene in me, I wouldn't have been much of a human being if Niko hadn't been around all my life. Mom would've needed a dictionary to look up the phrase "good influence."

"But now I feel it, felt it when I saw Grimm. I want to kill the bastard because he's Auphe, a murderer, a monster, because it's justice, but I also want to . . . play."

"If one of you kills the other, how does that help the son of a bitch's plan?" Niko asked with an edge of confusion and of that anger he rarely showed . . . until Kalakos had shown up, which was yet another problem to be handled.

"If he kills me, I wasn't good enough to be part of the Second Coming or father the new race. If I kill him, he wouldn't be good enough either. It's a test too. Like him siccing Janus on me is a test." I gave up on the food. I'd eat after I showered. "But mainly it's a game he hopes we'll survive long enough to complete his plan."

"You can't think that it's actually . . ."

"Fun?" The grin crawled across my face of its own volition. I tried to hold it back, but I couldn't. "It is so much *fucking* fun I can hardly goddamn stand it."

And I could see then that while I didn't regret handing over a slice of my human pie to save Niko's life, he did. "Shit." I exhaled. "Ah, shit. I'm sorry. But I couldn't let you die, Nik. I couldn't do it."

"I know." He wrapped a rough arm around my neck, squeezed, and bumped his forehead lightly against mine. "I'd have done the same damn thing. It might not be the right thing for the world, but sometimes the world has to take a backseat."

He straightened. "You're not worried as much that Grimm will kill you; you're worried that he's . . ." He searched for the right word, Nik who knew every word, all the time. I think he didn't want to say it.

I said it for him. "Contagious. The asshole is contagious." I'd seen him once now and I was running down the dark road as fast as I could go, and there was no slowing down. I'd tried. Part of me was running, part of me was pushing, and part of me was trying to turn around. That last part was small now, too small to have a chance of holding its own. It was slowing me some, though. All parts of me were stubborn, large or small.

"I'm less worried about him turning Janus loose on us again than just *seeing* the bastard." Ah, the hell with it. If I let this shit stop me from eating, I'd starve to death in a week, because we weren't solving the Grimm situation that quickly or easily. I pulled the bowl back and went to work.

"If he finds out you're limited to three gates—two, actually—that could be much more of a problem."

Unworthy and spoiled, crippled and useless.

I shook my head and smiled at him. A real smile, the kind I saved for the brother who'd raised me and no one else. It was completely human and completely genuine. "He won't find out," I lied, because how could I know? But the lie was the best thing I could give Nik. I didn't want him blaming himself for the gates. If he hadn't given Rafferty the okay to rewire me, limit me, I might have gone all Auphe by now, reached the bottom of the road a long time ago. Chances were high.

Besides, Nik was wrong—it wouldn't be a problem if Grimm found out.

He'd kill me.

But Niko was also right. Sometimes with family the world takes a backseat, but sometimes it doesn't—not when you were the family, the solution, and the problem ... *problems*.

And when your problems are going full monster and helping create a new race to enslave or slaughter humanity ...

Death solves them all.

It wouldn't be long before Janus found us. Tonight, maybe tomorrow night. Grimm's tests and games were nowhere close to being done. That's why when Kalakos finished and Niko took his place in the shower, I thought it was time to wrap up the loose ends. We might not have a chance to again if Janus crushed each Vayash like a cockroach. Robin was making his way through the honey-fragrant lighter fluid cup by cup, and how he wasn't dead or blind by the time he reached the fourth bottle, I didn't know. There was tolerance and then there was taking to heart that embalming fluid shortage Jackie had told us about. After one last cup, he sprawled on the couch and was out. Not passed out. He was drinking the

Chinese version of moonshine, but it'd take a barrel of it to knock him out. He was asleep, tired same as we all were.

Talk about your long day. Gods, monsters, minefields of metal, and too much ass-kicking to recall.

I was ready for my shower and a spot on the floor to sleep too, but first there was something I had to do. Kalakos sat on the floor by the low table—there was no room for anything larger. He crossed his legs the same as Niko always did, and helped himself to the leftover food. The bastard resembled Nik so much, *they* should've been brothers, instead of father and son. And he had saved Nik from the Cyclops.

As little as I cared about Kalakos, I did care about my brother.

Shit.

"Do you want to talk to your son?" I demanded abruptly, the last word the painful bite of tinfoil on my tongue.

"I do," Kalakos answered simply. He hadn't taken his first bite yet, and put down his fork.

"Okay," I said brusquely. "I talked to Niko when we were driving to Bridgeport." The real reason I'd insisted on separate cars. "I think I convinced him to talk to you long enough to ask you some questions."

"I'm surprised you would do that, with all that has happened. Blood under the bridge, so to speak"—again with the similar quirk of the lips I saw daily from Nik—"but I am grateful."

"Don't think this means he thinks of you as his father or a human being, for that matter, although he might give you the benefit of the doubt on the last one. Niko thinks anyone is capable of change. But I'm not Niko. I know who you are. I know *what* you are."

I didn't have to have an Auphe sense of smell to scent my own kind—branded by violence. "All the apologies in the world aren't going to change that. Even saving his life won't change it. You're no different from Sophia." I smiled and it wasn't the one I'd given Niko. This was as cold as the inside of a morgue drawer. "Funny, though, considering what you think or say you once thought of me, you're no different than I am in the very worst of my ways."

I, on the other hand, was different from him or our mother in the one way that counted. They had nothing in them that wasn't tainted and completely selfish. I had Niko. I had Robin. I had Promise and Ishiah, not in the same way, but still, a way I refused to let myself believe Kalakos had, wanted, or was capable of. It was too late for him, but I'd let Niko decide for himself, and watch his back while he did.

"So if he does want to ask you something, say if he has any other brothers or sisters out there—because no other relatives would be capable of being the disappointment you are—you'd damn well better answer him. Try to manipulate him, try to get something out of him for the information and he'll simply walk away. That's Niko's way." I stood and let the blade up my sleeve fall into my hand. I flipped it, a mercury-silver pinwheel, to point at him.

"And after he does I'll be waiting in the shadows to slit your goddamn throat. That's *my* way."

"Is that the Auphe in you speaking?" Kalakos asked, his mind on me, but his eyes on the knife.

"No, you asshole," I snapped. "It's the brother in me."

I faded off toward the shower as Niko stepped out. He'd have heard the discussion. The room was too small not to. He did deserve to know if he had other brothers or sisters out there, if nothing else. I hope he stuck with the decision I'd dragged out of him in the car. If he did have any siblings, it wouldn't make him any less my brother. Would I be jealous? Hell, yeah. But I wouldn't begrudge him human brothers and sisters—the kind that hadn't once freaked out and killed and eaten a raw deer in the woods.

Then again, maybe one sibling was all he thought he could handle.

I stood in the small bathroom with the door open, leaning against the frame—watching and listening. I'd meant what I'd said to Kalakos. Every word, which meant I wanted to hear every one of his.

Niko had sat on the floor in the spot I'd vacated . . . the other end of the table. His hair was wet but already braided. He hadn't put on his shirt yet. He was letting his tattoo speak for him.

As he wasn't going to start, Kalakos did. "You're right in what you think about me. But I see you with Caliba . . . Cal"—he paused and chose his words carefully—"and for all that you suffered and survived with Sophia, the Auphe, protecting your brother, becoming a man almost before you had become a child. I had no such obstacles to approach anything close to that in my life, and I'm a cold man. A man without honor to his own blood, without worth. As were my father and his father—a chain of unfeeling bastards were we all. Had I taken you with me I wonder if you would be who you are today. The fact that I am . . . that I was such a callous bastard may have been the making of you, Niko. You who are the best man I've come to know."

He linked his fingers, the light sparking off the silver ring he wore on his right hand. "I have no excuse, but I think you wouldn't be who you are if you had learned from me. You made your own way, a better way. Had I taken you, your brother would've been alone with Sophia. I travel always. It was years after his birth before I knew of it. I can guess that you are the better for not being raised in my image, but I *know* he is the better for being raised by you."

That was true enough and it had nothing to do with my being better or not. If I hadn't had Niko, the Auphe plan would've worked. I would've unmade this world by sending them back. Humans would be scarce and hiding in caves now or extinct, the Auphe would rule, and those were the hard facts.

But when it came to family, facts were meaningless.

Niko stared at him, and if I were sensitive to feelings and auras and all that new age/old age bullshit, I'd say the room got colder. "Amazing how the hindsight of a saint is twenty/twenty and every word a smug explanation of how your being a bastard was the making of me and the saving of Cal." He stood. "I would've liked to have known if I had other brothers, perhaps sisters, but that's not the one thing that I wanted from you the most. I wanted what you owed me. Two words, and instead you would have me *thank* you for what you did and what you didn't do."

I shadowed out of the bathroom with the knife. Despite my threat, I didn't think I would get to cut Kalakos's throat. He had it coming, but Niko wouldn't like it or let me. He would think it would darken the humanity I had left. I didn't think so. If anything, as a punishment, it fell short of what his father deserved.

Kalakos took off his ring and placed it in the center of the table. "You're right. It doesn't make a difference if it turned out for the best or the worst. What matters is, I was wrong." He touched the ring with the tip of his finger. "All Vayash men are given one when they become a man. My actions have shown I never became one. I was wrong, and I'm sorry. You don't abandon your family. For any reason. Even a bastard like me should've known that."

The two words Niko had wanted. Needed.

I'm sorry.

So . . .

Fine. I wouldn't try to cut his throat.

Damn it.

Niko didn't have any other brothers or sisters, I found out after I was done with my shower. I used up the tepid water until it was ice-cold and kept going until my fingers and toes were blue. It took that long to soak off the dried blood from my legs and feet, thanks to Hephaestus and his floor of militarized cheese shredders. I was rubbing antibiotic ointment on my legs and wasn't bothering with bandages. There weren't enough in all the first-aid kits and I wouldn't get pants over that mummy effect.

The door opened without a knock, which only two people would do. Robin—looking to beef up his porn site material—or Niko, who'd seen it all before from the day I popped out of the oven.

"What's taking so long?" he started with a scowl, then a frown when he took in the sight of my legs and the bloody water still circling the shower drain. "When the Cyclops took me under, you ran for me. From across the room, you ran."

I tossed him the empty tube of ointment before grabbing a towel to scrub at my dripping hair. "Yeah, I ran. Sort of a given, Nik."

"Kalakos was closer and he ran carefully, picking his way through the metal. From the looks of you, you did not. You look as if you've been ... flayed. Damn it, Cal, it wouldn't kill you to be as careful as him once in a while."

"No, but it might have killed you, and I keep saying it, but I have never heard you curse this much in your life, much less in two days," I said, voice muffled by the towel. "Well? Any brothers or sisters?"

"If you'd fallen, you could've cut your own throat five times over and no, no siblings but you."

I peered from under the towel, my lips curving in a wicked smirk. "Did you cry? In relief, I mean. At least one tear?"

"I thanked every major religious figure I could think of. I thanked Goodfellow as well, as he once pretended to be a god. I wanted to cover all the bases." His face showed nothing but absolute sincerity.

I grinned wider and went back to drying my hair, then dumped the towel in the sink. I avoided the mirror as always and carelessly finger-combed my hair. "Do you think he meant it? That he's sorry?"

"Probably not, but he made an effort and that may count. Fractionally. I have to think on it." His lips tightened. "My God, your legs."

"Looked at yourself lately?" He'd cleaned off the blood from himself in the car while it was still fresh. It didn't change the fact that he appeared to have been attacked by five or six tiny dominatrices with small whips. And it wasn't his legs, although they were now covered with pants, but his arms, his chest, his neck, and a few cuts on his face, from being pulled down through the floor by the Cyclops. I'd seen it in the car and here. We were all sliced and diced, some more than others and some less. Niko and I had the most. Kalakos and Robin the least. Kalakos because he was careful. I swallowed the growl. Robin, in spite of running full-out, because he had a few millennia of practice at dodging sharp objects. I respected the puck's skill. I didn't respect Kalakos's investment in keeping his skin whole.

But whichever half you fell into, the more or the less, the four of us were all injured, Niko had pointed out. "The subject of the first class for blind butchers wouldn't have fared as badly as we did." That was a Nik joke. Not the type that are funny because they're true, but the type that aren't funny because they're *too* true.

"Tired?"

I groaned. "You have no idea."

Five minutes later he'd kicked Robin off the one couch in the room and had me on it with pillow and blanket before I had half pulled on a Chen-donated pair of cotton pajama pants. Goodfellow complained; I didn't blame him. The cushions were soft and comfortable. The floor wasn't going to be either one. But I heard Nik telling him it was time for his shower and first aid assisted by Niko himself.

My brother, he knew how to take one for the team.

"Monogamous or not, I am horrifically wounded and need all the first-aid assistance I can get," Robin agreed promptly. "Ish would want that. For my health ... my best interest. I'm sure of it."

Ishiah wasn't on a mission. He'd gone to Vegas to hole up in a hotel room and recover. Or flown farther, to Mexico, where they sell Viagra in barrels, not bottles. Whichever it was, I knew he had sun, and nothing trying to eat his feathered ass. I wished we could say the same.

Knife under my pillow, I slept instantly and hard and dreamed of Grimm. Of living his life shackled and chained. Tortured and craving the taste of raw meat. Dreamed of freedom and traveling a land I didn't know existed. Learning things I hadn't suspected, but knew I needed once I saw the world . . . the real world. I had a nightmare of killing a teacher, but I couldn't remember what she looked like or what her name was or why she kept talking when she should've been dead. I dreamed grim and Grimm, but no more than five or six times.

Maybe seven.

Isn't that the lucky number?

16

I was swatted awake the next morning by a paper in the face. It was rolled up and I wondered briefly if I'd piddled on the couch. "Up and at 'em, couch thief. Janus came back last night and wiped out about half an acre of Central Park. At least I'd say it's a reasonable assumption it was Janus, as the unnatural and unseen tornado out of a clear sky makes less sense, but is a weatherman's wet dream. One drop of rain and they're on TV yap-yap-yap, counting every drop, predicting the planet-threatening sprinkle but a mere five days away."

I snatched the paper from Goodfellow's hand as he kept yap-yap-yapping himself, to find it was in Chinese, which left me out. But there was a picture zoomed in on a circle of trees splintered and flattened. "Shit." Central Park. "The boggles." I'd come to the conclusion that Grimm wouldn't mess with family or friends, but I hadn't considered enemies. Some enemies can be more useful than friends on occasion. Then there were the kids. . . . "Jesus," I groaned, and sat up, every muscle aching.

"You were right. Grimm is intelligent, too intelligent." Niko was handing me some kind of sticky pastry with a napkin wrapped around it and a cup of coffee. I looked at both blankly for a good minute before I recognized what they were and what to do with them. Morning was not my thing. "He may have gone after something we value but can't claim as family. It's a fine line, if it's one he's indeed walking."

I grunted and ate. "Go?"

"Yes, I think we should. The area that was destroyed isn't close to the boggle pit, but it's not far enough for comfort either. And there is no other reason for Janus to have been there. We weren't."

"Games." One in which Grimm was several moves ahead of me. Did he think I cared enough about the boggles to come after him? Or that I cared that they were too useful for him to be screwing with? He was outlining the boundaries, dipping a toe in the water to see if Caliban the shark snapped at his leg and pulled him under. He wanted to know how far he could push, yet keep the possibility of my changing teams. Observation had shown him how I felt about family and friends; now he wanted to know how I felt about others.

Did I know myself? You can spend enough time with a monster that would rip off your arm like a turkey leg if you eventually let yourself get used to it. A give and take that goes on for years. Information for pay. Sparring for experience. As long as you're equally matched and you both can walk away ... some were convenient to have around. Like Boggle and her litter.

"I need more coffee," I mumbled. "Lots more coffee."

At first I thought the mud pit was empty. To be polite we'd shouted we were coming for a "consultation" with Mama Boggle when we were several hundred feet away in the deepest part of the woods of the park. It wasn't necessary. She had a nose as good as a Wolf's, but temperamental was a boggle's nature. That and predatory, homicidal, and they liked bright, shiny things. Mama Boggle was nine feet of scales, claws, pumpkin orange eyes. She was a humanoid alligator with the backward bite of a shark's mouth, and a magpie's attraction to gold and gems. When she was mildly annoyed, she'd uproot full-grown trees and throw them at you. If you were a mugger or a lost jogger, she ate you.

As informants went, she was a good one. If she knew anything and you bought her a bag full of Tiffany's best, she'd tell you. If she didn't know anything, she'd ignore you ... or go back to throwing trees at you. If she hadn't had the kids to feed and teach to hunt, she would've been more interested in killing us, but keeping her litter in line took a lot of time and energy. They looked just like their mom, but only seven feet tall and not that bright. They'd outgrow it. And when they did, I wasn't sure what would happen. One boggle in Central Park was survivable. One with a litter of boglets—they were occupied teaching and learning, also doable. But when the boglets became full-grown, I didn't think Central Park could sustain that many adult boggles. I knew we couldn't take on that many if worse came to worst.

Unless they stayed on the dim side.

I crouched by the pit and knocked on the edge of the mud. It wasn't as crusted around the edge, thanks to yesterday's storm that had finally cleared up around late afternoon. I lifted my hand and wiped the coating of mud on the grass. "Boggle?" I swiveled my head to look up at Nik and the others. "I smell sulfur. Janus. But not strong. Not like it was here. More like the boggles brought the scent back on them."

"I don't care for the sound of that. Unless they did us

a favor and took Janus apart to keep his bright and spar-kly pieces for souvenirs," Robin said with a yawn as he stood beside me, leaning on his sword. The floor hadn't been conducive to sleep, he'd said . . . repeatedly. That was intended to make me feel guilty.

It didn't.

I was about to knock again when the pit erupted and widely sweeping arms wrapped around Goodfellow and me and dragged us under. So much for the neighborly visit. My last sight was Kalakos holding Niko back, yell-ing, "It's too late! You can't fight that! And there are oth-ers. . . ."

I didn't hear any more about the others as mud filled my ears, nose, but not my mouth. I kept that shut. It was true that enemies could be more useful than friends once in a while, but that didn't mean you ever forgot what they were. You'd be tempted to . . . with every inter-action you survived, but if you let yourself forget, you'd be delivered from that temptation in a less than biblical way. I'd always known that about Mama Boggle. The first time you dropped your guard, she'd take you down.

Which is why, when I'd knocked with one hand, I'd been aiming my Glock with the other dead center at the pit. I was firing as soon as her scaled arm started to wrap around me. I couldn't avoid it—not with her speed—but I could react. Male boggles were bad fucking news, and fast. Female boggles were bigger, stronger, faster, and bad fucking news to the tenth power. They were of the "shoot first, ask questions never" kind if they came after you.

I was emptying the clip as fast as it would go, which, as I'd learned how to convert semiautomatics to full-auto when I was seventeen, I think equaled Mama Bog-gle's speed. Goodfellow would be using his sword with all the skill possible in a liquid pool of mud. All in all, we were probably going to die anyway, but she'd feel it when we did.

I like being right, but I also like being wrong. This was one of the times that wrong was my pick of the day. There was a tremendous push and I was out of the mud and back in the air again. Flying through it, but breathing it too. I landed hard against a tree trunk and fell to the ground on my side. Robin was next to me on his stomach, although lucky enough to have missed the tree. Both of us were covered in mud—rank, *rank* mud that reeked of decomposition.

With the Auphe scenting skills of a predator, I'd had a problem with things like that in the past. When a human came across a whiff of the bloated gaseous dead, it was disgusting. When I did, the same whiff was multiplied by fifty. It was the difference between driving past roadkill and shoving a rancid portion of it up your nose. "Hard to deal with" would be a huge understatement. I was getting more control of it now, though. I went ahead and puked twice. In the old days, I'd have vomited for fifteen minutes at least.

Robin was already on his feet and trying to pull me up as well, but his muddy hand kept sliding off my similarly covered shirt. "I hope you didn't break your back when you hit the tree, because now is the time for running. And I can't carry you and outrun a boggle. One or the other, but not both." He was optimistic. A Kentucky Derby winner couldn't outrun an adult boggle.

I wiped the mud from my face as I staggered up with his slippery help, then automatically ejected the Glock's empty clip and jammed in a new one. Glocks were sturdy enough to handle a little mud—if I was lucky. It was liquid, which helped, but it was thick, which didn't.

Mama Boggle was half in and half out of the pit, one of her harvest-moon eyes gone. Muddy pulp. She seemed determined to end us, but I felt a pang nonetheless. Boggles, like the alligators and sharks they resembled, weren't beautiful, National Geographic glorious, or anything less than freaking flat-headed, black-taloned evil with the smell of dead humans on their breath. But if they did have one redeeming physical quality, it was their eyes. Big, brilliant, and orange as a Halloween pumpkin. They were like the gems they desired, and either I or Robin had destroyed one. I regretted it.

Goddamn pussy.

Next to that mouthy part of me, some piece of me might be, but I had memories of lying in fields in the fall when I was seven or eight with my brother and seeing moons as round and as bright in color. I felt as if I'd torn it from the sky and it wouldn't be seen again. Every autumn would pass, but that miracle of nature wouldn't light the sky again.

Everything passes. Everything.

But not today.

I scanned the area for Niko and felt a stronger pang of relief when I saw him. He was less than thirty feet away with his sword buried in Kalakos's shoulder. The five boglets loosely surrounding him he was keeping at bay with the xiphos in his other hand. He had seen me thrown clear of the pit. I knew because the katana blade was in his father's shoulder and not his heart. Kalakos had Niko's best interest in mind, but Kalakos didn't have any idea that my brother was as extreme as I was when it came to some subjects. Keeping me alive was Niko's number one subject, A-plus, and more degrees in it than a Nobel Prize committee could handle.

Interfering with that would get you stabbed. The result of your interference would determine where you were stabbed. If I hadn't been tossed out of the pit that rapidly, Kalakos wouldn't have had to worry about the best interests of anyone again.

Niko was his son. I'd been, by his eyes, bait for a prehistoric crocodile and already swallowed. But that didn't mean that no good deed went unpunished. Step between brothers, for any reason—good or bad—and you might find a high price to pay.

"I'll take Mama. Go help Nik with the boglets." I gave Goodfellow a push, but no warning. He knew how lethally dangerous they could be. He also knew they were nothing compared to the one who whelped them.

"You think you're more able to fight her off than I am?" He may have lifted his eyebrows, but as he was a talking mud pie, I couldn't tell.

"I think I can hit her other eye without having to get anywhere as close as you'd have to." I pointed my gun at his sword.

"Good point. Spanking the kiddies, it is." He ran toward Niko, Kalakos, and the boglets with sword leveled and ready. "Spanking" was a euphemism for the end of days for boggles in Central Park. They were teens in monster terms and I didn't like it.

Liar.

All right. The best part of me didn't like it, but whatever had happened had set them off and there was nothing left to be done. It was us or them. You could dump a few pints of Mother Teresa genes in me to counteract the Auphe, but when it was an us-or-them situation, it was always going to be them. I'd hike up that nun habit and keep shooting.

I had the Glock aimed at Mama's remaining sundown eye and was halfway through the exhalation that would end in pulling the trigger—until she flung six hundred pounds of herself on the ground beside the pit and screamed. When you think scream, you think chick or kid or man with his balls crushed with a pair of pliers. High-pitched and hopeless. Boggle's wasn't that. Hers was deep-throated, wailing, a crocodile/she-lion/bear mourning in an agony fierce enough to banish the day and bring an endless night. The sound shook the leaves from the trees to fall as if the first frost had come early. It was a bellow of pain and of loss. Woman or boggle, the loss was the same. It was the shrieking sorrow of dead children snatched to the empty heavens itself.

When the boglets heard it, they deserted Niko and his father and gathered around the pit and wailed with their grieving mother. One eye was gone, but she didn't care. I didn't think she had noticed after the first explosion of agony. Her arms disappeared under the mud again, this time to pull free one dead boglet and then another. It took more than two attempts. They weren't whole. One had his head hacked off by metal claws and one had his entire body separated at the waist. Both had the faint scent of sulfur on them.

Janus.

"They hunt." Boggle gathered the pieces of them to her. Limp arms and legs. A head and only that cradled against her chest. Intestines resting on top of the mud and spilling forth further as she huddled over them. Hands and talons tried to shove them back together, to scoop up the guts and shove them back inside. To grind a head back onto the shattered vertebrae of its neck. "They hunt but they do not come back. We search and we see it. Atrocity." Her lips writhed to reveal the inward-curving shark teeth. "Not sheep. Not *paien*. Thing. It was a thing of metal and fire and wrong. Not of this time. Not of this place. *Wrong*."

Monsters love their children too. Not all of them, but some or there wouldn't be any monsters left. Enemy or informant, the death of Boggle's children was our fault. My fault.

Grimm's fault.

I felt his gate and I felt him, all at once. I searched up where Boggle's desolate cries had gone. There he was, crouching in the top of a tree. "Want to take a shot?" His teeth were silver again as he grinned. I didn't see the red of his eyes. He had his impenetrable black sunglasses back in place. "See if I can gate faster than you can pull the trigger? Or if *you* can gate faster than I can pull the trigger." He had another gun and it was aimed at my chest. Another Desert Eagle, the same matte black as the one he'd stolen from me and I'd stolen back.

"You should work on getting a personality of your own," I said, aiming my own gun, but at his head. A chest shot was for amateurs; a head shot was for professionals. "It's pretty pathetic when you're no more than a copy of me. I'm surprised you haven't dyed your hair to get it all." I gave him a matching grin, challenging and dark. "But when you're a failure, when you're not the Auphe chosen savior—one and fucking only—imitating the real thing is all you can hope for, huh, loser? They were right to put you in a cage. You want to one-up the Auphe, the *First*, with the offspring of a half-breed and some snakes? Ones that were so pitifully easy to kill they may as well have been *human*?"

I wanted him mad. I wanted him furious. It was the one way I could think of for him to make a mistake. He'd been arrogant in the basement and I'd taken advantage of it. But Grimm's life and existence were testament to how fast he learned. Making the same mistake most likely wouldn't happen. Fool him once . . .

He wasn't making this one either. "I am a copy in that I covet what you covet. Black. Leather. Things that kill. Good taste runs in the family. But all is superficial. A Caliban costume for the game. I *am* your opposite in the ways of the real world. It's how it should be. Black to white." Our hair. "Pale to brown." Our skin. "Storm clouds to spilled blood." Our eyes. "But we do have one thing that is the same. We have an identical need. We will make the Second Coming not one or the other of what we are, but the whole of what we can be." Without any sign or warning, he fired and I felt the bullet burn the skin on the side of my neck as he shifted aim while pulling the trigger. For intimidation, not killing.

Good shooting?

You goddamn betcha.

"The whole of what we *will* be." He tapped what had to be the still-hot muzzle against his silver hair, no concern I'd shoot back.

"The baddest motherfuckers on the planet?" I said with a shell of boredom I wouldn't let him see through. I would've shot back, but I knew the answer to his quiz. He could gate faster than a bullet could fly.

He laughed. "The way you play the game, brother, I won't mind when all is said and done and the Bae rule, if you finally win over me."

"It won't take that long, trust me, and I don't have your *need*." While he remained calm and patient, I was the one losing my temper. The fake wall of boredom was beginning to crack, but I held it together with everything I had in me. I didn't have a choice. Grimm dressed like me and carried a gun the same as one of mine, but he'd said it. That was superficial. The way he shot—that wasn't. If he wasn't my equal, he was close. Or vice versa.

"You know you do, Caliban. Ahhh, you know you do. Your cattle brother knows. Your goat knows. But they don't know how strong your need is and how *tired* you are of denying it." The grin went back to human. "But right now my need is for a drink." This time there was a tornado, a sideways swirl that opened behind him. "I know how you feel about your so-called enemies. Don't make me find out how you feel about your fellow workers. Neither of us would care for that. I've never liked chicken." He fell backward into the gray and it swallowed him up, but his last words—the bastard always had the last word—lingered behind. "But I am curious: When you twist a peri's head off, how long do they run around, flapping their wings, before they finally fall down?"

Shit. I could call the bar and clear it out, but it was too late. He was already there.

I pushed down the anger. He'd wait awhile. He'd think it was part of the game and he liked the way I played it. He'd like it less if he found out the reason I was unpredictable was because I couldn't gate. Three more days, counting today and I'd gate him inside out.

The fight had gone out of the boggles, if they'd had it at all. Boggles were predators without remorse, butchers and devourers of criminals and careless humans, but they knew the concept of family. They continued to mourn. The boglets rocking back and forth. The mother trying repeatedly to put her two dead children back together. She tore at the dirt outside the pit to make thicker mud and attempt to paste the head of the one boglet on his neck. The one sliced apart at the waist, she buried the lower half again and then its upper half to its chest. "Alive? Alive?" She would prop it up and croon, grooming the neck scales with her teeth. But its head flopped and though the mud up to its armpits kept it from falling over, the shoulders slumped, its chin rested against its chest, and the eyes had gone from fire to ash.

Enemies, but enemies I'd dragged into something they had no part of. Two of their family had been viciously torn apart because of me. Two dead children—size and bloodthirsty disposition was meaningless. They'd been half-grown children all the same. There was no sorry for that. No asking for forgiveness.

"Alive? Alive?" The hope was dying.

There was destroying the creature that had done it and the monster, the monster too much like me, who had pushed it into action.

That was it. It wouldn't be enough. Yet all I could do.

"Alive?" Fading.

I put my gun away as Niko unsheathed the metal from Kalakos's shoulder.

"Alive?" All but gone.

"Grimm is right," I said distantly. "I need a drink."

17

We'd gone home. All of us. We needed it. A respite. Several near-deaths and death itself called for it. Home was the closest thing to putting you right, particularly when you'd spent most of your life on the run: your mother from the cops, you from the Auphe. When you do find a place you can stop, *own* things that are more than can be packed in a garbage bag, you don't take it for granted.

Robin went back to his condo and mummified cats. Niko and I returned to the garage apartment that was drenched in two or three inches of water from a new skylight, a gift of Janus. Everything in the main area was ruined ... except the couch that I'd gated to Goodfellow's condo when the automaton had come through our roof. The TV was dead from the rain that had run down the wall. I didn't mourn as the boggles mourned, but I wasn't happy about it either. The workout mats were underwater, as was the rest of the floor. Everything was wet and already smelling of mold.

It made no difference in the end. It was home. Correction: It was home for two of us. The third, Kalakos, it was not his home. But until Janus was taken care of, he had no intention of staying in a hotel.

That he was around to *have* intentions or a lack of them, he should've been damn thankful. He'd made an attempt to keep Niko from going after Robin and me in Boggle's pit. He'd said it was too late. We were gone and they had the boglets coming for them. He was doing what he could to save Niko as he'd saved him before from the Cyclops.

He could've thought he was doing the right thing. He hadn't seen Niko grow up, but in the past two days I'd have thought he'd have learned that, hell, no, what he did wasn't the right thing. When it came to Niko's manner of thinking, what he'd done was a crime, a sword the punishment, the homicide justifiable, and the justice karmic.

But bottom line to the philosophy of Niko's morals and what flipped them upside down was simple: Don't insult his brother, don't fuck with his brother, and don't get between him and his brother.

"I was doing what I could to keep him alive. I thought you and the puck were beyond hope. Do you think I was wrong?"

My bedroom was relatively dry, thanks to my habit of keeping my dirty laundry as well as most of my clean laundry on the floor. It was a system. It worked and it had soaked up the water that we splashed through in every other room.

Coming home was necessary and going into my room was a second homecoming. I was able to wear my own clothes after showering off the mud from the park. I'd lucked out and done a load of laundry the morning before Janus had attacked us. I'd dumped half of it on and half off my unmade bed. I wouldn't have to wear something off the floor that'd have to dry on my body. I put on my holster and shrugged into my jacket. The first had been ripped to shreds by Janus when he'd attacked me outside the Ninth Circle. But I had backups. The holsters and jackets were the two things I didn't leave on the floor. I hung them from four hooks I'd jammed into the wall. I had three of each, three holsters and three jackets. The holsters hung on one hook, but each jacket had its own. I used hangers, believe it or not, but I took my jackets seriously.

"Was I wrong?" Kalakos demanded with a sharpness that was a clue to how he went about his business ... with impatience that would lead to threats and on to the results of those threats. Then the inevitable boring cleanup of whatever was left. When it came to personality and ethics (too much of one and not enough of the other), he should've been my father. He was nothing like Niko.

"I heard you," I answered. "I'm thinking. Shut up and wait."

The jacket felt good. Leather, comfortable, and ready to load up. I was me again. A man wasn't a man without a cool jacket ... the coolness factor measured by the fact that while wearing one I could carry enough weapons to make me my own walking WMD.

"Nope. I don't think you were wrong." I had thought, but I doubted Kalakos would get it. How do you explain the color red to someone who's been blind since birth?

I reached under my bed and pulled out a locker. It was army-sized, but waterproof. Opening it, I chose the Desert Eagle I'd taken back from Grimm, Eagle against Eagle, because I had no doubt he had one of his own. I backed it up with my SIG Sauer. "Keeping Nik safe is it. Number one priority for me." I started shoving clips in my pockets.

"Then you see." He yanked the tie from his hair and shoved fingers through it in clear frustration. "Then why won't he? I want my son back. We were making progress and now this." I felt his eyes on me, questioning. I didn't meet them. He'd been gone twenty-six years. That was too late for wanting big-eyed fucking tearful reassurance from me. "If it had been you I'd have held back," Kalakos pushed, "with Niko already beyond reach and gone, you would've understood."

When I'd moved the locker from under my bed, I'd turned it and myself to the side to keep Kalakos in the periphery of my vision from where he stood in the doorway. Force of habit with any stranger . . . and the majority of those I knew. I trusted my back to four . . . eh, two people. That was it. "Oh yeah, I'd understand," I said without emotion. "If you'd tried to hold me back from getting to Nik, no matter what the odds, I'd understand you'd be breathing through a bullet hole in your throat."

From the locker, I picked three knives: serrated combat, two throwing blades, and left room for the xiphos. A small sword, it fit in my jacket in a holster that held two guns and a smallish sword against my back. It wasn't comfortable, but it made the grade of concealed weapon. Lastly I slipped a switchblade in my pocket with the ammunition clips. Unfortunately I'd used my last grenade in the black market on that mutated octopus. I hadn't stocked up on those lately. Getting lazy. I didn't bother with the flamethrower. Janus was made of impervious metal and filled with some type of lavalike substance. It'd think a flamethrower was a refreshing shower or a damn sex toy.

Shoving the trunk back under my bed with a solid kick, I stood from my crouch. My combat boots were wet, but they would've been wet from walking through the several inches of water anyway. They'd dry. "I'm going to cut you a break because you did save Nik at least once. But I know you won't get it. You look like Nik, but you're not half as smart, and wanting to invest in emotions for your son now? Is 'too late' not in your vocabulary? But since you want to try . . ."

It was Nik. I didn't know what he wanted when it came to Kalakos, because *he* didn't know what he wanted. I'd do my best to leave the door open, though—in case that's what he decided.

"So listen, Kalakos. Concentrate." Now I did meet his eyes, and he didn't care for it. It didn't matter that Niko and I had eyes of the same gray. The color wasn't what counted. There were things in my eyes that no one would ever see in Nik's. That no one would see in anyone's eyes . . . except maybe Grimm's.

"I'd do anything to save my brother. *Anything.*" I'd proven that. Some lived to regret it, most didn't, and I hadn't given a rat's ass once.

"And he'd do the same for me. He has done the same," I went on. "Think it through. He risks his life for mine. Then I see the mess he's gotten himself into while pulling my ass out of the fire, and I'm right back in after him. Same risk. Same mess. Then back it goes again. Vicious circle, I think they call it."

"That's all but suicide," he snapped. He was stunned, angry, and me? I was not giving a rat's ass all over again. If he wanted a say in Niko's life, he would've shown up sooner.

I ignored the comment. "And if we're too far from each other and it's too late"—I shrugged—"vengeance has nothing to do with the Lord. Cain was wrong. I am my brother's keeper. And Niko's mine."

"That *is* suicide, plain and simple."

"You said it yourself, Father Kalakos. Niko is who he is because of me. I am who I am because of him. For me that won't stop. I'm terminal and Nik is my chemo. He keeps me human and he keeps me sane." For as long as he could. I walked toward the door and Kalakos took a few reluctant steps back. He'd said I wasn't a monster like the Bae, but I didn't think he or I actually believed it.

"Niko," I reflected, "I don't know what he would've been without me. Not you. Absolutely not you. Better off? Maybe. Able to love, like he loves Promise? To trust, like he trusts Goodfellow? I don't know. And neither does he."

"It's insane. Friends and family grieve and go on when people die. They don't jump in the grave after them. People live on."

"Yeah, people do." I brushed past him in the hall and left him behind. People mourn and move on.

Certain monsters and heroes don't.

Leaving Kalakos at our place, we took a cab to the Ninth Circle. There was no worrying over the driver hearing us. He couldn't hear us. He was an Ullikummi. They were from the Middle East, their skin the same color as cooled volcanic rock, blind eyes hidden behind sunglasses, and they were deaf to go along with the rest. Despite being blind, they navigated somehow. I hadn't seen one get a ticket once or run over anyone unless it was on purpose.

"As plans go, this is lacking in everything that one consists of," Niko said, also back in his own clothes and content with his own weapons. "Facts, arrangements, a goal in general."

An Auphe had once killed one of Ishiah's peris before to get to me. I wasn't going to let that happen again.

"Plan or not," I said, "Grimm has us by the balls." We had nothing, but Grimm—he had a plan ... for years. Complex and with every chance of working, of taking back the world, that was his plan. *My* plan had been surviving as long as I could. Trying not to kill too many people when it came to the end, and holding back the end as long as I was able. I'd thought it was a plan. It wasn't.

It was fucking irresponsible.

Of course, I might not be the end I thought I'd be. Grimm had a hell of a bigger shot at that than I did. His objective was different and he was all about the Second Coming. If he had five or six backup plans to the Coming, I wouldn't have been surprised.

"If we don't have a plan, then a fact-finding mission will do," Nik decided, running a finger around his steel mala bead bracelet.

"You and your obsessive need to label shit." I started to elbow his ribs as usual, but remembered we all had weeks to go before we weren't the next-best thing to pork cutlets. I wanted to give him a hard time, but not double him over in pain. "How about some unknown facts? We don't know how many Bae there are. Grimm's been on the loose for twelve years. . . ."

"But he would've had to acclimate, learn to blend into the human population, find out the Auphe were dead, depriving him of revenge and forcing him to come up with a new plan," Niko took over.

"And a goddamn plan like that takes time to set up," I thought aloud.

"We also don't know how many succubae he's keeping prisoner, how long he's had them, or how many Bae a pregnant succabae would deliver at one time. One? Three?"

I had no idea about any of it and didn't particularly want to know. There could be anywhere from twenty or fifty Bae out there. *Fifty*. God. They were young and no Auphe, but every year they'd be tougher opponents. Every year they'd learn and sharpen their killing skills. If one year was enough for a Bae to mature to full-grown status, think what it could become in five years. Every year equal to eighteen or twenty years of added intelligence and reflexes. In a decade, they would be Auphe and more.

Undefeatable.

"How are your legs?" Niko asked. Grimm's seeing me limping wasn't what we wanted. "Did you take the pills?"

I grinned. "Oh yeah." I'd dosed up on Vicodin to the max and then some before we left home. "I'm pretty sure I have legs, but I'm not feeling them." The wounded don't get to play the game. The wounded are broken Monopoly pieces thrown in the garbage. Grimm couldn't know, which changed the winding road of my thoughts to the one that was waiting for me. I felt him like he'd feel me. The entertainment factor of that thought was higher than sitting in a cab discussing plans we didn't know and facts we didn't have. My chances of dying were higher as well, but that was the game.

Time to play.

Yeah, time to play.

The cab was stopping at the bar. "He's there. I can feel him." I reached for the handle while Nik paid. "I'll talk to him. That's what he wants, right? To drink, talk, and to convince me to be the second founding father of the Bae. But, Nik, you can't sit with us. Take a table across the room, all right? Behind me." Watching my back as always.

"Why?" was followed and erased by, "No. Absolutely not."

"It's the game. Him and me. Only Auphe get to play. There are two rules and that's one of them." I slid out and slammed the door behind me.

"We could take him together. It's a possibility." Niko slammed his own door, considerably harder.

"And he could gate however many Bae he's fathered into the bar and wipe out everyone. If it looks like he's going to kill me, I would appreciate your coming over and joining in. Swear. But if I don't at least try the game, prove myself—then it's all over. He'll know I'm not as good as he is." Or the same as he was. And I wasn't.

Not yet.

"And it'll be hell-in-a-handbasket time then," I finished.

"I don't like it," he said, standing between the door and me. He could've been made of obstinacy instead of flesh and blood.

"And you wonder why I'm stubborn. I come by it honestly, Big Brother." I snorted. I stepped up on the curb and then stopped. "Be ready and don't move." I added reluctantly. "The second rule of the game."

This time his question was silent, but as forceful.

The second rule. "We're going to hurt each other, him and me. Not fatally, at least not now. But like the park." I rubbed at the bullet burn along the side of my neck. "Don't come over with your sword to make sure all new baby Bae are born with two assholes, one carved by a katana, okay? The game always hurts. Whether you're playing to play or playing to win, it'll always hurt."

"Why?" It was an echo of his earlier questions.

I didn't answer this time. I didn't want to tell him the truth.

If it doesn't hurt, it's not fun. If someone doesn't bleed, it's not the game.

I'd learned that when the Auphe had me in Tumulus. I didn't remember it, but I knew it. Felt it.

"Just a fact-finding mission. Right?" I said.

He didn't respond to the verbal poke, holding the bar door shut, before saying something I hadn't expected to hear from him. Not in my lifetime. "I've seen you, Cal, when you're Caliban, which is more often than you think. Don't ever doubt you can take him." It was the first time Nik had admitted there was a Caliban, that I was Auphe as much as or more than human. Cal and Caliban, not two. One. In the past I'd have been ashamed that he'd let himself believe it—the brother who always thought the best of me. Now I understood that this was how it should be and for the rest of my life how it had to be. He accepted me, all of me, with no denying of what I might become and what I might do.

"You're my brother, every part of you. Don't you forget that. And if you have to, then kick his goddamn ass, because I know you can," he ordered, opening the door and following me through it.

"How many times do I have to say that this non-Niko cursing is beginning to worry me," I started to say before I saw Grimm two tables over from the door. Niko kept walking to take a table against the back wall. He didn't look at me again or indicate anything other than that he just happened to be here at the same time as me. Grimm wouldn't touch him, but being careful not to do anything to change that frame of warped half-Auphe mind was a good idea.

Samyel and Kushial were working the bar and neither one seemed too happy. I didn't blame them. They didn't know what Grimm was, but they would have a good guess. They knew what he looked like, with his white hair, clawed glove, and red eyes, his sunglasses discarded.

He looked Auphe—part Auphe. Like me, only more so. That would normally make you want to leave, but turning your back on an Auphe of any kind, half, a quarter, was the same: asking for claws buried in your back or tearing out your throat. If it wasn't trying to eat you at the moment, staying calm and as motionless as possible was the best choice you could make to keep it uninterested in you.

And the last thing you wanted was for it to be interested in you.

There were no Wolves in the bar. Lamia, revenants, vodyanoi, vamps, but no Wolves. This was a big Wolf hangout. If there wasn't a Wolf in here, the reason was sitting at the table to my right. They'd smelled him ten blocks away and found a different bar. I guessed he didn't smell like me then, or the difference was slight but enough for a Wolf to detect. They were used to my being behind the bar. Grimm they weren't used to and didn't want to be, from the lack of leg humping and clumps of fur on the floor.

The other bar patrons couldn't smell an Auphe or hadn't seen one in their lives. They knew he wasn't human, but there were so many races of *paien* around that they didn't know all of them. Drinking and laughing, clawing and snarling, it was party time as usual for them.

I knew he'd felt me coming for a while. I moved to the table and turned the chair around to straddle it, same as he'd already done—which I'd bet he'd copied from watching me—and sat across the table from Grimm. He had a black-gloved hand, the one without the claws, lying casually on the table next to a half-empty pretzel bowl. He liked pretzels or he ate out of boredom. I did both. I reached for one. He tilted his head, irises red but as opaque as if he had kept on his sunglasses. "We should talk," he said cheerfully as he slammed an ice pick into my left hand, pinning it to the center of the table.

"Yeah, we should." That's what he heard *after* my switchblade had skewered his hand in place as well, next to the pretzel bowl of both our downfalls.

"Fast," he approved. "I didn't see it coming. Someone's been practicing. I'd clap, but, well . . ." He grinned, his human one, and raised his free hand for a round of drinks. The metal cat-claw glove wouldn't have drawn any attention in the Ninth Circle unless you knew what was wearing them . . . as the peris did.

Behind me, I'd heard the scrape of a chair against the floor, but Niko, after the first involuntary movement, kept his seat. He was trusting me on this, because on this no one knew as much except for Grimm himself.

"Practicing." I rolled the word around and I was juiced by the scent of the blood, the successful nailing of his hand, the pain inflicted, all part and parcel of the dark road. "No. Just not holding back as much to make the game last longer. You aren't the player I thought you were. Sending Janus after half-grown boggles? If you're that damn desperate, I should get a Chihuahua to kick, if that'll make you feel king of the Auphe."

"King is right. Bow down whenever you pull your hand free." He nodded at my shirt. "I like that. Where can I get one?"

"Free my hand? Why? Doesn't bother me." I drawled with an insulting ocean of fake sympathy, "Does yours bother you?"

As for the shirt, I'd dug it out of a drawer where I'd hidden several "attitudinal" tees. I knew Niko wouldn't find them there. Put shirts in a drawer? I didn't know what a drawer was, in his opinion. I'd retired them after he'd threatened to burn them all, but once in a while you need an ego boost. This one, my favorite, read, KING OF THE FUCKING UNIVERSE.

And I did feel like the king of the fucking universe. Grimm had gotten me, but I'd matched him. That was the game. Although my hand ached mildly, it didn't hurt as much as it should, whether I counted the normal few minutes of shock or not.

That's because I was cheating. If you want to win the game, you have to be willing to go the extra mile. Like cheating—I had no problem with it whatsoever. The triple dose of Vicodin hadn't been for my legs alone. I could handle pain if I had to, but showing none at all . . . you were a true player. The pills had helped my legs, but they'd also been for the pain I'd known was coming in one form or another.

Cheater. Cheater. Aren't you proud?

Couldn't have been prouder. If he was going to force me to play, I was going to play to win, and cheating was nothing compared to what I'd do.

No rules but two. You must be Auphe. There must be pain.

But there wasn't pain. I didn't plan on cheating Grimm. I planned on cheating the game too. The Auphe in me didn't know whether to be amused or pissed off by that. I didn't care. Grimm thought he was better than they had been, and after listening to and fighting him, I did as well. I was not an Auphe. I was something different and if I played games, they'd be my games. The Auphe said no rules but two?

Bullshit.

I said no rules, period.

Grimm flashed a scarlet glance at my hand. He could look all day . . . or at least until the Vicodin wore off. Of the two of us, he'd remove the blade from his hand first.

Fact. "I don't care what your idiotic shirt says, I am king. Did you come to prove me better, Cal-i-ban, by playing my game?"

Surprisingly my wound wasn't as bad as I'd suspected. The ice pick could've hit nerves or tendons or broken some metacarpal bones and screwed up my hand but good. It hadn't. It had gone in parallel to the bones and between them, closer to my fingers than my wrist. I'd have another two holes to stitch up, but I'd be tossing blades and pulling triggers in no time. Besides, it wasn't my dominant hand. You don't reach for pretzels with that one.

Either Niko or Chuck Norris had said that.

"I'll prove you a thousand times better. Auphe don't play *the* game, not *your* game, over bar snacks. That's degrading. Pathetic. And boring." I took the bottle of beer Samyel brought over as he did his best to ignore two hands impaled to the table. "Besides we both know we can gate away and this will have been for nothing." One of us could gate away, at least.

"Gate? Why?" He took a swallow of his beer right behind me. If a half-Auphe could be mellow, it mellowed him, or the game had shifted. "We haven't talked. It's important that family talk." There was that Auphe silver grin again. "I saw that on *Oprah*."

"Oprah?" I said, both skeptical and rather disgusted.

"Judgmental to have been raised by cattle, aren't you?" He put down the bottle of beer and swiped a finger across the top of my pinned hand. There wasn't much blood, but enough for a taste. "We are the same, but we're different too. The best of both . . . or so you should be hoping."

He returned to the beer. "Daytime TV can be helpful. I have the kiddies to raise. A single father needs all the advice he can get. And chewing through their throats when they screw up doesn't work. They make more mistakes then. Then there's more punishment and more mistakes. On it goes. If this keeps up, I'll have to start from scratch."

The ache in my hand was growing slightly. The shock had faded. Without being signaled, Samyel came over with two whiskies with a beer back—a different kind of painkiller. Samyel was a good guy, his wings flashing in and out of existence in nervousness, but I'd already had Niko warn him. This was between Grimm and me. No sweeping in like a feathered cavalry. Being a good guy didn't mean Samyel wouldn't end up dead if he tried. In some ways Samyel was a little too good.

I tossed the whiskey back and felt the burn. I didn't like whiskey, but it could take the edge off an ice pick through your hand like nothing else except Vicodin. It assisted that considerably. I put the empty glass back down and gave Grimm a grin to match his earlier one. The Bae. His plan with them had a flaw.

"Oh, Daddy Grimm's done fucked up." That made me happy as you could be. "Your little Auphe-bae are afraid. And each time you kill one for messing up you make the others more afraid. The more afraid they are the more likely they are to mess up again and on and on. Maybe I should call in a social worker. Daddy has a temper."

Grimm had switched from beer to whiskey. He swallowed half of it. He didn't need the whole glass I'd finished in one swallow. Eighteen years of torture had given him a pain tolerance I knew would've exceeded mine if I hadn't thought ahead to dope up. He'd earned his righteously, though. I gave him that. His metal teeth descended to crack the edge of the glass. "Auphe do not fear. Our bastard fathers did not fear. Their blood overcame the human in us and we do not fear. I do not fear. There can be no fear in the Second Coming."

I dipped a finger in his blood. Turnabout was fair play—the only fair play you'd see here. And it was his blood that had created the Bae, after all. I drew on the table. "The Auphe were pure." I talked as I drew a *Y* with lines of equal length. "We are half and the Auphe made us, own us, even past their death. We can't escape our breeding."

"Now . . ." I put a bloody *S* in the top *V* of the *Y*. "Succubae." To one side of the letter an *H*. "Human." On the other side of the line an *A* for "Auphe." My grin widened. "Simple for a monster educated in simple multiplication, or did you miss that day? You and I are half Auphe, half human. That was enough Auphe to breed out fear. But your delinquents are one-fourth Auphe, one-fourth human, and one-*half* succubae. And you don't have the balls or the Auphe to overcome that biology. Succubae know fear and you bred that fear into your miserable Bae bastards."

He snarled and reached over to jerk the ice pick out of my hand and let it fall to the table. He wouldn't concede my victory by freeing his own hand first. He took back his weapon instead; then he ripped my switchblade out of his hand. "Give it up," I growled back. "You lost this round. Don't be a Bae and be *afraid* to admit it. Give up the game, Grimm, because, goddamn, you suck at it."

"Next time I put the ice pick through your tongue. We *will* play the game until you join the Coming or one of us loses. It could go on for years. Think about it, Caliban. Death, *me* waiting around every corner. It could be every month, every day, every second."

He was right. I thought I could outplay him and maybe I could, but it wouldn't be today. Until one of us died, this was the way it would be.

There was also a way it wouldn't be.

"Play your game with me. I'll go along and who's to say I don't like it as much as you?" I said, and meant it, but was doing my best not to.

"But not my family. My real family or my friends. You don't play your game with Niko, Robin, Ishiah, or Promise. The second you do, I'll take my Glock and I'll blow my brains out."

Deadly serious, I continued, "And who will you play with then? How are you going to get up a dead dick to make your chickenshit Bae?" It was the only threat I thought . . . *knew* would work. Grimm was smarter than the Auphe. He believed in the consequences if he broke that rule. He believed it because he knew I meant it. He'd watched me long enough now; he'd heard my history, stories of the things I'd done. I would do exactly what I said and there went all the fun and the Second Coming too.

"They're not your family. They're cattle, goats, pigeons, and leeches. I don't waste time playing with cattle anymore, and goats and the others aren't that much more entertaining. I'll leave your herd alone." His eyes brightened to the point that I wished he'd put on his sunglasses. It was like looking at the sun. Searing. "It's only you and me, Caliban. In this game, this family, this soon-to-be new world, it is only us."

"Unless one of us kills the other first, which is what will happen. I won't choose the Coming. I won't choose you or the Bae over my family. Hell, over anything," I said flatly.

"But you will. You are more Auphe than you were

two days ago. What will you be in a month? You'll choose us. I hope there is a spark of the human *Cal* left in there when you do come to our side. I want him to know what he's done—a thing he could once never imagine doing. I hope I can see that speck of him in your eyes screaming as he blinks out of existence. And even then I won't kill your fake family. You know why?" This twist of lips and flash of teeth were too god-awful to be called any kind of grin. It was an executioner's ax, one of flesh and metal and painted on a face no one could mistake for human then.

"Because I know *you* will." He finished his drink. "And you'll enjoy it. The blood, the taste, the betrayal and pain—because of you and for you."

He held my switchblade and tasted his blood and my metal. "Good. I like the mix."

Not done with me yet, he pointed the blade at the bathroom in the back of the bar. He'd seen the quick consideration I'd given it, no more than a tic of my head in that direction. "And don't think you can stop any of this by going back there right now, a wolf trying so hard to be cattle, and blow your human-*tainted* brains over the walls. You do that and my word is done. I'll *make* your nightmare happen, your so-called family die before your body hits the piss-covered floor. Three gates and you not there to warn them as I claw air and reality apart and then claw through them as easily. You wouldn't be giving your 'family' any chance then."

He held the switchblade in front of me. "A different game, Caliban, with your one more rule, but I'll make fucking do." The black and gray spun around him this time, not behind or in front—a demon's aura. "Come to Fort Tilden tonight. You say you won this round. It's my turn for the next move. Janus is a damned bitch to keep penned up. Let's see what you can do with my toy. Better than last time or I wouldn't have your genes in the Bae. Defective bast . . ."

Not bothering to finish the word, he dropped his eyes to see the katana blade that had passed through his back, anything in between, and exited where a human's heart would be. "That is impressive. For cattle, you would've made a half-decent Auphe. My highest compliment." The gate closed around him and he disappeared with about a third of Niko's blade.

Half-Auphe were different. My heart was where a human's would be, and the majority of the half-breeds I'd killed in Nevah's Landing had been the same, but not all were that way. Some, like Grimm, took after the pure Auphe, who had kept theirs elsewhere.

"I thought"—I caught the towel Samyel threw me and wrapped it around my sluggishly bleeding hand— "you were going to let me handle this?"

Niko dropped the handle of the ruined katana in disgust and took the towel I was wrapping with one hand and tied it briskly and with enough pressure to stop the bleeding. "When did I say that?"

I scowled. "When I told you how the game worked, to take the back table, and to interfere only if he was going to kill me."

"Yes, you said quite a few things, but I don't recall agreeing to any of them." He must have gone out the side door to the alley, back in the front, and Grimm and I were focused with such intensity on the game, neither had heard him or the door. Grimm was right. He wouldn't make a half-bad Auphe.

My scowl deepened. Grimm was heavy shit, but he was *my* heavy shit. I might be hurt thanks to him, but no one else would be. With something like this, something worse than Auphe, Niko had to listen to me. For once in my life I knew more than he did.

"When did you stop following my directions?" I asked. He raised an eyebrow at the question with a comeback that was uncomfortably true.

"When did you start following mine?"

18

Black Sheep

If I could respect cattle, an impossible, stupid notion, but if I could, I might almost respect the human Caliban claimed to be his brother. He was devious and sly. I liked both of those qualities. He wasn't bad with a sword either, but he was cattle and I couldn't respect one of them whatever their talent. And he was human, and that was the reason he wasn't Caliban's brother.

As if a human could be part of us. That made me want to gag. Their blood was in us, I knew, but it was disappearing. The Auphe cells are more efficient than any virus in existence. They touched the human cells or enveloped them or excreted a contagion. . . . I didn't know or think about it as long as it worked.

And it did work. It turned them. Human became Auphe. We ate humans in this form, a farmer surprised in his field—he'd tasted of pork, and our cells ate human cells in turn on the inside of the form. It was a slow process by human standards, but a whirlwind to an Auphe or a half Auphe who planned to live as long as the First.

Efficiency beats fear and war on every occasion. The Auphe hadn't known that.

Stupid. Stupid. Stupid.

They had the tools, but not the schooling. Instead they attempted to make a thing that could make a gate and the last of the First would meet the first of the First to end humans before they barely began, or keep them cave-bound and low in numbers. They had determination and luck and then bad luck.

One of my teachers had taught that invaluable lesson on efficiency by combining biology and history. He told us of some human seaport close to a thousand years ago with walls too thick to breach . . . for humans. The attacking army came down with the plague and, smarter than your average cow, catapulted their diseased dead over the walls into the city. Those cowering there were then infected and that battle was over. That teacher—I had so many, learned so much—went on to say it did little good in the end, as the plague swept the continent and most of the humans died.

Flying humans: dead, rotting, and crawling with contamination. An entire continent all but wiped out. Cattle inventing a new way to kill, cunning enough to do tricks not unlike dogs do for treats.

All that comedy, and I missed it. It would've been hilarious.

I ate that teacher too, but I did pat him on his balding head first for the excellent job he'd done. He'd tasted of roots and rice and beans. A vegetarian. One bite and I'd spit it out. Evil. No good deed goes unpunished. That was my first and last plant eater.

I could taste the vegatation now and wished I'd broken every bone in his body instead of only his neck. And I took back the pat. Grass eaters could have all the knowl-

edge in the world, but no one who tasted that bad deserved a pat.

Disappointing, and the memory of his flavor was making me want to vomit. I sighed and continued to wrap a bandage around my chest. I'd leave it until the edges of the two sword cuts meshed back together. I healed faster than the other half Auphe had. I thought I healed faster than the Auphe themselves had. I laughed at that. More proof I was above them. I'd told Caliban we were evolution in motion.

Or had I told myself that?

Or the Bae?

Who knew?

I didn't worry. My memory was fine. Top of my class. Top ... of ... my ... class. I didn't remember, because I didn't care. I was all that mattered. My plan all that mattered. Memories came and went, but I didn't forget a single part of the plan. The plan that was born of the only beautiful thing I'd known in my life: biology. There was more to it than plague and flying bodies.

Although those were as beautiful too.

I'd always been the most Auphe of the others in Nevah's Landing—insane and weak every one—and years later the Auphe in me had grown, then continued to grow and spread. When I took biology ... I'd enjoyed throwing the irritating lab tech off the roof. Him I had no desire to eat. He was greasy and flabby with the stench of STDs following him like a cloud. How he'd gotten anyone, even a whore, to give them to him was a mystery. And loud. He was loud enough to puncture my eardrums. Off he had to go. I didn't leave that class. I wasn't finished and he was an obvious suicide. He covered the sidewalk in an explosion of bacon-grease-coated syphilis. He ...

Where was I? Where was I? Where ...

Biology.

I'd learned and what I learned combined with what I knew and felt happening in me. It wasn't hard to figure out. The Auphe were the first predators of merit on earth. Didn't Sidle the warden tell us that enough? Brown-nosing, cocksucking shit.

The Auphe genes had survived and evolved the longest. Mixed with any others, they couldn't lose. You could start out half Auphe, but given years—I didn't know how many, but I could wait—all the human would be gone from the inside. Consumed. Perhaps the outside too. We'd see.

With time, you would become pure Auphe. And with us, better—smarter. Able to learn and knowing it necessary to learn. Auphe times two. The Second Coming.

Caliban's cattle companion taught college classes. I'd watched. He'd taught Caliban because that's what cattle companions, loyal and true, do. They would both know biology as I did. They would have seen the changes in Caliban over the years.

They knew.

But they didn't know.

Because they didn't want to know.

And so they would refuse to know.

Caliban could tell he was becoming more Auphe, but completely Auphe? He wouldn't believe that. He'd think monster . . . stupid word . . . predator, crazed, thoughts and actions of an abnormal beast. Close to an Auphe, but not an Auphe. He was right, but not in the way he wanted to be. We would make the myth of Auphe forgotten with what we would be and the things we would do.

The Auphe would be nothing next to us.

Caliban would've been happier to be pure Auphe if he knew that.

But all he saw were snakes and a half-breed. He'd be-
lieve one day. Denial didn't last forever when your hair
turned silver, eyes red, your fake family became a pool of
blood and flesh at your doing.

Denial couldn't turn its back against that.

I rested against the Bae's cavern wall. The separated
succubae, can you imagine, weren't fond of me. The rap-
ists didn't like the raper. Hypocritical worms. I pointed at
the nearest Bae. "I'm hungry."

It nodded and disappeared into the murk. The only
light was from the small opening far above us. It was
cooler down here. I enjoyed it. I liked the warmth, but up
above was too warm a good deal of the time. I examined
my hand that Caliban had put a blade through almost at
the same moment I'd put mine through his. I'd played
nice. I needed him for the Coming, whole, not a cripple—
although he'd healed fast from Janus's attack. I put the ice
pick center and parallel in his hand. My need to accelerate
the Coming made me weak in that one action.

Caliban hadn't been. He'd slammed his blade home
transverse. He'd broken bone, torn tendon, sliced through
nerves—doing the worst damage he could. He'd said he'd
won that round. The son of a bitch had been right. While
I needed things from him, he didn't need a thing from me.
And if I broke his new rule—stay away from his cattle—he
would splatter his brain with whatever gun he happened
to have in hand.

But I'd known that before he told me. Watching, watch-
ing, thinking. He was still the smallest measure too human
to let that go. I'd always planned to let him solve the cattle
problem himself when he was ready, and he would when
he finally became what he'd always been born to be. What
the Auphe themselves had never imagined could exist be-
yond them.

I tried to move my hand, but I could hardly twitch my fingers. I could try for anger, but . . . he was a worthwhile opponent. The only one I'd had. I'd heal sooner or later and the game was the game. If it didn't hurt, if you were positive you wouldn't die, why the hell would you play?

"Food, Father." The Bae was back with a large chunk of meat. It had been skinned, but one whiff said what it was. Wolf. Not desert wolf, but werewolf. They were one of my favorites. They weren't difficult to catch or slaughter, but they had a strong taste. Wolves had an appetite for anything. When you ate one of them, it was a regular buffet of tastes. Human and non.

I took it and dropped it in my lap before whipping out Caliban's switchblade and pressing it against the Bae's neck. "Are you afraid?"

It opened its mouth to hiss at me, black cobra fangs ready, red eyes unblinking. "No, Father. It's the game. We play it too . . . some of us. From your stories."

I narrowed my eyes in thought. "How old are you?"

"Ten years, Father."

Ah, one of my first. "When does the fear go? How many years before the corruption of your breeding lizard bitches passes?" Caliban and his shitty assessment of my new race. Fearful. Little snakes. If he couldn't force himself to accept what he was becoming, he couldn't accept what my children would become, and, as rapidly as they matured, faster than he could think.

Imagine any of it, he couldn't yet.

Lie, lie, lie, lie to yourself. That will only lose you the game and by then maybe make you eager to join the Coming. You can't fight what is in you if you cannot admit it's there.

"Five, Father. Some four. Some six. Some never. But at five years the fear usually goes."

I was thinking how I'd like to be in Caliban's face to tell him that—while perhaps cutting out that lying tongue—but a rumbling from outside distracted me. Janus. Time to put him back down until tonight. For a machine made for nothing but murder, my favorite hobby, it was nothing but an unholy pain in the ass to keep penned.

After tonight that wasn't my worry anymore.

If anyone was still alive after this round, it was my gift to them.

Merry Second Coming.

19

Tonight at Fort Tilden. There went the two more days I needed to gate Janus to Tumulus, inescapable graveyard of radioactive bones and assholes like this that couldn't die. We could run to get those two days, but Grimm would take it out on someone. Someone I couldn't claim to care about to include in my protective circle, someone I might not know, but someone who didn't deserve to die.

Or might. Taking that attitude would turn the dark road into a vertical slide. Holding on to the human in me was what I had. I'd use it to my last goddamn breath.

"Niko, I know Grimm, Christ, in a way you can't. You have to listen when I tell you what to do when it comes to him," I said as I tried to call Goodfellow. I didn't get through but he had changed his voice mail message to say that if this was the Hardy Boys, he'd had another idea about Janus. He'd call us when he found out something. After three more calls, I gave up. I left the info on Fort Tilden and Janus. He'd call back sooner or later. His facing Janus with us was nothing compared to what we'd faced with the puck reunion.

"Again, when do you listen to me?" Niko demanded with a snort when I flipped the phone shut. "Particularly if someone stabbed me in the hand and seemed inclined to chew off my face with metal teeth?" On the way home from the bar, he'd bought a laptop with an extra battery, as the rain that had filled the place had knocked out the electricity. "We listen, but if we see an opportunity, we take it. I saw one. I took it." He magnified the picture on the screen. "I was wary of trying to cut off his head. I thought he might see the swing of the blade out of the corner of his eye. I was in the right. Stop complaining."

"Then why do I have to listen to you bitch for hours if I see a big fat opportunity and don't do what you say?" I demanded.

"Big-brother prerogative." He was staring at the screen, a satellite close-up of Fort Tilden. He was memorizing it. He had all that crap on his phone too, but bigger is better for imprinting rough terrain on your brain cells.

"You are such an ass," I grouched before pushing up to sit on the breakfast counter beside him. "How'd you do it anyway? Neither one of us saw you, heard the door ... although you have the ninja-stealth thing going on, but we didn't smell you either. That much closer to us and we should've noticed how much stronger your scent was. You were like frigging Houdini."

"I was able to do it because you and that misbegotten megalomaniacal would-be ruler of the world have three things in common." He handed me the computer. "Arrange to meet that supplier of yours, Rapture. We'll need all the explosives she has in stock."

I sent an innocent, *Let's grab pizza today at five. My treat*, e-mail. "Let's grab lunch" meant I was in the market to buy. "Today" meant today or not again, and no one could afford to lose my business in weaponry. "My treat" meant I was willing to pay double if the shit was good, exotic, and plentiful.

"Okay, done. Now tell me what Grimm and I have in common." His being aware that I could have been Grimm in another life was not what I wanted to know, but I could live with it. Not comfortably, but it was do-able, knowing that except for one omission of Sidle's to the Auphe a possibility would've been a stone-cold certainty. Past is past. Telling Nik and the others the way things might have been was one thing. Having my brother tell me the same was a knife in the gut. He was the one who told me it wasn't true. That was what got me through and made me believe it part of the time.

"Not what I wish you'd shown back then." He looked at my hand when he said the words, the large puncture flushed, stitched, and wrapped in a bandage cleaner than a bar towel. And there'd been another shot instead of ointment. Hands were more prone to infection than most body parts. Nushi didn't have to teach Nik that. We'd seen that ourselves years before Nushi and we both remembered. Niko had come close to dying from a bite. Not a Wolf bite, but a dog bite.

Like he'd said, back then . . .

Hell, the dog had been a beagle, but the infection had set in by the next day. His arm had swollen and turned bright red. The bite had been on the wrist. In three days the infection was an inch away from his elbow. He was eight. I was four. Sophia was working two conventions back-to-back, emphasis on the "back." I was four and I knew what that meant from the smirking kids down the street, but medicine and nonmicrowaved food, those I didn't know anything about.

She wouldn't have done anything anyway.

I'd wanted to go to the house next door from where we rented. A nurse lived there. Or she'd been a nurse, but then she wasn't. Nik had said she stole medicine from the hospital and was fired. Everyone in the neighborhood knew it. I'd brightened when I remembered that and said she'd help us. She was a nurse. She had to have tons of medicine because she stole it. The same as we had tons of things Sophia stole, but useless stuff. No medicine. Nik had shaken his head. "That's not the kind of medicine she has, kiddo."

I'd stood by the rickety table where Niko was doing his homework. It was hot, but he wore long sleeves to cover his arm. It was the first time I'd had to help Nik like this, but not the last, and it was the first time he told me: *Don't tell. Don't tell teachers about Sophia. Don't tell the counselor. Don't tell anyone. They'll take us away.* I'd thought being taken away from Sophia sounded great … until Niko had said that then they might take us away from each other. There might not be enough room in foster homes for two kids at once. They were crowded all the time.

Take us away? Niko gone? When he'd said that I'd blinked hard to keep from crying. I was four years old and I was a big boy. Big boys didn't cry.

"Never tell. I'll never tell. I won't forget," I'd chanted, rubbing the first tear away hard before it had a chance to reach my cheek. "I promise. I *promise*."

Niko had looked sicker than he already had. His dusky skin was lighter, kind of gray. After my promise, it had turned as white as his could. He wrapped the arm that wasn't hurt around me and hugged me tightly. His longish blond hair—no money for haircuts and no trusting Sophia's shaky hands with a pair of scissors—fell against my cheek. "I'm sorry, little brother. It won't happen. I won't leave you. They can't make me. I promise. Okay? I promise and you know I never lie."

I'd hugged him back, careful not to touch his bad arm. No, Nik never lied. If he said it wouldn't happen, it wouldn't happen. He sometimes ducked the truth or circled it somehow, but not to me. He was *good*, in the way adults were on TV, but sometimes he was too good. Already I knew if you needed something, needed it really badly, being good didn't work.

I'd offered to microwave him some soup. He said he wasn't hungry. He hadn't eaten since yesterday and then just crackers. I'd said okay and that I'd go outside to play. But I didn't. I'd gone next door to talk to the used-to-be-a-nurse. She'd opened the door wearing flip-flops and sweatpants and a top that was small enough that I could see her pasty belly pooch out. Her hair was straw blond, her eyes bloodshot brown, and she had a cigarette hanging from her lip. She didn't look like any nurse on TV. She stared at me and then started to shut the door without saying anything.

"Wait!" I pushed against the door and slipped inside just before it shut. "It's my brother. He's sick. A dog bit him and his arm is huge and red and he's hot. He has a fever." How high I didn't know. We didn't have a thermometer. "He needs medicine. Everyone says you have medicine."

"Go to the doctor, kid." She flopped on the couch to blankly watch TV. "My folks might've named me Happy, the bastards, but I ain't no charity and I ain't got the kind of medicine to help no dog bite."

"But maybe you could get it?" Four-year-olds didn't cry. Big boys didn't cry. I didn't cry . . . unless I wanted to. And I did. I'd cried and cried. My face was wet, my shirt, part of my hair. I didn't whine. Whining was a mistake and adults didn't like whining. Adults told me how cute I was. Playing outside, shopping in the grocery store with Nik, buying clothes at the Salvation Army. Black hair, pale skin, huge solemn gray eyes. They hadn't seen a little boy as cute as me. When cute little boys cry, most adults run to help. "Please," I'd begged, my voice hitching. I was sad and scared. Really, really sad. Really, really scared. No one could not see that. "He's sick. We can't go to the doctor, and he's so sick."

She yawned. "Yeah, and it's a damn shame, but I don't have what you need and if I did, what're you gonna give me for it? A Tonka truck? Go home."

Oh. She was one of those kinds of adults. She was a Sophia. Fake tears wouldn't help. The same with fake sad and fake scared. I wasn't sad or scared anymore. I hadn't been since I'd known what to do. I'd stopped crying instantly, dried my face with the front of my shirt, and asked, showing all the mean I felt in me, "What do you want? We have five bottles of scotch, a stolen diamond ring, a pearl necklace," stolen too, but Sophia wasn't sure if it was real or not, "and a motorcycle. The big ones that cost a lot. A Harley-Davidman." It was a whole lot of mean as I added, "And I know how to call nine-one-one. Cops don't like people that steal. They don't like people who hit little kids either. Or touch them in bad places like it says on TV."

"Jesus fucking Christ, kid." She stared at me, then finally clicked off the TV with the remote. "A Harley-Davidman, huh? Stolen too?"

I'd smiled. Not a cute kid smile. She was a bad lady. She didn't deserve a smile at all. But I'd seen Sophia do business, and though Nik wasn't like her and I wasn't like her, I was something else. Not good like my brother, and not rotten like Sophia, but maybe in between. And even at four I'd known sometimes you have to do not-so-good things. I knew Niko would've done it for me, but he'd have moped over it forever and ever. That people weren't better, that life wasn't better, that you had to do wrong things to do right things.

Sometimes Niko wasn't very . . . practical.

He'd taught me that word last week. It was weird how I knew what it meant right away and he was four years older and didn't know. He could spell it and explain it to me, but inside, he didn't know it. No. That wasn't right. Not really. He knew, but it was hard for him to do it? Um . . . *be* it? Maybe when he was older it'd be easier.

He was a hero. Heroes on TV, where I learned most stuff, usually weren't practical either. It got them into all sorts of trouble. I was practical and I didn't care about anybody like I cared about my brother. "You're some strange-ass kid, you know that? Creepy as hell too, you little blackmailing asshole." Like I'd cared. They were just words. I'd heard a whole lot worse from my mother. They didn't matter. What mattered was that Nurse Happy stood up. "But I'll go get an antibiotic. If it's practically his whole arm, he'll need a shot. That'll take a little longer to get."

I couldn't tell time yet. It was hard to learn even with Nik teaching me. But she didn't know that. "In an hour I'll pour a bottle of whiskey down the sink. In two hours I'll flush the diamond ring down the toilet. In three hours . . ."

She'd made it before my favorite cartoon was over. Nik said that lasted half of an hour. He'd liked that I was interested in learning to tell time again and was trying to give me a lesson when Nurse Happy showed up. She'd given a confused Niko a shot and a bottle of pills to take twice a day. I'd hidden them in a rusty lunch box under the porch steps where the rats were. Sophia hated rats. She wouldn't go there. She wouldn't find them. "Thanks for doing this," he had told her, although pinching me for disobeying him. "It's very nice of you. What's your name?"

"You don't know? Your ... No one told you?" she said, her eyes sliding sideways to look at me. She saw the finger I put to my lips, but Nik didn't. He was too sick to be worrying that she'd tell on me for doing a kind of naughty thing. She wouldn't tell because she knew I hadn't lied. I did know how to call 911. I knew that she hadn't cared about my tears, but cops would. And I knew who cops would believe between a cute, crying kid and someone who'd been fired for stealing medicine from sick people.

"Happy," she answered. "Good joke on me by my parents, huh?" She snapped her fingers at me. "Pay up."

I'd made Nik rest on the couch with a blanket over him—that's what they did on TV when you were sick, covered you with blankets—and ignored his questions about paying. That he didn't come after me through the house meant he was as sick as I'd thought and maybe more. The kind-of-naughty thing didn't seem at all naughty then.

I'd shown Nurse Happy where Sophia thought she hid her whiskey. Under the bed in shoe boxes covered with magazines of men with no clothes on. That wasn't hiding. That was saying, *I'm trying so hard to hide you have to see me.* Then the diamond ring and pearl necklace. "The motorcycle's in the garage. You'll have to push it. Sophia did when she stole it. She doesn't have a key. She'll be back in four days. Hide it good or sell it before then. You're not nice. My brother's like that Forrest Gump guy. He thinks everyone can be nice if they want. I know that's not the way things are. You might be mean like a snake; I don't know. But Sophia is worse than not nice. If she comes home and sees you with any of her stuff, she'll hurt you. With a knife. She's done it before. She cut a guy's pinkie off once. People who steal don't like people who steal from them. My brother says that's called no honor among thieves." She was as pale as Nik now. "But if it's all gone by then, I'll say we were robbed while Nik was at school and I was at Mrs. Thomasina's with the other kids till Nik got home."

She'd held the stuff gathered in her arms and backed away from me. "You're not a strange kid after all. You're a goddamned scary kid."

"And you're not nice. So now *you* go away."

She'd slammed the door behind her and I'd crawled up to sit on Niko's blanket-covered lap. "You'll get better now. And I'll make you soup and a cheese sandwich," I said. "You won't die and we'll stay together and it's fixed, right? It's fixed." I rested my head against his chest. He was taller than most eight-year-olds and I was smaller than most kids my age. He made a perfect pillow.

"It's fixed," he'd said slowly, smoothing my hair down. All the fake crying was real water and had turned my straight hair damp and messy. "What'd you do, Cal? I mean, I see what you did, but what made you think of that?" He'd seen part of what I'd done with the paying. That was enough. Maybe someday I'd tell him the rest when he got over his mopey phase.

I'd smiled up at him. My real smile. Proud and wanting him to be proud of me. He took care of me and now I took care of him.

"I was practical."

"Where did the two of you go?"

"Where you weren't," I said with now automatic accusation as I rested my punctured hand palm up on my leg, the Vicodin for the game having long worn off. Nik nudged me and handed me two more automatically. Getting off the childproof cap on the bottle with one hand made it difficult to open without tossing pills everywhere like candy from a piñata; we both knew that from personal experience.

"I see. Ancient history." Kalakos rubbed the finger where he'd once worn the Vayash ring of manhood. The paler strip of skin was his shame. He'd given the ring to Niko at Goodfellow's rental in Mr. Chen's subbasement. Niko'd refused it. Robin solved the problem by swiping it.

Efficiency, thy name is Goodfellow.

"You were both where you shouldn't have been," Kalakos continued. "Where no child should've been. And on my shoulders that will stay forever." The bitterness that I heard was for the first time directed inward, and the Vayash appeared brutally unforgiving of himself. Niko hadn't been able in twenty-four years of trying to make me believe that it was possible that people could change who they were and would be in the future. But now . . . if Kalakos could accomplish that, Nik damn well warranted it.

I didn't have a look or another comment for Kalakos's metaphorical "coming to God" as he leaned against the wall, the water he was standing in only half an inch deep now. That I had nothing for him wasn't due to the fact that all of this wasn't his fault. It *was* his fault if you went back far enough. Regret didn't change that.

But I was thinking of other things, such as how at four I'd already shown a little Auphe when I hadn't known what they were yet. Sophia told me I was a monster from the day I was born, before I knew what words were. Niko told me she was crazy and spiteful and there were no such things as monsters. He knew there were, but I'd believed him . . . for a while. It wasn't a lie I'd hold against him, then or now.

Niko did have a look for his father, though, the recrimination in the tightening of his jaw, but then it loosened into a frustrated exhalation. The man had saved his life and thought he was saving it twice. My brother had eventually learned to do practical and do it well, but he'd not grown to like it. The guilt that went with it had faded, yet a sliver would always remain. To him that would mean that if his father could feel guilt, he might be salvageable as a human being.

What people . . . what Kalakos had done in the past, however . . . they couldn't undo. I'd go along with what Niko wanted, but I wouldn't forget that. Kalakos didn't have the patent on being brutally unforgiving.

I returned to the original subject. "What three things do Grimm and I have in common that let you sneak up on us?"

Niko poured the rest of the pills into a small pocket on my jacket lying between us and zipped it. The night was going to be long or short, depending on how successful or unsuccessful we were. I might need them. "First, and you said it yourself: You're both arrogant. Grimm doesn't think anyone or anything can take him. You're the same, except when it comes to me." True. Niko had taught me to fight. He knew what I'd do before I did it. Without gates, Niko could and had taken me down.

"Second: competition. Right now you use the game. When you play the game, neither of you sees anything else. You see each other, the pain, the blood. Competition blinds you to all but the game." He was right when it came to that too. Once I'd smelled Grimm's blood, the rest of the bar had been lost in a fog.

He slid off the counter. "I suggest we grab an hour or two of rest before we meet your combustible contact." The roof of the bedrooms had remained intact. The floor was wet, but the beds were dry. "Kalakos, I'll give you a blanket if you can find something mostly dry to sleep on."

"Hey, what's the third one?" I asked. "You said we had three things in common."

"I'd thought that obvious. You're both idiots." That wasn't a joke. He was serious. "He taunts you; you taunt him back. Forget he's making baby Bae right and left; it's all about the game. Forget you might kill him and ruin his plan. Forget all those potentially life-ending, world-ending issues. 'We're part Auphe. We have to play. Born to play. So much fun I can't fucking stand it.'" He quoted me with a mixture of anger and frustration.

"But you're both lying to yourself. It's not a game. It's suicide. Grimm thinks he wants to take over everything, but the entire damn world? He doesn't know that he can. He *is* smart enough to know that maybe he can't. He'll be a failure like he was before." He jammed a finger into my chest. "And you think you want to stop him and this is how to do it. It takes an Auphe to beat an Auphe. You two think the game is the Auphe part of you. It's not. The blood is. The pain is. Even the game, but you're not playing it how the Auphe would play. The rest of it, the winner and the loser when it comes to you two, isn't Auphe. That's the human in you. It's the easy way out and you know it is. The game is what you let it be."

That wasn't right, was it?

"Grimm would sooner die than fail again, and you think that you could've been Grimm, that you will be

Grimm someday. You'd sooner die than be that, to get that far. I know you don't trust yourself, but, Cal, trust me. I won't let it happen. That's *my* promise."

This time he slapped me. It wasn't a real slap but the *Godfather* kind. The "whatta I'm gonna do with this boy?" light one. The anger was gone. The frustration remained, but it was tempered with empathy. "As I said: idiots. Using an Auphe game for a human reason."

He opened my hand and put something in it, concealing the object until he closed my fingers around it. "You're twenty-four, twenty-five next month. You're a man, Cal. You have been long before you could drive. Be as practical as you were when you were four, little brother. You don't play to win. You just *win* and screw the games."

He lifted a bunch of the hair hanging in front of my eyes and added, "And for the love of all that is holy, will you do something with your damn hair? You can fight blind, but your chances are better if you don't."

Orders given, he went to his room. When his door shut, I opened my hand and saw a ring. It wasn't the Vayash solid-silver ring of manhood. The top half was black metal and the bottom half bronze. Or the other way around, depending how you flipped it.

Black for me, bronze for Niko, and it may as well have been case-hardened steel. We wouldn't be Vayash; neither of us would want a ring attached to that name. He might mean this as my "Leandros" ring of manhood. Niko putting the lie to the black-market monsters who accused me of being much more of a nightmare than they were. Niko denying Grimm's games and plans and lures.

My genes didn't matter one way or the other in what Nik knew and had always known. I wasn't a monster.

I was a man.

He must've bought it from Mr. Chen before we left. It fit my middle finger, which would be at the forefront of any punch I threw. It not only said I was a man, but it was ... I grinned.

Practical.

20

Three hours later we were going into a bakery on Melbourne Avenue. Robin hadn't called back yet and that was beginning to worry me. Niko had called Promise to check on his condo and we were waiting to hear back from her. It wasn't like Goodfellow. Okay, honestly, it was like him with everyone else, but not with us and not now.

The bakery wasn't much to look at. Plain. Blue and pink cupcakes had been painted on the smallish window by hand, and not a good one. The paint was peeling now, giving them a slowly advancing case of sugar leprosy. But as with most dives, that's where the food was the best. When I opened the door, the smell was unbelievable. Bread, pies, fudge, and ten kinds of cake. The place was called Rapture's Buns. The paint on that was flaking too, but it wasn't making the business suffer. The place was full of people lined up at a glass case, squabbling over who was first in line and snatching free samples off the top of the counter.

Repeat customers like me didn't have to go through that. Rapture bumped them to the front, actually the back technically, as soon as you walked in. She saw me as she was putting a cake in a box and handed it over to one of the guys who worked for her. They were all guys. All tough, some with prison tats, but all good-looking. Rapture liked her baking harem.

She beckoned impatiently toward the door in the back. "*Bebé*, where have you and your *hermano, el buenorro,* been? My best customers and you desert me. Where is the *lealtad* these days? Ay, the world, she is falling apart when my children starve because your wallet is too tight to buy some of my sweets." She didn't have kids, but it was a good line when bargaining.

Rapture had been thrown into hooking when she was sixteen, two years after coming over from Puerto Rico. Her favorite line had been, "My name be Rapture, honey. I'm so good, sugar pie, I'll make you see God." I think she came up with the line first and then picked her street name. I had no idea how big she'd been then, but she was large enough now to bring her chosen name to the whole world or at least an entire continent. I had a feeling she'd been close to the same big and beautiful three hundred and fifty some-odd pounds she was now as when she'd shot her pimp's cousin at the same time she sat on her pimp's head and suffocated him. She said they called him Tiny Tino for a reason. It was a good story and I believed it.

After two years of hooking she'd decided it was time for a career change. She loved telling her success story. It gave hope to other whores with stupid pimps, she said. Tino had a cousin who sold weapons, and he made money Tino couldn't dream of. And he didn't have to give blow jobs in alleys. She watched and learned and made that profit when she brought the Rapture to Tino and shot the cousin with one of his own guns. Of course,

then it was her gun and that was a quicker profit than a
BJ any day. Now Rapture was thirty-five and not the
only gunrunner in the city, but one of the top ones. And
she gave you a free cupcake with every purchase. How
the hell can you beat that?

We'd left Kalakos driving the car around a few blocks
until we were finished. With what I was buying, those
random checks on public transportation these days
would give a transit cop a heart attack and have us running before the government buried us so far under that
the word "lawyer" was a myth.

She closed the door behind us and stripped off her
baker's jacket and hairnet. The last thing she'd want was
the health department coming around and finding even
the rats carried Uzis. She fluffed her curly black hair and
pulled down a sequined tube top that Niko, Kalakos, and
I all three could've stood in. "I had the boob job. What
do you think? I have money. Why should I not give the
angels a look at what they're missing?"

They were perky, and as she was half an alphabet past
a D cup, that made me both doubt gravity existed and
think she had one damn talented doctor . . . who used concrete instead of silicone. "They're . . . damn. I'll bet men
fight to the death for you when you walk down the street."
Hey, I didn't want to get shot by my supplier. If they made
her happy, good for her. For someone who sold guns and
had put a few people six feet under, she wasn't bad.

She hugged me thoroughly until my bones creaked
and I was inhaling sequins. I heard the click in Niko's
throat he made when he was desperately trying not to
laugh. His laughter was rare and I'd have wanted to hear
it if it weren't at my expense and would get him shot as
well. Rapture let go of me, pulled up the glittering top
again, and then waved her arms. "So? What is it you

need? Wait. My book." Opening the book, she flipped pages and ran a finger down.

"Ah, here. *Cachorro Gruñón*." She didn't know any of her customers' real names in case the police ever tracked her down. She gave us code names, and I got Grouchy Puppy, as I'd started buying from her when we'd first moved to New York. I'd been seventeen. Apparently that had gotten me "Puppy." "Grouchy" I'd earned on my own. She always tried to get me to smile. At that point I was being chased by the entire Auphe race. I didn't have a lot to smile about.

"Yes, *tsk*, you take vacation? You should be low on everything. Explosive rounds. Jaivin made a good batch last night. Your usual forty?"

"Nah. Thirty should do it. They're not quite getting it done on my current job. What I really need is about twenty grenades," I'd want some spares around if we survived Janus. "C4 with military detonators, all you have. A grenade launcher. A little more distance than my pitching arm would be a good thing."

Her round face beamed. "With this, I might get the butt lift too. Very popular in Brazil." She wrote a couple of check marks in her book and then, unusually, scribbled what looked like three words. "I am sorry, *Cachorro*. I sold my last grenade launcher last week. Am waiting on new batch to fall off truck. But lucky, lucky you, *bebé*, I have something that would have you spit on that. I have a thing of such beauty. For almost a year, it sits sad and unwanted on the shelf. I should know you would be the one to buy it. To appreciate the *virilidad magnifico*."

I knew a few Spanish words, but that wasn't one of them. I glanced at Nik. "Virility," he supplied dryly. That sounded right. If it swung a bigger metaphorical dick than a grenade launcher, bring it on.

She opened yet another door at the back of the room and shouted, "Marco, bring us the Javelin."

That word I knew, and not in the Olympic throwing-competition category. "You have an antitank *rocket*?" I asked, incredulous at that as I was at the fact that her tube top was staying up.

"An antitank system." She planted a kiss on my cheek. I could feel the thick coating of bright red lipstick. I carefully waited to wipe it off until she was focused on Niko. Do not offend the woman with the antitank system. "Your puppy brother. He has vision and like all good men knows the perfect tool for the job."

Niko said, "You mean as a terrorist would?"

She waved her hands vigorously. "I sell to no terrorist and your brother has good heart. He doesn't want to think so. He hides it. But one day, you will see, your brother is a hero. One day he might save the world. My *abuela* had the sight. Me some too. You will see."

Before I could tell her she'd better get some glasses for that sight, as she was way off about world saving and hearts, she was shouting again. "Marco, you lazy, worthless bastard. I have the order of the week. Are you back there with the porno magazines pulling on your *polla* again? I told you next time I would cut it off and bake it in a turkey-apple cobbler." That was the Thanksgiving special. "This is work time, not *pervertido* time."

Marco was up for the list in less than five seconds and his belt was buckled in the wrong hole, pants bagging low on his hips. I wouldn't be eating the cobbler here for a while, on Thanksgiving or otherwise. While he was back pulling the inventory, Rapture added up the bill. "Since you are good customer, *Cachorro*, I will give you discount." That and the fact that she was having a hard time selling the antitank rocket. Discount or no, it was about half a year's pay. It was a good thing I'd brought almost all the cash we had on hand, because at this rate we'd be lucky to pay the six-fifty toll on our way to Tilden.

When we left, I was carrying three large bakery bags by white twine handles. Each bag had pink boxes with RAPTURE'S BUNS written in flowing white script. The boxes were cake-size but held C4, detonators, grenades, and a small box of explosive rounds. Niko was carrying the Javelin on his shoulder. It was wrapped in brown paper painted and dried ahead of time with garlic butter. As far as anyone was concerned, he was toting a piece of Italian bread almost four feet long . . . and close to thirty pounds.

"Grouchy Puppy." This time Niko did laugh as we walked along the sidewalk waiting for Kalakos to come by. "She labeled you impeccably on your first visit."

"I wouldn't push it." I snorted. "She thinks you're my 'hot brother.' She's got brand-new boobs ready to try out. I could tell her you're up for some mountain climbing."

Before he could get me back, and he would have, his cell rang. It was Promise. Robin's condo was empty; his phone was gone; nothing appeared out of the ordinary except that our couch was still beside his. Salome and Spartacus weren't perturbed. What would perturb a dead cat, I didn't know, but they were batting around an old skull Goodfellow had given them. Yorick. It was their favorite toy. It seemed as if Goodfellow had taken his cell phone and gone. "What about his coat?" I prodded Niko. "He wouldn't go out without his coat to cover his sword."

Promise's answer to that was that he had so many coats that Armani flew him free to Italy every year for the new line, and how could she possibly know if he'd gone on his own with a coat and sword or unwillingly without either.

Shit. Now I was worried. But it was Janus and Grimm prep time. Niko asked Promise to try to find the puck. We needed her help, but Robin might need it more. She said she would do her best. I heard her voice from Niko's cell. Her best didn't sound too enthusiastic. Granted, Goodfellow had tried to steal Niko from her, but Niko was straight. She should be over that. He had stolen some jewelry from her, had orgies in her penthouse when he'd been hiding out there on the run from an ancient Arabian death squad. He'd tried to give her two undead mummified cats out of the eleven I'd dumped in his condo. When she turned them down, he'd waited until she was out at dinner with Niko one night and given her three instead. Each had engraved collars: Vlad, Spike, and Elvira.

And they wouldn't leave. As strong and quick as vampires are, Promise hadn't been able to catch a single one. She was stuck with them and not a cat person. Every cat person knows that not liking them makes cats like you and enjoy torturing you all the more. I had no sympathy. If you weren't an undead mummified cat person, there was something wrong with you.

"She sounded pissed," I said after he disconnected.

"She is—a good deal lately."

Women, can't live with them. Can't screw them without passing on monster-Auphe babies. It wasn't fair.

"Maybe it's because the cats line up on her headboard and watch the two of you when you have sex?" I suggested. "Jesus, finally. There's Kalakos." I waved him down.

"How did you . . ." Niko frowned. "I meant, that does not happen."

I grinned at him. "Mummy cats talk, and I don't know how, but Salome talks to Goodfellow." I didn't think she actually did. It was another trickster lie for the entertainment of it. "He had some tips for the two of you, but I told him if he wanted to keep his head, he might want to forget about that." I put the bags in the trunk and went around to the passenger seat. Kalakos moved to the back and had the antitank rocket dumped in his lap by Nik. Hard. Who was the grouchy puppy now?

Niko got in the driver's seat, silent until we were at the Brooklyn Bridge. "That son of a bitch."

"He did say there was a position called the Seventh Posture from a book called *The Perfumed Garden* that for the not very skilled would improve—" I ducked and his hand smacked the window glass of the passenger door instead of me.

"One more word and that antitank rocket will be used on you, not Janus," he threatened. He wasn't serious, not completely serious. The thought of the puck having eyes and ears in your bedroom, that was worse than a sex tape on the Internet. That might be worse than anything in creation.

"We have an antitank rocket?" Kalakos asked, lifting his hands cautiously off the package that lay across his lap.

"You are definitely not in the union. When this is over, you should retire and go home to roll dice with the old men," I said lazily, before tossing him one of the dozen cupcakes Rapture had given us. "A rocket is nothing.

"We once had a nuke."

21

It was about seven when we made it past Rockaway Boulevard, turned left, and found a well-hidden restricted road. Restricted meaning: Park Here, Please. Niko drove around the horizontal metal pole that acted as a gate and his junkmobile disappeared into the tall grass. There was salt water saturating the air, and the sun hung low in a clear violet sky. If you were into nature, it was the place to visit.

Goodfellow hadn't visited. He hadn't shown up or called and Promise hadn't found him yet at any of his usual haunts. Worried as I was, there was nothing we could do. Janus and Grimm would be coming soon. When the sun set would be a good guess. Grimm would think the dark would give him an advantage, but around Janus it wasn't completely dark, with the red light pouring from its eyes and the cracks between the metal shields that constructed its outer shell.

I checked my phone one more time in case somehow I'd missed a call. Nothing. *Shit.* We were all, him and us, on our own now. At least he wasn't going to be around Janus. That was something. A bleak hope but better than none at all. We hoisted the bakery bags and our other equipment and started hiking through the grass. It was taller than waist-high, not good terrain for the type of fighting we planned on. Or Nik and I planned on. Kalakos was protective of Niko now and a damn good sword fighter, but I'd told him before: He was out of his league. He was a babe in the woods with this gear, and babies didn't need to be touching explosives or things that set them off.

When we reached the Battery Harris East portal we pried open the gates with a crowbar and not a lot of effort. Nothing erodes like salt water. We walked down the middle of the battery corridor and the two metal frames of what had once been working train tracks. My footsteps gritted against the concrete dust. Niko and Kalakos were ghosts. "What was this place?" Kalakos studied the passage and the graffiti on the walls.

"The Battery Harris. A battery for a gun, one of two large ones, during World War Two. The cannons were sixteen-inch bore, something for their time. The east and west batteries are about two hundred feet long, fifty feet tall, and eventually covered in concrete to keep the guns from being used against the country back then." When Grimm had said Fort Tilden was the place, Niko had researched it until there was nothing he didn't know about it. "It's a tourist attraction now during the day."

I jiggled our bags. "But maybe not after tomorrow."

"Behave. Don't bounce the weapons of mass destruction," Niko said.

"It's C4," I complained. "Stable as it comes. More a weapon of minidestruction." Depending on how much you had. If we weren't used to keeping our identity hidden and avoiding credit cards, real or fake, like the plague, I'd have said we would've maxed them out on what I was hauling. All right, I'd give it to Nik . . . mass destruction wasn't totally out of the ballpark.

Coming out into the open between the east and west batteries we kept moving as I said, "This is good. Like you said, Nik. It's practically a small coliseum. Grimm will eat this up. Lions and Christians, bread and circuses." The two structures about two hundred or more feet from each other hemmed in either end, and vegetation, thick and tightly intertwined, had grown tall enough to provide a natural wall on each side. It really was the next-best thing to a coliseum. Where was Russell Crowe in his leather skirt when you needed him?

Grimm hadn't specified where at Fort Tilden he wanted us, but he wouldn't have any difficulty. Either he would pick up our scent or Janus would find us, however Janus did that. We had problems, but that wasn't one of them. After walking another hundred feet out of the first battery, I put down the bags and started opening cake boxes to mold gray bricks around the base of the powder magazine that sat square on the combination concrete road and track. It was about twenty feet high and had a large square entrance that the ammunition train would've gone through.

"How do you know for certain that's where they'll be?" Niko asked.

"Looking down on my victims, held up like an emperor, with my unstoppable gladiator beside me. It's where I'd stand . . . if I were Grimm. Arrogant, remember?" I activated the receivers and handed Niko one of the two detonators I had. "Just in case."

In case I lost mine or had no heartbeat or fingers left to press the button. The customary precautions. Then I took one of the two duffel bags we'd given a mystified Kalakos to carry and took out a can of spray paint. Neon glow-in-the-dark red. Another prop to Grimm's ego. Niko had been right.

Practical was the way to go.

Playing the Auphe game for a human reason wasn't.

And I thought people couldn't change. This was me changing my ways.

As Niko observed, I shook the can and sprayed a large circle around the magazine. I'd stomped down the shorter grass that had sprung up through the cracks in the concrete and the paint went on fairly evenly. Outside of the circle I sprayed symbols. They looped, came to odd points, tangled with one another, turned jagged, insane, and forbidding as anything written.

"And that would be?" he questioned. I hadn't mentioned this part to Nik. It wasn't a weapon, unless you counted psychological ones. It might not do shit, but then again it might. If ever there was a time to pull out all the stops, this was it.

"Grimm can't speak Auphe." I started spraying the English translation in yet another ring around it. "He hates that. He hates that I can. From the two years they had me, I know some. I don't remember it, like I don't remember anything else from then. If I tried to say something in it now, I couldn't. It just comes to me . . . sometimes. But Grimm doesn't know that." He'd know . . . *know* that I thought I was more Auphe than he was, mouthing their dead words, but Grimm didn't know anything about what I felt when it came to that.

It didn't mean it wouldn't burn his *ass*.

For a guy who thought he was superior to the Auphe, he had a thing about which of us had the most of them in us. He was a conflicted son of a bitch. Black sheep often were. Your family of monsters throws you in a cage and has you tortured and you hate them for it. Your family of monsters throws you in a cage and has you tortured, but you want their acceptance.

Now, *that* was pathetically human.

"How often is sometimes?" Niko inquired, hiding that he was uneasy about that. But not hiding it very well.

"Hardly ever. Like two or three times when I was really pissed off, but only with Auphe." Or the Auphe in me. "Nobody else brings it out." I finished up and stood to look at my masterpiece. The English read, "It's only an illiterate human half-breed with the cock of a herpes-ridden, snake-raping sheep who can't speak or read the tongue of the First."

"Grammatically atrocious, but effective," Niko admitted.

"Grimm is as conceited as you"—I elbowed my brother—"about his intelligence. This has a chance of pissing him off so badly that control will be the last thing on his mind."

Kalakos glanced at the circles and rapidly away. "Evil magic," he said with dark accusation. "Those are the words of demons. They will drive us to madness."

"Unless I spray it in your eyes, it won't do shit to you or anyone." I snorted and tossed the empty can of paint to Nik. "The Auphe spoke, but they didn't write. No written language. I copied this from that spooky little girl two blocks down who's always writing on the sidewalk. It's gibberish."

"Actually I think it's Hungarian." Niko tilted his head.

Huh. "Could be. Her place smells of goulash a lot. The good spicy kind."

He put the paint can in his bag, folded up the bakery boxes and bags, and stuffed them in there too before splitting the grenades between the two of us. "I'll be at twelve o'clock. Kalakos at eight. You at four. Let's not make goulash of one another. Kalakos, stay back as far as you can until we blow it all. Once the C4 goes—and if it doesn't do the job—you won't have accurate enough hearing to count the grenades." He started to offer the Javelin to me, but I shook my head.

"Grimm will definitely be after me. Janus could be after us all. Better you have it. The instruction manual's taped to the side." One last joke.

"And I get nothing?" Kalakos demanded. "I can and have fought with the best of them. I helped Niko escape the Cyclops. If this is all you expect of me, you should've left me in the car until it was done."

"You ever used a grenade?" I asked. "A rocket? A goddamn nuke? I didn't think so. If I'm going to be killed, I'd rather it be by Janus or Grimm than because you miscounted and threw a grenade down my throat. So hang back. Niko and I will be doing the same thing. And if we're screwed and none of the explosives do the job—here." I gave him back his xiphos. "So far it's the only thing that has made Janus think twice."

I slapped Niko on his shoulder. "See you when I see you."

He cuffed the back of my head as he walked behind me to pick up his bag. "The Javelin has night sight. I'll be seeing you the whole time."

"Wait." I pulled a ponytail holder out of my pocket . . . the hell with Kalakos's identical one . . . and yanked my hair back tightly. Praise Jesus. I could see. "And now I can see you. Later, big brother."

He lifted his hand, his lips curled smugly, having gotten his way. "Later, little brother."

We all separated and headed into three different directions, burrowing into the greenery. It was almost impossible, it being as unyielding and densely woven as a prison fence, but using my combat knife, I made my way in about six feet. Grimm would know I was there. He would find me by scent and feel me as well. But knowing I was there and knowing where I was within several feet weren't the same.

Six feet back, he wouldn't see me, as the branches, leaves, and grass had all sprung back into place—which was important. He wore those sunglasses all the time for a reason, and not just because his eyes were red. I hadn't inherited the Auphe heightened ability to see in the dark, but it was safe to say he had. Six feet back and hidden by nature. Six feet close and ready to blow the C4 with backup grenades in the smallish bag that I had looped from left shoulder to right hip. It woudn't interfere much if I had to unholster my Glock with my left hand while either setting off the detonator with my right or using it to throw grenades. All assuming my left hand cooperated.

I flexed it and gritted my teeth. I straightened it, then flexed it again. This time I tasted the blood of a teeth-torn bottom lip. Now I knew. Cooperation was not on the menu, but I'd make do. If it's not broken or severed, you can make it work and the hell with the pain. I wasn't taking the pain pills. I'd rather hurt than lose my edge. I checked my phone one more time. It was the same. Nothing. *Goddamn it, Goodfellow,* I thought, *your horny ass had better be alive.* Then I turned the phone to vibrate and slipped it in my front jeans pocket.

The sun set and Mars rose. Mosquitoes swarmed about, but after one bit me, it and the others buzzed off. Like that succubus had once made clear: They did not like the way I tasted. I was about to check the phone again when I felt him.

Grimm was here. On the beach maybe. I didn't try to

see. It would be impossible through the New York version of the Amazon jungle. And if he was on the beach, he wouldn't be there long. I was right. I could feel him moving . . . gating . . . triangulating our scent. There was the familiar flash of gray, silver, and black light on top of the Battery East and then they were there . . . on the powder magazine.

The king of the Second Coming and his malignant windup toy.

It was dark, but the night wasn't as deep as you'd think. Janus glowed. I thought it would, but not like this. The crimson, in heat and color, that outlined each metal shield that scaled him like a dragon lit up the entire top of the powder magazine. Its eyes were lamps to lead the dead, and the face with the grinning mouth and pointed ebony teeth was half turned my way. I could see the liquid twin to lava running slowly out of its mouth. Whatever had made this had made it in a volcano and you couldn't tell me any different. Its mouth wasn't big enough to throw virgins into, but other than that . . . volcano god.

"I like this place, Caliban," Grimm said as the gate died around him and Janus. "If nothing else, you take the game higher with every throw of the dice and rattle of the bones." The light from Janus was enough to let me see the half Auphe take a step to see over the side of their royal stage. He wanted a three-sixty view of his victory ring. He got something else instead. He walked the top, all four sides, reading the Hungarian goulash recipe and the English pseudo-translation that went with it. Every word that shone on the ground.

Graffiti to outrage the ego.

When he finished, he halted, facing me precisely. I'd been wrong that he couldn't nail down my precise location, but I hadn't been wrong about his being pissed. His eyes made the long-set sun as nothing. His Auphe teeth were down, the silver reflecting the red aura around the magazine, turning the metal needles into flickering flames.

"Why would I want to befoul my tongue or my eyes with the scribbling of a race that let one miserable half human destroy what was left of it?" He didn't gate to the ground. He leaped, hitting the dirt at the base of the magazine. He made the jump down as if it had been three feet instead of twenty. It threw me off. My thumb was on the detonator, but I'd expected to see the swirl of a gate as I pressed the button. The physical action of it rather then the Auphe one put me off for a fraction of a second before I recovered.

The detonator Rapture had sold me had an inch-tall antenna and was small enough to fit in the palm of my hand. I'd dealt with C4 once or twice—some monsters are bigger than others—but I hadn't used this much of it before on any job. It should have an approximate blast zone of thirty feet. I pressed the button on the detonator and blew that motherfucker before Grimm could gate this time or take a single step. There was a very nonstereotypical war-movie boom. Or rather . . .

BOOM!

Holy shit. As far back as I'd been, six feet into the weeds, which was a good fifty feet from the powder magazine, I was thrown back farther. I didn't have any idea how far. The branches and twigs of the wild bushes whipped at me as I was tossed, but didn't make it through my jacket. As I'd been crouching when I set off the explosive, my back was clearing a path for me. When I landed, I considered myself pretty damn lucky.

And then something else landed . . . on top of me.

Grimm. The son of a bitch had escaped a mess of C4. *Outgated* an explosion that to human eyes would be instantaneous. Why the hell he wanted my help, I was beginning to wonder. Why he was enraged I could speak Auphe and he couldn't, that I knew. The Auphe had made him and thrown him away like garbage. Said he was garbage. He hated them, but he wanted to prove to them they were wrong. He was something they couldn't have thought possible to create: He was the first of nature's second big fucking mistake, not the Bae. No supernatural creature thought the Auphe evolved—why would the perfect predator need to evolve? Yet they had. Grimm wanted to prove it to them, except they were gone and I was the only thing left of them. But why he thought I could be his equal, was almost his equal, was fit to wipe his royal Bae-siring ass, much less help breed his race, I didn't know.

Outgated a fucking explosion. *Jesus.*

His man-made curved claws dug into my shoulder, his knee bearing all his weight was wedged against my crotch, and his hundreds of hypodermic-needle teeth were pressed against mine. I was grimacing. He was smiling. The fact that pain was peeling my lips back and rage his nevertheless had the same effect. "You insult me. You insult yourself. You're a fool, but a fool I will give one last chance. Come to the Bae or I'll rip off your face and your balls. But I won't kill you. Not for hours. Not until there is nothing to remove from your bones." His breath had the sweet fragrance of raw meat on it. The warmth of copper. The odor of death.

Sweet. It smelled sweet.

Things that are meant for you. Tell him yes. Be the Bae with him. The Second Coming is for you and him. And you want it. To rule. To kill. To make it better than before.

I held tight to the control that hadn't let me down yet. Those thoughts weren't true. Not unless I let them be. *Not true,* I repeated silently to myself. *Not true.* I had the power to deny them and I would. But they were . . .

Practical.

Be practical.

If you couldn't keep that part of you from whispering slyly, demanding harshly, stop ignoring it—*use* it.

Temporarily and with a different type of control.

Four years old and I'd known what to do. I damn sure wasn't going to do any less at twenty-four.

I didn't fight it. Grimm was better than me—now. Fighting what was in me wouldn't change that, and fighting it didn't make me more human, only not as Auphe as I could be. And I could be much, much more. I'd tainted a good deal of my soul, if it existed, for control and now I was going to intentionally give it up, turn it off, push it aside. I'd have to have faith I'd be able to get it back. I'd have to believe *I'd* come back. A child's assurance told me I would. I chose to believe him.

I let it go.

Let . . . it . . . go.

Things changed. My desire to join Grimm changed and it changed in all the best ways.

Join him? The laughter echoed in me—derisive, disgusted. *He is a failure. No matter what he can do* now, *there will come a* then. *Auphe are not wrong in our judgments. He was a failure once. He will be a failure again. The Bae and the Second Coming are not his. They are mine. They are mine because I will take them and fix them.*

Building is the sheep way. Taking is the Auphe way.

I'd been fishing my hand in the bag on the ground by my hip. He was watching for a move toward my holsters. I gave him a different one. I pulled the ring on a grenade and shoved it down the front of his jeans. "They can sew my balls back on. They'll need a microscope to find what's left of yours," I snarled. "Good luck knocking up the snakes by wishing real fucking hard."

His snarl matched mine and he flung himself off of me, retrieved the grenade, and tossed it where it exploded off in the brush. He could've gated out of his clothes, leaving the grenade behind too, but that would be Auphe. Fighting naked—the highest of predators, but animals too. No clothes. No history and education to refine your plans. The highest, yes, but unchanged for millions of years. They didn't advance in their ways, didn't retreat. A human would think that primitive.

Caliban would think it practical. Didn't I? Why do you need weapons when you are one? Why do you need clothing when you can kill and luxuriate in the warmth among the bodies of your fresh prey? Why learn when you are the only thing worth learning about in a world that belongs to you?

"*Sheep*." I said it in Auphe that the failure couldn't understand.

"Never even a black sheep, failure. Only a malformed human sheep." I said that in English so that he would understand it this time—to hear his shame, one no greater. "You *are* human, the Auphe in you barely a single cell. Any race you create with succubae is already polluted twice over. Yet I can make them right."

By wiping them out.

I had the patience the failure only thought he had. I could wait until I finally became all Auphe. The Auphe genes in me wouldn't stop their progress—ever. A trillion clocks ticking away inside until the day I was pure Auphe.

I would take his succubae, and then I would undo his

Bae until they were nothing but piles of bloody *parts* and start again when the time came. Make them as Auphe as they could be until they too one day became pure. The mongrels he'd created—I could be patient, but I didn't have a million years for them to turn. Half-pure—my race would be whole far sooner than that.

"You think you can do better than I have?" he growled.

"I know I can." This time I pulled the Eagle and emptied the clip at his head. "Because I am Auphe."

Inside now and, with time enough, I would be outside as well.

I gave him a grin and then the worst threat tailor-made for him. "The single one left. Auphe live free to kill." I grinned wider. "Human failures go back to their *cages*."

He'd gated as I pulled the trigger, but I was already turning, faster than I'd ever moved in my life, to where I felt reality ripple behind me. I was firing the Glock this time before the gate even opened. I hit him several times in the chest in that one second before he disappeared again.

"So long, *brother*." The sneer wasn't on my face, but the word was soaked with it. I didn't think he'd be coming back for a while if at all. That gave me time.

Things to do. Track him or his corpse down. Him and his Bae bastards, his succubae breeding ground. My succubae breeding ground. They were long-lived. They could wait as long as I could for my last human cell to die, gobbled up and transformed to something far superior. Then the first race to walk the earth, the first to discover the pleasure of murder, the Cains of the supernatural world—we would return.

No.

I cocked my head to the side. What was that?

I'd heard ... What had I heard? A voice. Small, but determined.

No. Caliban time is over. No more practical today. It's Cal time again. They were the words of a four-year-old. Familiar. Firm. Undeniable.

Me.

I hissed with rage as I felt the shadows creep away at the order of a four-year-old kid twice as smart as Cal. I stubbornly refused to reach for the control they revealed. It reached for me instead. Caliban became Cal again—if we'd been separate to begin with. I hadn't lost control as I used to in the past. I'd purposely put it aside, but it remained a hard-won part of me as much as the Auphe was a part. As I'd known since my last visit to Nevah's Landing, we were one, a disagreeable, highly conflicted one, but one.

The kid I had once been was right. I would come back from any future trips to Auphe land and those trips could be nothing but deliberate and by choice.

For now.

How long would now last?

But it wasn't time for thinking about the future when the present had gone to hell, no road of good intentions needed to lead the way. I heard, "Cal, move!" and jerked my head up in time to see Janus, wreathed with smoke, but still intact except for the original missing claw-hand. He was rushing me, and Niko was behind him with the antitank rocket.

It reminded me bizarrely of the old Road Runner cartoons. Explosives, grenades, antitank rocket and a determined coyote, and it was then that it struck me that the poor furry bastard had gotten screwed by Acme's products every damn time and we weren't doing any better.

I lunged sideways, heard the rocket fire and hit Janus in the back. It knocked it forward, but not off its feet. It went down to all fours, claws digging into the earth, its head spinning slowly. One face smiling, one frowning. Over and over.

Scrambling off to the other side away from Niko where we wouldn't be one concentrated target, I shouted, "You've got to be shitting me! C4 and the rocket?"

"And all of my grenades. Don't bother wasting yours," Niko called back grimly.

But I did have to when Janus staggered back up, shaking the ground, and came after me again. Mr. Popularity, that was me. I ran. I wasn't as fast as when I'd been Caliban, and that was a problem, because Janus was quick enough that he was a blur of metal and flame. Throwing another grenade, I kept going, barely avoiding the claws reaching for my legs. One more explosion to Janus, and nothing compared to the C4 and rocket. He went down and was up again faster this time.

That's when Niko ran between us, his xiphos up. He was trying to distract Janus from me and annoy him with the xiphos, which was the full extent of its powers I'd seen so far. And where the fuck was Kalakos? He wanted his role in the battle. Well, here it was. I started to yell his name when Niko found a way to make the sword do something else than only annoy the automaton. He arched his arm back and threw it directly in the boiling red left eye. There was a sound, metallic and buzzing but louder, as if Janus had swallowed a hundred chain saws. It staggered in a weaving circle. Niko pushed at me. "We have to find Kalakos and his sword."

I was already moving, but as I ran I felt it in my pocket. My cell phone was vibrating. I snatched it and held it to my ear. "Way to go with the goddamn impeccable timing, Goodfellow!" I snapped. I heard frantic noises, but they weren't loud enough to register as words. *Shit.* I couldn't imagine it could be as important as being halfway to dead, and shoved it back in my pocket, still running. It vibrated again.

"Motherf—" I cut myself off. I could be wrong. With Robin it might be that important. I switched to text and read as I ran and yelled for Kalakos all at once. After I read it again, I stopped and I didn't shout for Kalakos again. From what I was reading, he was the last person we wanted around.

I was on the other side of the powder magazine, and with one eye black and dead, as I'd done to Boggle, Janus was walking through the rubble of it that now stood less than four feet high. I was on the automaton's blind side until its head started to turn again. I crouched down in the bushes. Kalakos, the son of a bitch, stood, rising opposite me on the other side of the clearing. Only the red light and his dark blond hair let me spot him. For all his complaining, it didn't look like he was in any hurry to join the fight.

And I knew why.

"I saw you, Caliban." With my pale skin, no one had much problem seeing me.

Kalakos had shouted, but his voice was piercing, deep, and full of the contempt I'd expected at the beginning when he'd first shown up at our door.

A Vayash, proving you should always judge a book by its cover. "I saw you on your phone. You looked surprised, although not as surprised as I expected. A father touches his son, who in turn touches his brother. You accepted me if only for him. Family can be a joyous and yet woefully naïve thing."

His smile was my smile, the one I gave the worst of

my enemies . . . the moment before I ended them in metal and mortality, guts and gore. I should've been his son, not Niko.

"That horny goat who's been missing, let me guess. He had something to tell you, didn't he?"

Robin had. There had been a secret code, commands in a long-lost language, but with each new buyer, they were changed to the new language. Mutable, as Dodger had said. Adusted to the new owner's language of choice. And wouldn't that make sense? You don't sell a car but refuse to give over the keys. The commands had been changed to Rom when Hephaestus had given Janus to the Vayash for safekeeping, and hardly a burden when you thought about it. He was an unplugged toaster for all the guarding or care he needed. The Vayash knew turning him on in this modern day and age wasn't an option. And they weren't murderers. Some were con artists, bounty hunters; some got by doing honest odd jobs; some were thieves. They were all different, the same as any other people.

Except when it came to their real burden. Then they were all killers with one truly exceptional assassin, a man who could fight like Niko but lacking the conscience of his son, and he was ready to do what had to be done. Grimm hadn't stolen Janus from the Rom. No one had.

We were separated now, the four of us. We stood at the four points of a rectangle. If I could hear again from the rocket's explosion—well enough, anyway—Niko would be able to as well. If I wished him deaf for a few minutes, I thought he would understand. He was staring at Kalakos now. He had heard what was said about Goodfellow and the derision that had been unmatched by the *paien* in the black market. The monsters didn't hate me as much as my former clan did.

"Janus is not the Vayash burden I came for." He pointed his sword at me. "While some burdens are to be kept, some duties to be honored, some are to be destroyed. Janus is an obedient tool if used wisely; you, Auphe freak, are a chaotic nightmare and we will carry you no more."

"Goodfellow says the Rom can waken Janus by the blood from the death of one of their own clan. Their burden. Their blood. You killed your own clan members just to flip a switch and turn him on like a goddamn vacuum cleaner?" I growled.

"Only the one. There was no second victim. That was an embellishment to the story, as all good stories have. I was certain I could do you on my own ... easily. I am Achilles reborn, but the others insisted I use Janus. Their fear of you is that deep that they cannot believe a human would be a match for you. That meant the sacrifice was necessary. Lots were drawn. It was a good death. A death to restore his clan's honor among the other Rom. He went willingly and I made it painless."

His smile wasn't mine any longer. It wasn't the imitation of Nik's. It was that of a ruthless murderer, one who'd slaughtered more than one before coming after me; I knew it. It was the smile of someone who belonged on death row with a needle in his arm. An arrogant, sociopathic asshole who should be put in a grave and nowhere else.

"Relatively painless, at least. And he was sixteen without having stuck his dick in a woman yet. As lives go, his was a waste anyway. If he screamed and cried for his mother"—that smile let me know he had—"blame yourself. It'd been a long time between hunts, and that is thanks to you, freak. No Rom will speak to us or hire me. We are dead to them. We have been cast out by all the clans due to our shame, so our shame must end that our exile can end." That goddamn smile. I'd cut it off his face. "I do miss my work. Killing and raping at random is good for fending off boredom, but it doesn't pay. I want my old life back. All the Vayash do."

"And for that Cal has to end," Niko said. "You fooled us so well. No, you fooled me. Nothing but suspicion from the beginning and you still fooled me. Let me guess. You healed Cal so we wouldn't begin moving him to hide him from your machine. It would give Janus time to find us again."

"Which would've worked perfectly if the abomination hadn't used his unholy door to carry us away to the house of the goat," he growled. The smile was gone now, his sword twisting back and forth in his hand. "Then worse, yet *another* abomination appears and steals Janus. Pulling it here and there through that same unholy doorway. Leaves it in the park to do what war machines do when their target isn't there: mangle and destroy whatever is."

Grimm *had* stolen Janus, but not for long and not in the beginning. He'd seen a toy and a way to taunt me and he'd taken it, probably from our place after it had attacked us there. Grimm and his goddamn binoculars. He could see me, but I couldn't feel him.

He hadn't directed the titan or known how. He simply turned it loose to see what it would do, and death and destruction was it. He didn't know it was centered on me or he would've turned it loose a little closer . . . just to see what I would do. No one played games like Grimm, even accidentally.

"You targeted it on Cal." Now Niko's other sword was in his hand. "Specifically. You came to me. You asked for my help. You saved my life with Hephaestus. You tried to save my life with the boggles, or pretended to, so Cal along with Goodfellow would drown in mud or be killed by the Boggle below. You asked to claim me as a son. And you did it all to murder my brother."

"Never have I told so many lies that made me want to bite off my tongue. You're the son of a slut and a whore. Why would I claim you? I saved you to gain further acceptance. To stay with you. I was at the point where I was going to slit the freak's throat myself no matter what the clan wanted. I could stand no more of you demons. Sharing the same space with you, eating with you—all of you unclean and debase. Your kind and all you touch contaminate me. It was disgusting enough that I think I deserve a bonus for all of this. I'll bury the burden myself, but first I'll have Janus wipe the world of my first and only mistake." He turned and said something in rapid-fire Rom to the automaton and then pointed the xiphos at Niko.

Janus had been reprogrammed.

Kalakos was dead. Achilles reborn, my fucking ass. He was *dead*.

Somehow.

Niko didn't stand around waiting for his fate. He ran. Quicker than Cal could, but not as quickly as when I let out the Auphe in me. But neither human nor Auphe matched the titan. I was running too, and although fast as shit, I wouldn't break any world records with it. But I could throw like a son of a bitch. Could've been a baseball star in another life. "Nik!" I pulled off the bag and strap and tossed it farther than I could ever run.

He caught it and didn't stop running and dodging claws scoring the ground behind him. He took one grenade from the bag, flipped the spoon, pulled the pin, and dropped it back in the bag with the others. Then he somersaulted sideways as Janus's last tangle of metal talons buried themselves up to its wrist in the dirt where Niko had been less than a moment before. Nik didn't take advantage to get more space between them. He propelled himself toward the automaton, which had dropped to one knee to pull its killing claws free. Niko used that. He—counting off the grenade's six seconds, because I sure as hell was—planted a foot on Janus's knee and, taking advantage of its blind eye with the sword embedded in it, used the thrust of the forward motion to leap high enough to hang the bag around the titan's neck.

I blinked and he was gone, already running as I'd not seen him run before, and Niko was the fastest human I'd seen in my lifetime. Counting the short three to four seconds he had left, he would make it out of the blast zone. I knew it.

I knew it because if there was an Achilles reborn it wasn't that bastard Kalakos.

It was my brother.

A warrior from the womb. A reluctant warrior, but a warrior like the world hadn't seen in thousands of years.

I threw myself on the ground right before the grenades blew, closing my eyes against the fierce light and heat, and opening them immediately after to see Nik down, but because he'd done the same. He'd made it. I'd made it.

And so had that goddamn Janus. An explosive collar on a demonic metal dog and it didn't stop it from freeing its claws and rising to its feet. The ground shook under the weight and its head spun to move the blinded eye. It saw Niko climbing to his feet and raced toward him as if nothing had happened. How could something that heavy and made of metal move that goddamn fast?

If we'd had that suitcase nuke from a year and a half

ago, I didn't think that would have done a damn thing. It was indestructible. We weren't. We were good at what we did, but with the biggest disadvantage around when we could die and it couldn't.

Niko was weaponless now except for his various swords that would do no good, the same as my guns. Useless. If he managed to get to Kalakos and use his sword to blind another eye, what would that do? Janus would have two left and that was enough.

It wouldn't have made a difference if it had had only two eyes. I could see it run as Niko turned and ran again. It would reach him before he could reach Kalakos. Better than human, better than a crippled Auphe, what do you do then?

Nothing . . . nothing that would work.

I didn't care if it would work. I did it anyway.

Other than hurling myself in front of Niko before the automaton could reach him, there wasn't anything I could do—and I was too far away from them both with the titan's speed to do even that. I pushed up off the ground and ran. It was hopeless, but I did it, because that's what you do. Deny reality. Deny you won't make it in time. You do your best to throw yourself between your brother and death whether it will save him or not. You shred your lungs, seizing more oxygen than is possible, tear tendons to gain ground with a flight that isn't there. You do the physically impossible.

You died for your brother or you died with your brother. *Watching* him die was the impossibility.

It was just what you fucking . . .

Goodfellow.

Goodfellow—he'd told me about Janus's commands. And about more. He'd found out how to wake Janus and how to put him back to sleep.

And they were the same.

I wasn't going to make it. I wasn't fast enough or close enough and had one more day before I could gate. One more damned day. The four-year-old me was wrong. There was time enough to be practical once more tonight. To trust myself one last time—the very last time. I didn't close my eyes. I didn't think about it or concentrate. I didn't focus. There was time to be four again, but there wasn't time for any of the rest.

I made the third gate.

The gate that would kill me.

Niko had stopped. He couldn't run anymore, but Niko was Niko. He would face death, not turn a cowardly back on it. He staggered and turned to face the blades of Janus's hand flying toward him. He faced it like the warrior he was. Across the circle, Kalakos, keeping his distance— another warrior but worthless, a fighter, but spineless— disappeared, haloed by dark-veined tarnished silver.

Wasn't that just too bad?

He *reappeared* in a haze of gray and black directly before Janus's outstretched claws thrusting through the air with such a swift velocity that the flash of them was only an afterimage. It was a titan. It had some abilities that couldn't be re-created these days. It was faster than an Auphe. . . .

But it wasn't an Auphe.

We had abilities too, and they beat speed-walking every fucking time.

The long-lost metal went completely through Kalakos to touch but not penetrate Niko's chest in the day's last red-stained impossibility. I saw Kalakos shudder, I saw his head fall back to gaze blindly at the sky, and I saw him die. With it I saw Janus go dark, the scarlet in it go black, and the automaton fall backward. Asleep again.

Vayash blood would awaken him and Vayash blood would send him back to sleep. For all that Kalakos had been a shit and a half, he had been Vayash. His blood did the trick, no problem. Niko. Niko I could see standing hardly a stone's throw away from it all.

Alive.

That was all I needed to see.

I closed my eyes as the darkness came.

All I needed . . .

22

"Cal, you didn't."

I heard Niko hitting the ground beside me where I lay on my back. It had all given way: my knees, my legs, my body. I'd fallen as well—as all monsters had, Janus and Kalakos, one with the earth. "*No*. You didn't do it. You didn't. Tell me. Tell me, you son of a bitch." This time he gripped my shoulders and shook them hard.

Being one with the earth wasn't as peaceful as you'd think.

He shook me again, with more force. "Cal, *tell* me.

"Tell me you wouldn't visit that nightmare on me." There was no resignation. There was demand, refusal, and fingers pressing to the bone in a grip that was absolute and eternal.

Painful as shit too.

"Yeah, sorry. I kind of did. And ow."

I opened my eyes and slid a hand under my head that my brother was knocking against the ground with the shaking. I had to give him a break on not picking up on the fact that I was breathing. With Janus inactive, it was dark now, and we'd been thoroughly conditioned to believe that making a third gate would burst my brain like an overfilled water balloon. Why wouldn't he think that I was gone?

And it had been true—about the third gate. I'd seen that when I'd tried to gate out of the basement when I was trapped with Grimm. A third gate had been impossible then, and impractical. I'd have killed myself but not him. But that had been two days ago.

"Buddha," he swore fervently. "How . . . No. Give me a moment." He felt my face for the blood a second gate would cause. There was a small nosebleed at best, less by far than the usual.

"I can wipe my own nose. I am a man after all, remember?" I held up my fist to show the ring he'd given me. You could hardly see it in the night gloom, but it was there. "I have proof." I brought my hand back and used the bandage on my left hand to soak up the slow-flowing smear of blood. "And I'm wiping, so why don't you take a break?"

"I think I will." He turned sideways and fell backward beside me. After a good five minutes, he said calmly, "I think you broke me."

"I can see that." If positions were reversed, I'd feel like a bag of shattered glass, slammed time and time again against a brick wall—every piece getting smaller and smaller. Disintegrating. "I had to, though. I didn't know it would work. Doubted like hell it would work, but I couldn't let them kill you. I . . . Hell, Nik . . . I couldn't, okay? When Janus almost killed me at the Ninth Circle, I didn't see you running for cover. It's no different."

"My father used me to try to murder you. It's different." There it was. The worst part of it all. Niko wouldn't have seen his father again if the man had been honest and the story the truth. It had been too late for that, but he would've had the memory of an apology and knowing that his father, whatever he was, was proud of him. Now he had worse than nothing. I had had a genuine monster for a father. Niko had had a human version of one.

"Neither of us has a father or a mother. Christ, Nik, haven't you always known that?" I finished soaking up the blood and watched the moon start to rise. "It's always been you and me growing up. No family except us. Why would it be different now?"

The grass rustled as he shook his head. "Why you pretend to be so lazy and a completely idiotic ass at times, I don't know. You're too smart for my own good. You're right. We're all the family we have or need."

"See? You should listen to me more often." I paused. "But I don't pretend to be lazy ... and I am an ass."

He laughed. It was a little choked but a laugh all the same. "How'd you do it? The third gate. How did it happen? Rafferty said his work on you couldn't be undone."

"It couldn't, I don't think. Not by anyone around now." There were sirens in the distance. Soon I'd have to gate us home and Kalakos and Janus to Tumulus for disposal, but not yet. It was warm; I could smell the ocean, maybe even see what I thought were stars. "Remember when we thought Rafferty was the best healer who had ever been born?"

"Difficult to forget," Niko said, now quietly somber. That had been a bad time.

"Remember how, after he rewired my gating ability and later fought Suyolak ..." Antihealer. The Plague of the World. Suyolak had thought he was hot shit, the hottest, and he'd been right. No one, including Rafferty, could match him. ". . . how Suyolak kicked his ass, dumping him down to second-best and almost dead healer?"

"Even more difficult to forget."

"When Kalakos gave you Suyolak's ointment, there was some left. Remember—"

"How you ran your finger around the box like it was an almost empty pudding bowl and ate it." He propped up on his elbows. "Quite a few 'remembers,' but I haven't forgotten."

I shrugged. "I didn't know if it would work and, if it did work, if it would take days, weeks, years. It was a shot in the dark."

What wasn't in our lives?

He let himself drop back again. "Random luck. What if it had taken weeks or months? Or not worked at all? You'd be dead." The sound of one hand clapping over his eyes lifted into the night. "God, I think you broke me twice now. You could be dead."

It was in no way his fault that his father was a homicidal psychopath, surprising me that he and Sophia hadn't gotten along better. He'd used Niko, and he'd used my wanting what was best for my brother to worm his way inside until he could kill me himself or recover Janus. I had meant it: Neither of us had parents. Kalakos was nothing more than a murderer, and if he'd been successful then I'd have been the equivalent of someone shot to death while mugged or eaten in Central Park. A victim of a monster. Nothing to do with Niko. Simply the wrong place, wrong time. But Niko would have to mull it over awhile before he let himelf off the hook. Until then he'd brood and feel guilty. He didn't deserve that, but he was stubborn and he'd hang on to that guilt but good. How'd you make that better?

"I could've died." I said it the same as I would say the sky was blue. Simple fact.

"Shut up," he snapped. "Just . . . shut up."

"Dying . . . scary fucking shit, right?"

"Shut *up*." That was Niko on the ragged edge.

I thought and uncrossed my arm from my chest and held it over to him. "Want to hold my hand? I think I'd feel better."

This time the laughter was real, the guilt was less, and I definitely saw stars above.

"You are such an ass." He snorted. He'd said that already, but I let it go.

"I told you not to trust a man who looked like that. Big nose. Blond hair and dark skin, that's just weird. Way too good with a sword. Obviously exercised too much. Probably liked bonsai trees and dating vampires too. Sign of a nut job right there."

He slapped me on the stomach and said it for the third time. "Complete and utter ass." This time we both laughed.

The stars were brighter than ever.

It was a great night.

"I can't believe you went back to Hephaestus to get the info on Janus." I put my feet up on the couch . . . it was in Robin's condo but it was still my couch. "And didn't tell us. He could've killed you. He should've killed you."

"You would've interfered. Besides, if I recall correctly, I outran every one of you on the first visit." He scratched Salome's bony butt as she hung around his neck while he peered in the refrigerator. "I'm starving. I save your lives and you don't even bring me a nice duck pizza home in gratitude."

"Sorry." I was damn hungry myself. I slid my phone out of my pocket, Grimm's claw marks in my shoulder howling in protest, but I felt too good otherwise to care. Grimm, Janus, and Kalakos: That was a hat trick nothing could ruin. "So ... when you went back to the armory, you pretended to be like Hob, thought like Hob to get Hephaestus to talk, didn't you? I know you didn't want to have to do that. Sorry," I repeated. I was too.

Robin closed the refrigerator door when he saw me ordering pizza and sat on his couch where Niko rested, Spartacus having half strangled himself in my brother's braid. "I didn't think like Hob. I won't do that. I cannot even step into his shoes. Walk the bloody road he traveled." So many of us with our dark and bloody roads. "It would suck me in. But I could do a pretense of a pretense. A poor imitation, the cheapest of Halloween masks, and his reputation preceded him. I was convincing enough to make Hephaestus think cooperation is a wonderful thing. He couldn't talk fast enough." His eyes were slitted at the memory. "He obviously had never crossed paths with the actual Hob. The first Hob."

"You were Hob once, weren't you?" The question, without judgment, came from Niko. As Niko was the one Hob had tried to sacrifice, it needed to.

"Yes." They were gone, the strange flashes that had obscured his normally wicked and sly ways. He'd always before clearly shown what he was. Not a fox with sour grapes—a fox with a ladder and someone dim enough to be convinced to climb it for him.

"The memories are long gone, but I know. First there was Hob and then there was me. The second puck to step foot to earth. Identical. Same body, same mind, same thoughts, same memories, same proclivities." Then again there was the quickest glitter in the eyes, but it passed. "Then, as all pucks do, I made new memories, developed my own singular personality, became not-Hob. But always I know what cast its reflection into me. Although I walked away, the mirror remains. If I stare into it, I'll see

my birth. I'll see what I was. If I see it, I'll remember it; if
I remember it, I'll become it . . . and Hob will live again."
He threw his own phone to me. "Forget the pizza. Call a
limo. We're going drinking and we're not stopping until
every damn drop of alcohol has been drunk and every
stripper spanked for being the bad, bad boy or girl they
are."

We let the subject drop as he wanted. After what he'd
done for us, we'd be bastards if we didn't.

"One thing bothers me. How did Grimm know Janus's name if he didn't steal him or know of his existence
to begin with?" Niko wondered. That brooding of my
brother's I'd worried about? It couldn't have lasted longer? No. *Crap.*

"I might have mentioned it in the basement where
Grimm had me," I mumbled. "He'd just said he gated
that metal monstrosity off of me in front of the bar, I said
'Janus,' and there you go. He was playing games with me,
testing me. I thought, Who more likely to steal something like that than a half Auphe? Little did I know it
was your dear old dad who was out to viciously mur . . .
Oh, hey, we need a limo at Rob Fellows's place." I didn't
bother to give an address. He was their most frequent
rider/drinker/horn-dog in the city. "Viciously murder
me," I went on after disconnecting. "I don't think one slip
of the tongue—"

"Leading us down a completely wrong path of investi-
gation while taking the real killer with us everywhere we
went," Niko completed caustically. Yeah, that guilt had
faded much quicker than I thought it would. "I was wrong.
You don't pretend to be lazy and idiotic. You *are* both."

"He held my hand when he thought I almost died," I
told Robin, tossing back the phone. "And although it was
too dark to see for sure, I think he might've cried."

"I did not. I shook you and pounded your head against the ground, which unfortunately didn't knock anything back into place." He frowned. I grinned. Giving up—a wise move on his part—he moved on. "Now, we may still have Grimm out there somewhere, and the Bae. He's been free twelve years. We guessed at best he could've reproduced thirty to fifty of the Bae. What do you think, Goodfellow? How many do we have to worry about?"

Robin shook his head. "I have no idea. Succubae usually lay only one egg when they reproduce. Who knows what will happen when they breed with a half Auphe? And how many succubae he has? I can't imagine it being more than fifty." He stood and grabbed his coat to head down for the limo. "Twelve years, and Artemis the fertile one knows how long it took him to find that succubae were compatible with a half Auphe. It couldn't have been more than eight years at the most. Fifty in eight years? I doubt it. Even I'm not that horny."

When Goodfellow was right, he was right.

It didn't get more logical than that.

23

Black Sheep

I had a teacher once. . . . I know. I had many, and many of them had tasted so good that I wondered if it was the meals I liked more than the learning. But one of my teachers had read a quote to his students by a human not as weak-minded as the others. I thought of it when I thought of my brother and the pain and burn of the bullet wounds in my chest. They would heal as all my wounds did and it was worth it to see what I'd seen. To hear what I'd heard. This long-dead human whose words were repeated to us should have met Caliban in the grass and fire, explosions and blood. Those words were something close to, "Whoever fights monsters should see to it that in the process he does not become a monster." That human would've known, seeing the face of Caliban, the flecks of red in the gray of his eyes, that his words had come far too late.

I smiled to myself, sitting on the ledge of the desert cavern, the full moon directly over the entrance turning the inside to winter. White walls, white floor, a huge mass of white slithering amongst one another, clawing and biting, snarling and playing the hunt, longing for the real thing. There were over a thousand of them. It was a start. I planned on hundreds of thousands. One day a million. But numbers didn't matter. I already had an unstoppable army. I had a way to go yet, but a brother who was my equal, perhaps more than, and soon would be as much a part of the Second Coming as we all were here. He would take convincing that the Auphe were gone beyond resurrection and that he was above them, as were the Bae, but I'd had all those teachers. Why couldn't I teach myself? I thought that, given a cage, a fiery poker, and a bucket of acid, he'd learn my lessons soon enough. See the light, or rather the dark. And then things would change.

The world would change.

Caliban thought the Second Coming was the future, thought there was time to stop it. He was wrong.

The Second Coming was here.

The Second Coming was now.

Those who remained would be something new, something old, something one day to be like everything on this earth.

Everyone the same as the next and the next and the next . . .

Bae.

And not a human to be found anywhere.

Now who was the failure?

ROB THURMAN

NIGHTLIFE

'There are monsters among us. There always have been and there always will be. I've known that since I can remember, just like I've always known that I was one ... Well, half of one anyway.'

Cal Leandros is nineteen. He eats junk food, he doesn't clean up after himself and he fights with his half brother Niko. It's a fairly normal life, but for the fact that Cal and Niko are constantly on the run. Cal's father has been after him for the last four years. And given that he's a monster whose dark lineage is the stuff of nightmares they really don't want him and his entire otherworldly race catching up with them. But Cal is about to learn why they want him, why they've always wanted him - he is the key to unleashing their hell on earth.

Meanwhile the bright lights of the Big Apple shine on, oblivious to the fact that the fate of the human world will be decided in the fight of Cal and Niko's lives ...

ROB THURMAN

MOONSHINE

'I was born a monster. Although truthfully, I was only half monster. Half monster or whole, in the end it didn't matter. I had my weaknesses, same as anyone else. And I was facing one of them now.'

Cal and his half-brother Niko's lives are settling back to normal after preventing their bloodthirsty relatives from bringing about the apocalypse. They've found a new apartment and even gainful employment by starting an investigative agency in partnership with a glamorous Upper East Side vampire. Of course, their clientele tends to be a little . . . unusual, but their money spends just the same.

Their latest job is undercover work for the Kin - New York's werewolf mafia - to sniff out proof of a set-up by a rival. The location is Moonshine, a gambling club for the otherworldly and Cal figures it will be an easy in-and-out sort of job. But as Niko likes to point out, nothing is more dangerous than overconfidence and when a brawl gets out of hand, it looks like he's right. Are Cal and Niko being set up themselves? And by people whose bite is much worse than their bark . . .

HUNGRY FOR FRESH
BLOOD ?

Then come and join us at
www.facebook.com/BerkleyUK,
where we're dedicated to keeping you
fully up to date on all of our SF, fantasy
and supernatural fiction releases.

- Author Q&As
- Exclusive cover reveals
- Exclusive competitions
- Advance readers' copies
- Guest blogs from our authors
- Excellent reading recommendations

And we'd love to hear from you, email
us at **berkleyuk@uk.penguingroup.com**

BERKLEY UK
PENGUIN